Whatever After
The Graphic Novel
~ FAIREST OF ALL ~

BY **SARAH MLYNOWSKI**

ADAPTED BY **MEREDITH RUSU**

ART BY **ANU CHOUHAN**

COLOR BY **BETHANY CRANDALL**

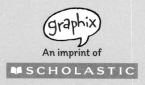

Graphix

An imprint of

SCHOLASTIC

For Jessica Braun
P.S. Read (forever!)
—S. M.

For my older sister Amrita,
the Abby to my Jonah.
—A. C.

Story and text copyright © 2024 by Sarah Mlynowski
Adaption by Meredith Rusu
Art copyright © 2024 by Anu Chouhan

Library of Congress Control Number available
ISBN 978-1-338-84510-5 (hardcover)
ISBN 978-1-338-84509-9 (paperback)

10 9 8 7 6 5 4 3 2 1   24 25 26 27 28

Printed in China   62
First edition, April 2024

Color Flats by Nicky Rodriguez
Color by Bethany Crandall
Lettering by Jesse Post
Edited by Aimee Friedman
Book Design by Carina Taylor
Creative Director: Phil Falco
Publisher: David Saylor

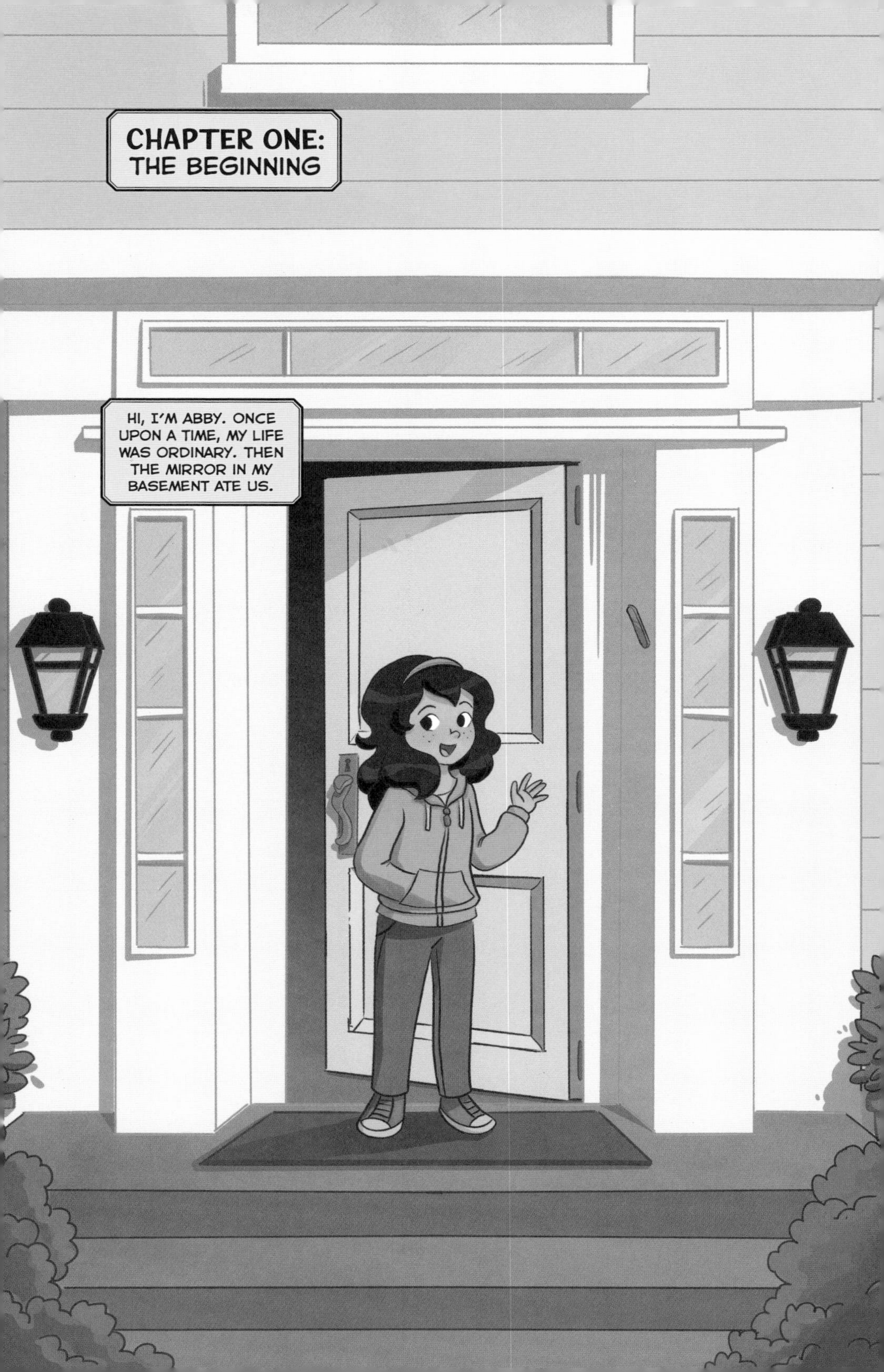
CHAPTER ONE: THE BEGINNING
HI, I'M ABBY. ONCE UPON A TIME, MY LIFE WAS ORDINARY. THEN THE MIRROR IN MY BASEMENT ATE US.

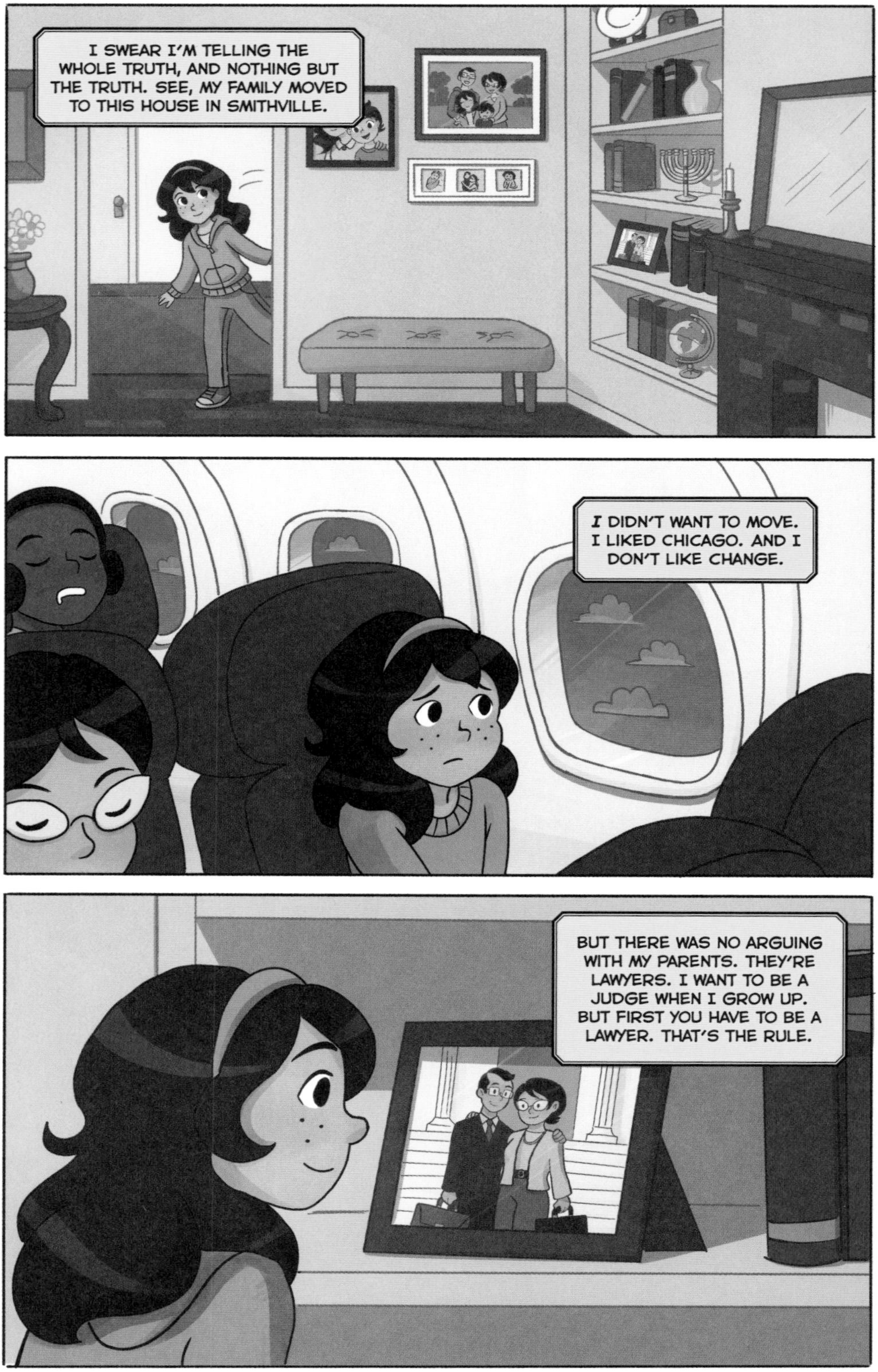
I SWEAR I'M TELLING THE WHOLE TRUTH, AND NOTHING BUT THE TRUTH. SEE, MY FAMILY MOVED TO THIS HOUSE IN SMITHVILLE.
I DIDN'T WANT TO MOVE. I LIKED CHICAGO. AND I DON'T LIKE CHANGE.
BUT THERE WAS NO ARGUING WITH MY PARENTS. THEY'RE LAWYERS. I WANT TO BE A JUDGE WHEN I GROW UP. BUT FIRST YOU HAVE TO BE A LAWYER. THAT'S THE RULE.

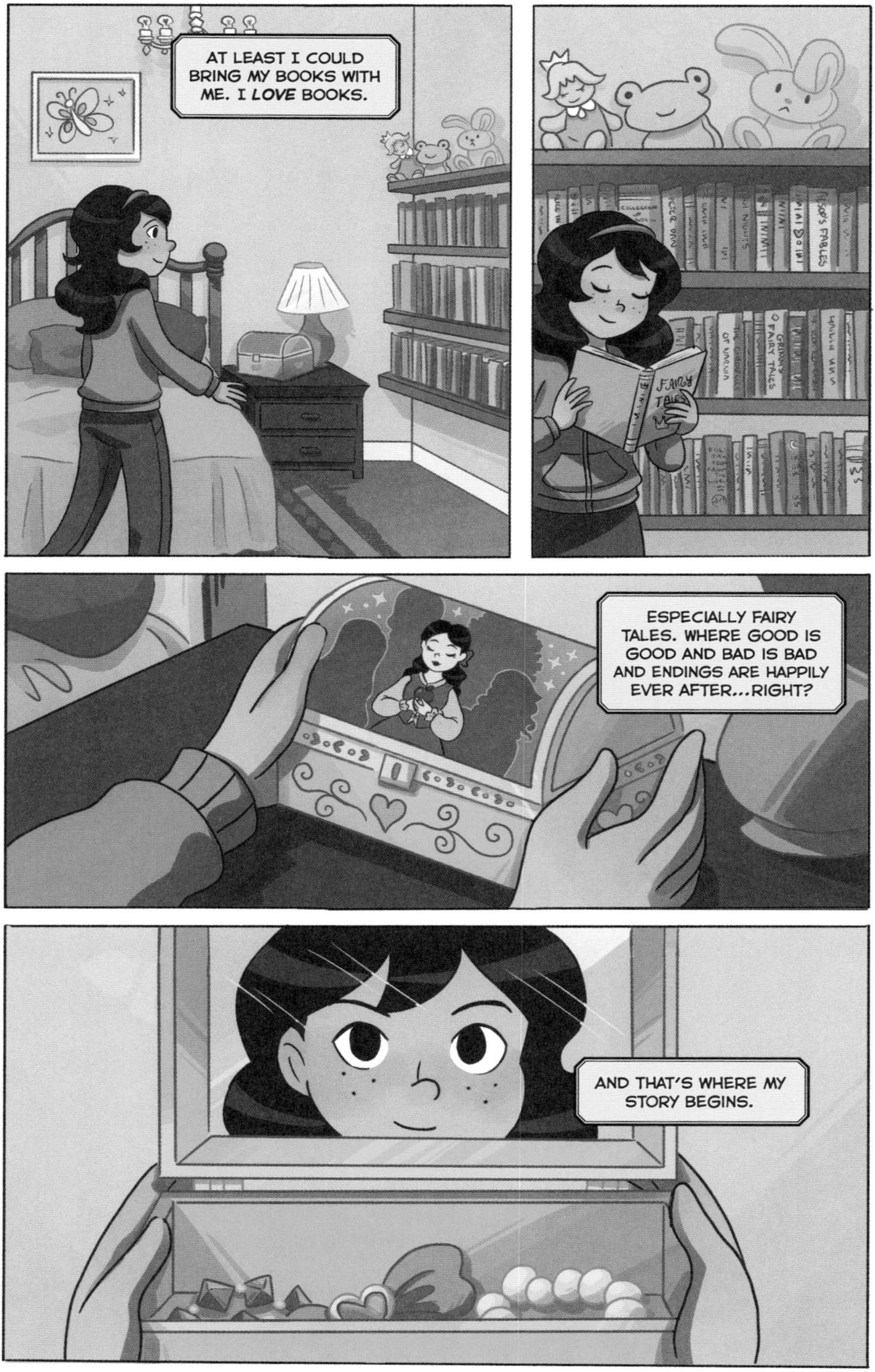
AT LEAST I COULD BRING MY BOOKS WITH ME. I *LOVE* BOOKS.
ESPECIALLY FAIRY TALES. WHERE GOOD IS GOOD AND BAD IS BAD AND ENDINGS ARE HAPPILY EVER AFTER...RIGHT?
AND THAT'S WHERE MY STORY BEGINS.

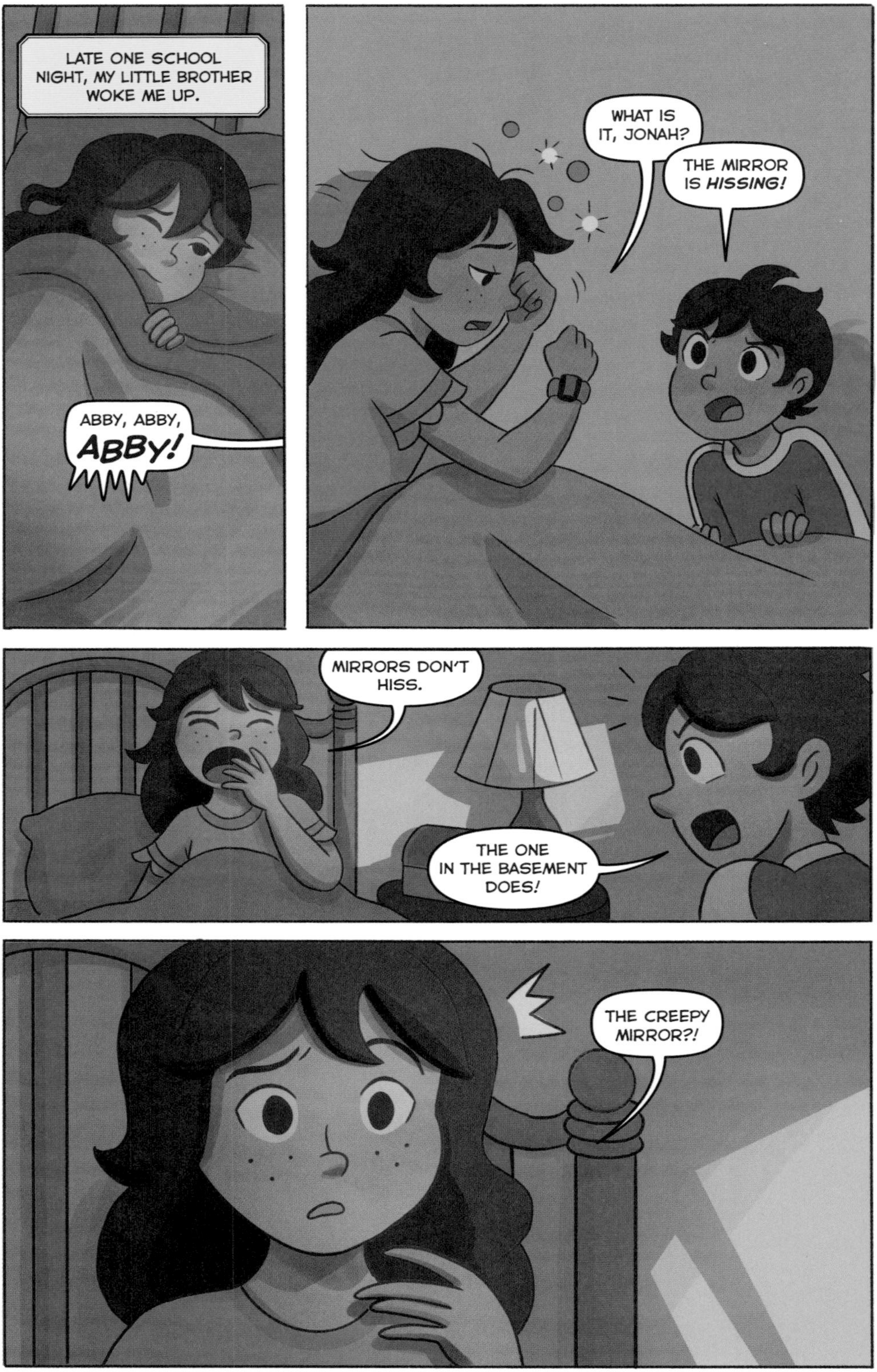
LATE ONE SCHOOL NIGHT, MY LITTLE BROTHER WOKE ME UP.
ABBY, ABBY, ABBY!
WHAT IS IT, JONAH?
THE MIRROR IS HISSING!
MIRRORS DON'T HISS.
THE ONE IN THE BASEMENT DOES!
THE CREEPY MIRROR?!

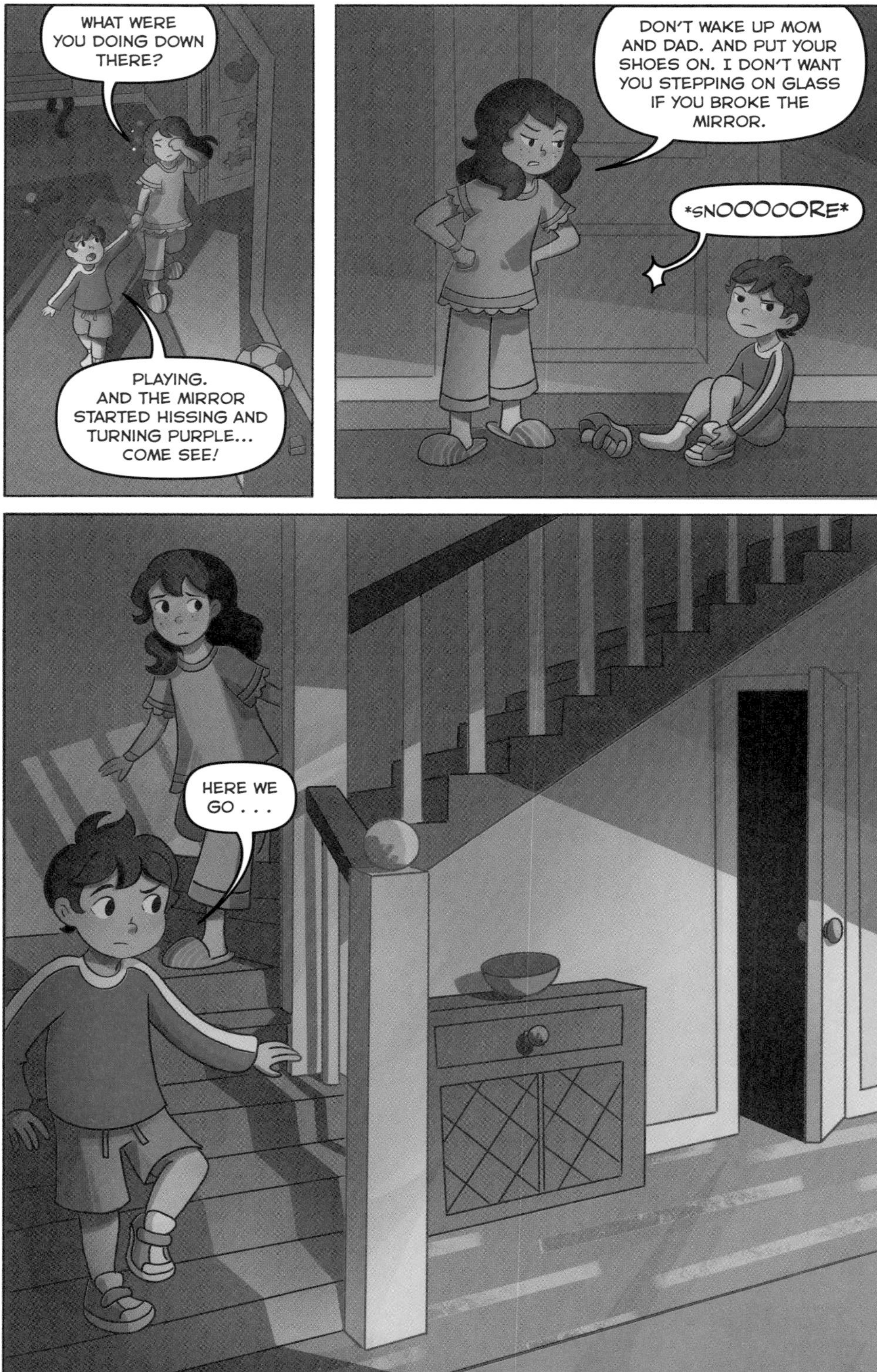
WHAT WERE YOU DOING DOWN THERE?
PLAYING. AND THE MIRROR STARTED HISSING AND TURNING PURPLE... COME SEE!
DON'T WAKE UP MOM AND DAD. AND PUT YOUR SHOES ON. I DON'T WANT YOU STEPPING ON GLASS IF YOU BROKE THE MIRROR.
SNOOOOORE
HERE WE GO . . .

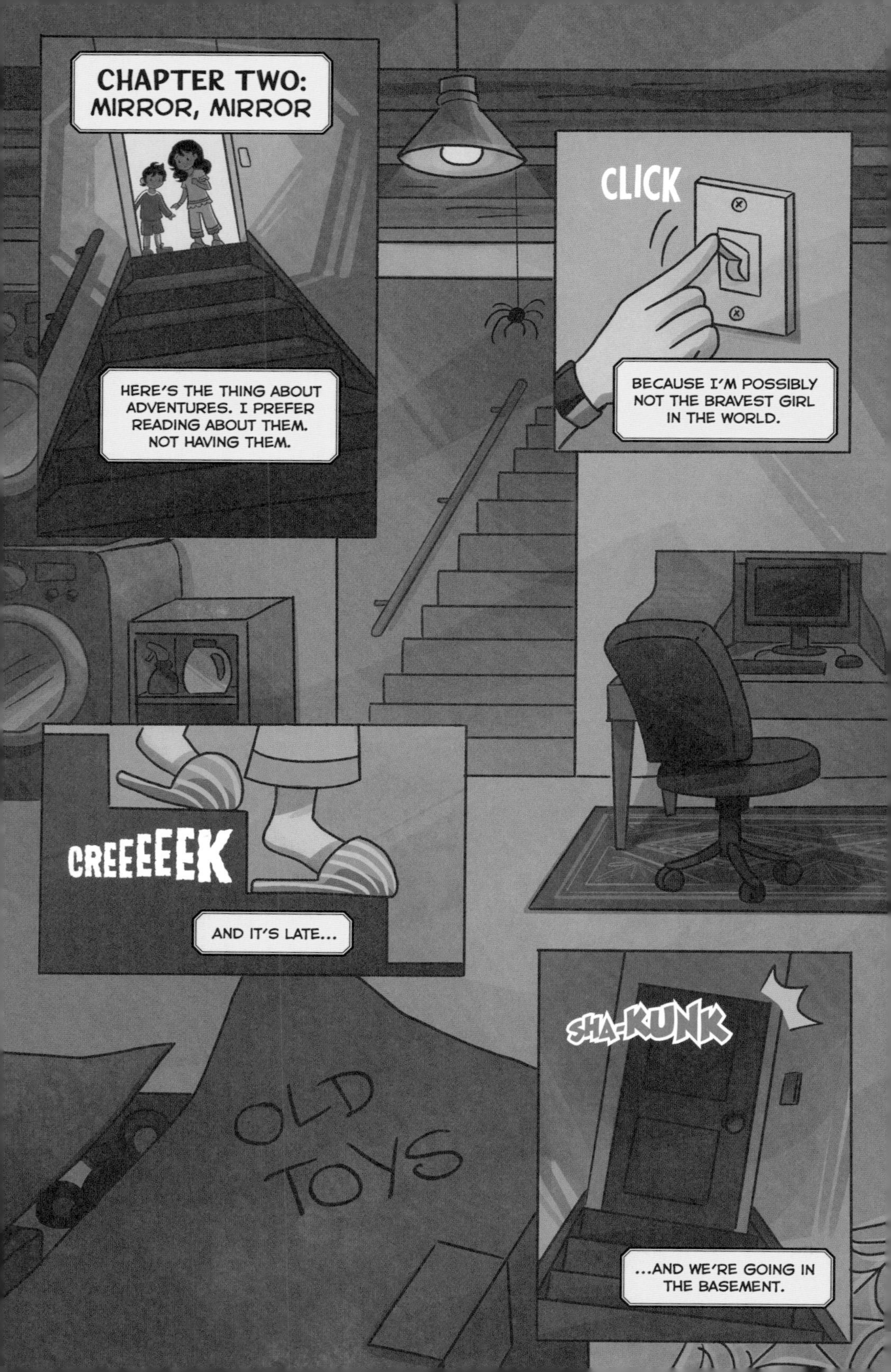
CHAPTER TWO:
MIRROR, MIRROR
HERE'S THE THING ABOUT ADVENTURES. I PREFER READING ABOUT THEM. NOT HAVING THEM.
CLICK
BECAUSE I'M POSSIBLY NOT THE BRAVEST GIRL IN THE WORLD.
CREEEEEK
AND IT'S LATE...
SHA-KUNK
...AND WE'RE GOING IN THE BASEMENT.
OLD TOYS

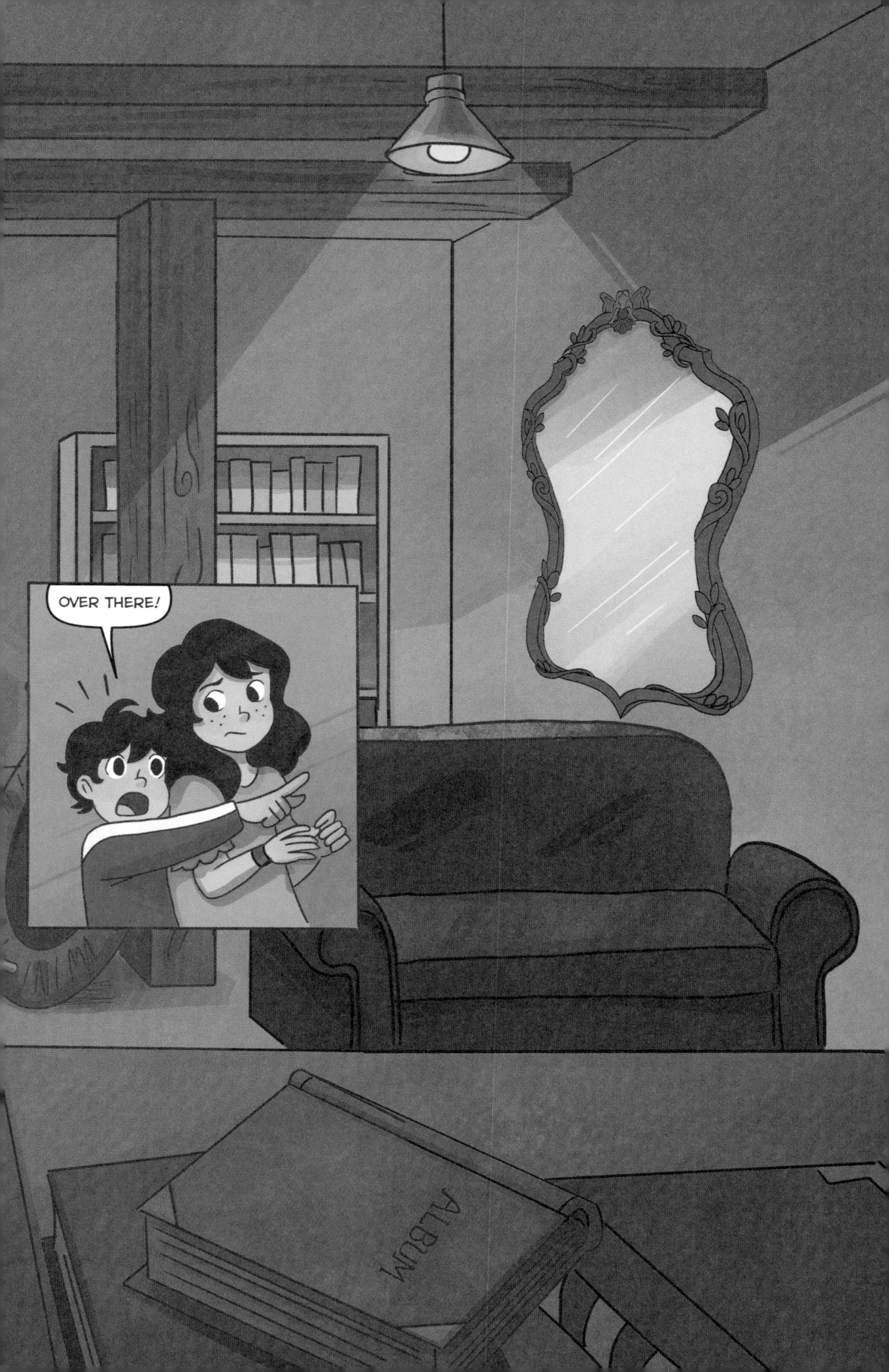
OVER THERE!
ALBUM

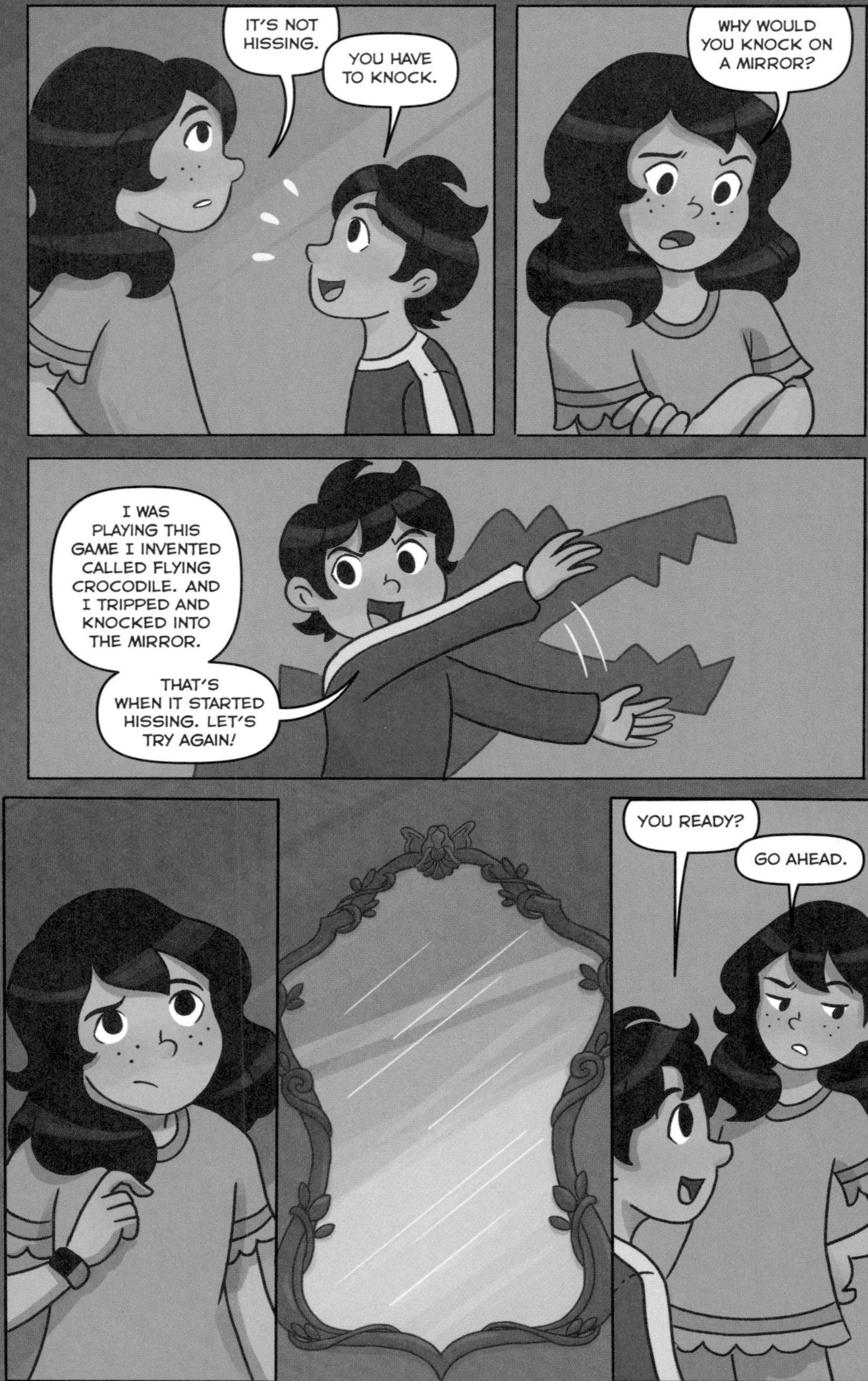
IT'S NOT HISSING.
YOU HAVE TO KNOCK.
WHY WOULD YOU KNOCK ON A MIRROR?
I WAS PLAYING THIS GAME I INVENTED CALLED FLYING CROCODILE. AND I TRIPPED AND KNOCKED INTO THE MIRROR.
THAT'S WHEN IT STARTED HISSING. LET'S TRY AGAIN!
YOU READY?
GO AHEAD.

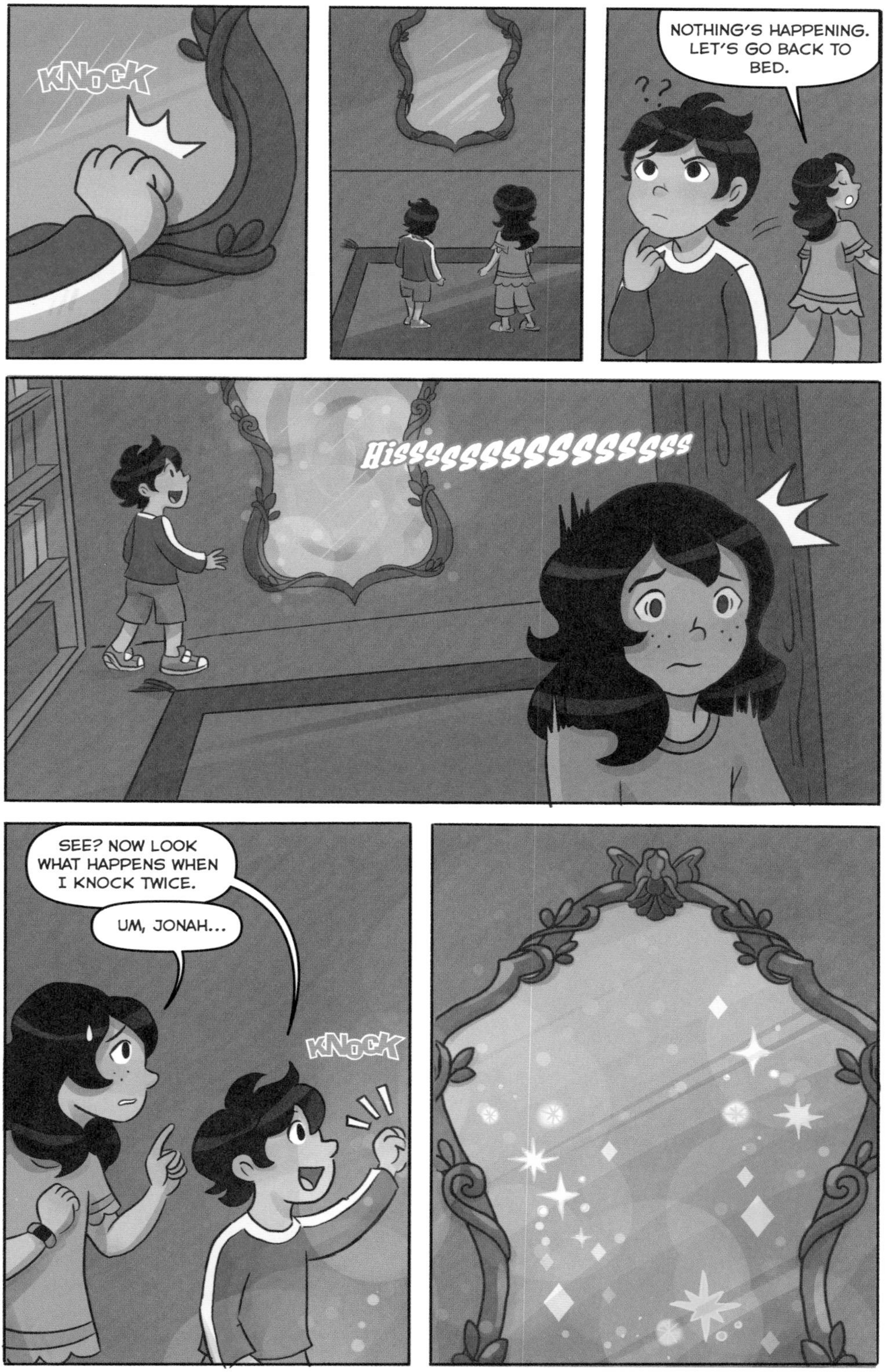
KNOCK
NOTHING'S HAPPENING. LET'S GO BACK TO BED.
HISSSSSSSSSSSSSSS
SEE? NOW LOOK WHAT HAPPENS WHEN I KNOCK TWICE.
UM, JONAH...
KNOCK

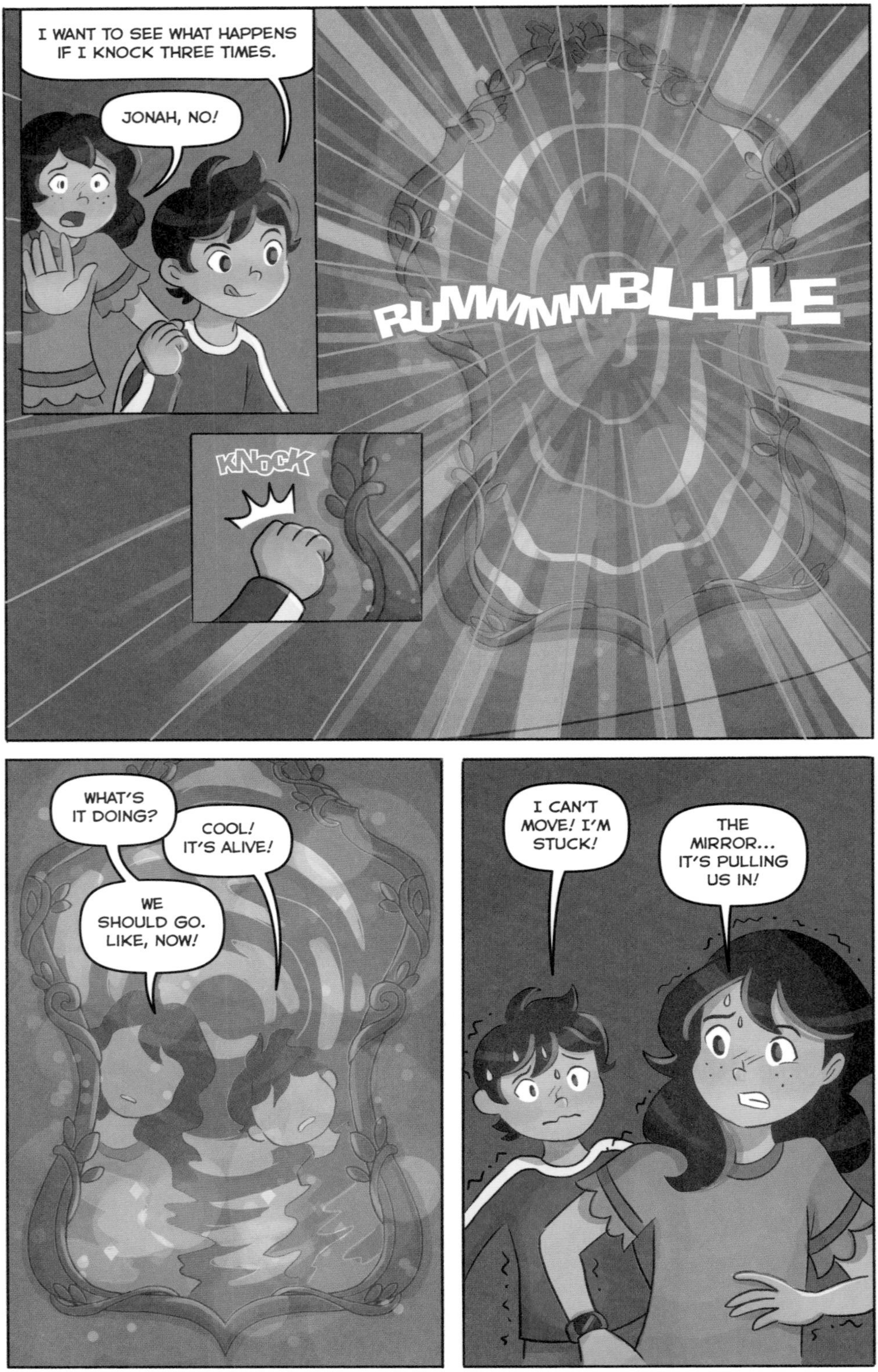
I WANT TO SEE WHAT HAPPENS IF I KNOCK THREE TIMES.
JONAH, NO!
KNOCK
RUMMMMMBLLLLE
WHAT'S IT DOING?
COOL! IT'S ALIVE!
WE SHOULD GO. LIKE, NOW!
I CAN'T MOVE! I'M STUCK!
THE MIRROR... IT'S PULLING US IN!

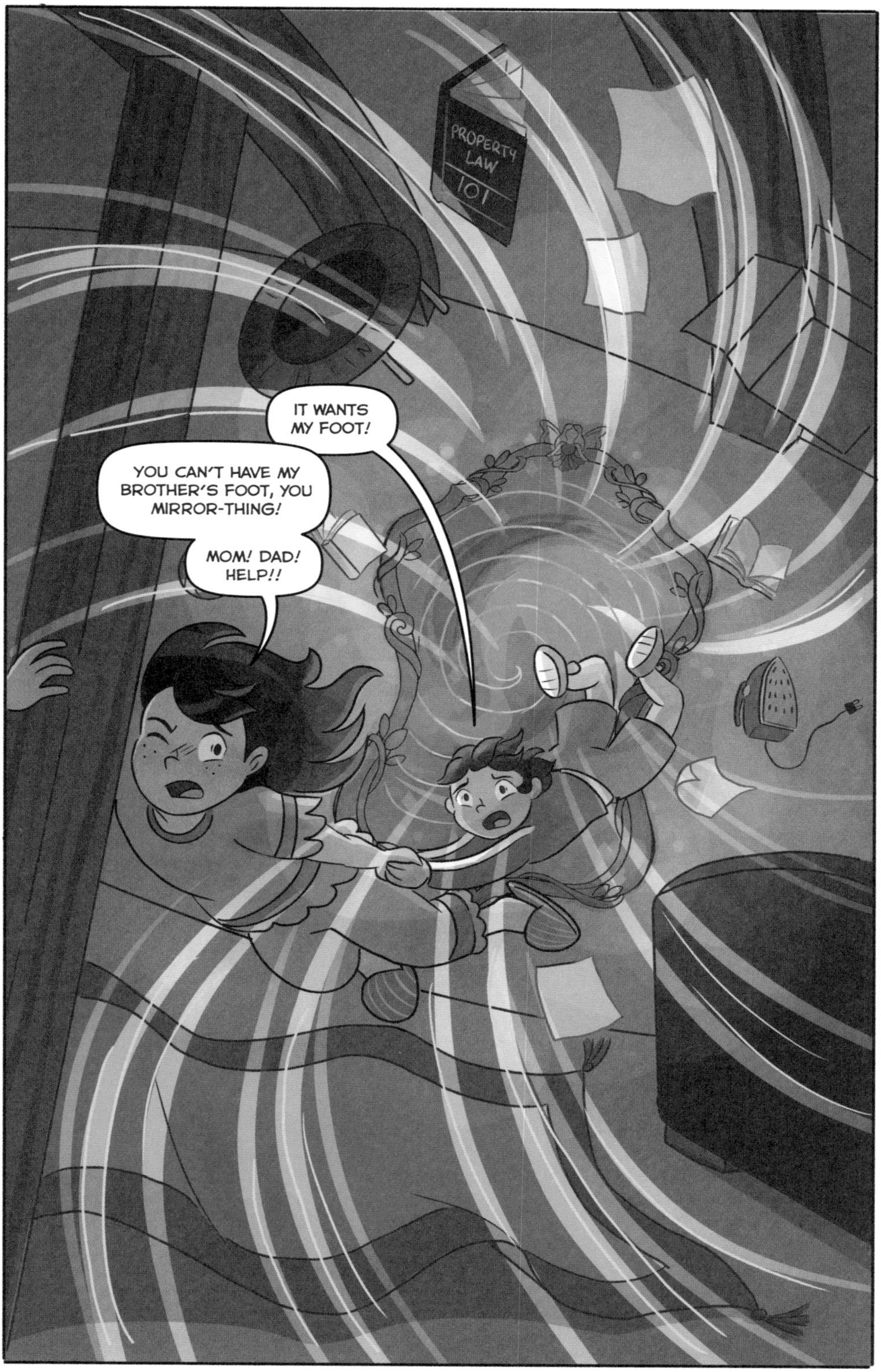
PROPERTY LAW 101
YOU CAN'T HAVE MY BROTHER'S FOOT, YOU MIRROR-THING!
IT WANTS MY FOOT!
MOM! DAD! HELP!!

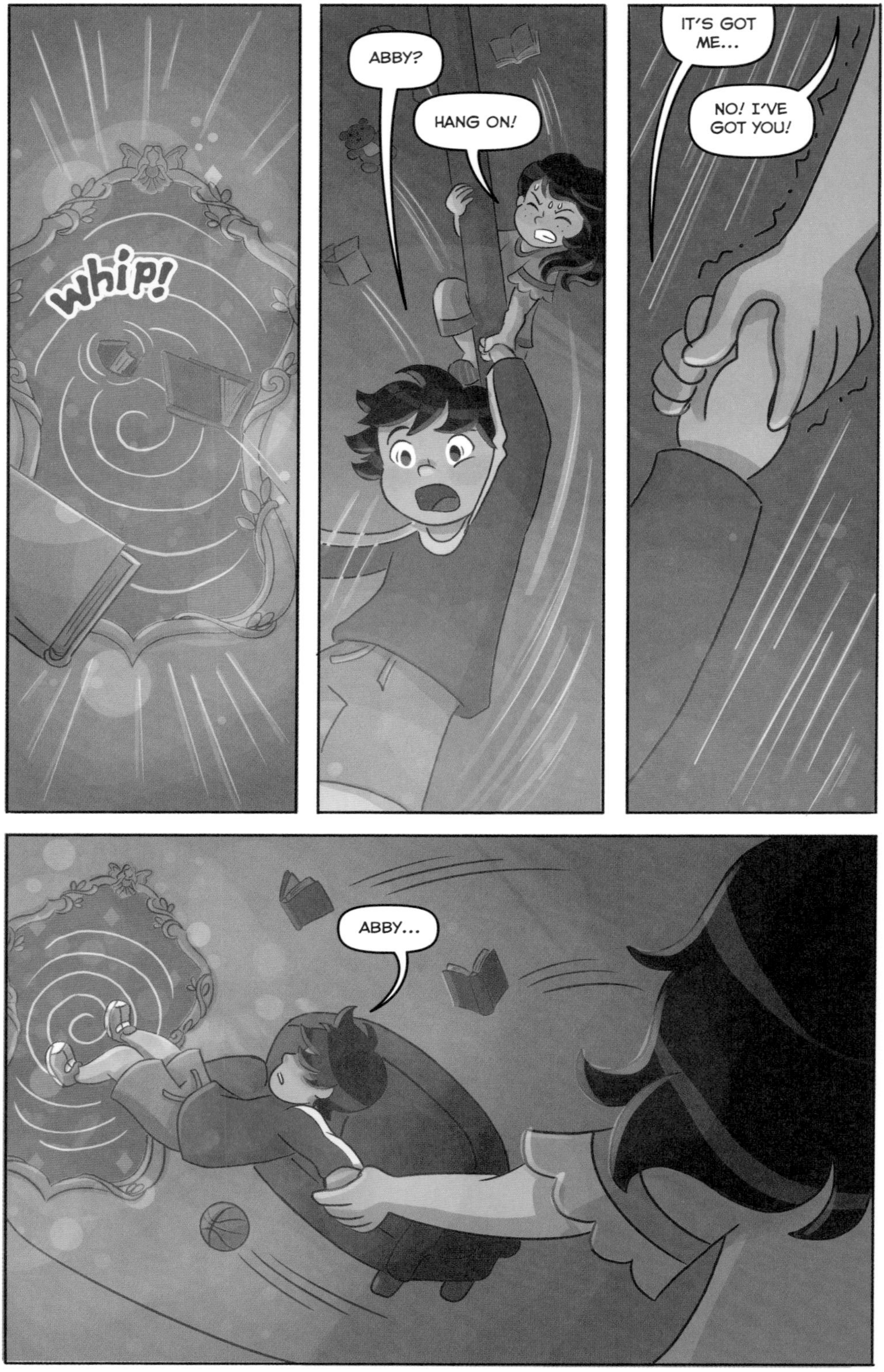
whip!
ABBY?
HANG ON!
IT'S GOT ME...
NO! I'VE GOT YOU!
ABBY...

NO!

NO, NO, NO! IF THE MIRROR WANTS YOU, THEN IT HAS TO TAKE ME, TOO!

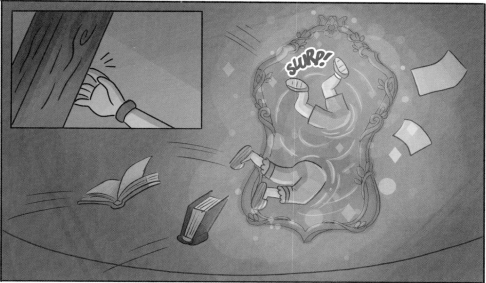

SLURP!

RUMMBLLE

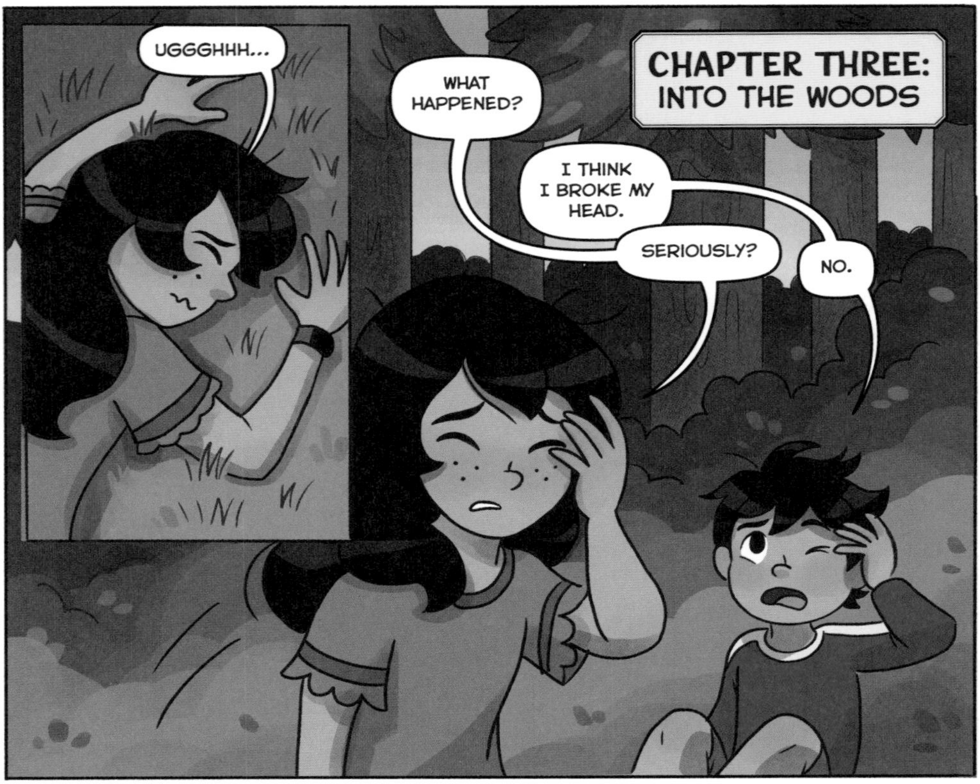
CHAPTER THREE:
INTO THE WOODS
UGGGHHH...
WHAT HAPPENED?
I THINK I BROKE MY HEAD.
SERIOUSLY?
NO.

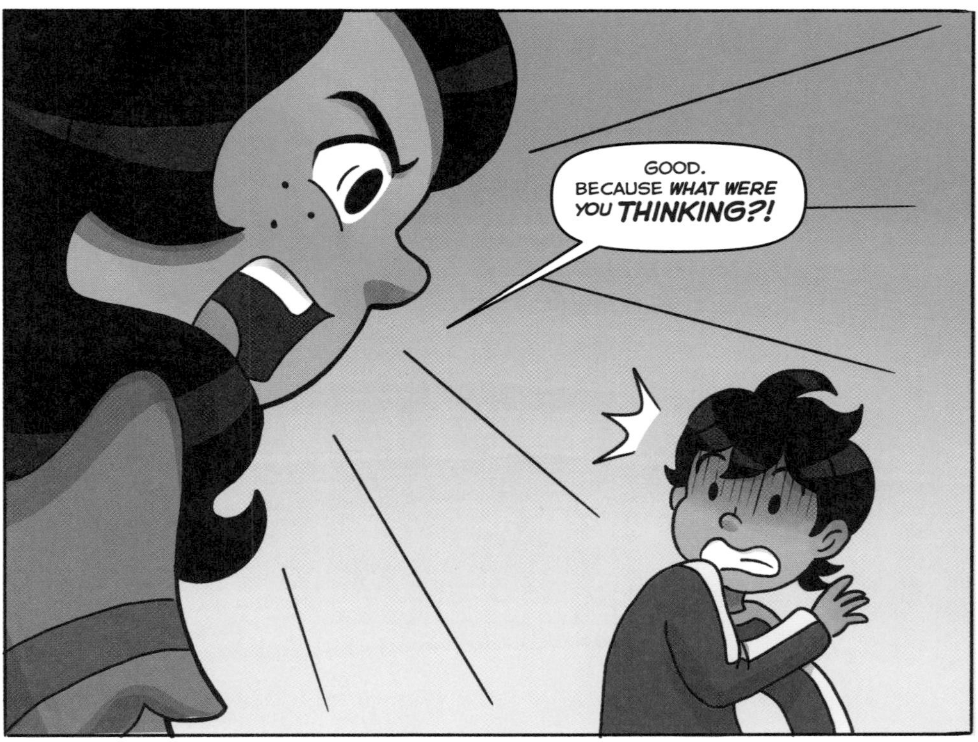
GOOD. BECAUSE *WHAT WERE YOU* ***THINKING?!***

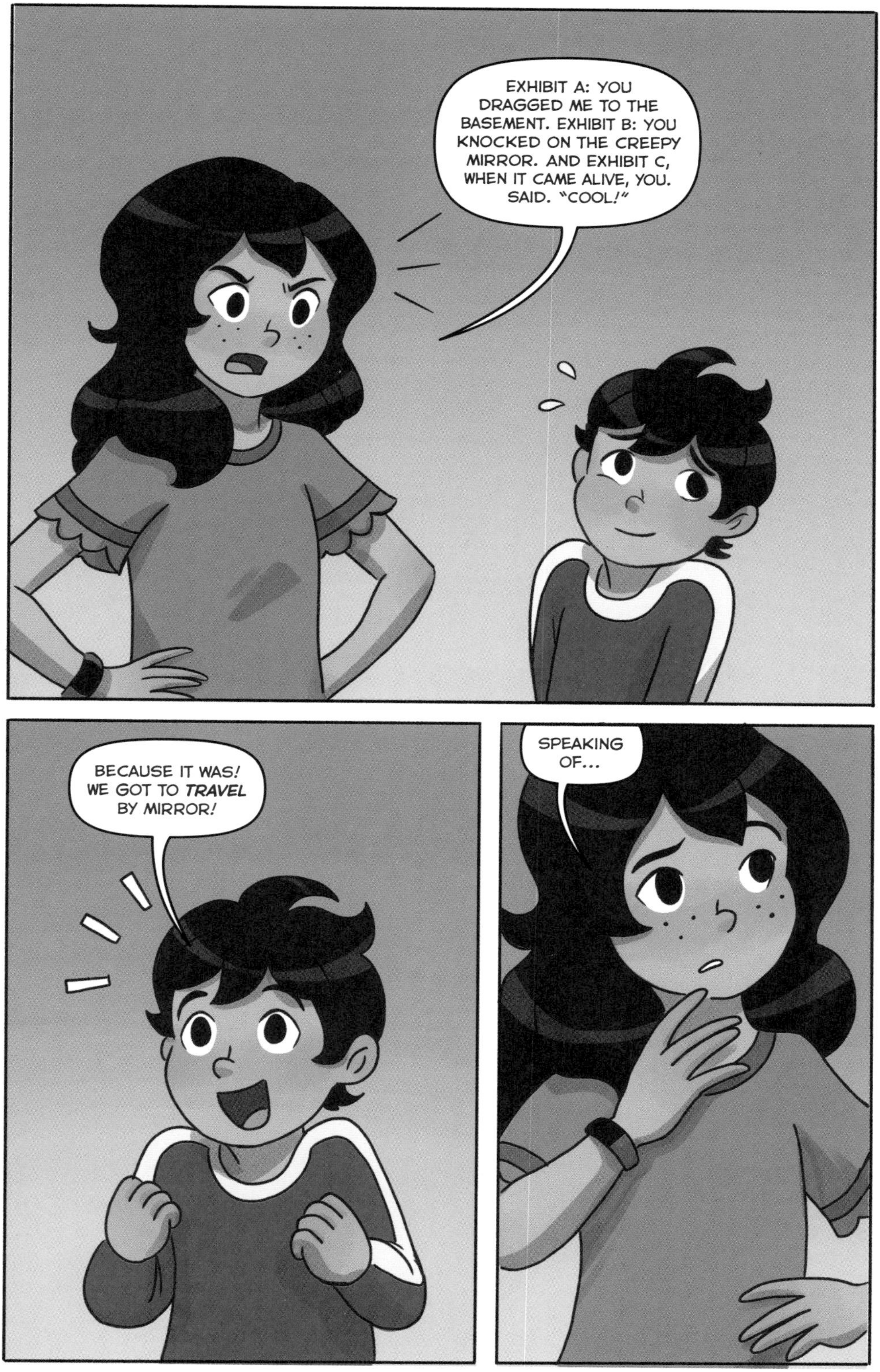
EXHIBIT A: YOU DRAGGED ME TO THE BASEMENT. EXHIBIT B: YOU KNOCKED ON THE CREEPY MIRROR. AND EXHIBIT C, WHEN IT CAME ALIVE, YOU. SAID. "COOL!"
BECAUSE IT WAS! WE GOT TO *TRAVEL* BY MIRROR!
SPEAKING OF...

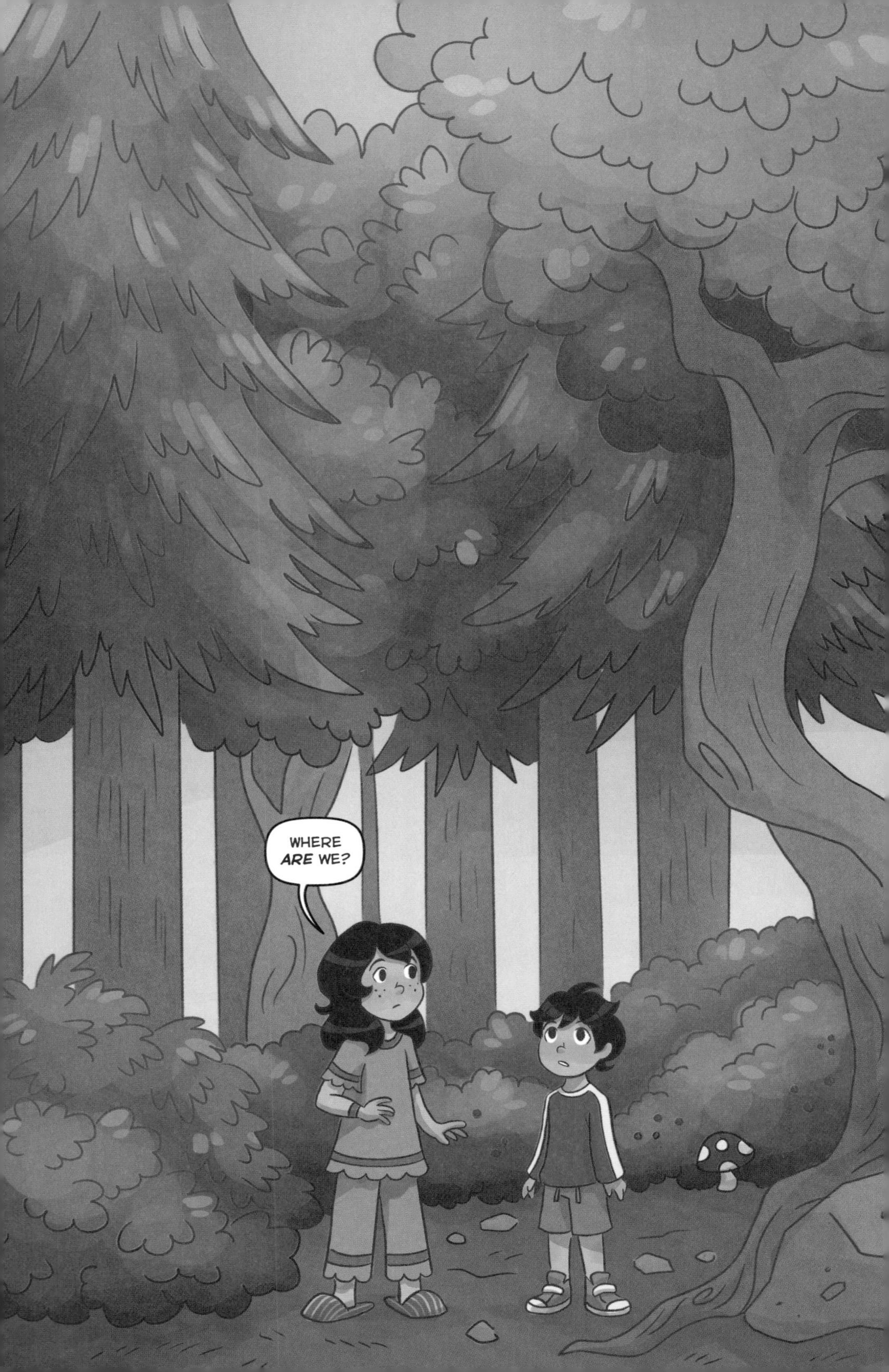
WHERE
ARE WE?

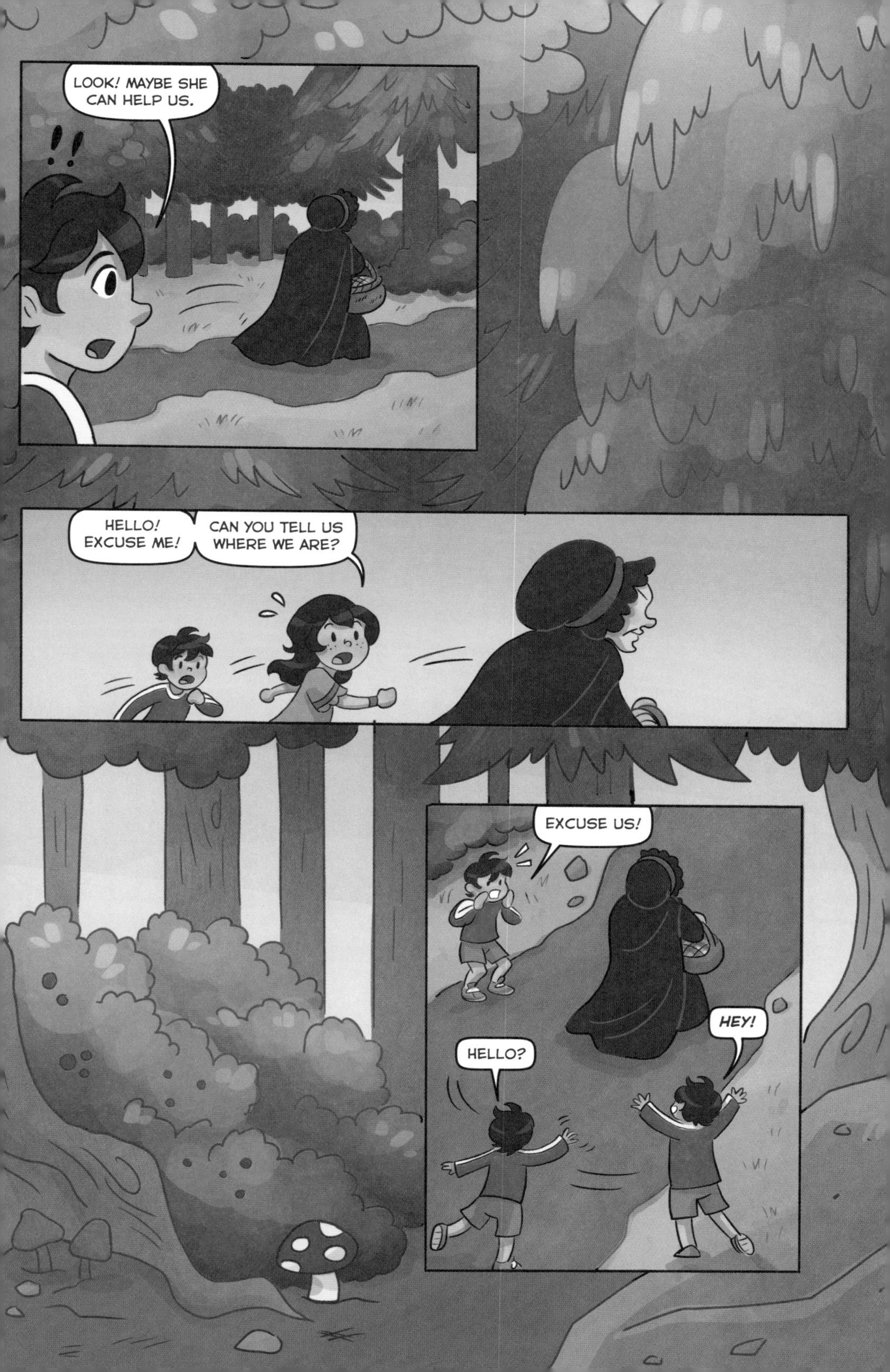
LOOK! MAYBE SHE CAN HELP US.
!!
HELLO! EXCUSE ME!
CAN YOU TELL US WHERE WE ARE?
EXCUSE US!
HEY!
HELLO?

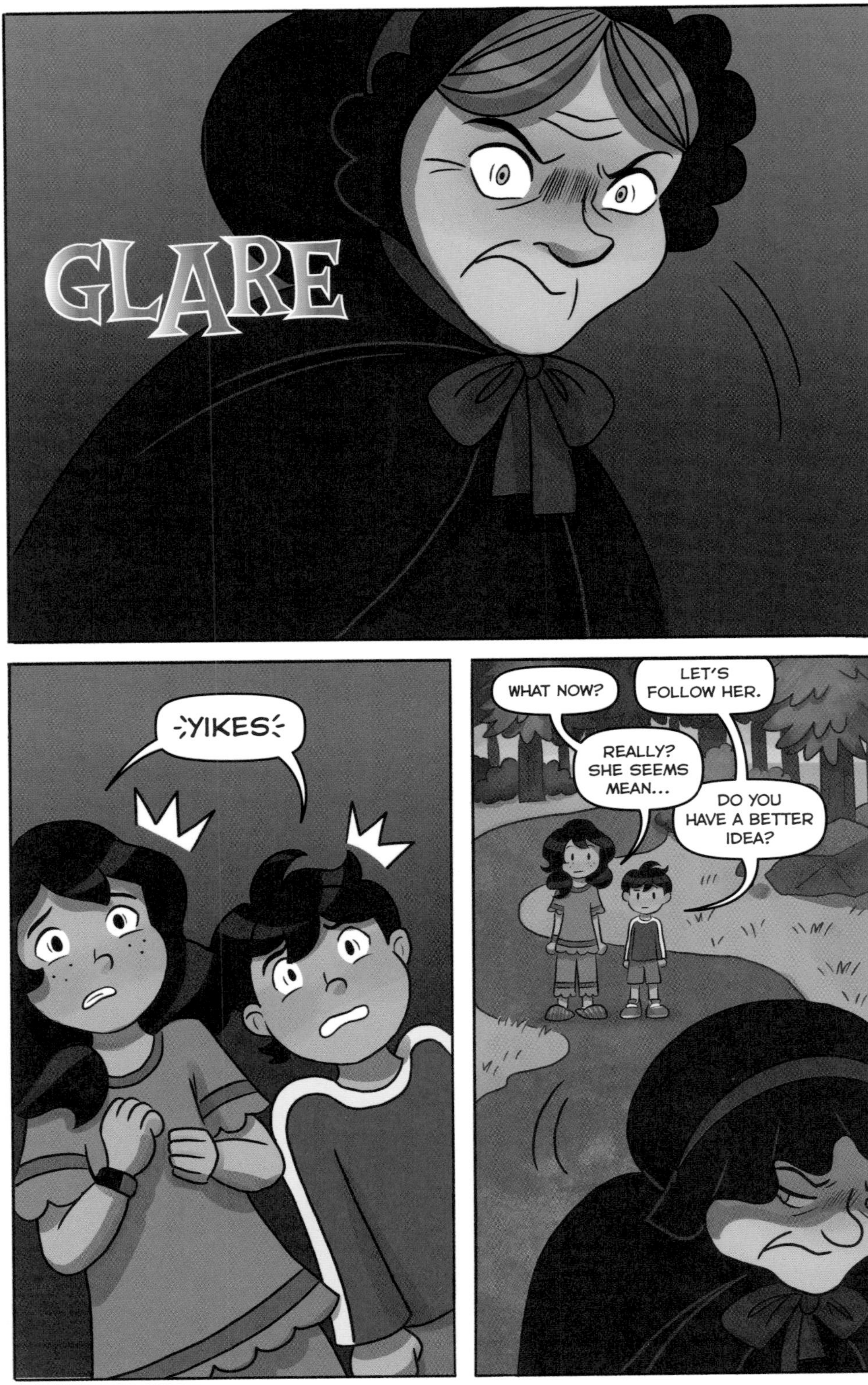
GLARE
YIKES
WHAT NOW?
LET'S FOLLOW HER.
REALLY? SHE SEEMS MEAN...
DO YOU HAVE A BETTER IDEA?

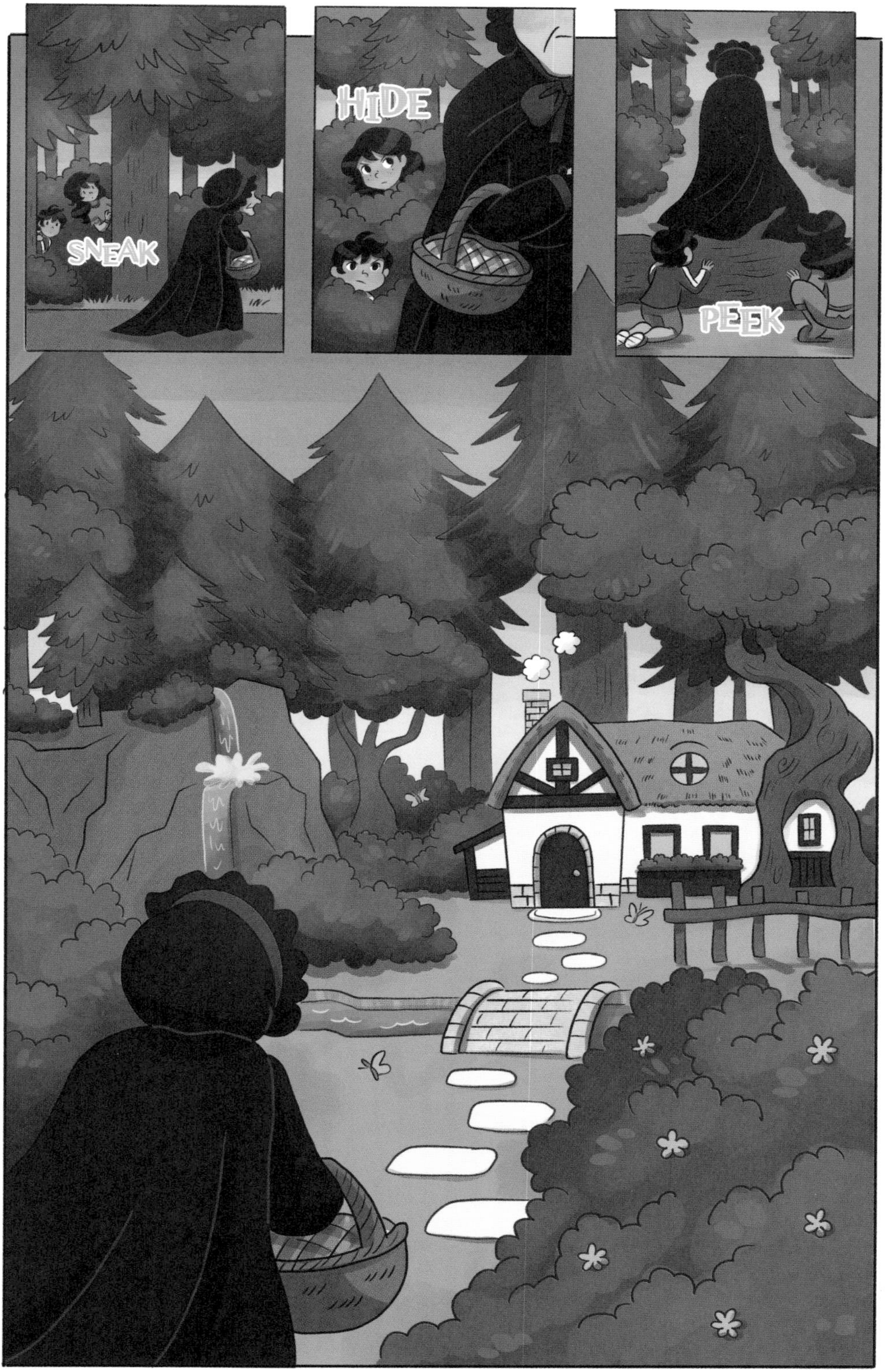
SNEAK
HIDE
PEEK

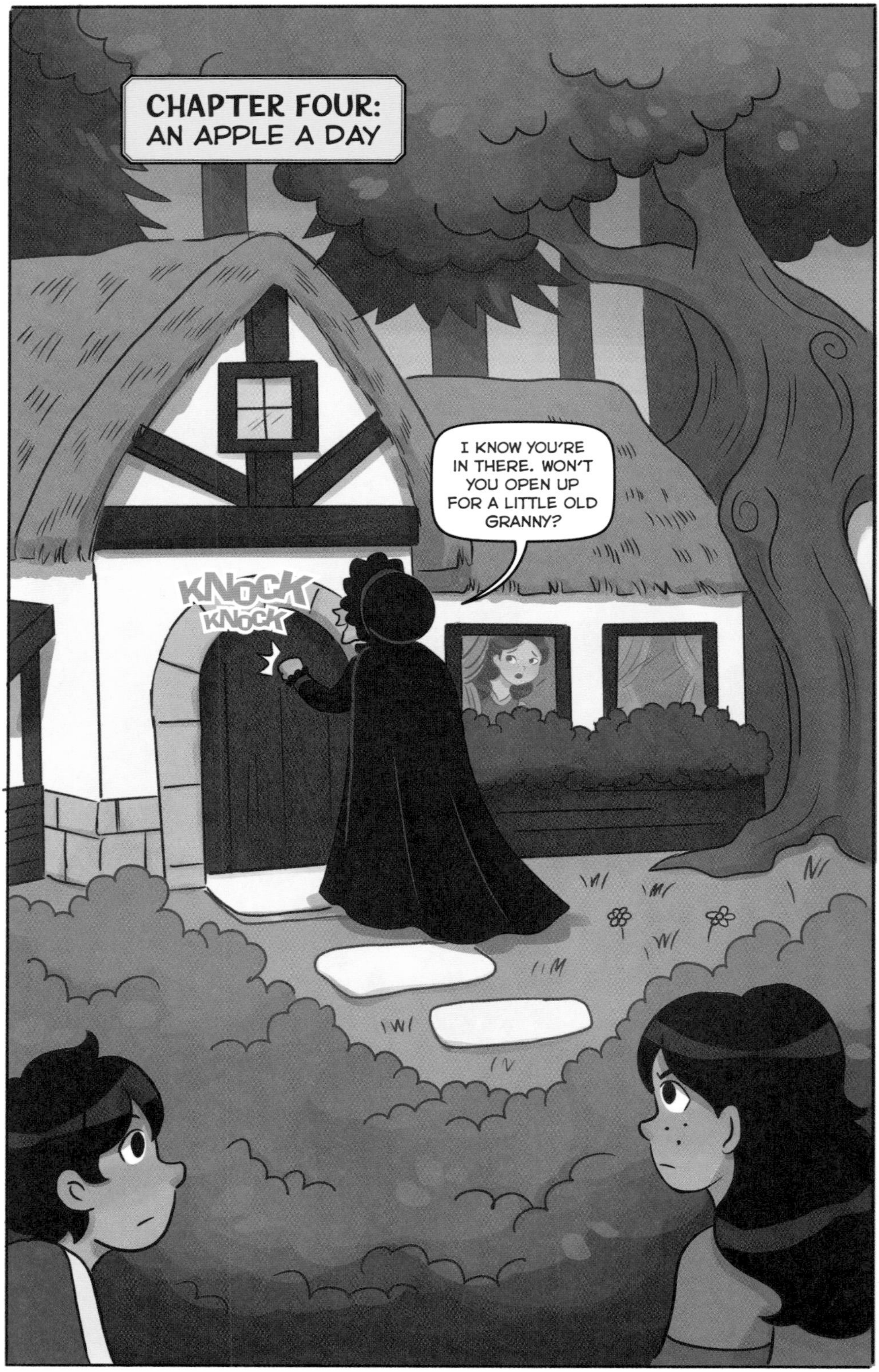
CHAPTER FOUR:
AN APPLE A DAY
I KNOW YOU'RE IN THERE. WON'T YOU OPEN UP FOR A LITTLE OLD GRANNY?
KNOCK
KNOCK

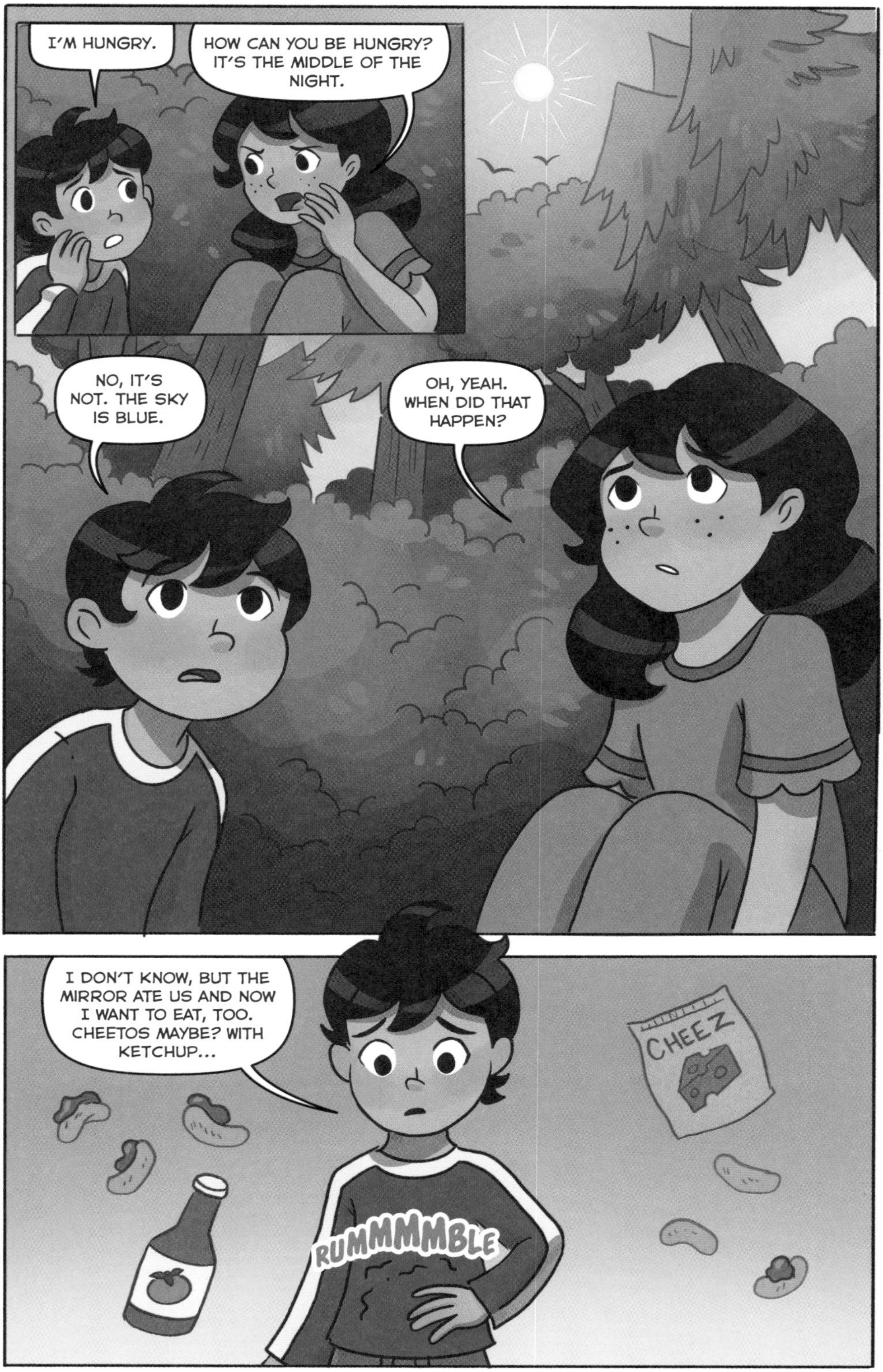
I'M HUNGRY.
HOW CAN YOU BE HUNGRY? IT'S THE MIDDLE OF THE NIGHT.
NO, IT'S NOT. THE SKY IS BLUE.
OH, YEAH. WHEN DID THAT HAPPEN?
I DON'T KNOW, BUT THE MIRROR ATE US AND NOW I WANT TO EAT, TOO. CHEETOS MAYBE? WITH KETCHUP...
CHEEZ
RUMMMMMBLE

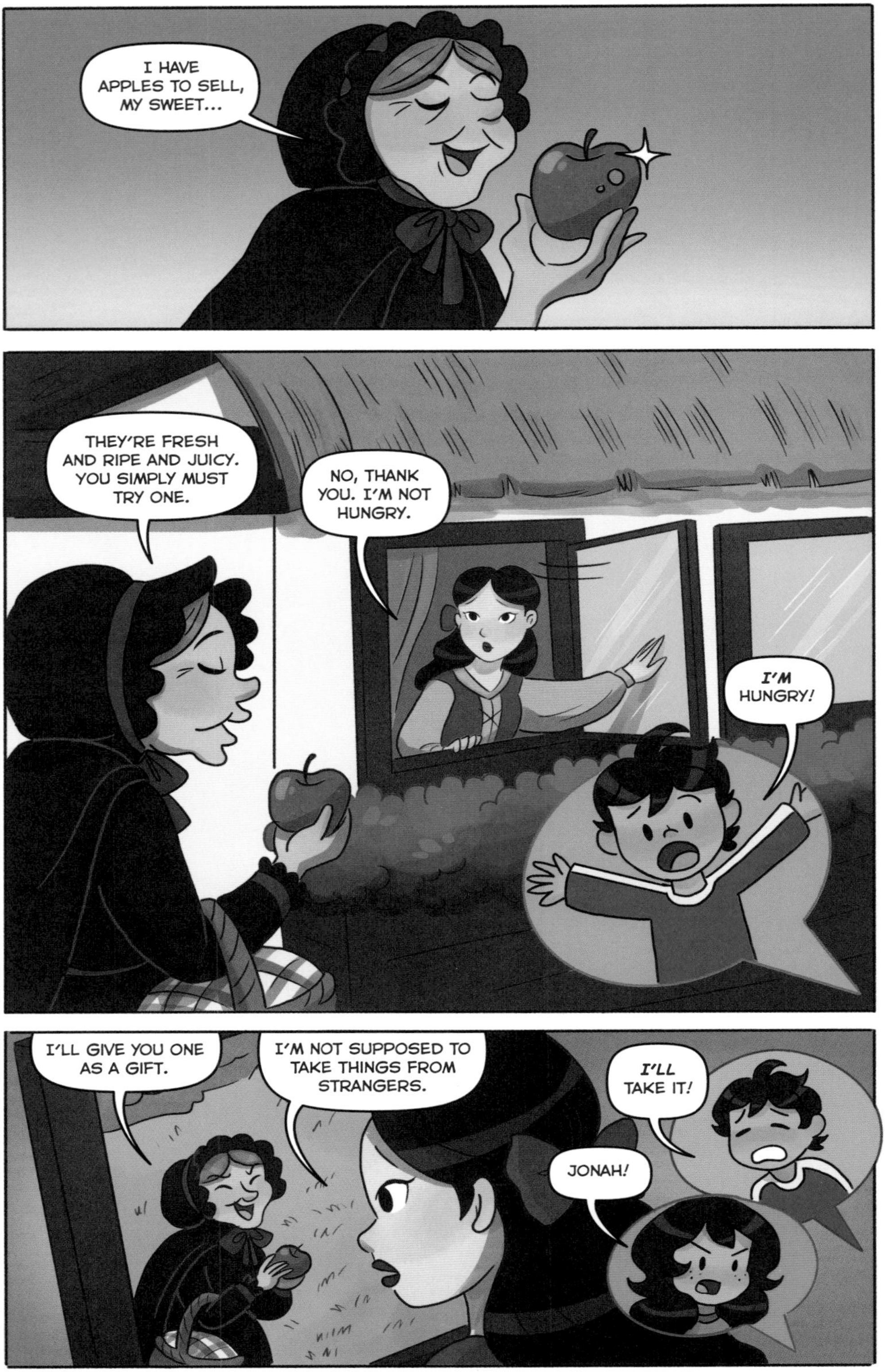
I HAVE APPLES TO SELL, MY SWEET...
THEY'RE FRESH AND RIPE AND JUICY. YOU SIMPLY MUST TRY ONE.
NO, THANK YOU. I'M NOT HUNGRY.
I'M HUNGRY!
I'LL GIVE YOU ONE AS A GIFT.
I'M NOT SUPPOSED TO TAKE THINGS FROM STRANGERS.
I'LL TAKE IT!
JONAH!

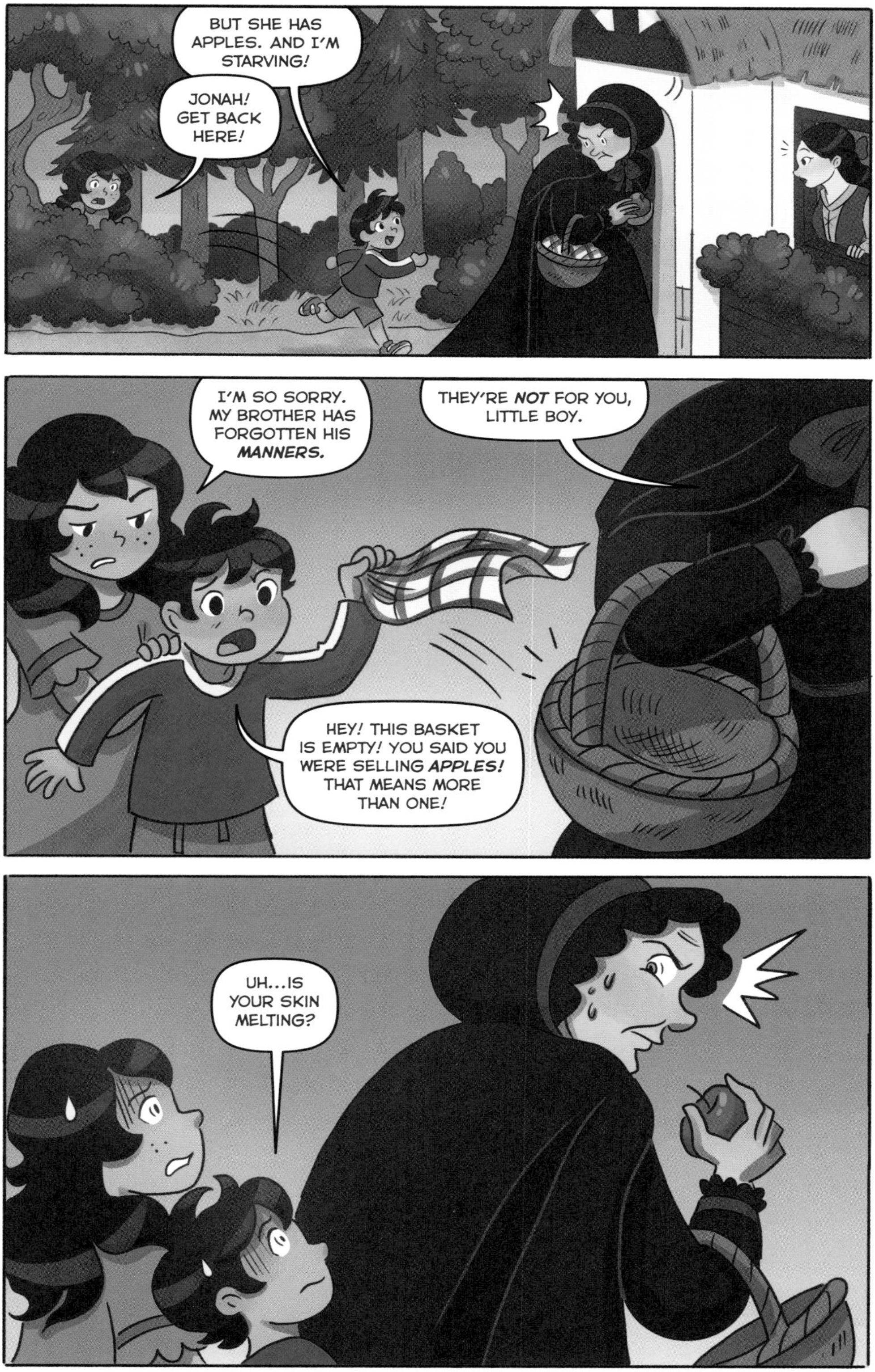
BUT SHE HAS APPLES. AND I'M STARVING!
JONAH! GET BACK HERE!
I'M SO SORRY. MY BROTHER HAS FORGOTTEN HIS MANNERS.
THEY'RE NOT FOR YOU, LITTLE BOY.
HEY! THIS BASKET IS EMPTY! YOU SAID YOU WERE SELLING APPLES! THAT MEANS MORE THAN ONE!
UH...IS YOUR SKIN MELTING?

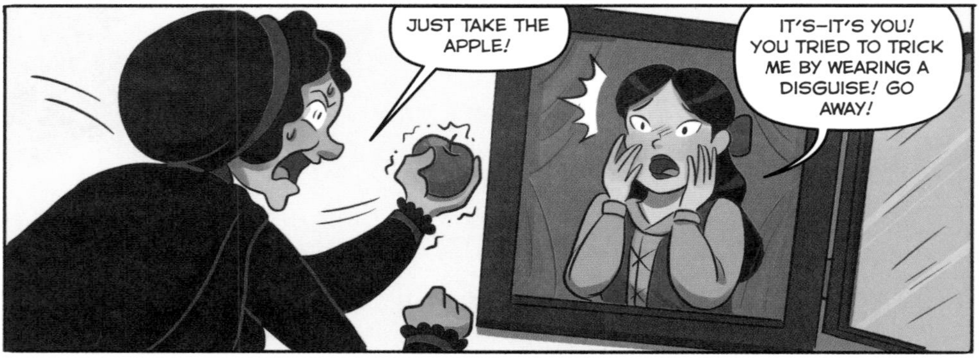
JUST TAKE THE APPLE!
IT'S–IT'S YOU! YOU TRIED TO TRICK ME BY WEARING A DISGUISE! GO AWAY!

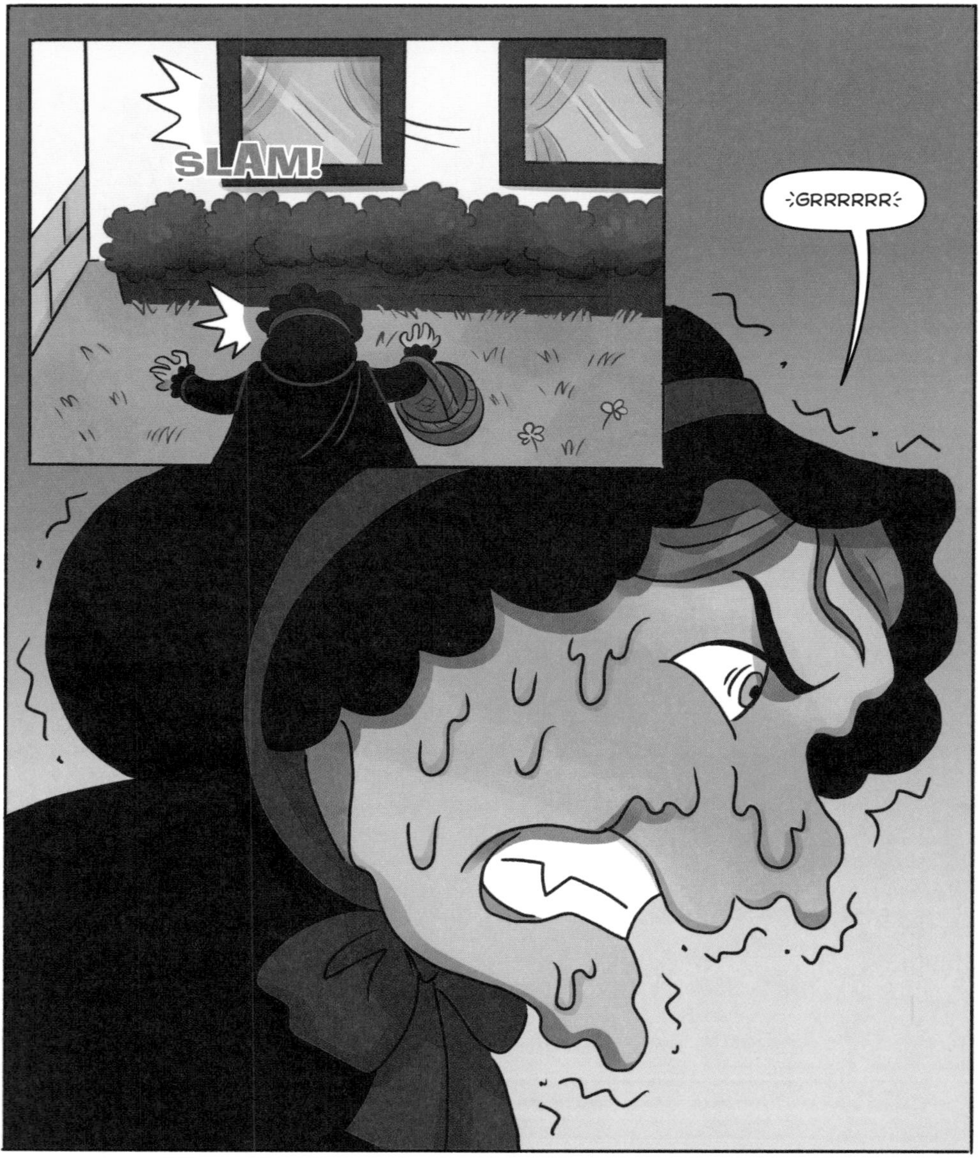
SLAM!
GRRRRRR

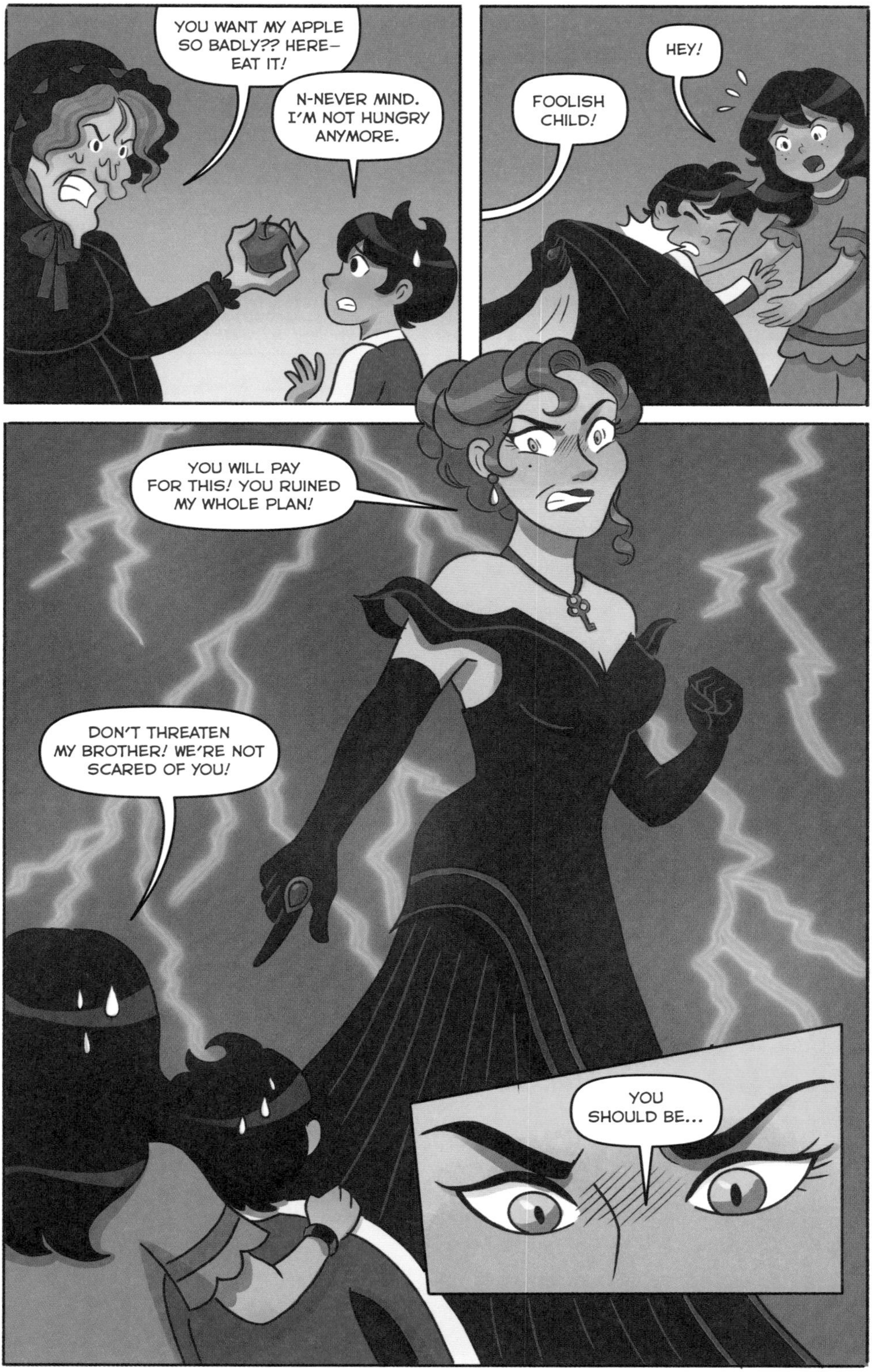
YOU WANT MY APPLE SO BADLY?? HERE— EAT IT!
N-NEVER MIND. I'M NOT HUNGRY ANYMORE.
HEY!
FOOLISH CHILD!
YOU WILL PAY FOR THIS! YOU RUINED MY WHOLE PLAN!
DON'T THREATEN MY BROTHER! WE'RE NOT SCARED OF YOU!
YOU SHOULD BE...

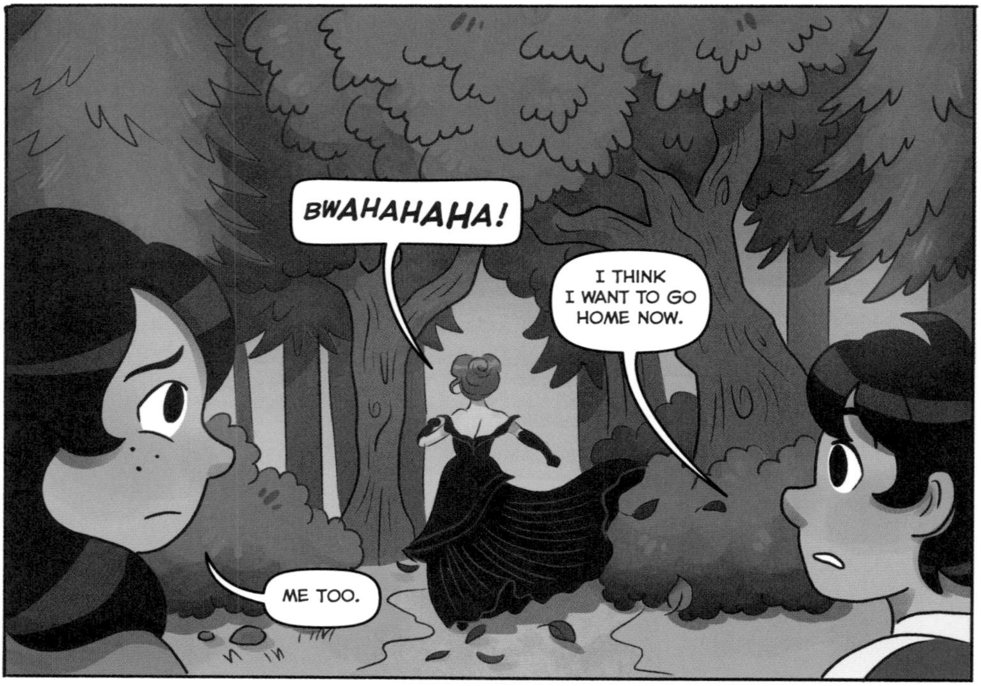
BWAHAHAHA!
I THINK I WANT TO GO HOME NOW.
ME TOO.

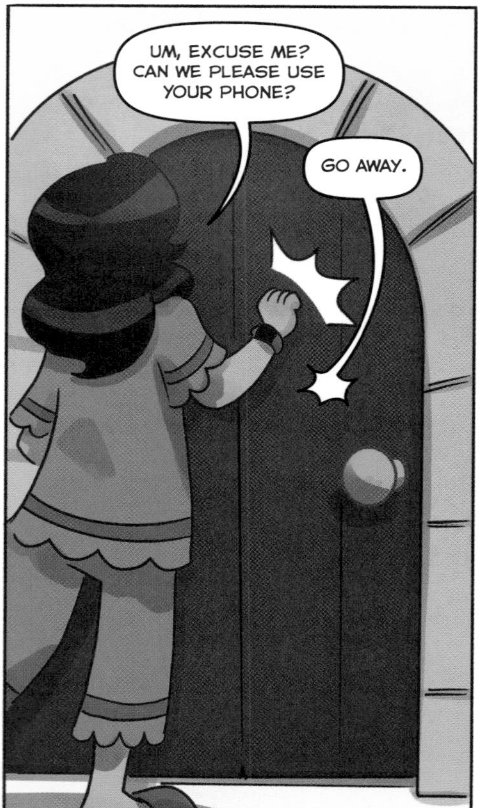
UM, EXCUSE ME? CAN WE PLEASE USE YOUR PHONE?
GO AWAY.

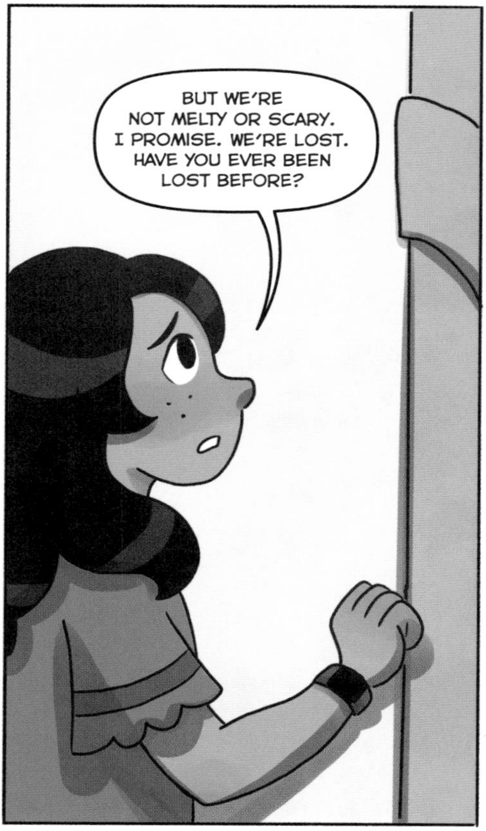
BUT WE'RE NOT MELTY OR SCARY. I PROMISE. WE'RE LOST. HAVE YOU EVER BEEN LOST BEFORE?

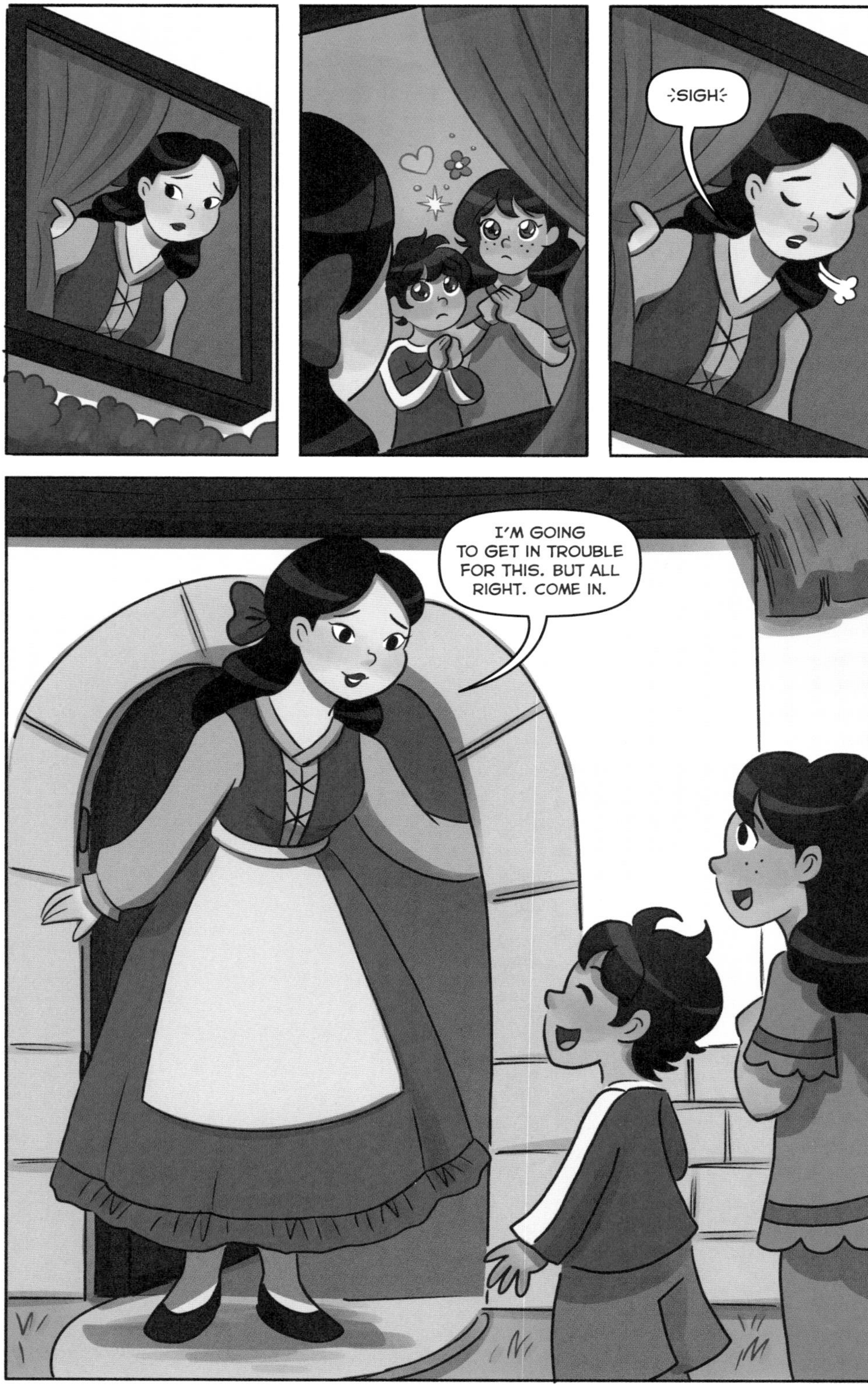

-SIGH-
I'M GOING TO GET IN TROUBLE FOR THIS. BUT ALL RIGHT. COME IN.

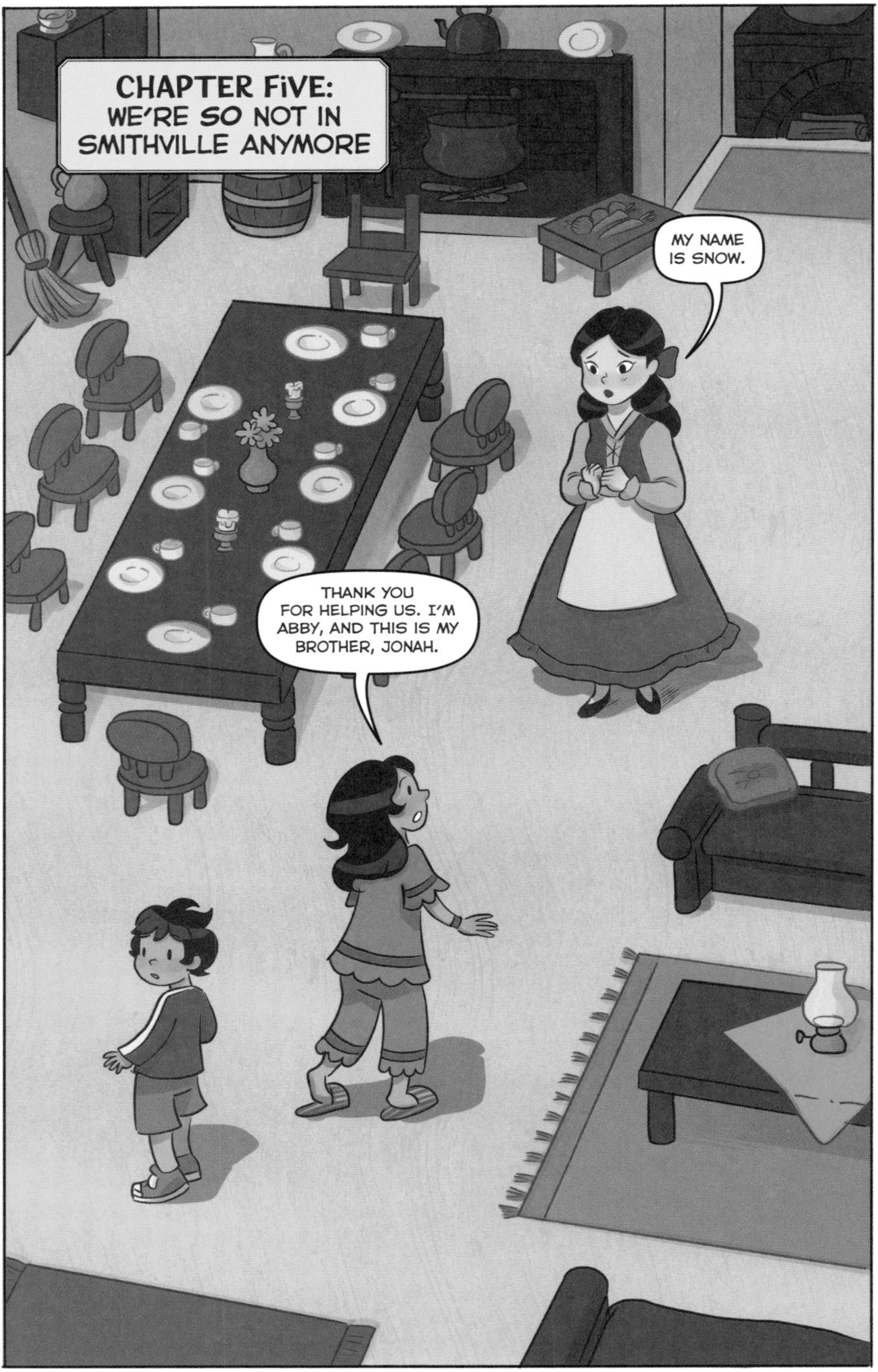
CHAPTER FiVE:
WE'RE SO NOT IN
SMITHVILLE ANYMORE
MY NAME IS SNOW.
THANK YOU FOR HELPING US. I'M ABBY, AND THIS IS MY BROTHER, JONAH.

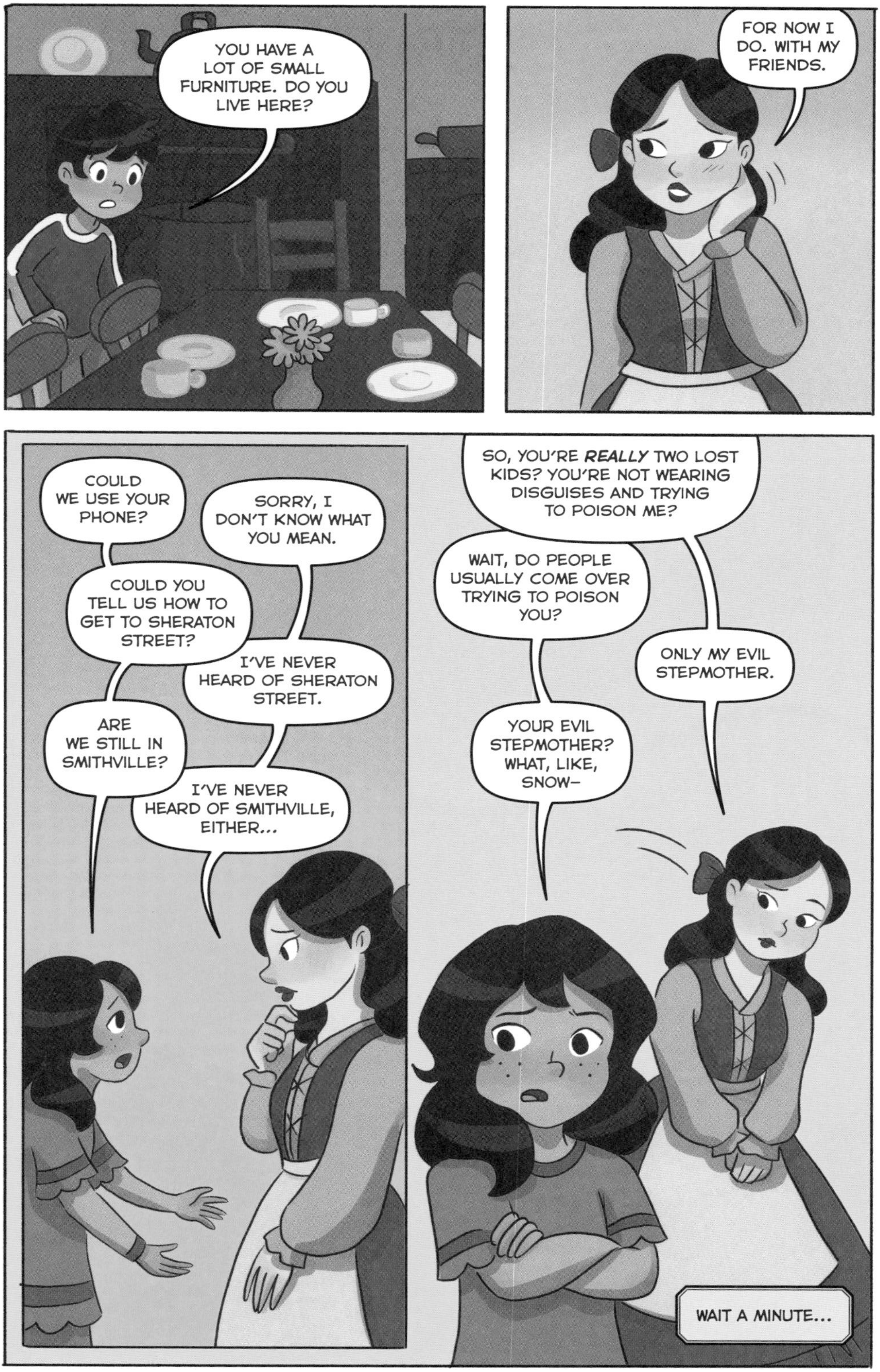
YOU HAVE A LOT OF SMALL FURNITURE. DO YOU LIVE HERE?
FOR NOW I DO. WITH MY FRIENDS.
COULD WE USE YOUR PHONE?
SORRY, I DON'T KNOW WHAT YOU MEAN.
COULD YOU TELL US HOW TO GET TO SHERATON STREET?
I'VE NEVER HEARD OF SHERATON STREET.
ARE WE STILL IN SMITHVILLE?
I'VE NEVER HEARD OF SMITHVILLE, EITHER...
SO, YOU'RE ***REALLY*** TWO LOST KIDS? YOU'RE NOT WEARING DISGUISES AND TRYING TO POISON ME?
WAIT, DO PEOPLE USUALLY COME OVER TRYING TO POISON YOU?
ONLY MY EVIL STEPMOTHER.
YOUR EVIL STEPMOTHER? WHAT, LIKE, SNOW–
WAIT A MINUTE...

FACT 1: The mirror took us to a forest.

FACT 2: This girl lives in a cottage with tiny furniture.

FACT 3: She's beautiful, and her name is Snow.

FACT 4: An old woman in a disguise tried to give her an apple.

FACT 5: She has an evil stepmother who's trying to poison her.

CONCLUSION:

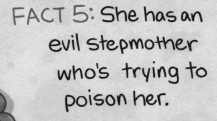

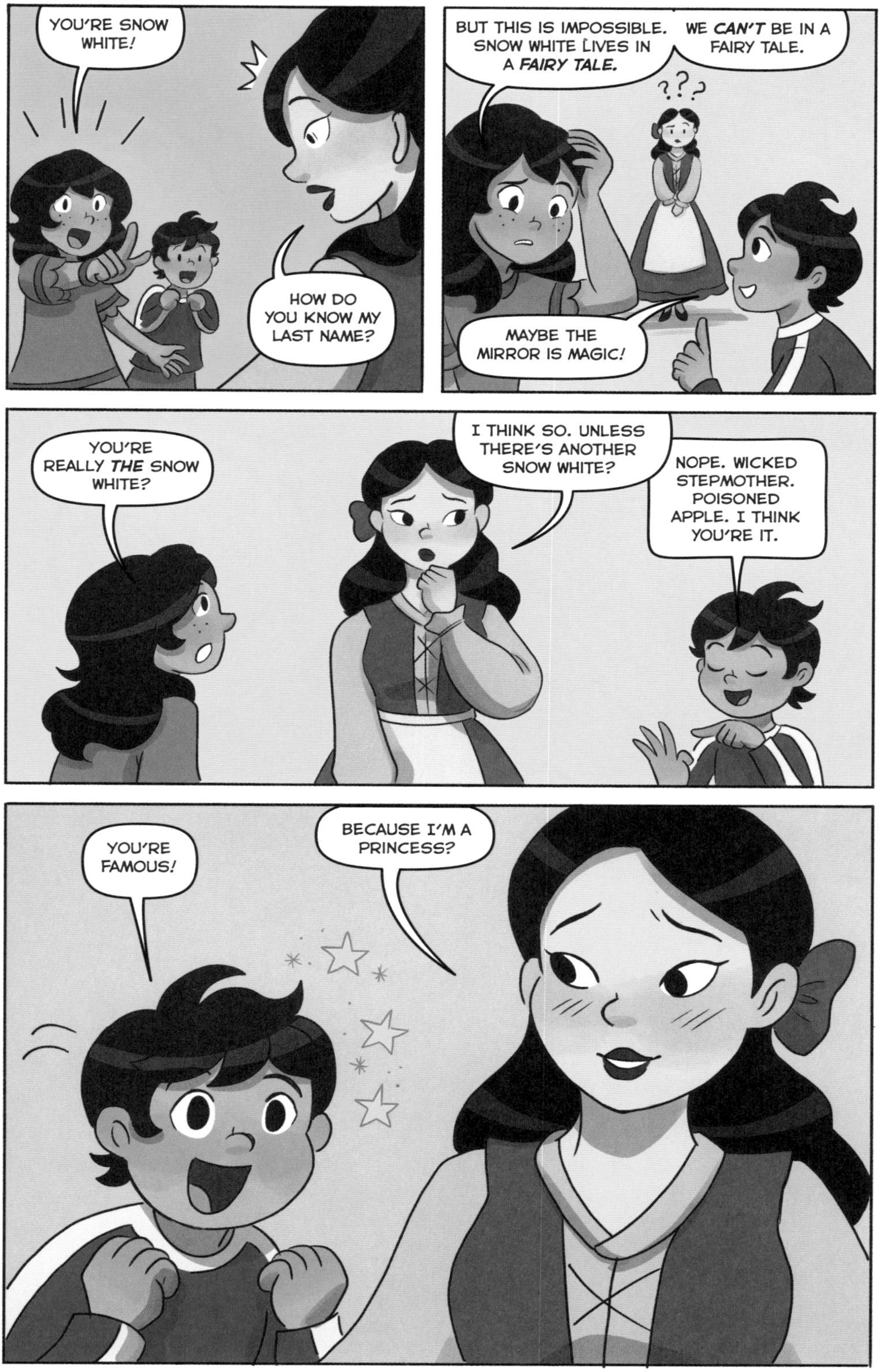
YOU'RE SNOW WHITE!
HOW DO YOU KNOW MY LAST NAME?
BUT THIS IS IMPOSSIBLE. SNOW WHITE LIVES IN A *FAIRY TALE.*
WE *CAN'T* BE IN A FAIRY TALE.
???
MAYBE THE MIRROR IS MAGIC!
YOU'RE REALLY *THE* SNOW WHITE?
I THINK SO. UNLESS THERE'S ANOTHER SNOW WHITE?
NOPE. WICKED STEPMOTHER. POISONED APPLE. I THINK YOU'RE IT.
YOU'RE FAMOUS!
BECAUSE I'M A PRINCESS?

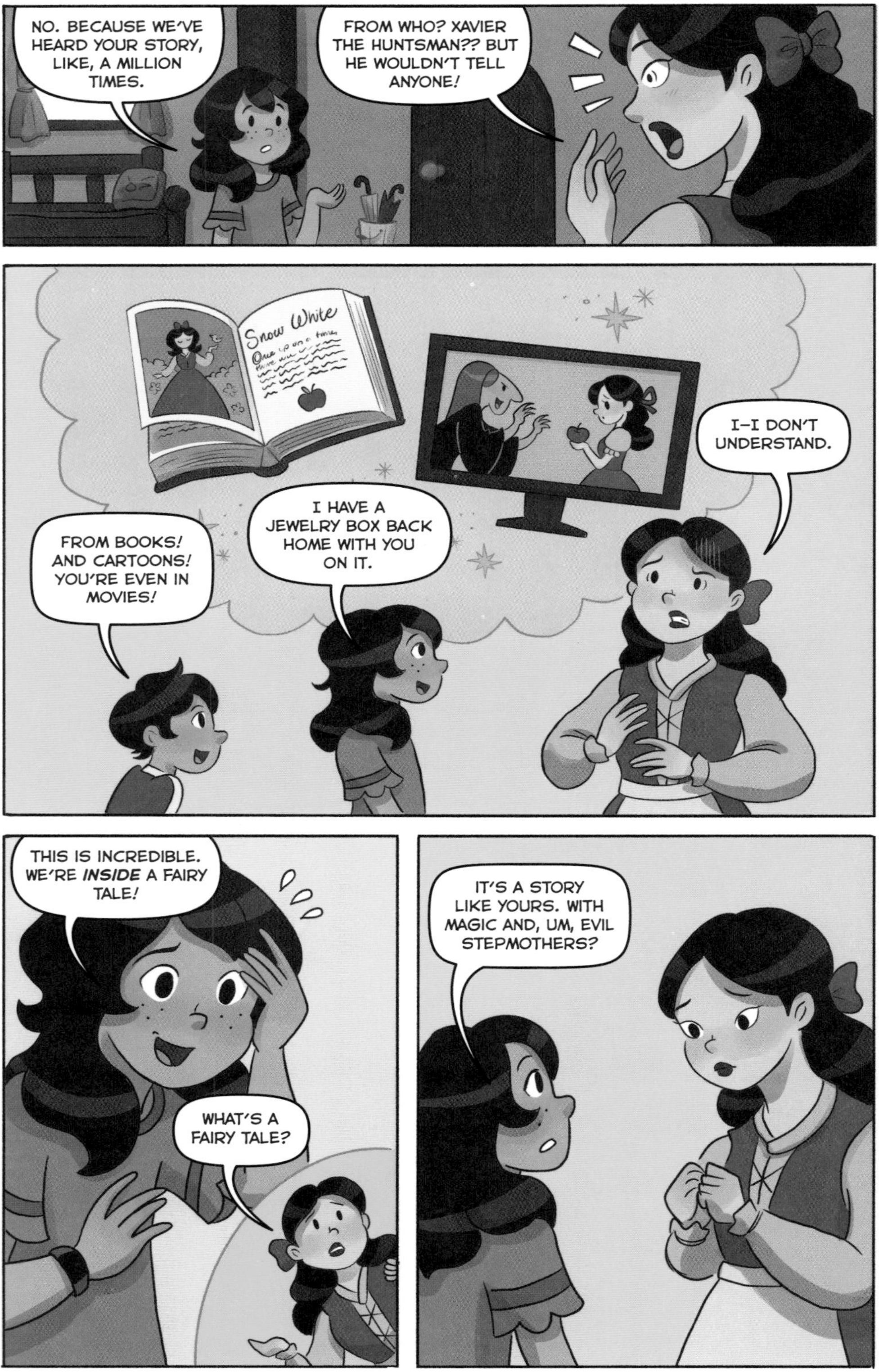
NO. BECAUSE WE'VE HEARD YOUR STORY, LIKE, A MILLION TIMES.
FROM WHO? XAVIER THE HUNTSMAN?? BUT HE WOULDN'T TELL ANYONE!
Snow White
I-I DON'T UNDERSTAND.
FROM BOOKS! AND CARTOONS! YOU'RE EVEN IN MOVIES!
I HAVE A JEWELRY BOX BACK HOME WITH YOU ON IT.
THIS IS INCREDIBLE. WE'RE *INSIDE* A FAIRY TALE!
WHAT'S A FAIRY TALE?
IT'S A STORY LIKE YOURS. WITH MAGIC AND, UM, EVIL STEPMOTHERS?

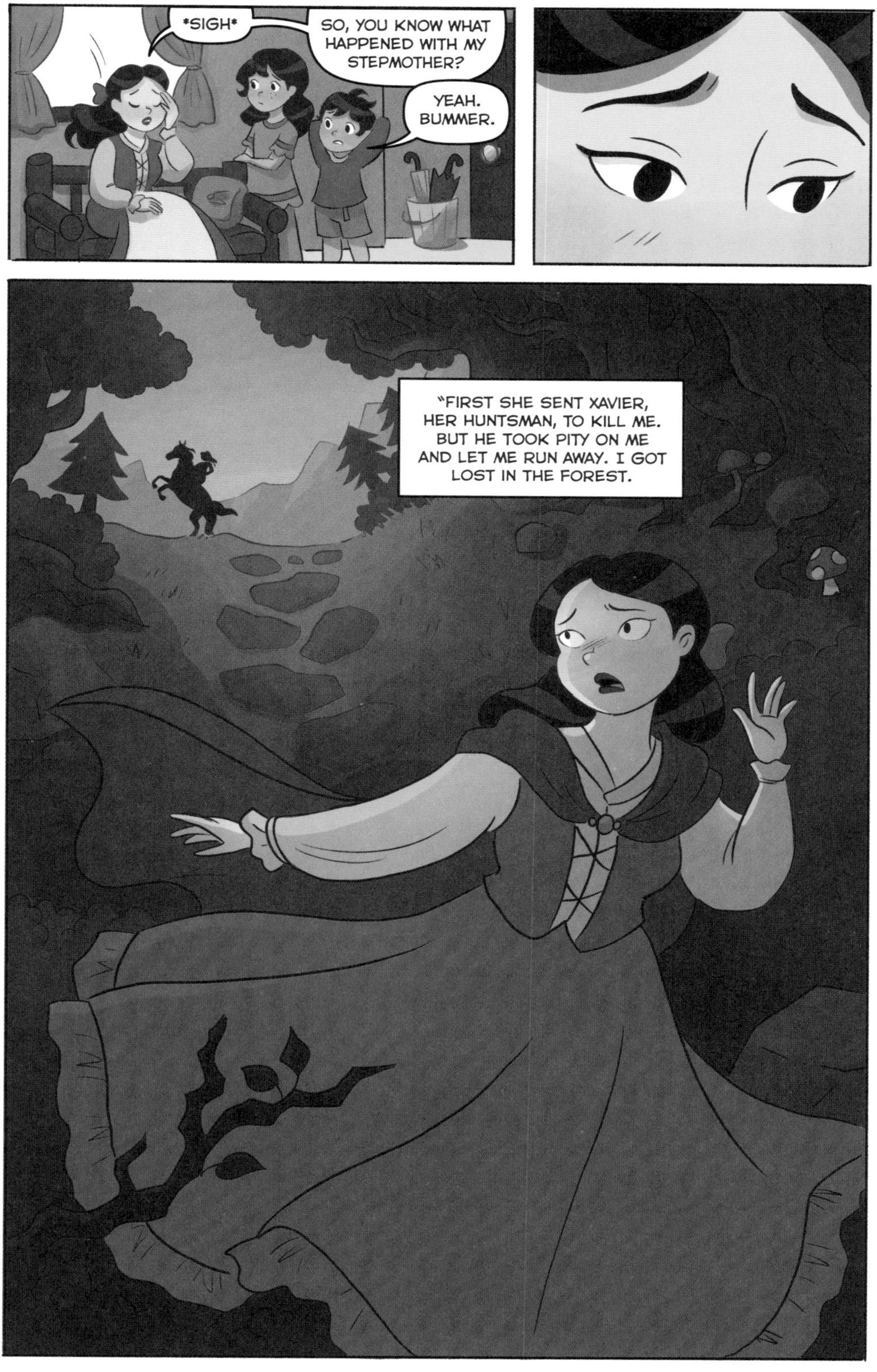
SIGH
SO, YOU KNOW WHAT HAPPENED WITH MY STEPMOTHER?
YEAH. BUMMER.
"FIRST SHE SENT XAVIER, HER HUNTSMAN, TO KILL ME. BUT HE TOOK PITY ON ME AND LET ME RUN AWAY. I GOT LOST IN THE FOREST.

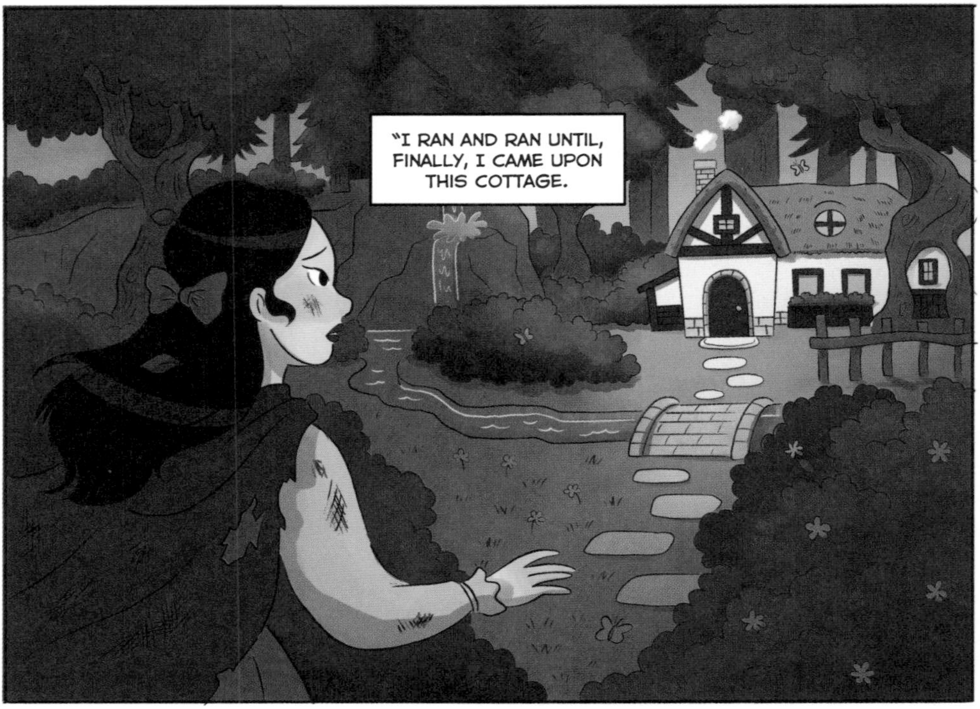
"I RAN AND RAN UNTIL, FINALLY, I CAME UPON THIS COTTAGE.

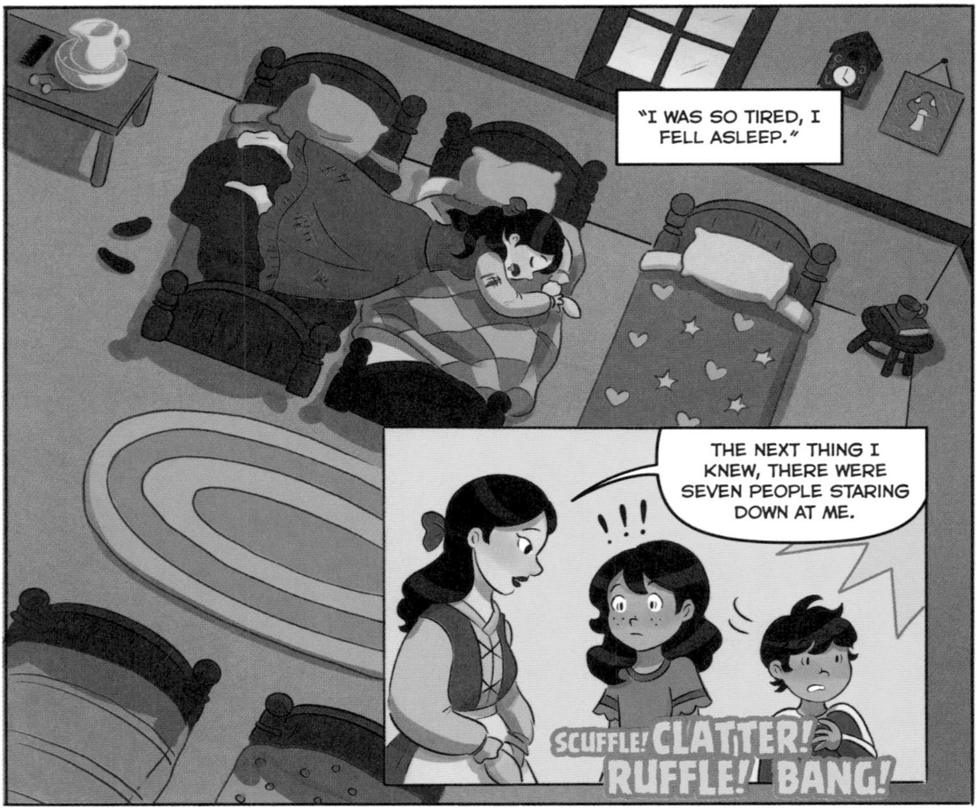
"I WAS SO TIRED, I FELL ASLEEP."
THE NEXT THING I KNEW, THERE WERE SEVEN PEOPLE STARING DOWN AT ME.
!!!
SCUFFLE! CLATTER!
RUFFLE! BANG!

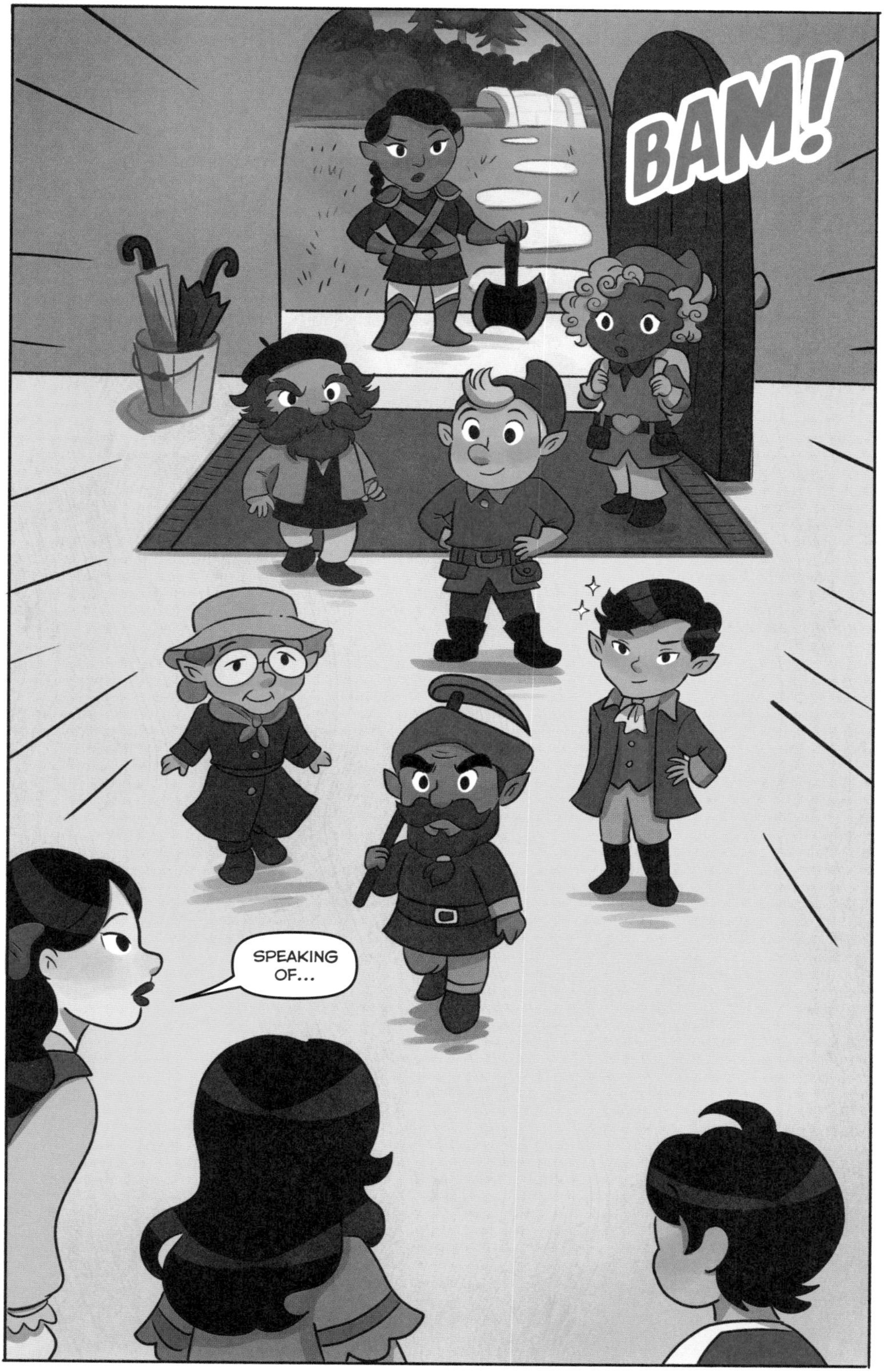
BAM!
SPEAKING OF...

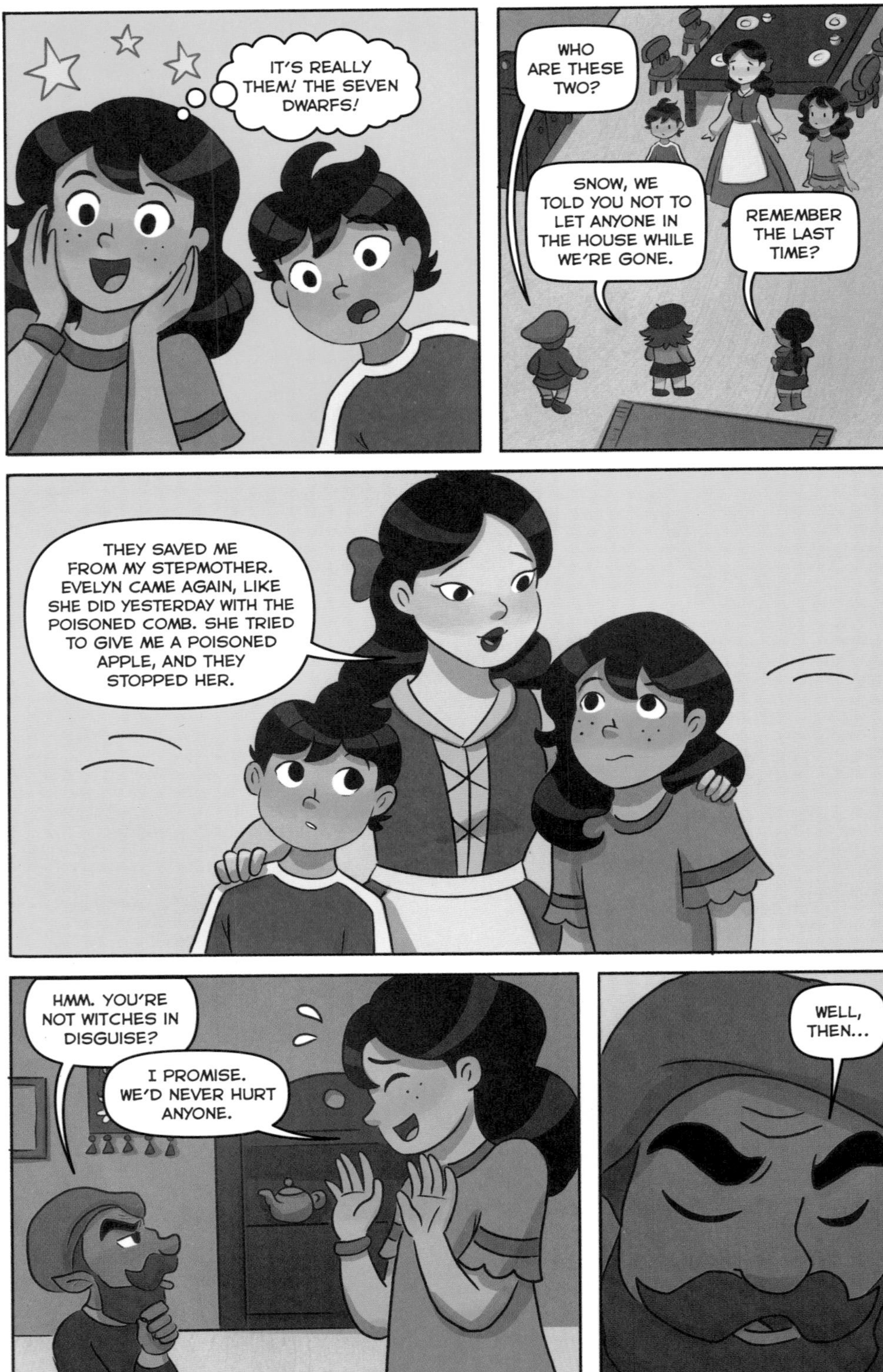
IT'S REALLY THEM! THE SEVEN DWARFS!
WHO ARE THESE TWO?
SNOW, WE TOLD YOU NOT TO LET ANYONE IN THE HOUSE WHILE WE'RE GONE.
REMEMBER THE LAST TIME?
THEY SAVED ME FROM MY STEPMOTHER. EVELYN CAME AGAIN, LIKE SHE DID YESTERDAY WITH THE POISONED COMB. SHE TRIED TO GIVE ME A POISONED APPLE, AND THEY STOPPED HER.
HMM. YOU'RE NOT WITCHES IN DISGUISE?
I PROMISE. WE'D NEVER HURT ANYONE.
WELL, THEN...

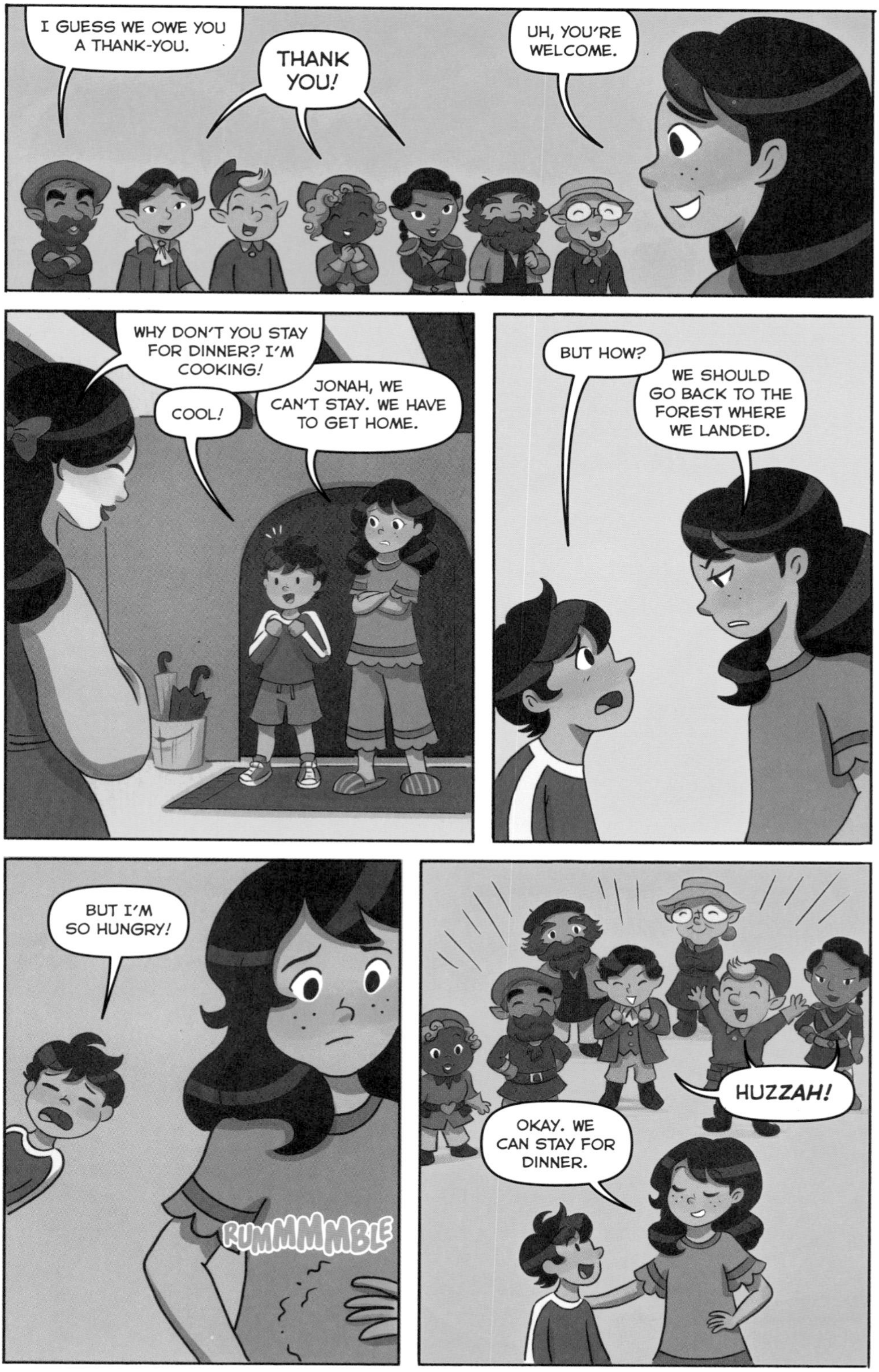
I GUESS WE OWE YOU A THANK-YOU.
THANK YOU!
UH, YOU'RE WELCOME.
WHY DON'T YOU STAY FOR DINNER? I'M COOKING!
COOL!
JONAH, WE CAN'T STAY. WE HAVE TO GET HOME.
BUT HOW?
WE SHOULD GO BACK TO THE FOREST WHERE WE LANDED.
BUT I'M SO HUNGRY!
RUMMMMBLE
HUZZAH!
OKAY. WE CAN STAY FOR DINNER.

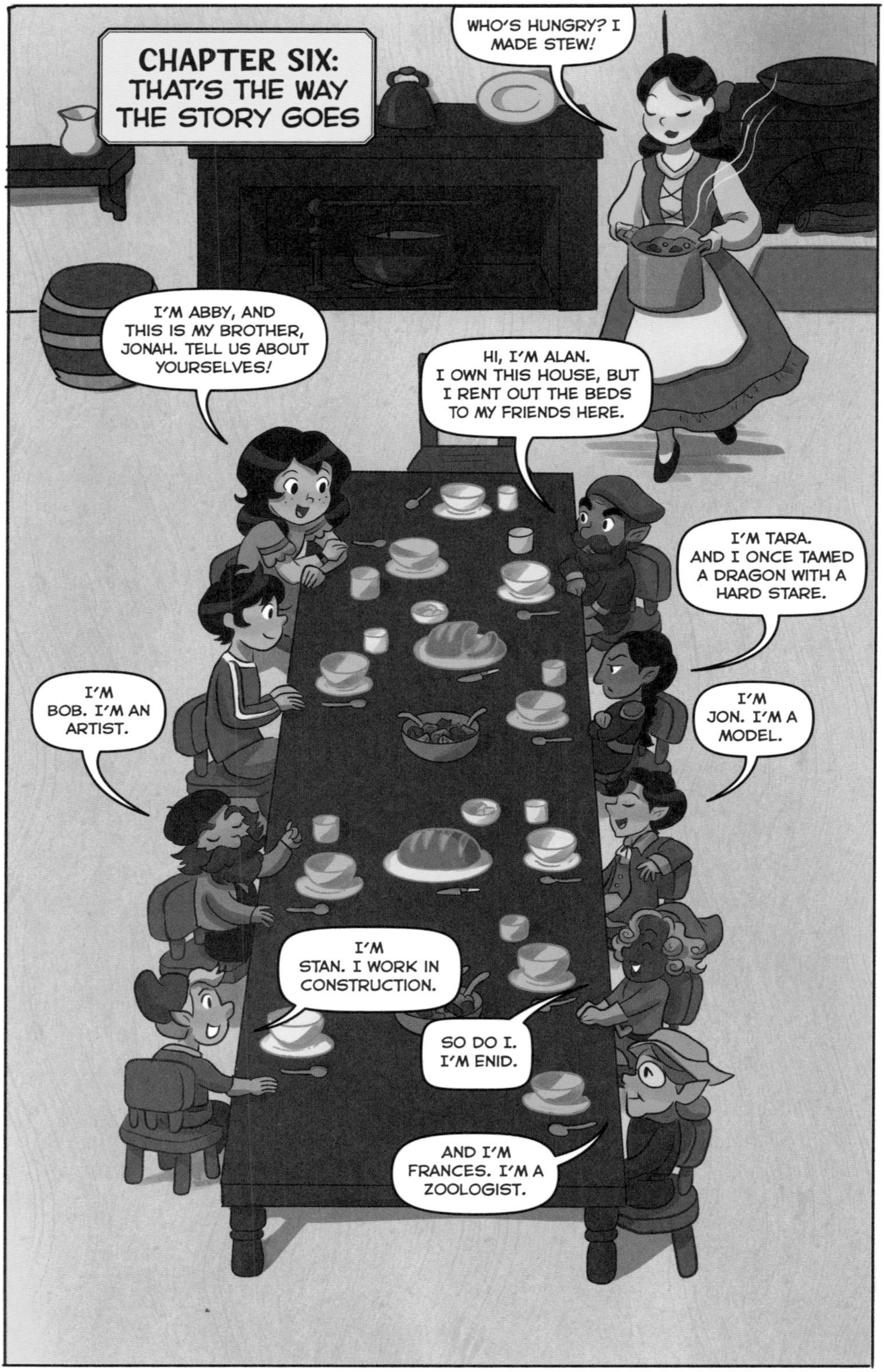
CHAPTER SIX:
THAT'S THE WAY THE STORY GOES
WHO'S HUNGRY? I MADE STEW!
I'M ABBY, AND THIS IS MY BROTHER, JONAH. TELL US ABOUT YOURSELVES!
HI, I'M ALAN. I OWN THIS HOUSE, BUT I RENT OUT THE BEDS TO MY FRIENDS HERE.
I'M TARA. AND I ONCE TAMED A DRAGON WITH A HARD STARE.
I'M BOB. I'M AN ARTIST.
I'M JON. I'M A MODEL.
I'M STAN. I WORK IN CONSTRUCTION.
SO DO I. I'M ENID.
AND I'M FRANCES. I'M A ZOOLOGIST.

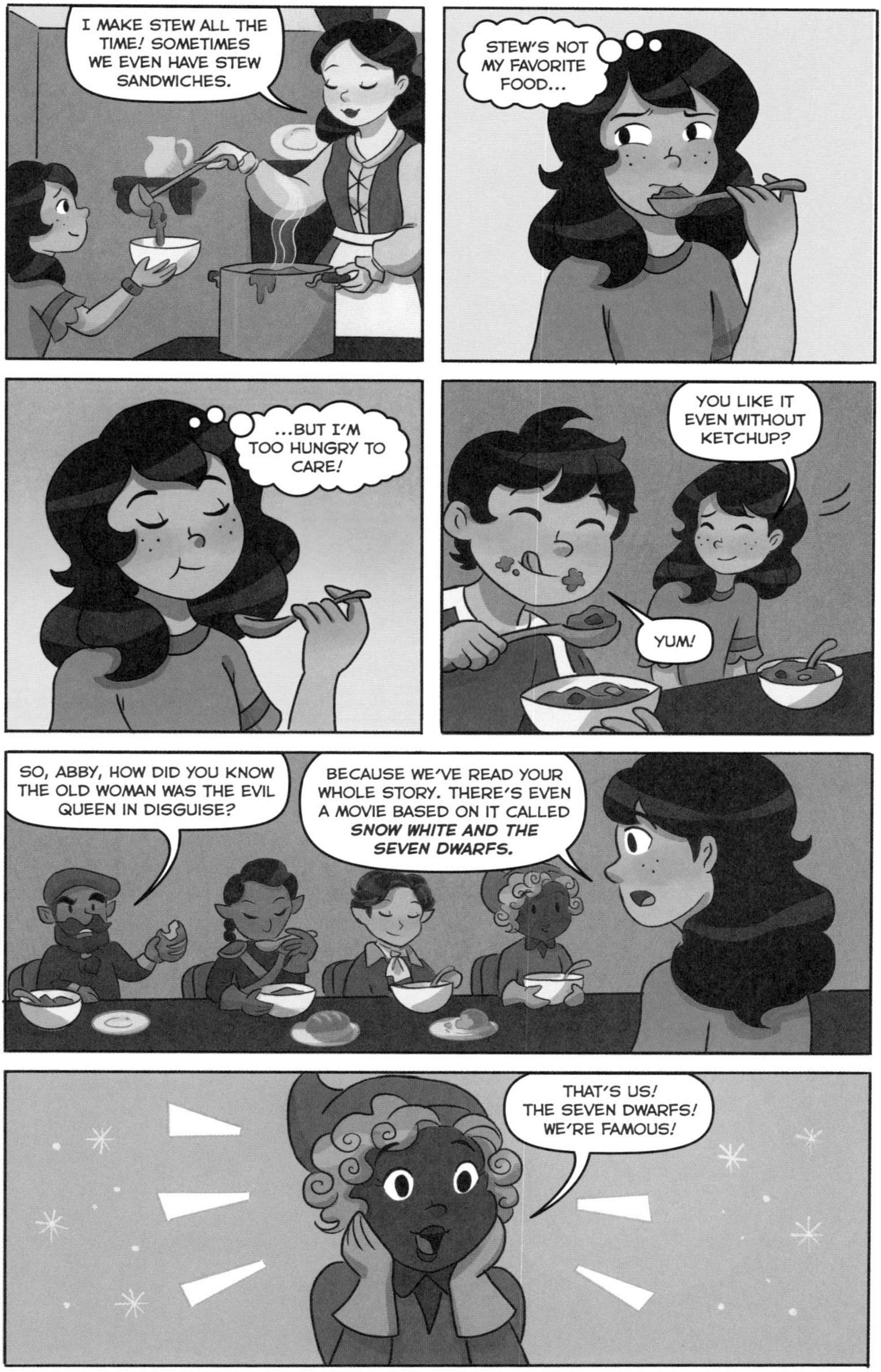
I MAKE STEW ALL THE TIME! SOMETIMES WE EVEN HAVE STEW SANDWICHES.
STEW'S NOT MY FAVORITE FOOD...
...BUT I'M TOO HUNGRY TO CARE!
YOU LIKE IT EVEN WITHOUT KETCHUP?
YUM!
SO, ABBY, HOW DID YOU KNOW THE OLD WOMAN WAS THE EVIL QUEEN IN DISGUISE?
BECAUSE WE'VE READ YOUR WHOLE STORY. THERE'S EVEN A MOVIE BASED ON IT CALLED ***SNOW WHITE AND THE SEVEN DWARFS.***
THAT'S US! THE SEVEN DWARFS! WE'RE FAMOUS!

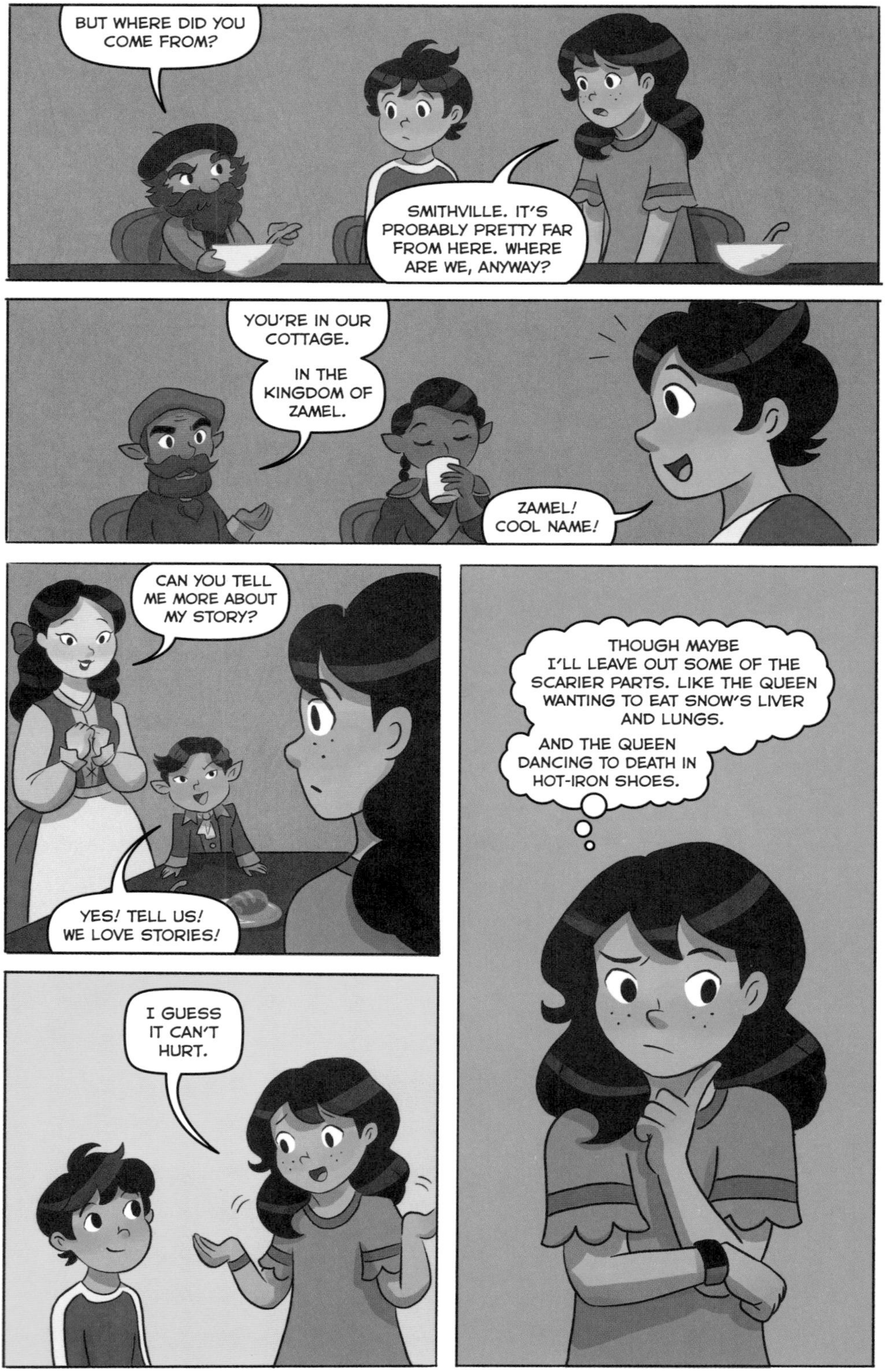

BUT WHERE DID YOU COME FROM?
SMITHVILLE. IT'S PROBABLY PRETTY FAR FROM HERE. WHERE ARE WE, ANYWAY?
YOU'RE IN OUR COTTAGE.
IN THE KINGDOM OF ZAMEL.
ZAMEL! COOL NAME!
CAN YOU TELL ME MORE ABOUT MY STORY?
YES! TELL US! WE LOVE STORIES!
I GUESS IT CAN'T HURT.
THOUGH MAYBE I'LL LEAVE OUT SOME OF THE SCARIER PARTS. LIKE THE QUEEN WANTING TO EAT SNOW'S LIVER AND LUNGS.
AND THE QUEEN DANCING TO DEATH IN HOT-IRON SHOES.

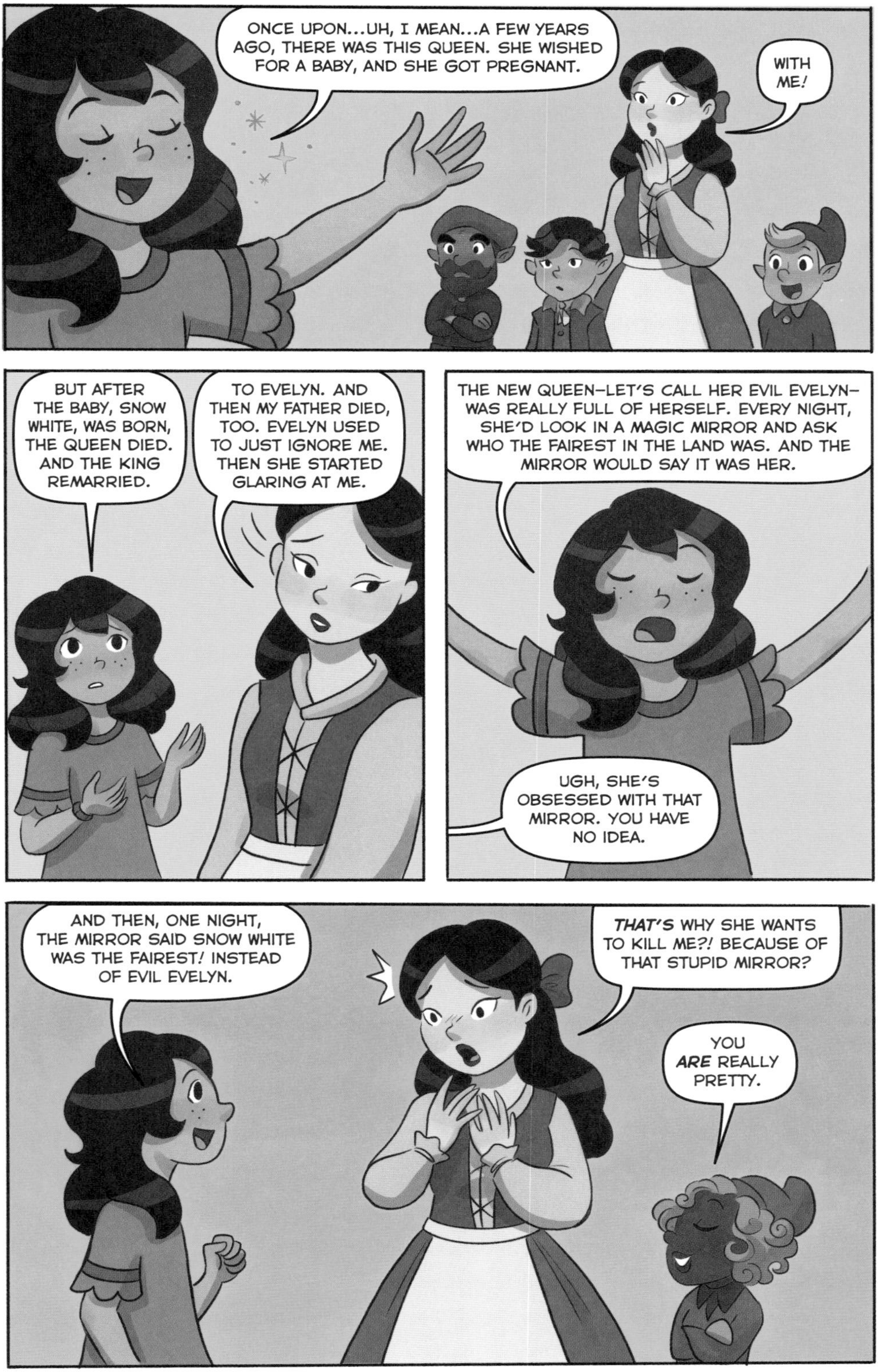
ONCE UPON...UH, I MEAN...A FEW YEARS AGO, THERE WAS THIS QUEEN. SHE WISHED FOR A BABY, AND SHE GOT PREGNANT.
WITH ME!
BUT AFTER THE BABY, SNOW WHITE, WAS BORN, THE QUEEN DIED. AND THE KING REMARRIED.
TO EVELYN. AND THEN MY FATHER DIED, TOO. EVELYN USED TO JUST IGNORE ME. THEN SHE STARTED GLARING AT ME.
THE NEW QUEEN—LET'S CALL HER EVIL EVELYN—WAS REALLY FULL OF HERSELF. EVERY NIGHT, SHE'D LOOK IN A MAGIC MIRROR AND ASK WHO THE FAIREST IN THE LAND WAS. AND THE MIRROR WOULD SAY IT WAS HER.
UGH, SHE'S OBSESSED WITH THAT MIRROR. YOU HAVE NO IDEA.
AND THEN, ONE NIGHT, THE MIRROR SAID SNOW WHITE WAS THE FAIREST! INSTEAD OF EVIL EVELYN.
THAT'S WHY SHE WANTS TO KILL ME?! BECAUSE OF THAT STUPID MIRROR?
YOU *ARE* REALLY PRETTY.

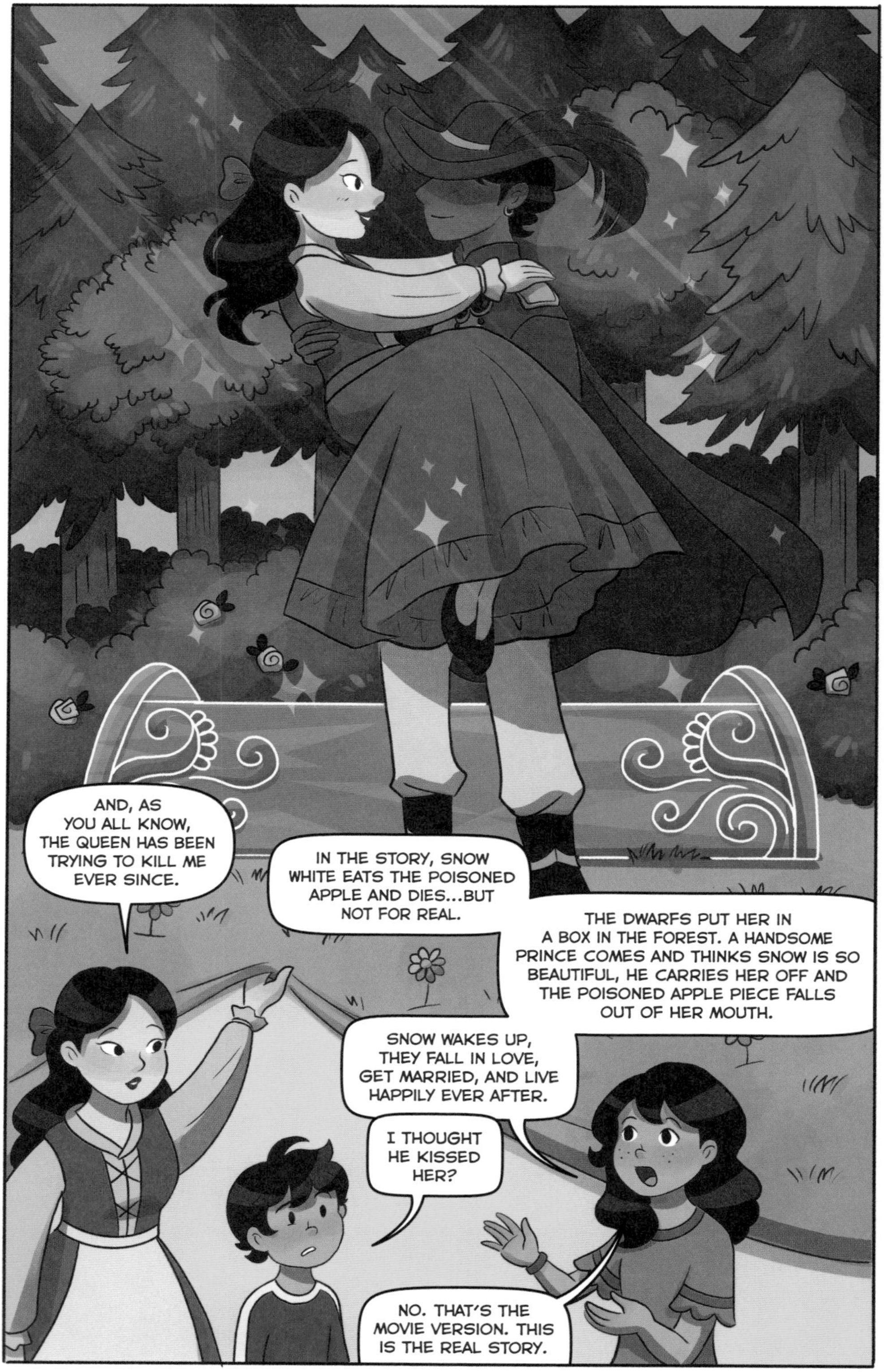
AND, AS YOU ALL KNOW, THE QUEEN HAS BEEN TRYING TO KILL ME EVER SINCE.
IN THE STORY, SNOW WHITE EATS THE POISONED APPLE AND DIES...BUT NOT FOR REAL.
THE DWARFS PUT HER IN A BOX IN THE FOREST. A HANDSOME PRINCE COMES AND THINKS SNOW IS SO BEAUTIFUL, HE CARRIES HER OFF AND THE POISONED APPLE PIECE FALLS OUT OF HER MOUTH.
SNOW WAKES UP, THEY FALL IN LOVE, GET MARRIED, AND LIVE HAPPILY EVER AFTER.
I THOUGHT HE KISSED HER?
NO. THAT'S THE MOVIE VERSION. THIS IS THE REAL STORY.

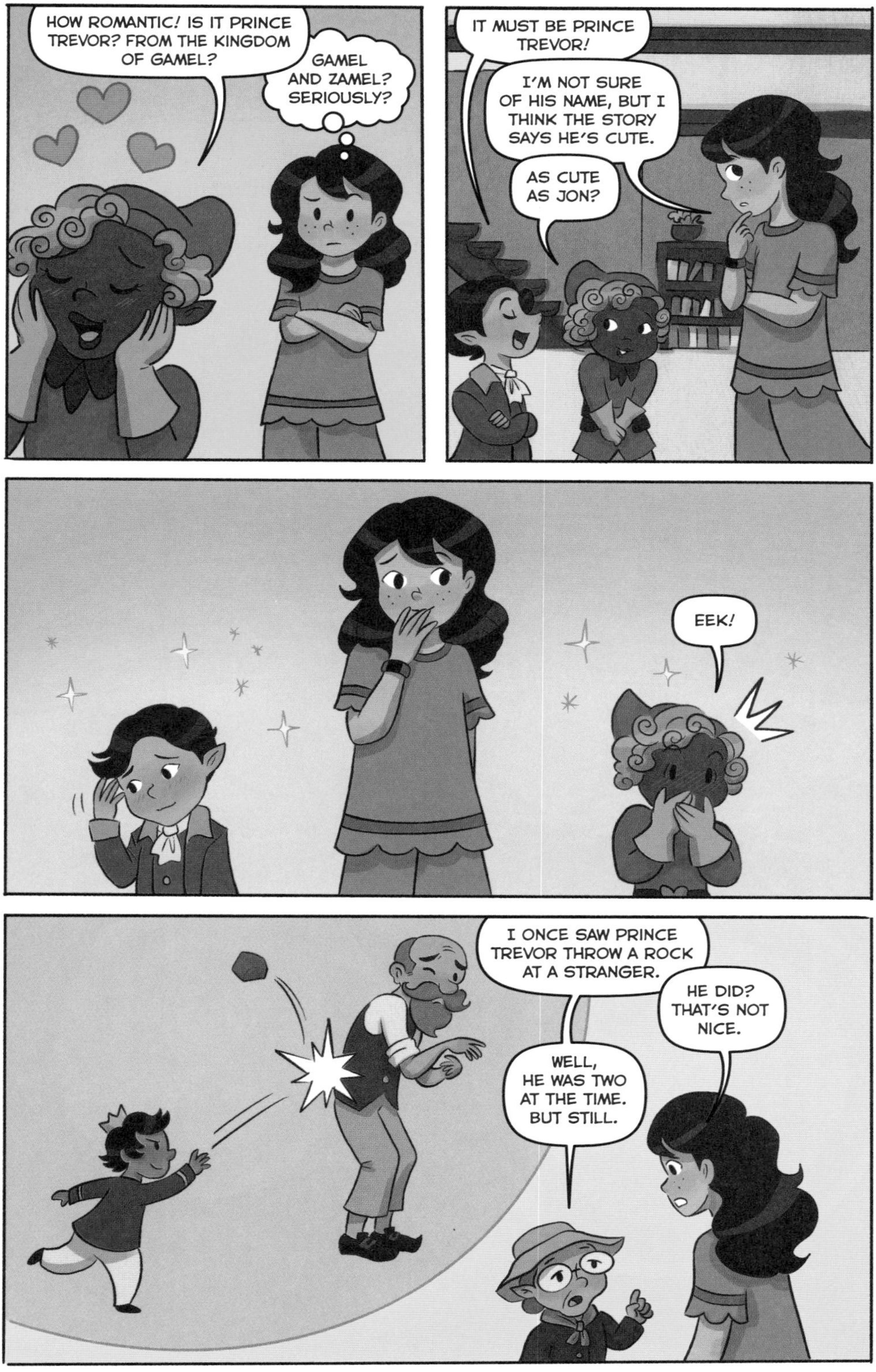
HOW ROMANTIC! IS IT PRINCE TREVOR? FROM THE KINGDOM OF GAMEL?
GAMEL AND ZAMEL? SERIOUSLY?
IT MUST BE PRINCE TREVOR!
I'M NOT SURE OF HIS NAME, BUT I THINK THE STORY SAYS HE'S CUTE.
AS CUTE AS JON?
EEK!
I ONCE SAW PRINCE TREVOR THROW A ROCK AT A STRANGER.
HE DID? THAT'S NOT NICE.
WELL, HE WAS TWO AT THE TIME. BUT STILL.

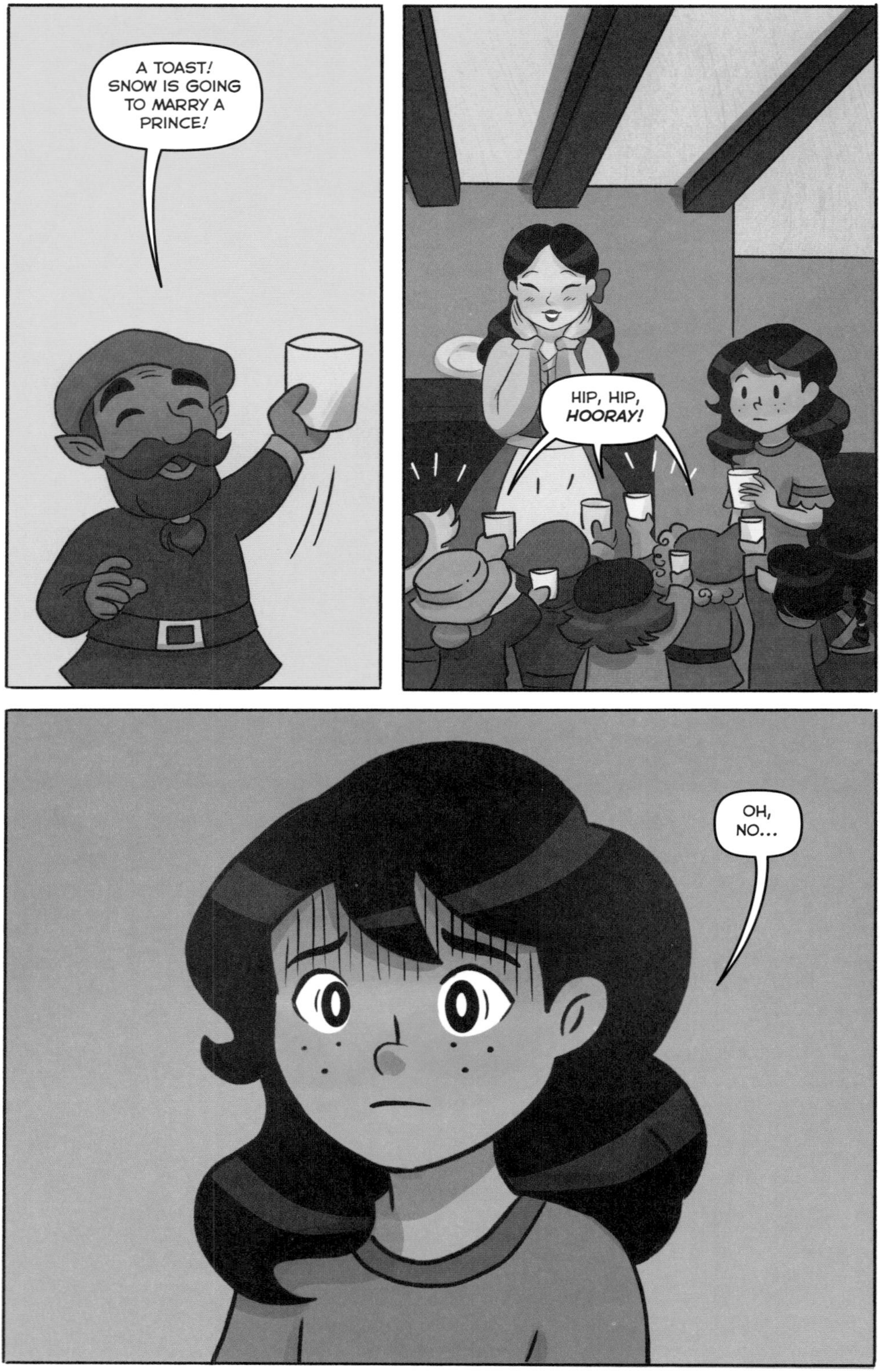
A TOAST! SNOW IS GOING TO MARRY A PRINCE!
HIP, HIP, HOORAY!
OH, NO...

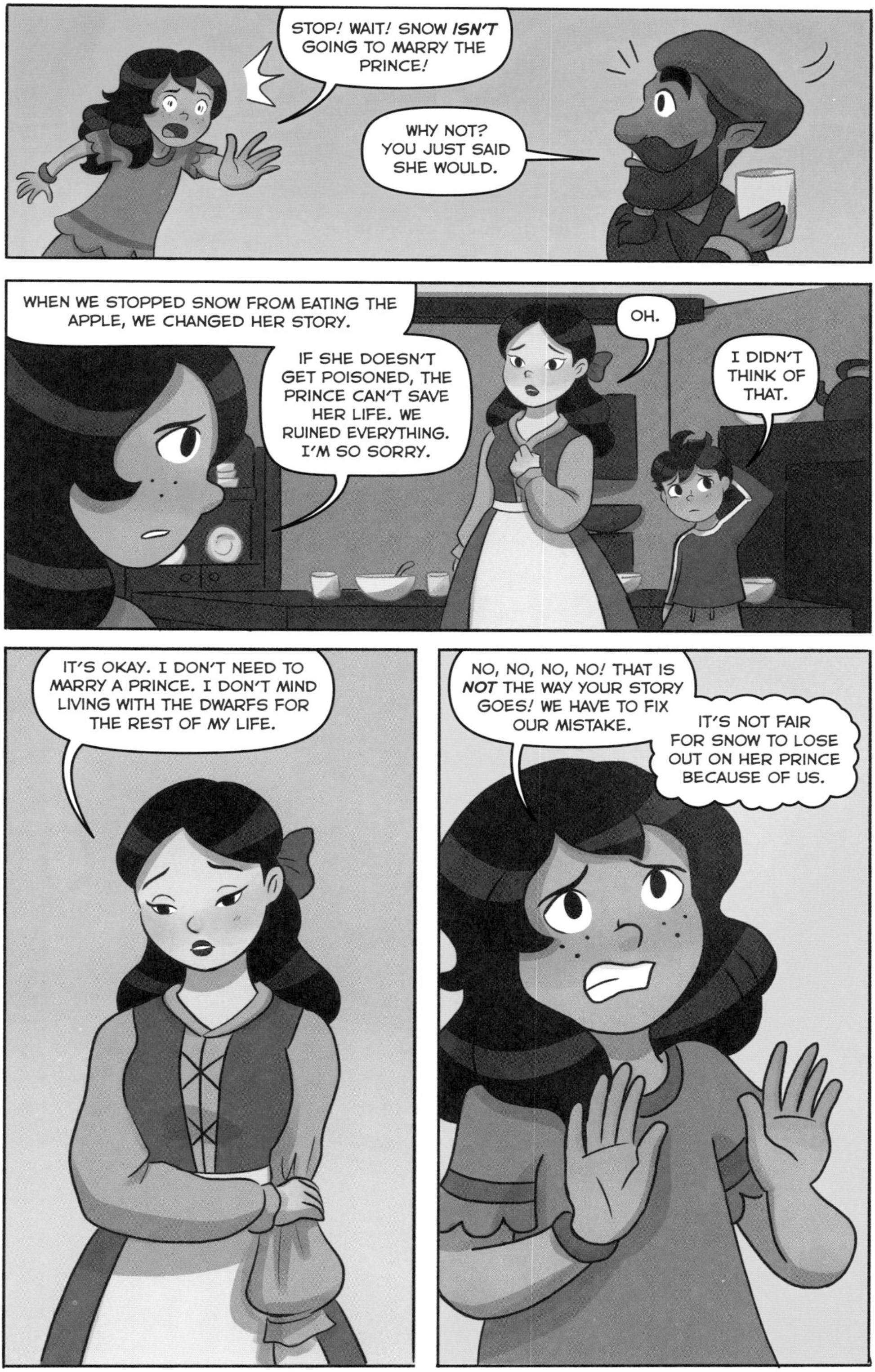
STOP! WAIT! SNOW **ISN'T** GOING TO MARRY THE PRINCE!
WHY NOT? YOU JUST SAID SHE WOULD.
WHEN WE STOPPED SNOW FROM EATING THE APPLE, WE CHANGED HER STORY.
IF SHE DOESN'T GET POISONED, THE PRINCE CAN'T SAVE HER LIFE. WE RUINED EVERYTHING. I'M SO SORRY.
OH.
I DIDN'T THINK OF THAT.
IT'S OKAY. I DON'T NEED TO MARRY A PRINCE. I DON'T MIND LIVING WITH THE DWARFS FOR THE REST OF MY LIFE.
NO, NO, NO, NO! THAT IS **NOT** THE WAY YOUR STORY GOES! WE HAVE TO FIX OUR MISTAKE.
IT'S NOT FAIR FOR SNOW TO LOSE OUT ON HER PRINCE BECAUSE OF US.

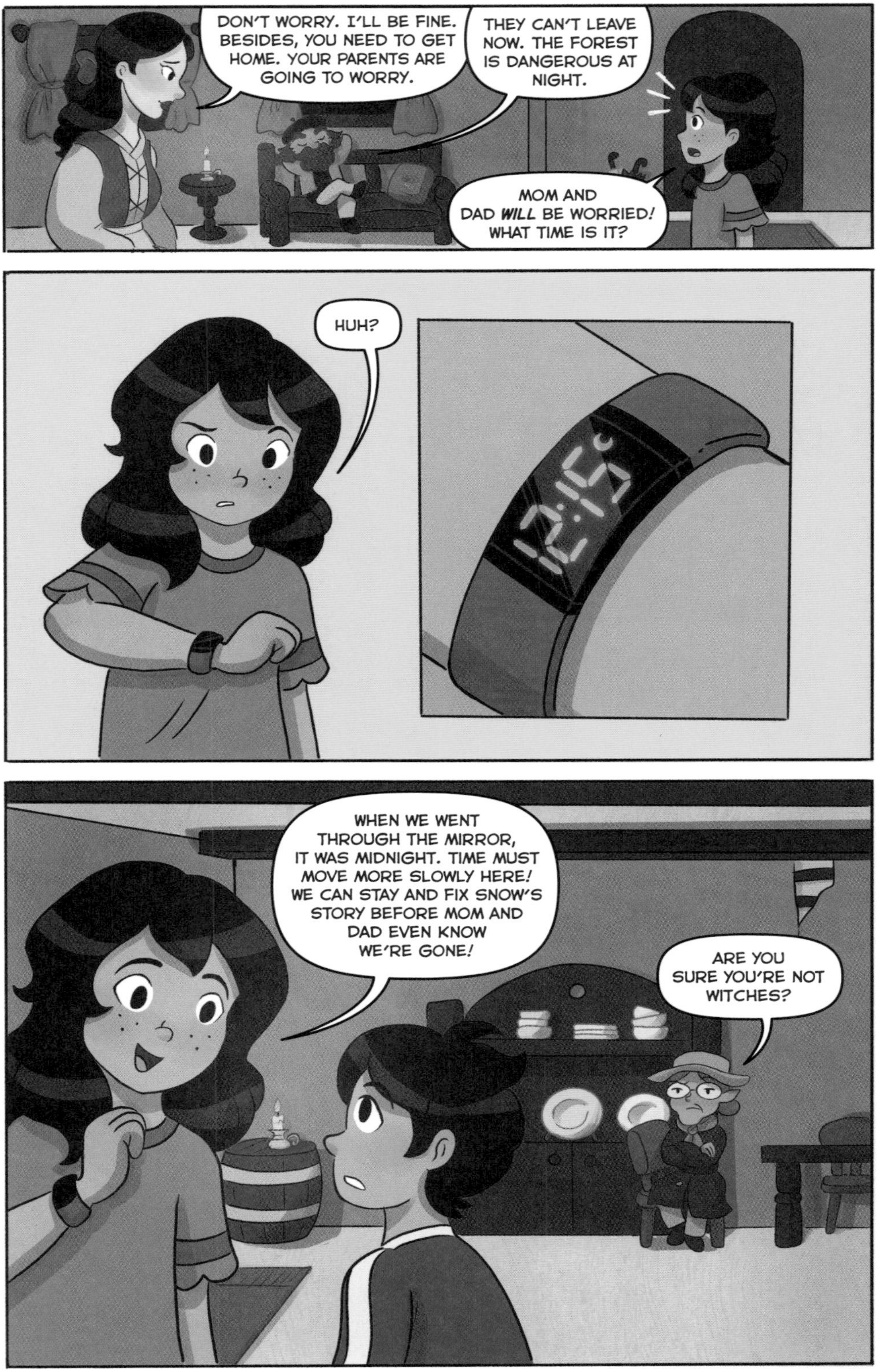
DON'T WORRY. I'LL BE FINE. BESIDES, YOU NEED TO GET HOME. YOUR PARENTS ARE GOING TO WORRY.
THEY CAN'T LEAVE NOW. THE FOREST IS DANGEROUS AT NIGHT.
MOM AND DAD ***WILL*** BE WORRIED! WHAT TIME IS IT?
HUH?
12:15
WHEN WE WENT THROUGH THE MIRROR, IT WAS MIDNIGHT. TIME MUST MOVE MORE SLOWLY HERE! WE CAN STAY AND FIX SNOW'S STORY BEFORE MOM AND DAD EVEN KNOW WE'RE GONE!
ARE YOU SURE YOU'RE NOT WITCHES?

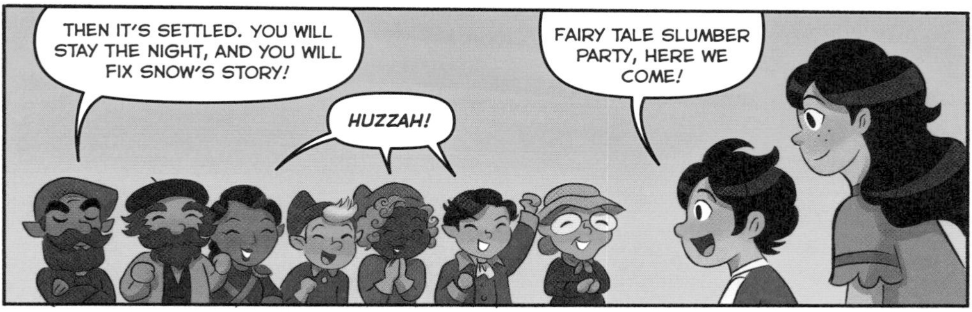
THEN IT'S SETTLED. YOU WILL STAY THE NIGHT, AND YOU WILL FIX SNOW'S STORY!
HUZZAH!
FAIRY TALE SLUMBER PARTY, HERE WE COME!

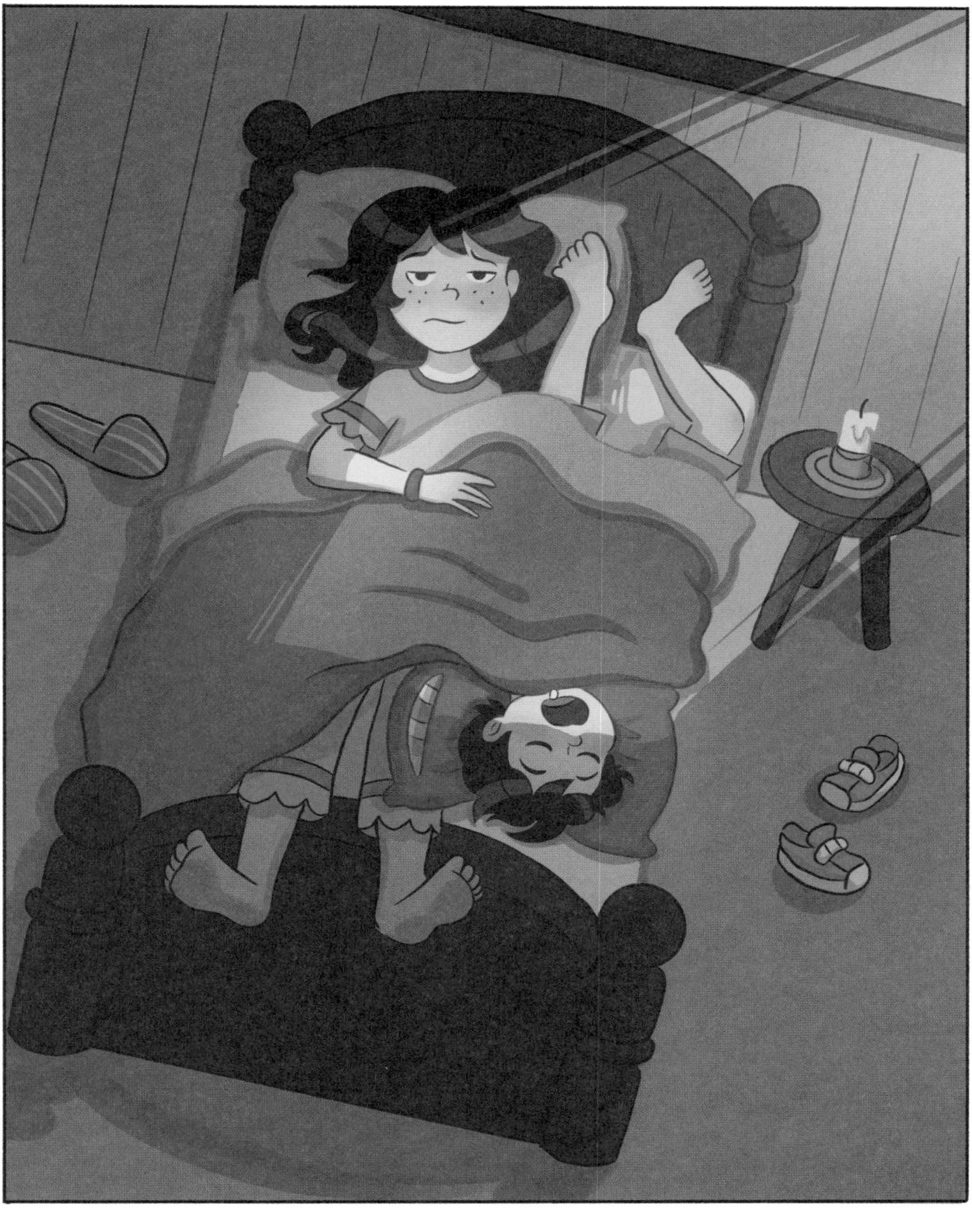

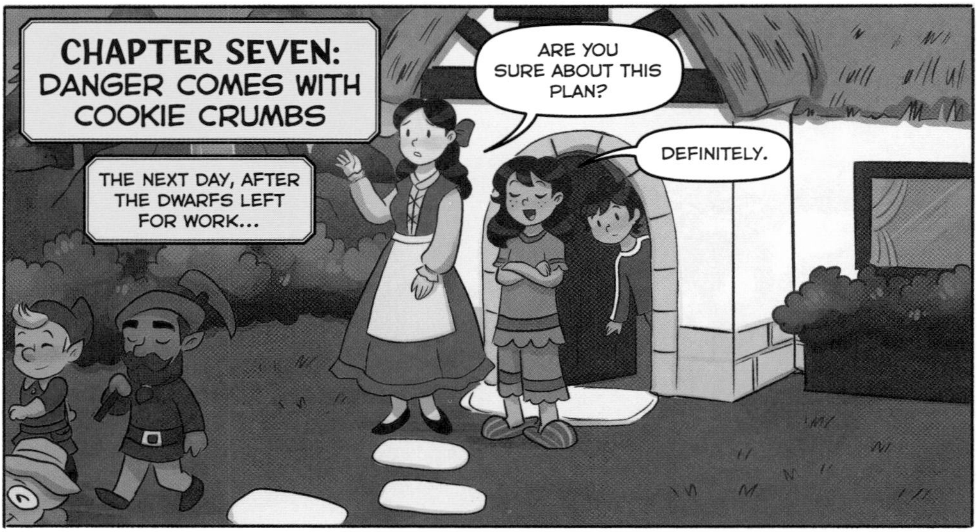
CHAPTER SEVEN: DANGER COMES WITH COOKIE CRUMBS
THE NEXT DAY, AFTER THE DWARFS LEFT FOR WORK...
ARE YOU SURE ABOUT THIS PLAN?
DEFINITELY.

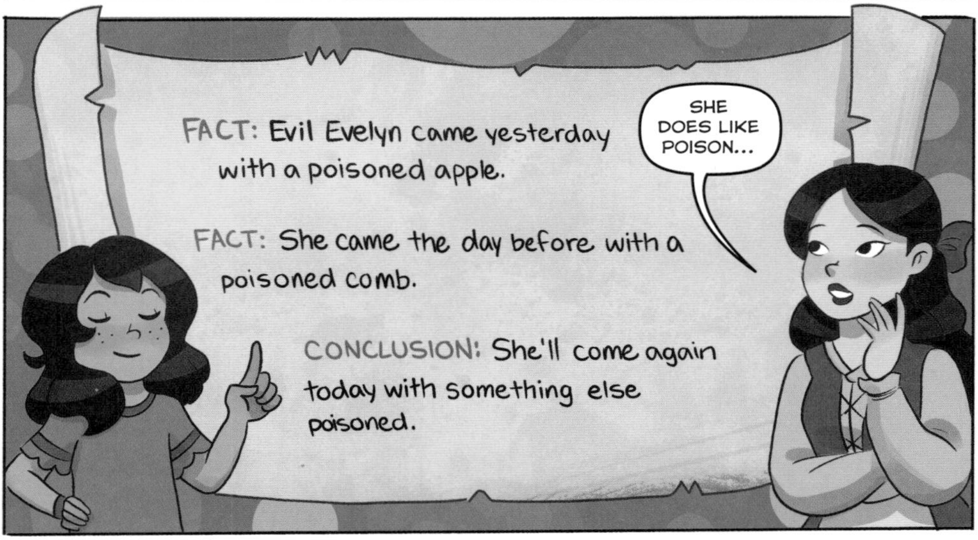
FACT: Evil Evelyn came yesterday with a poisoned apple.
FACT: She came the day before with a poisoned comb.
CONCLUSION: She'll come again today with something else poisoned.
SHE DOES LIKE POISON...

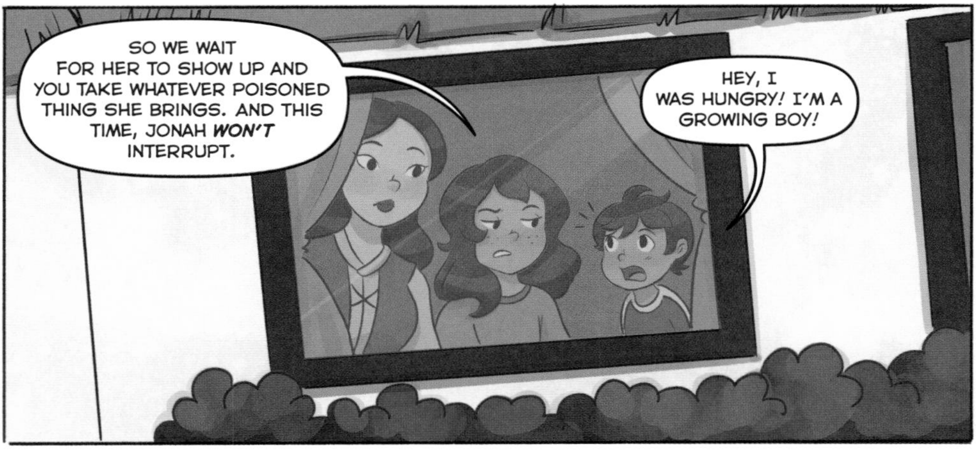
SO WE WAIT FOR HER TO SHOW UP AND YOU TAKE WHATEVER POISONED THING SHE BRINGS. AND THIS TIME, JONAH *WON'T* INTERRUPT.
HEY, I WAS HUNGRY! I'M A GROWING BOY!

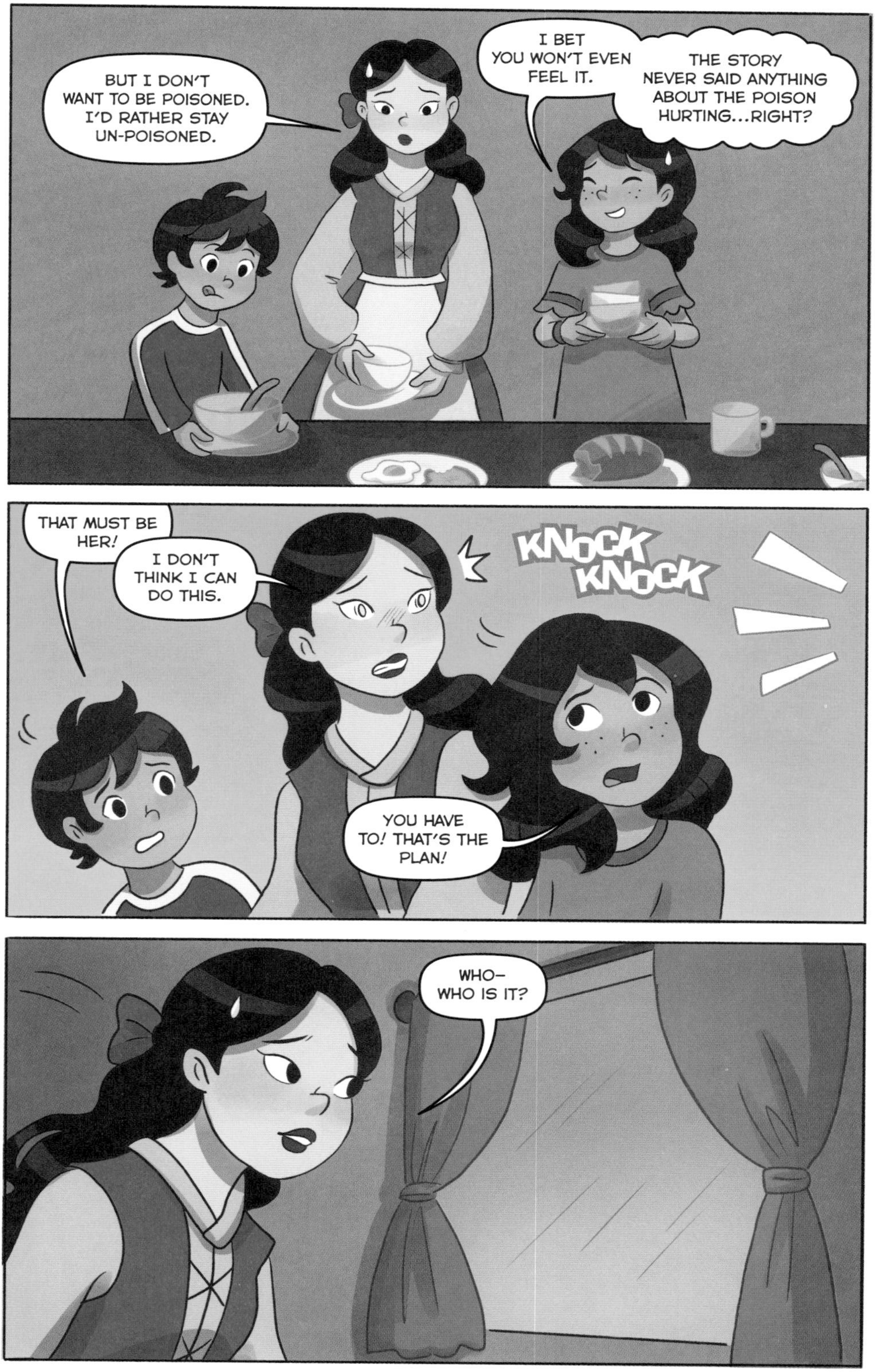
BUT I DON'T WANT TO BE POISONED. I'D RATHER STAY UN-POISONED.
I BET YOU WON'T EVEN FEEL IT.
THE STORY NEVER SAID ANYTHING ABOUT THE POISON HURTING...RIGHT?
KNOCK KNOCK
THAT MUST BE HER!
I DON'T THINK I CAN DO THIS.
YOU HAVE TO! THAT'S THE PLAN!
WHO— WHO IS IT?

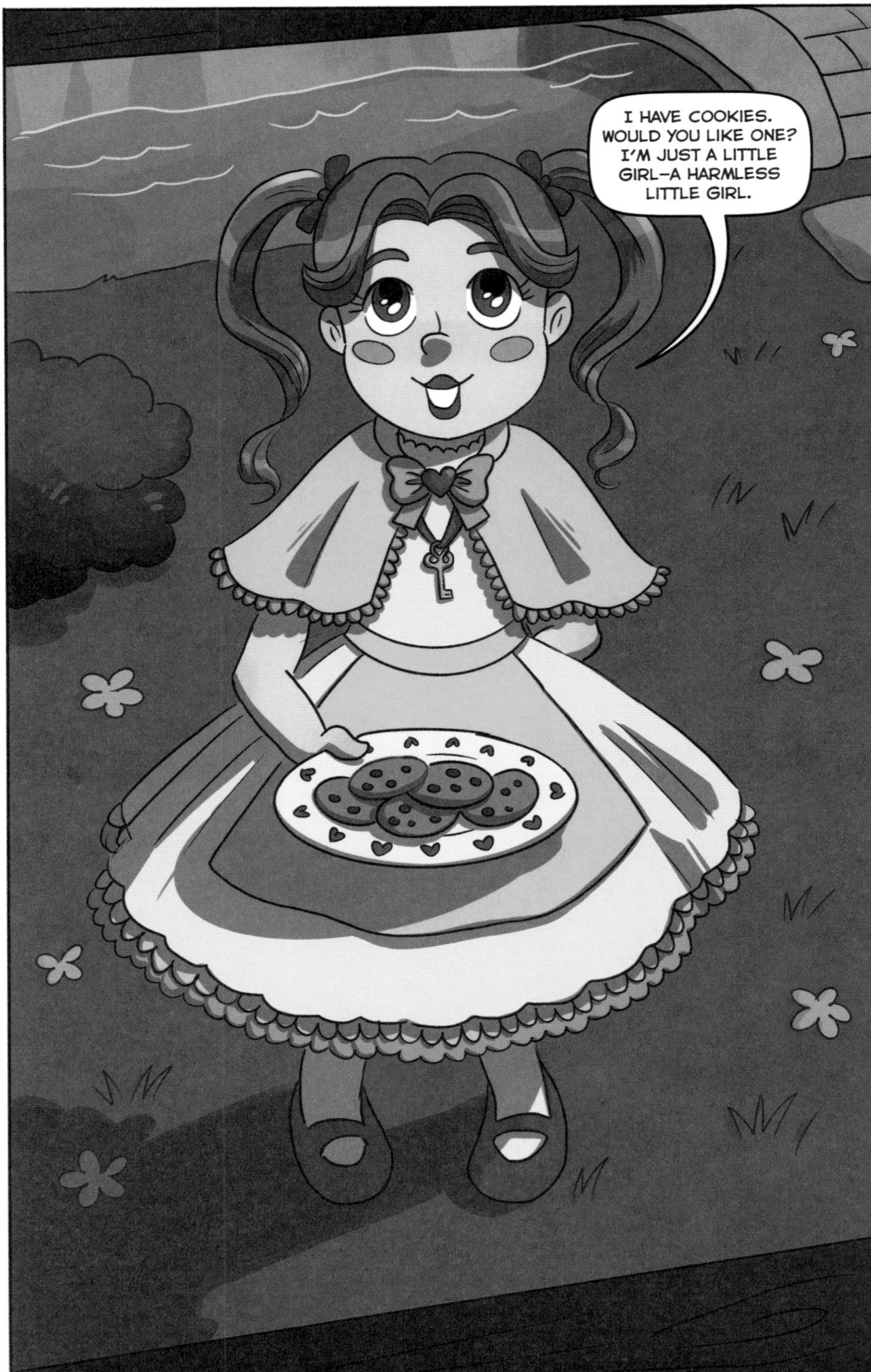
I HAVE COOKIES. WOULD YOU LIKE ONE? I'M JUST A LITTLE GIRL—A HARMLESS LITTLE GIRL.

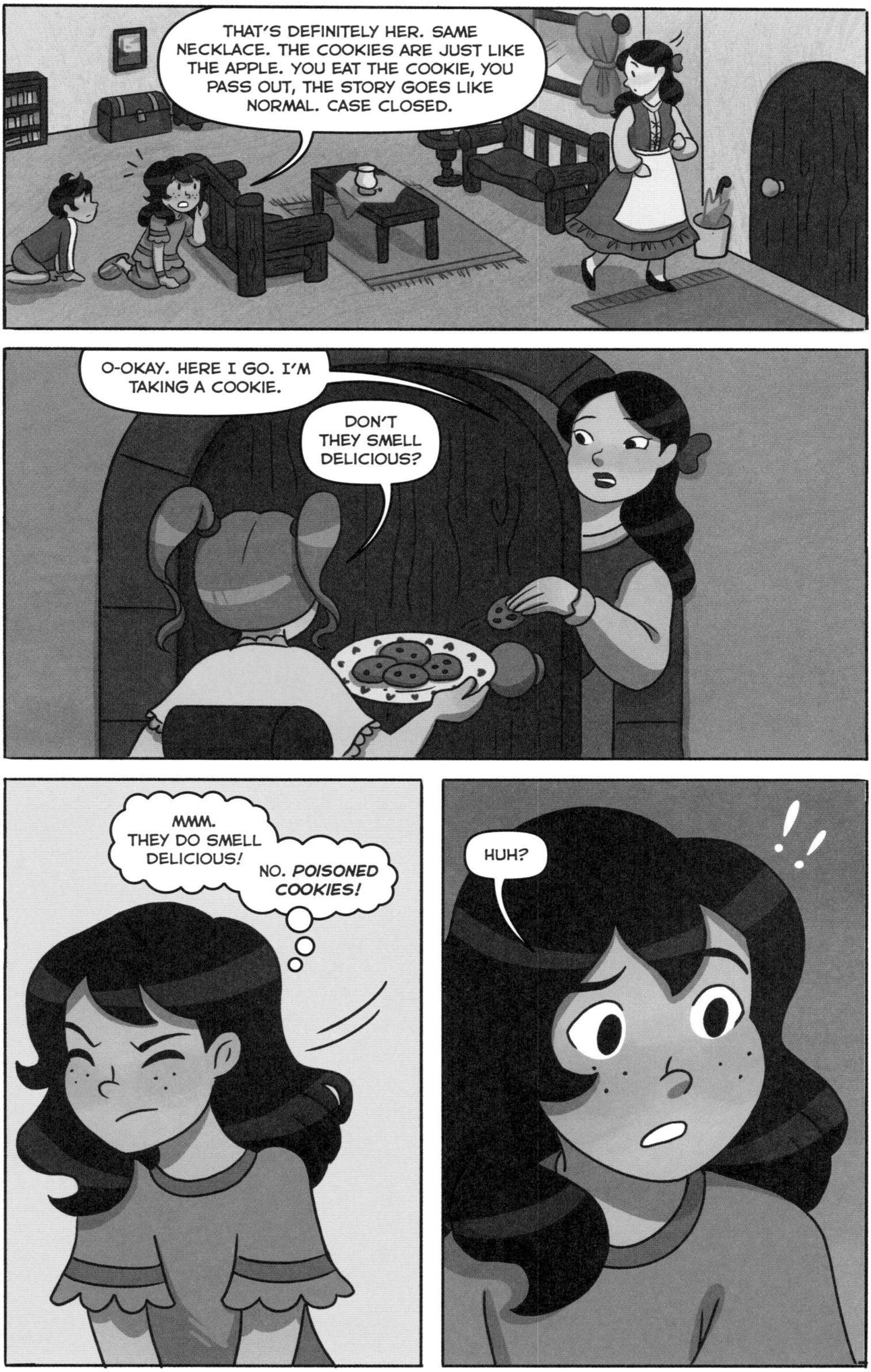
THAT'S DEFINITELY HER. SAME NECKLACE. THE COOKIES ARE JUST LIKE THE APPLE. YOU EAT THE COOKIE, YOU PASS OUT, THE STORY GOES LIKE NORMAL. CASE CLOSED.
O-OKAY. HERE I GO. I'M TAKING A COOKIE.
DON'T THEY SMELL DELICIOUS?
MMM. THEY DO SMELL DELICIOUS!
NO. *POISONED COOKIES!*
HUH?
! !

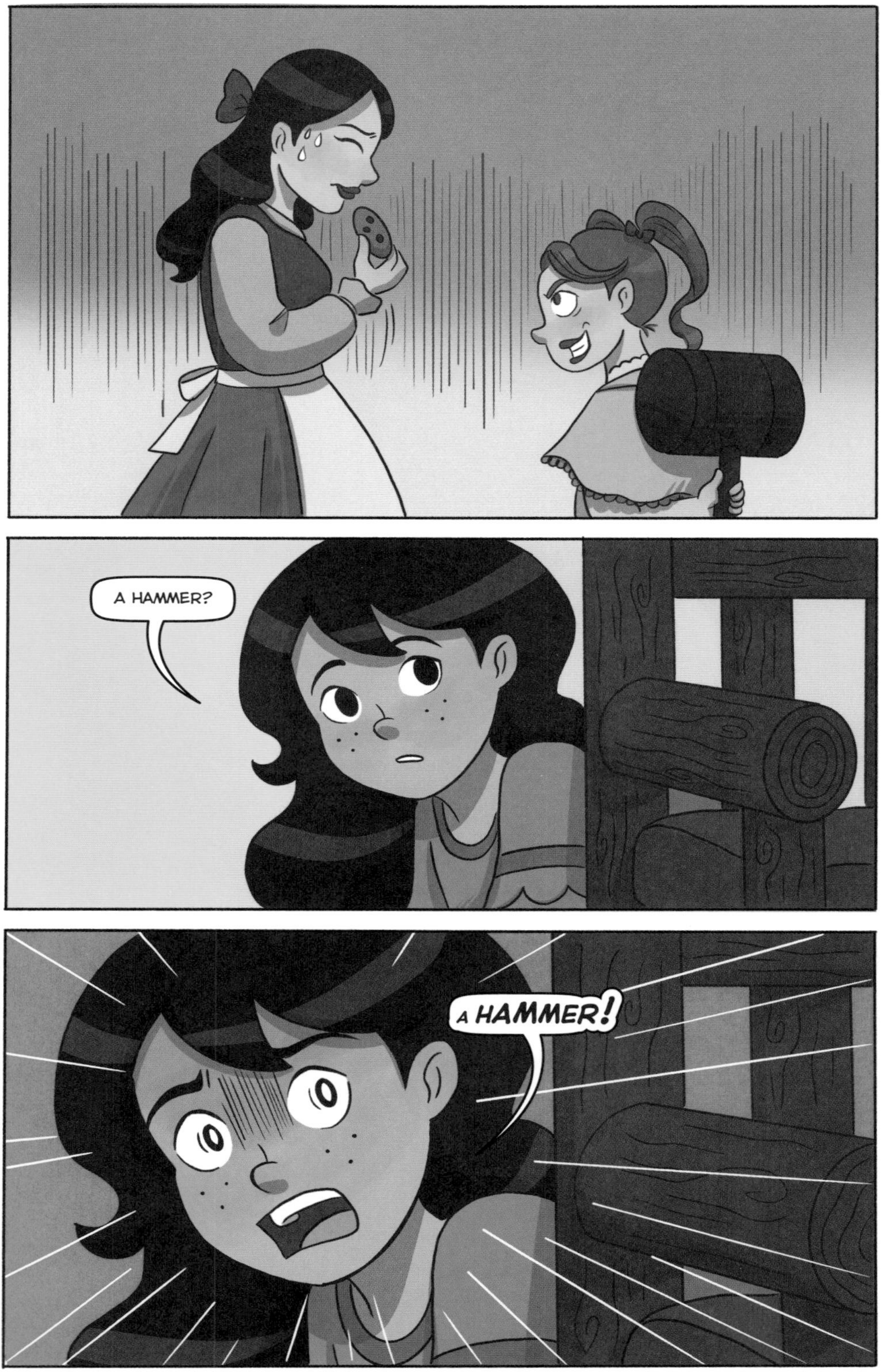
A HAMMER?
A HAMMER!

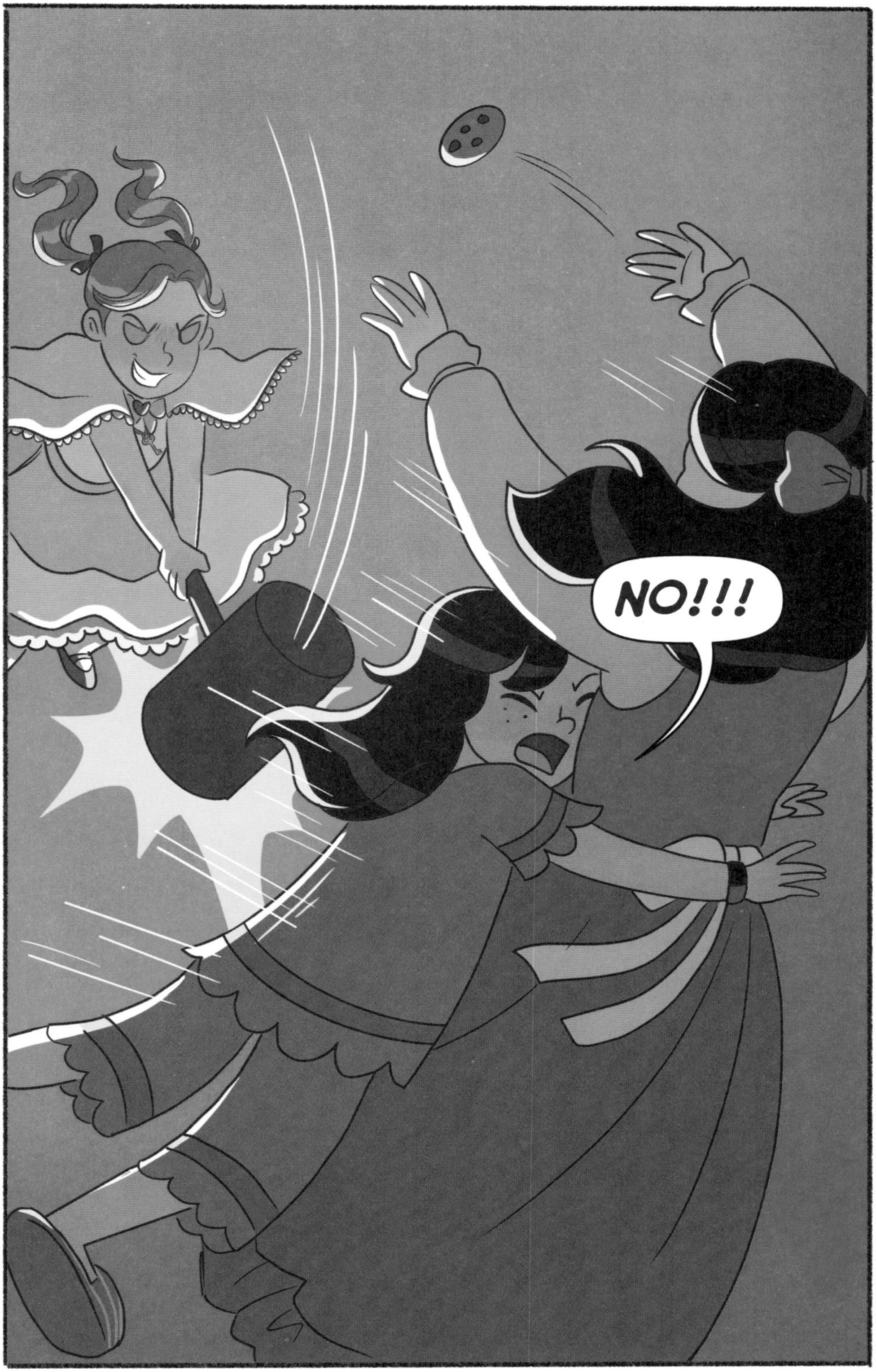
NO!!!

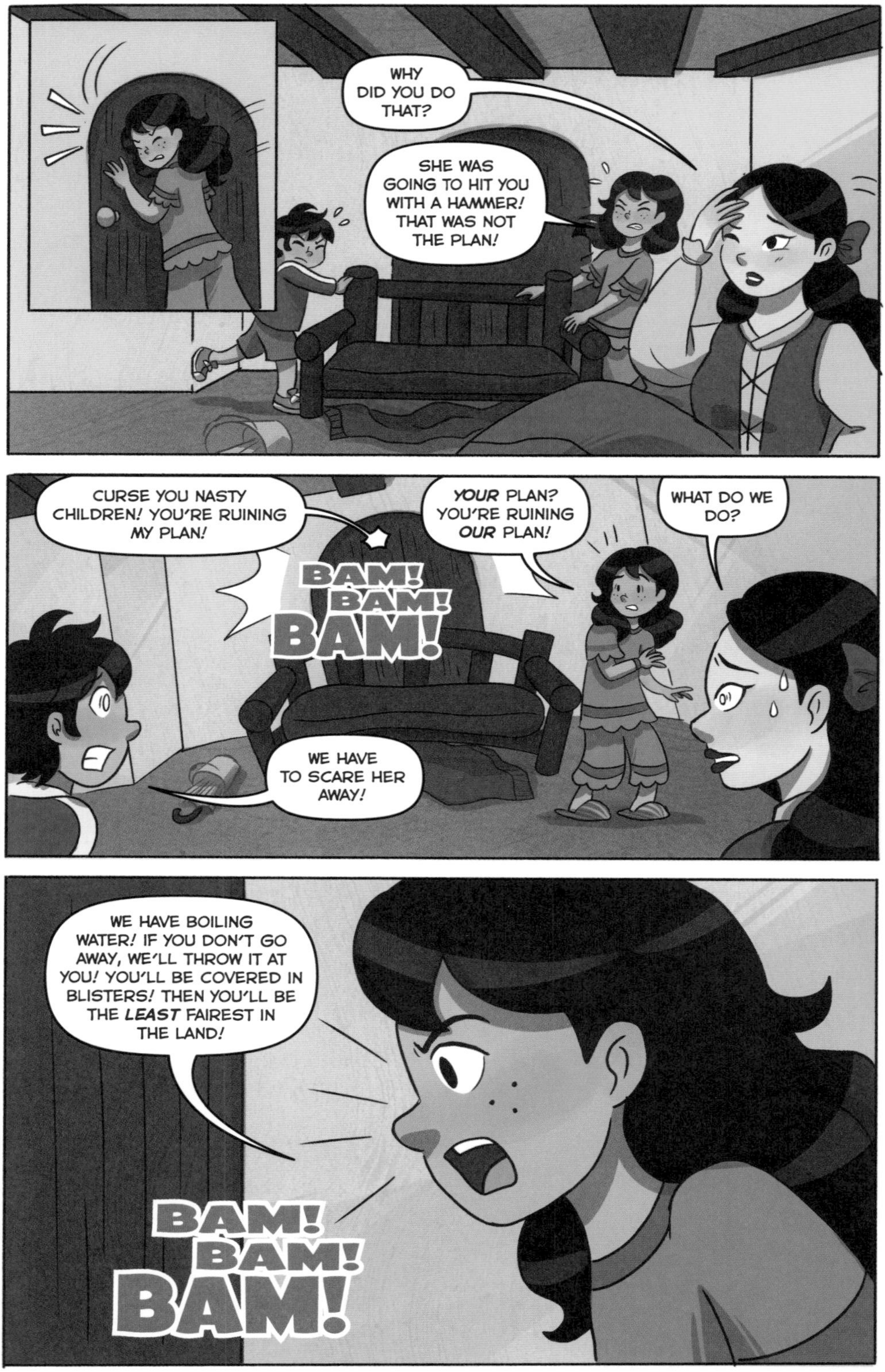
WHY DID YOU DO THAT?
SHE WAS GOING TO HIT YOU WITH A HAMMER! THAT WAS NOT THE PLAN!
CURSE YOU NASTY CHILDREN! YOU'RE RUINING *MY* PLAN!
BAM! BAM! BAM!
YOUR PLAN? YOU'RE RUINING *OUR* PLAN!
WHAT DO WE DO?
WE HAVE TO SCARE HER AWAY!
WE HAVE BOILING WATER! IF YOU DON'T GO AWAY, WE'LL THROW IT AT YOU! YOU'LL BE COVERED IN BLISTERS! THEN YOU'LL BE THE *LEAST* FAIREST IN THE LAND!
BAM! BAM! BAM!

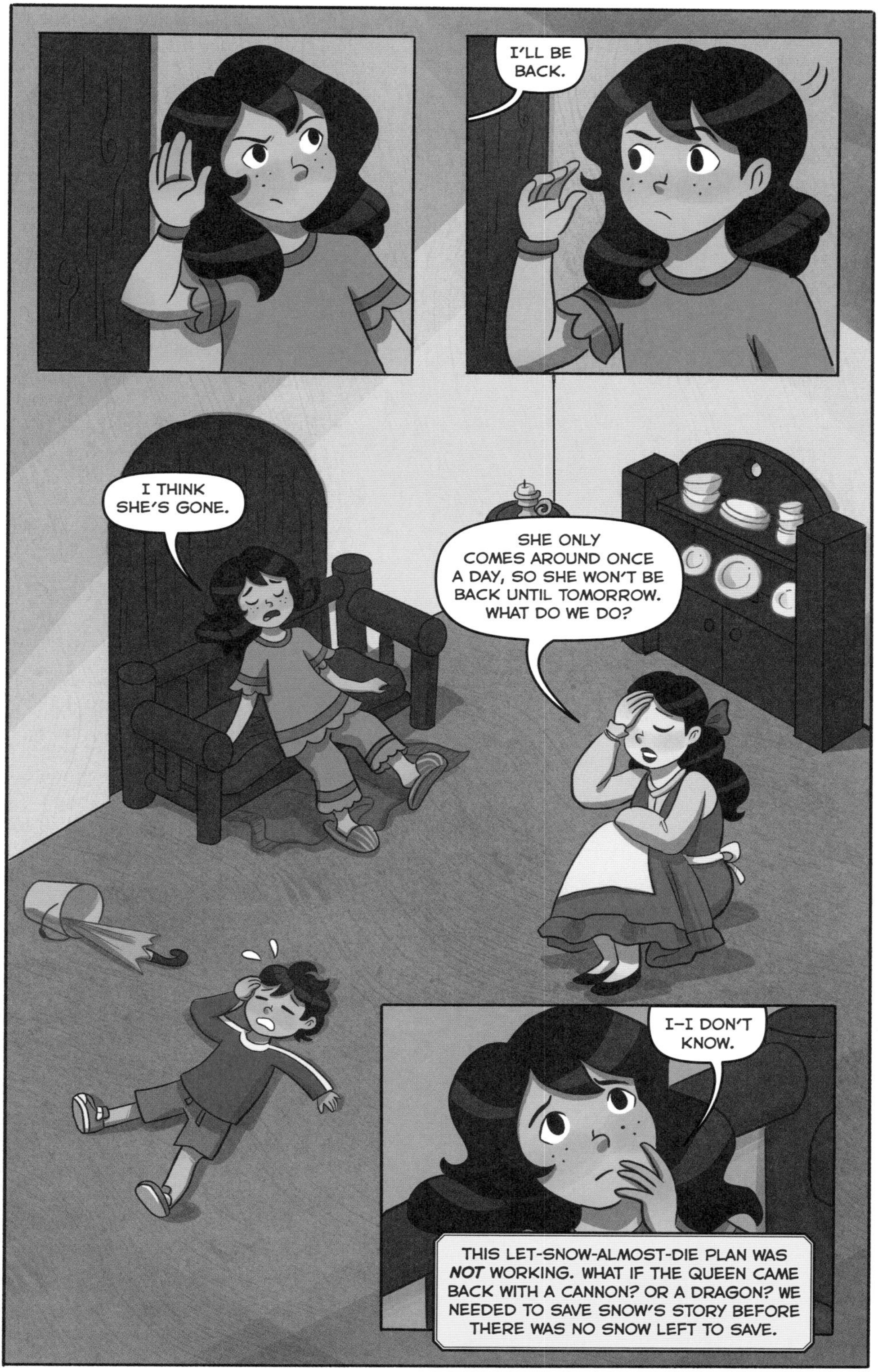
I'LL BE BACK.
I THINK SHE'S GONE.
SHE ONLY COMES AROUND ONCE A DAY, SO SHE WON'T BE BACK UNTIL TOMORROW. WHAT DO WE DO?
I–I DON'T KNOW.
THIS LET-SNOW-ALMOST-DIE PLAN WAS ***NOT*** WORKING. WHAT IF THE QUEEN CAME BACK WITH A CANNON? OR A DRAGON? WE NEEDED TO SAVE SNOW'S STORY BEFORE THERE WAS NO SNOW LEFT TO SAVE.

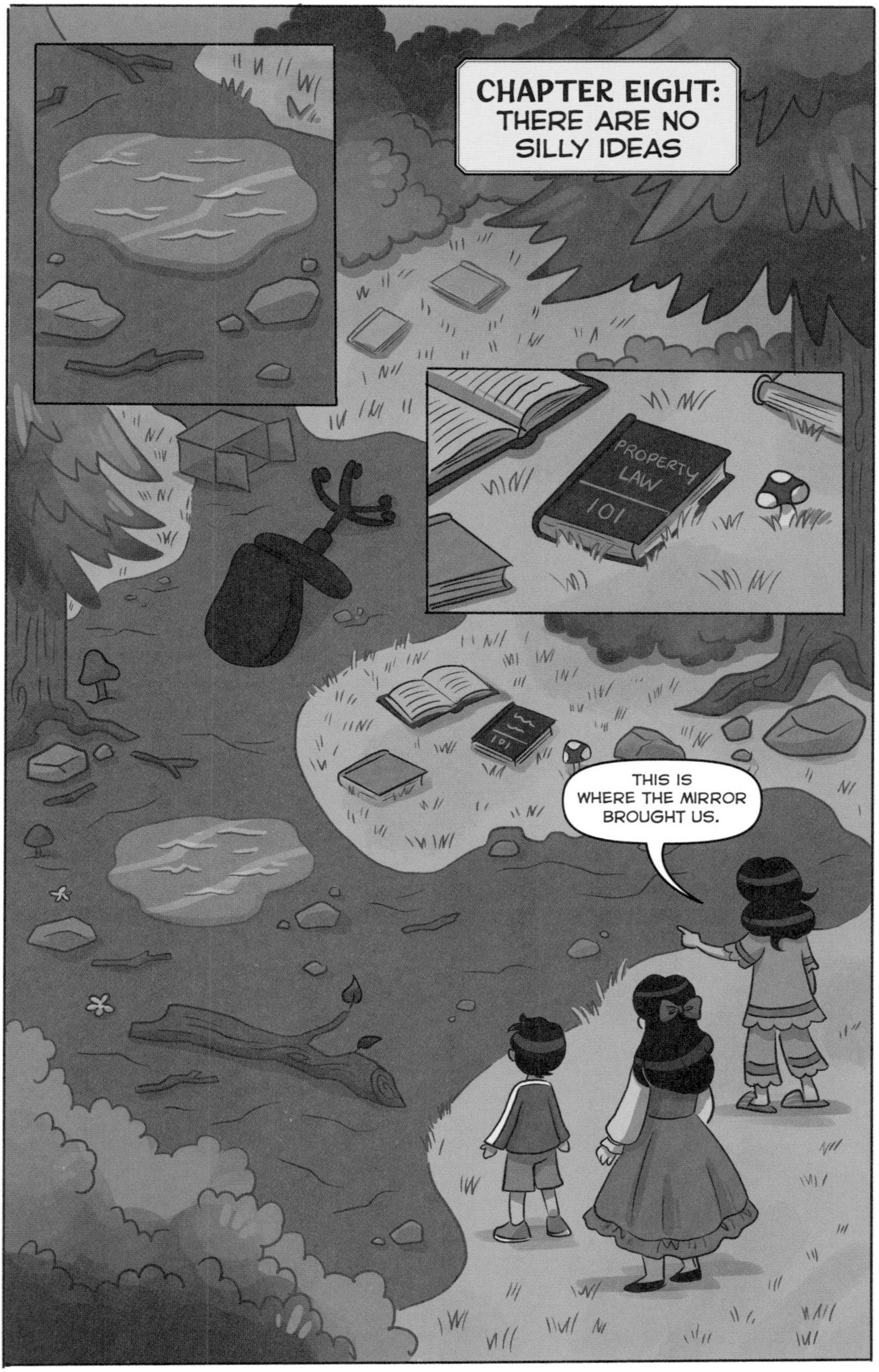
CHAPTER EIGHT:
THERE ARE NO
SILLY IDEAS
PROPERTY LAW 101
THIS IS WHERE THE MIRROR BROUGHT US.

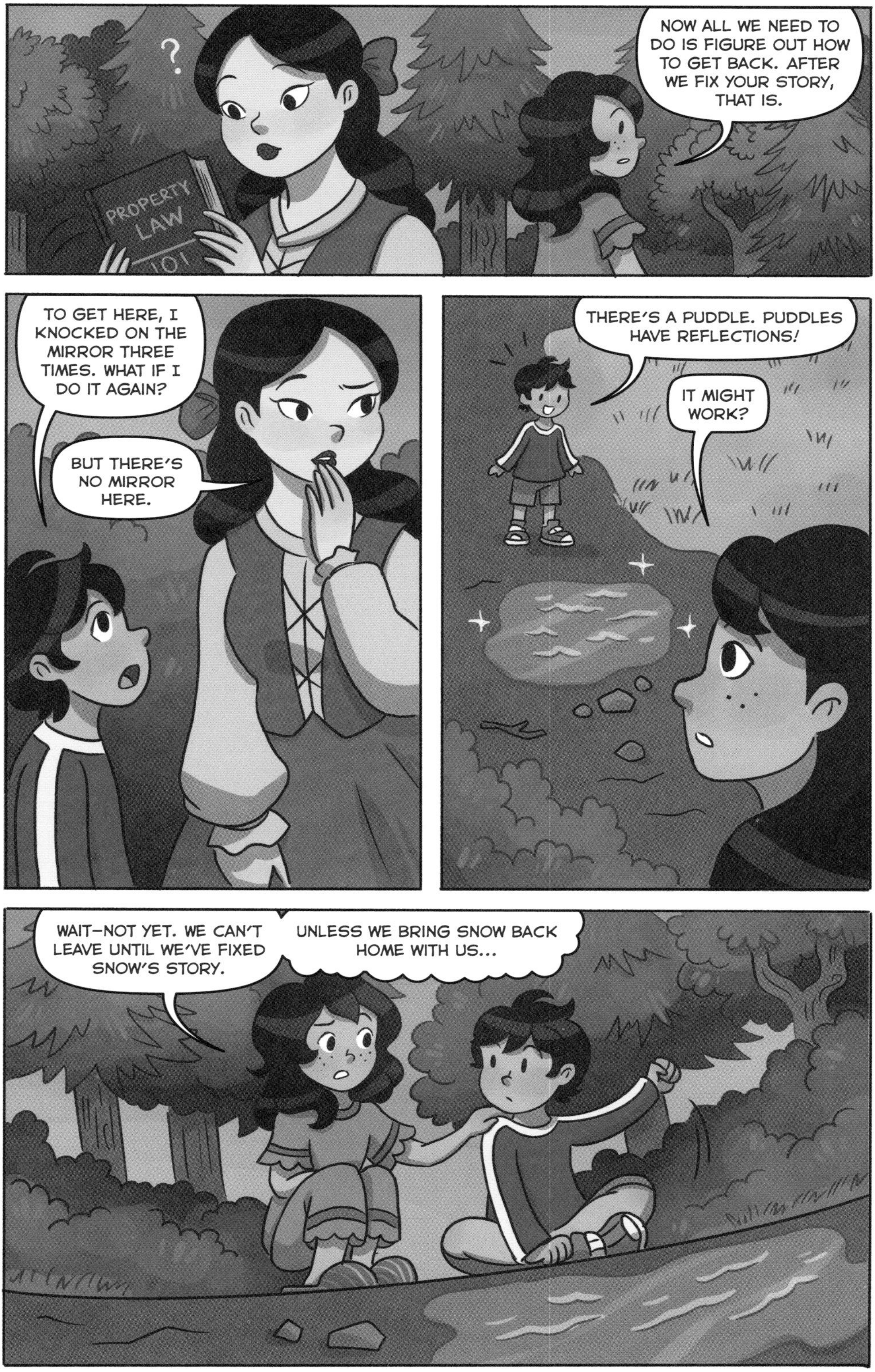
?
NOW ALL WE NEED TO DO IS FIGURE OUT HOW TO GET BACK. AFTER WE FIX YOUR STORY, THAT IS.
PROPERTY LAW 101
TO GET HERE, I KNOCKED ON THE MIRROR THREE TIMES. WHAT IF I DO IT AGAIN?
BUT THERE'S NO MIRROR HERE.
THERE'S A PUDDLE. PUDDLES HAVE REFLECTIONS!
IT MIGHT WORK?
WAIT—NOT YET. WE CAN'T LEAVE UNTIL WE'VE FIXED SNOW'S STORY.
UNLESS WE BRING SNOW BACK HOME WITH US...

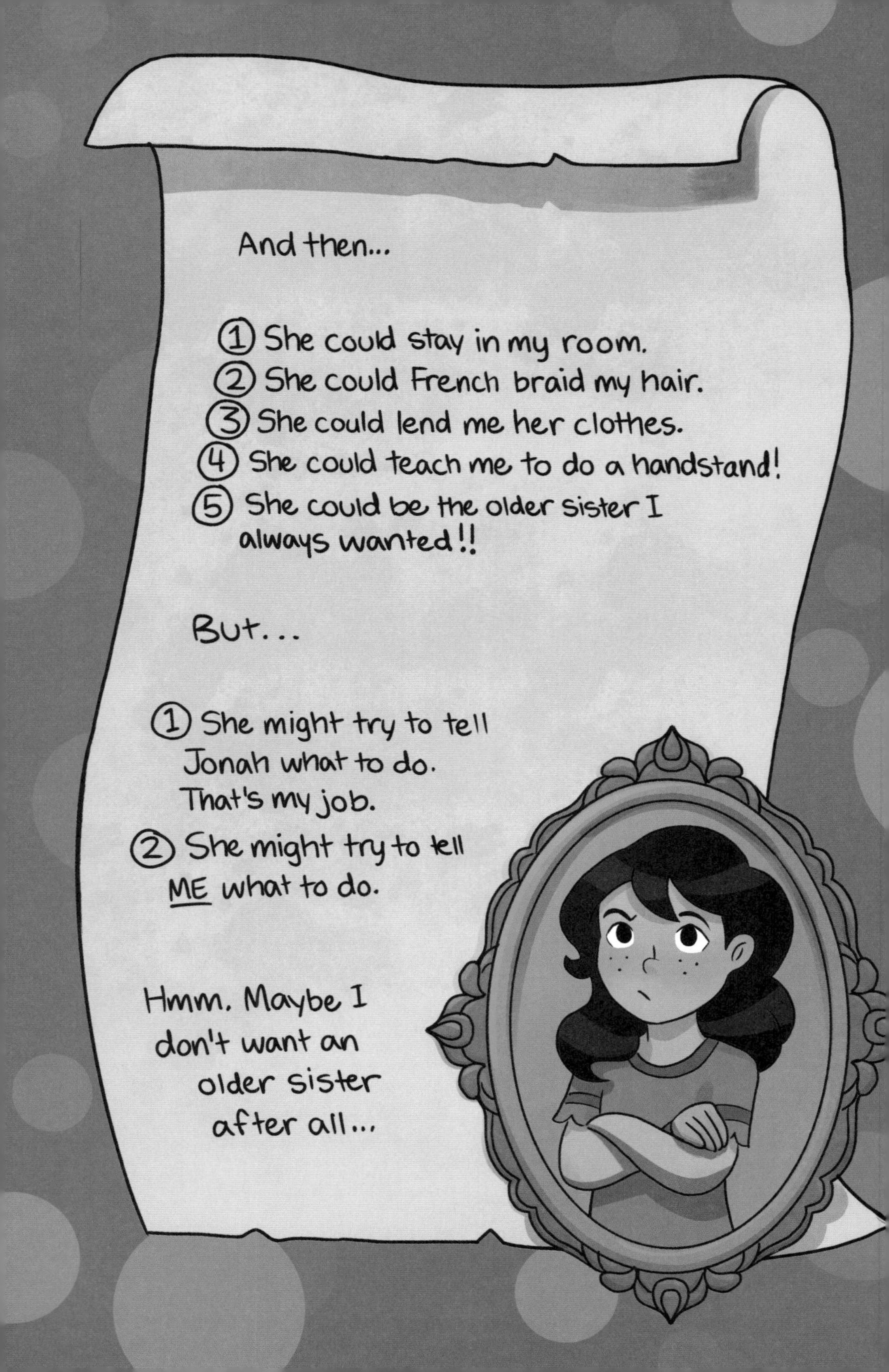
And then...
① She could stay in my room.
② She could French braid my hair.
③ She could lend me her clothes.
④ She could teach me to do a handstand!
⑤ She could be the older sister I always wanted!!
But...
① She might try to tell Jonah what to do. That's my job.
② She might try to tell ME what to do.
Hmm. Maybe I don't want an older sister after all...

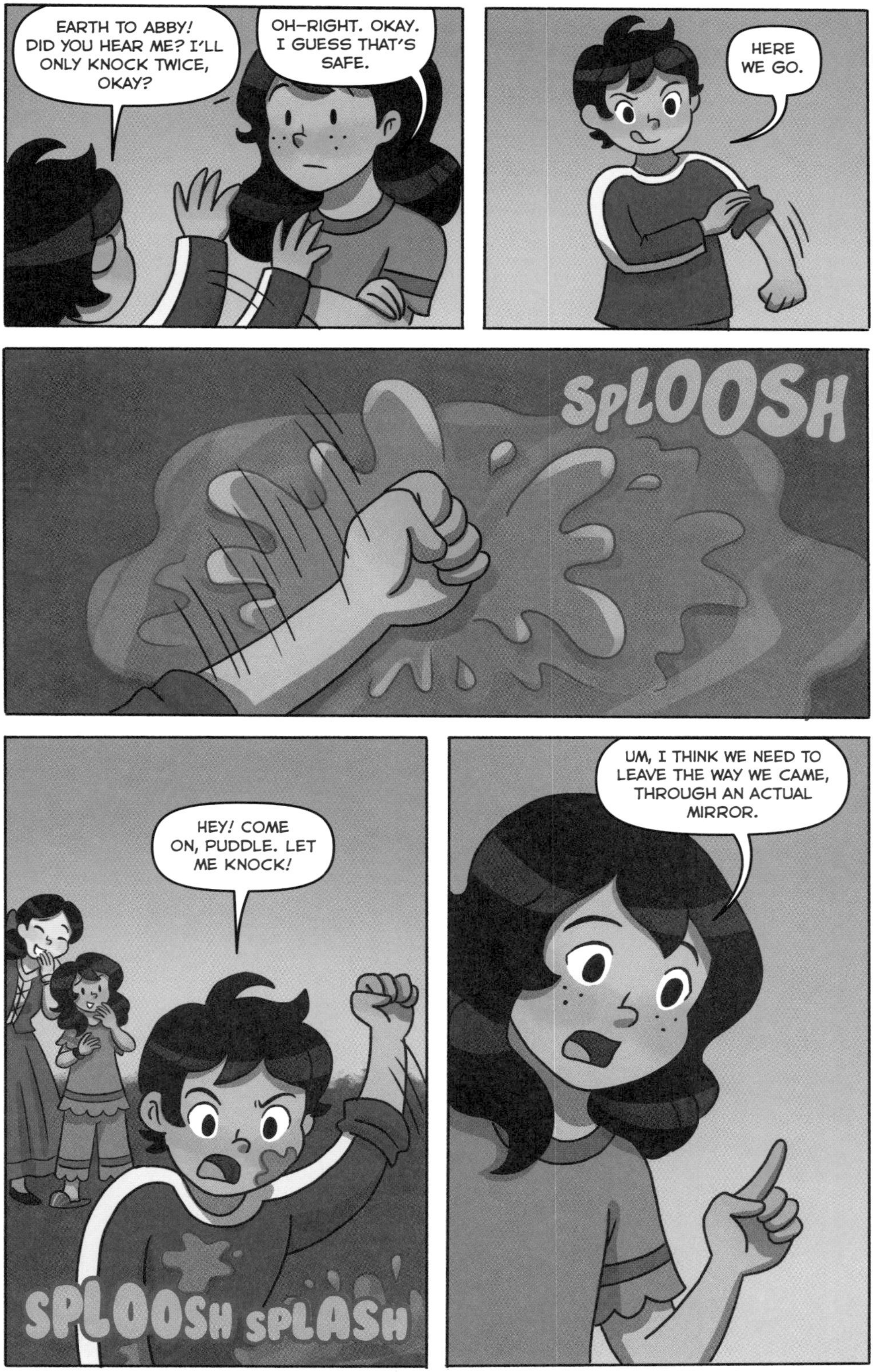
EARTH TO ABBY! DID YOU HEAR ME? I'LL ONLY KNOCK TWICE, OKAY?
OH–RIGHT. OKAY. I GUESS THAT'S SAFE.
HERE WE GO.
SPLOOSH
HEY! COME ON, PUDDLE. LET ME KNOCK!
SPLOOSH SPLASH
UM, I THINK WE NEED TO LEAVE THE WAY WE CAME, THROUGH AN ACTUAL MIRROR.

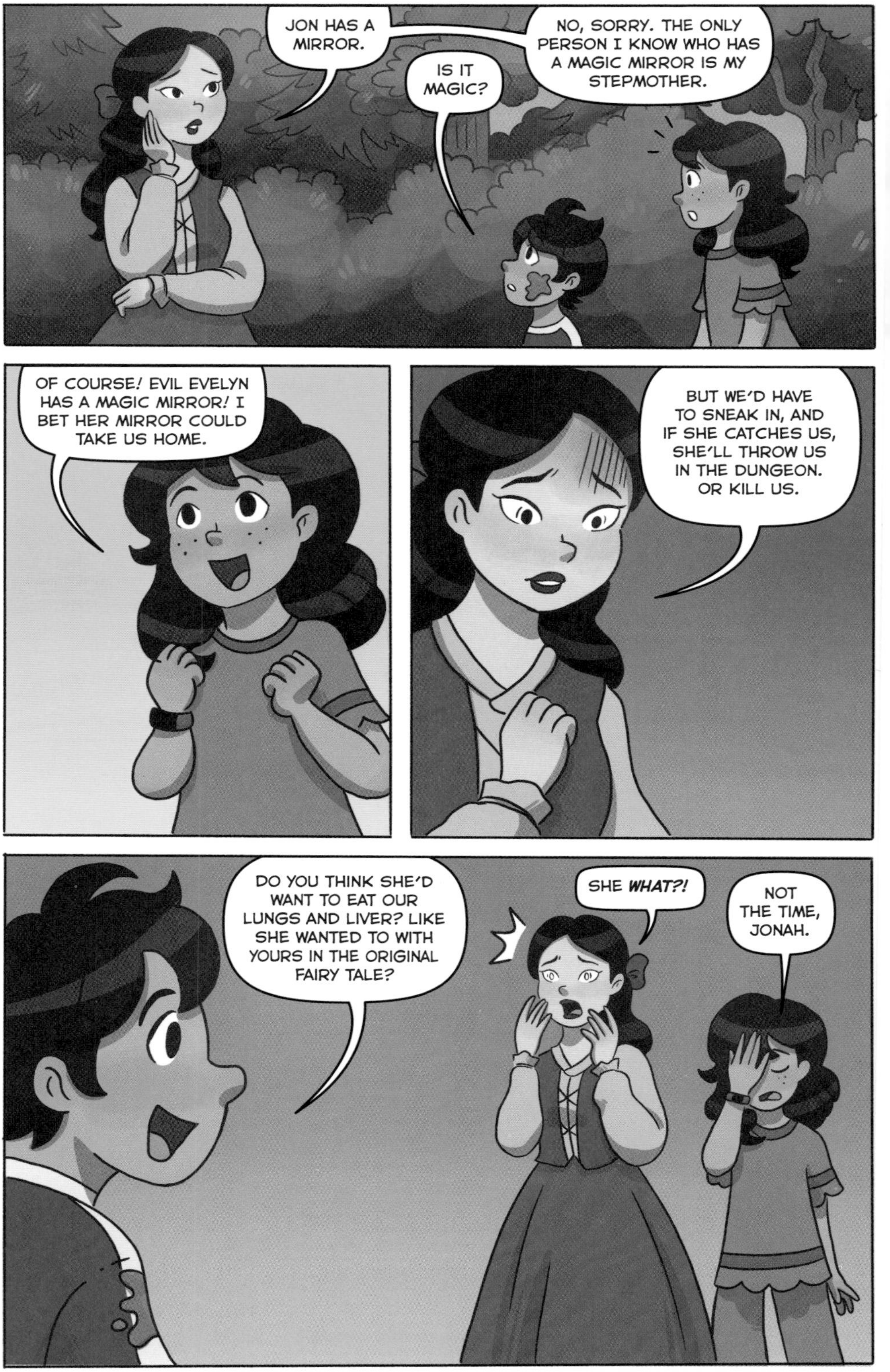
JON HAS A MIRROR.
IS IT MAGIC?
NO, SORRY. THE ONLY PERSON I KNOW WHO HAS A MAGIC MIRROR IS MY STEPMOTHER.
OF COURSE! EVIL EVELYN HAS A MAGIC MIRROR! I BET HER MIRROR COULD TAKE US HOME.
BUT WE'D HAVE TO SNEAK IN, AND IF SHE CATCHES US, SHE'LL THROW US IN THE DUNGEON. OR KILL US.
DO YOU THINK SHE'D WANT TO EAT OUR LUNGS AND LIVER? LIKE SHE WANTED TO WITH YOURS IN THE ORIGINAL FAIRY TALE?
SHE ***WHAT?!***
NOT THE TIME, JONAH.

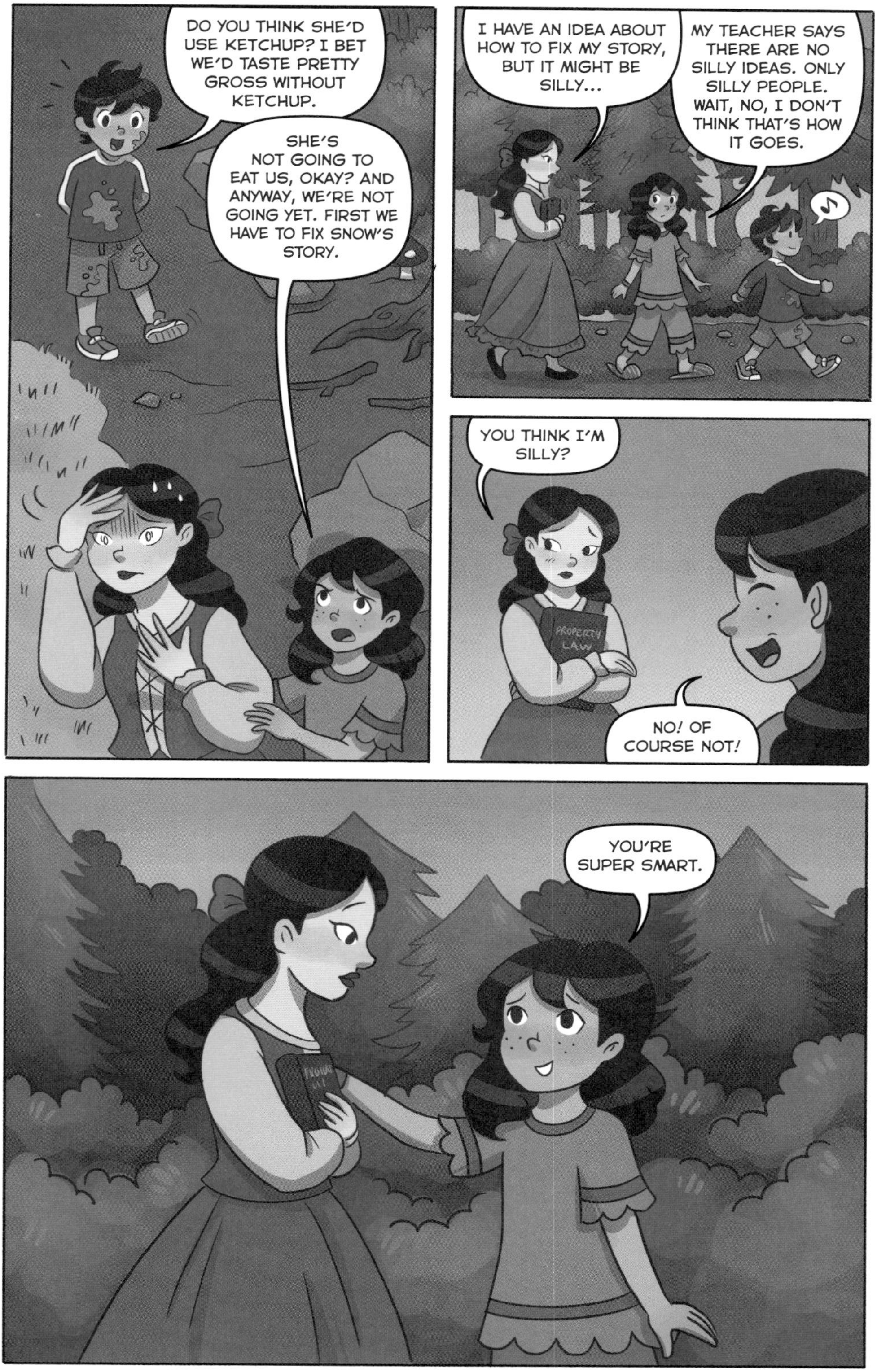
DO YOU THINK SHE'D USE KETCHUP? I BET WE'D TASTE PRETTY GROSS WITHOUT KETCHUP.
SHE'S NOT GOING TO EAT US, OKAY? AND ANYWAY, WE'RE NOT GOING YET. FIRST WE HAVE TO FIX SNOW'S STORY.
I HAVE AN IDEA ABOUT HOW TO FIX MY STORY, BUT IT MIGHT BE SILLY...
MY TEACHER SAYS THERE ARE NO SILLY IDEAS. ONLY SILLY PEOPLE. WAIT, NO, I DON'T THINK THAT'S HOW IT GOES.
YOU THINK I'M SILLY?
PROPERTY LAW
NO! OF COURSE NOT!
YOU'RE SUPER SMART.

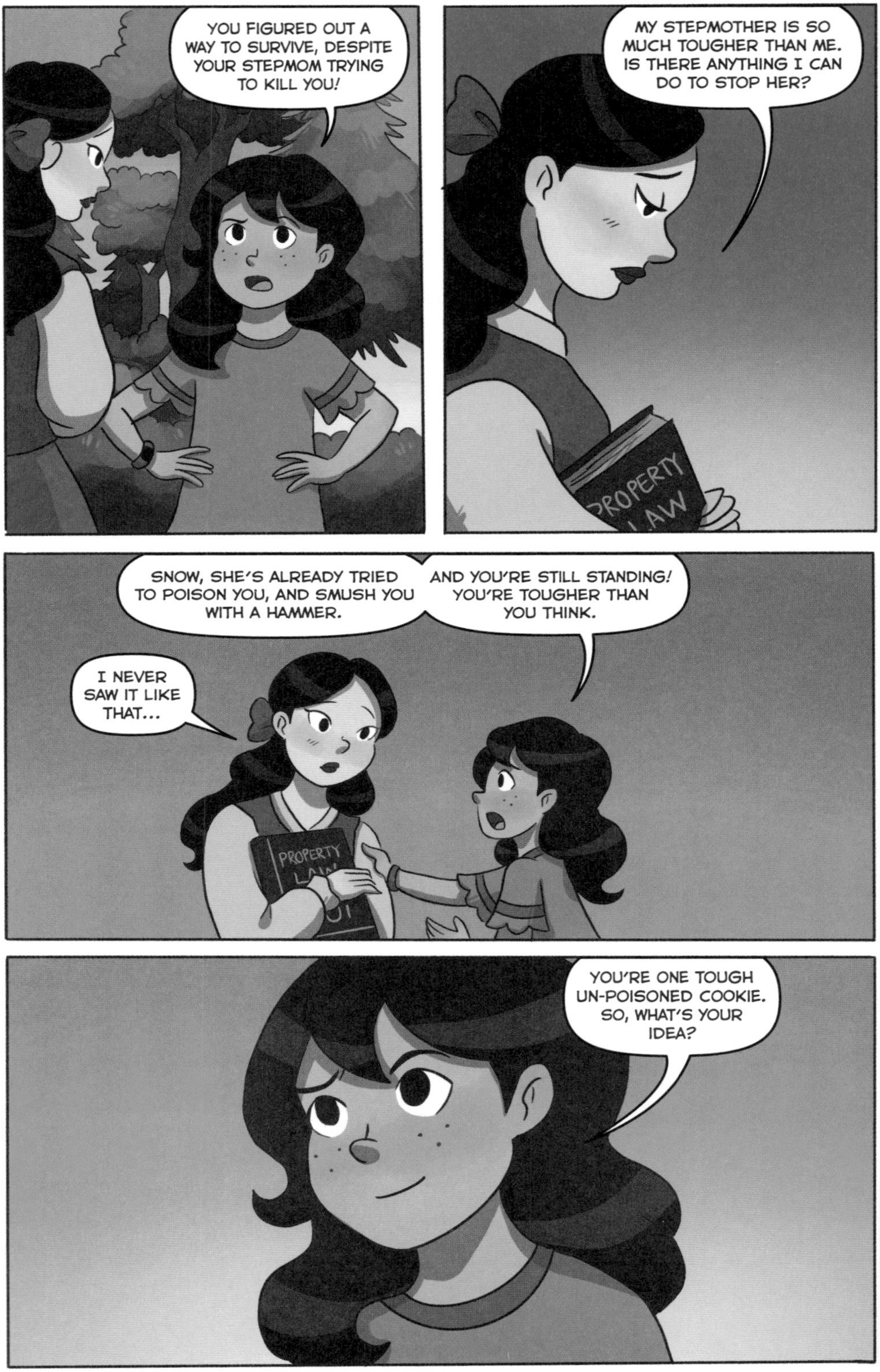
YOU FIGURED OUT A WAY TO SURVIVE, DESPITE YOUR STEPMOM TRYING TO KILL YOU!
MY STEPMOTHER IS SO MUCH TOUGHER THAN ME. IS THERE ANYTHING I CAN DO TO STOP HER?
PROPERTY LAW
SNOW, SHE'S ALREADY TRIED TO POISON YOU, AND SMUSH YOU WITH A HAMMER.
AND YOU'RE STILL STANDING! YOU'RE TOUGHER THAN YOU THINK.
I NEVER SAW IT LIKE THAT...
PROPERTY LAW
YOU'RE ONE TOUGH UN-POISONED COOKIE. SO, WHAT'S YOUR IDEA?

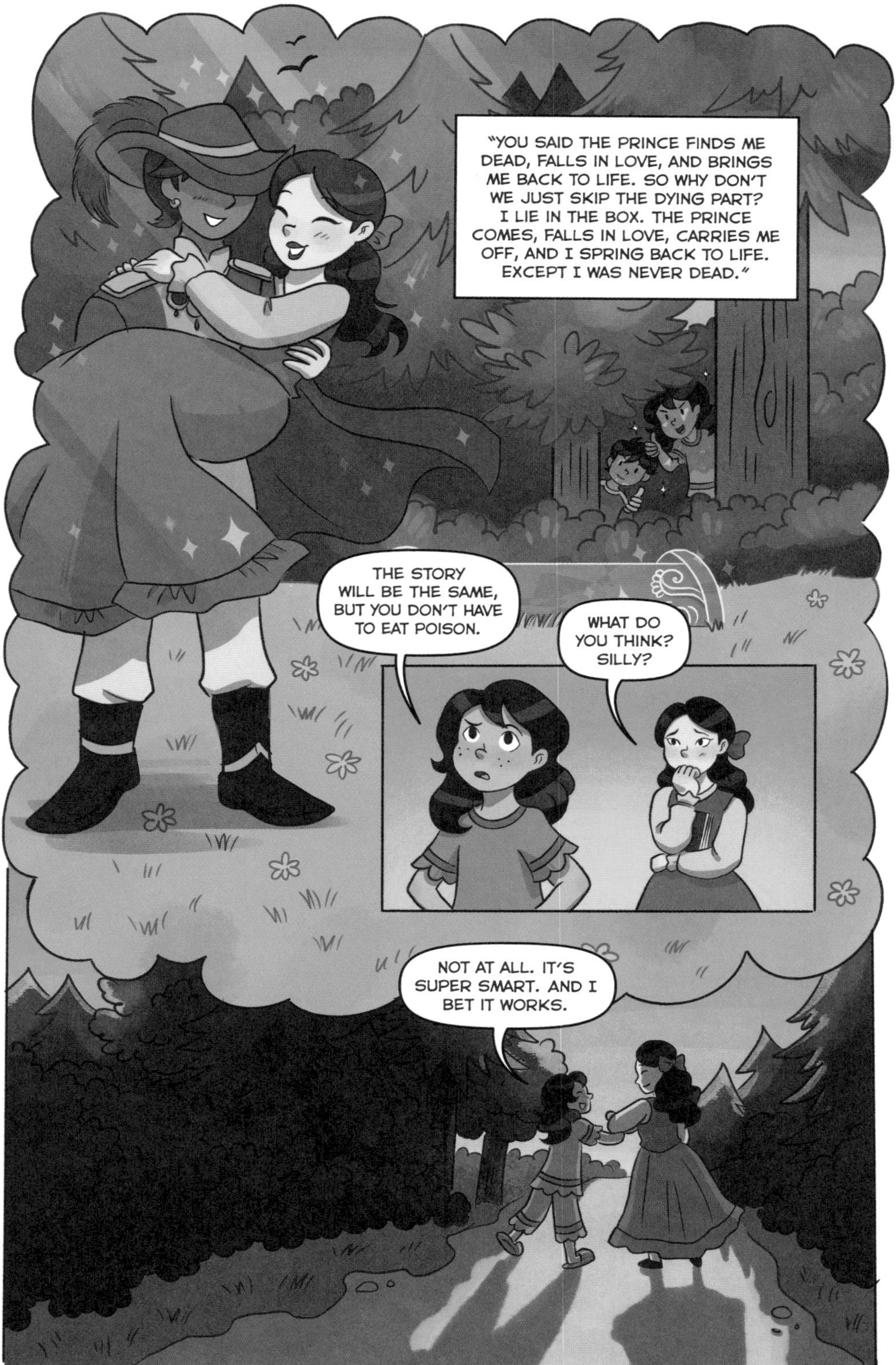
"YOU SAID THE PRINCE FINDS ME DEAD, FALLS IN LOVE, AND BRINGS ME BACK TO LIFE. SO WHY DON'T WE JUST SKIP THE DYING PART? I LIE IN THE BOX. THE PRINCE COMES, FALLS IN LOVE, CARRIES ME OFF, AND I SPRING BACK TO LIFE. EXCEPT I WAS NEVER DEAD."
THE STORY WILL BE THE SAME, BUT YOU DON'T HAVE TO EAT POISON.
WHAT DO YOU THINK? SILLY?
NOT AT ALL. IT'S SUPER SMART. AND I BET IT WORKS.

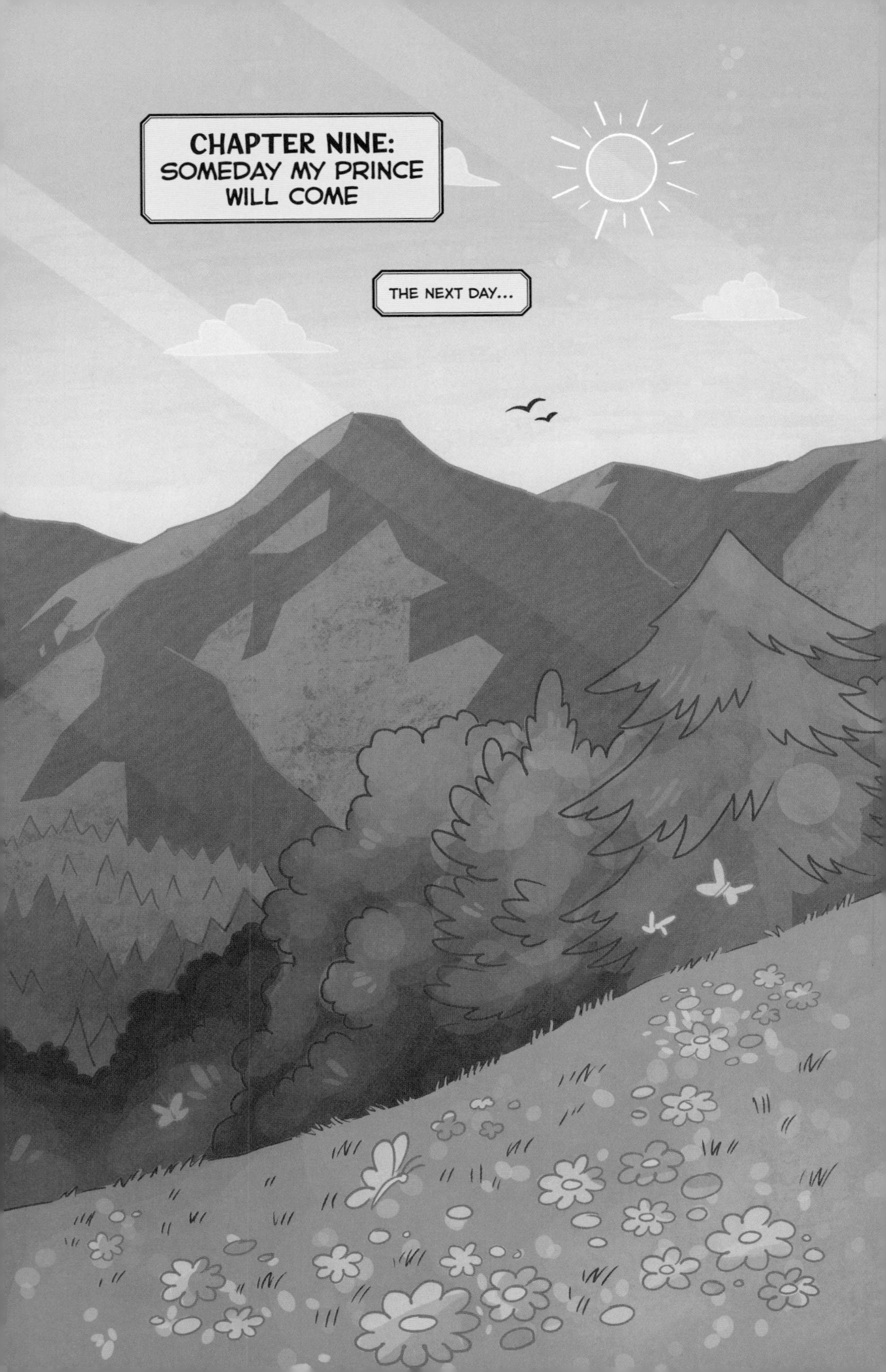
CHAPTER NINE:
SOMEDAY MY PRINCE WILL COME
THE NEXT DAY...

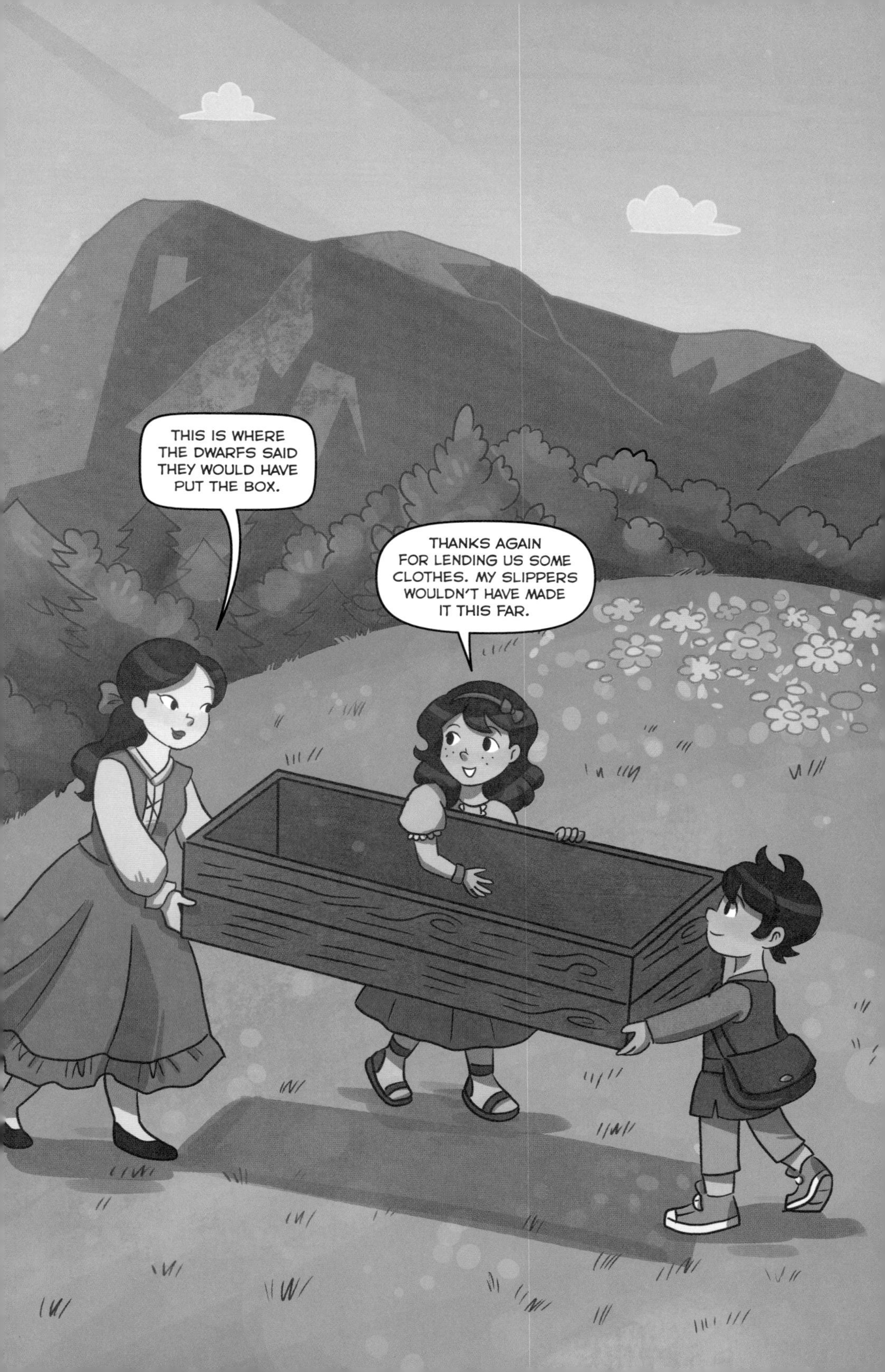
THIS IS WHERE THE DWARFS SAID THEY WOULD HAVE PUT THE BOX.
THANKS AGAIN FOR LENDING US SOME CLOTHES. MY SLIPPERS WOULDN'T HAVE MADE IT THIS FAR.

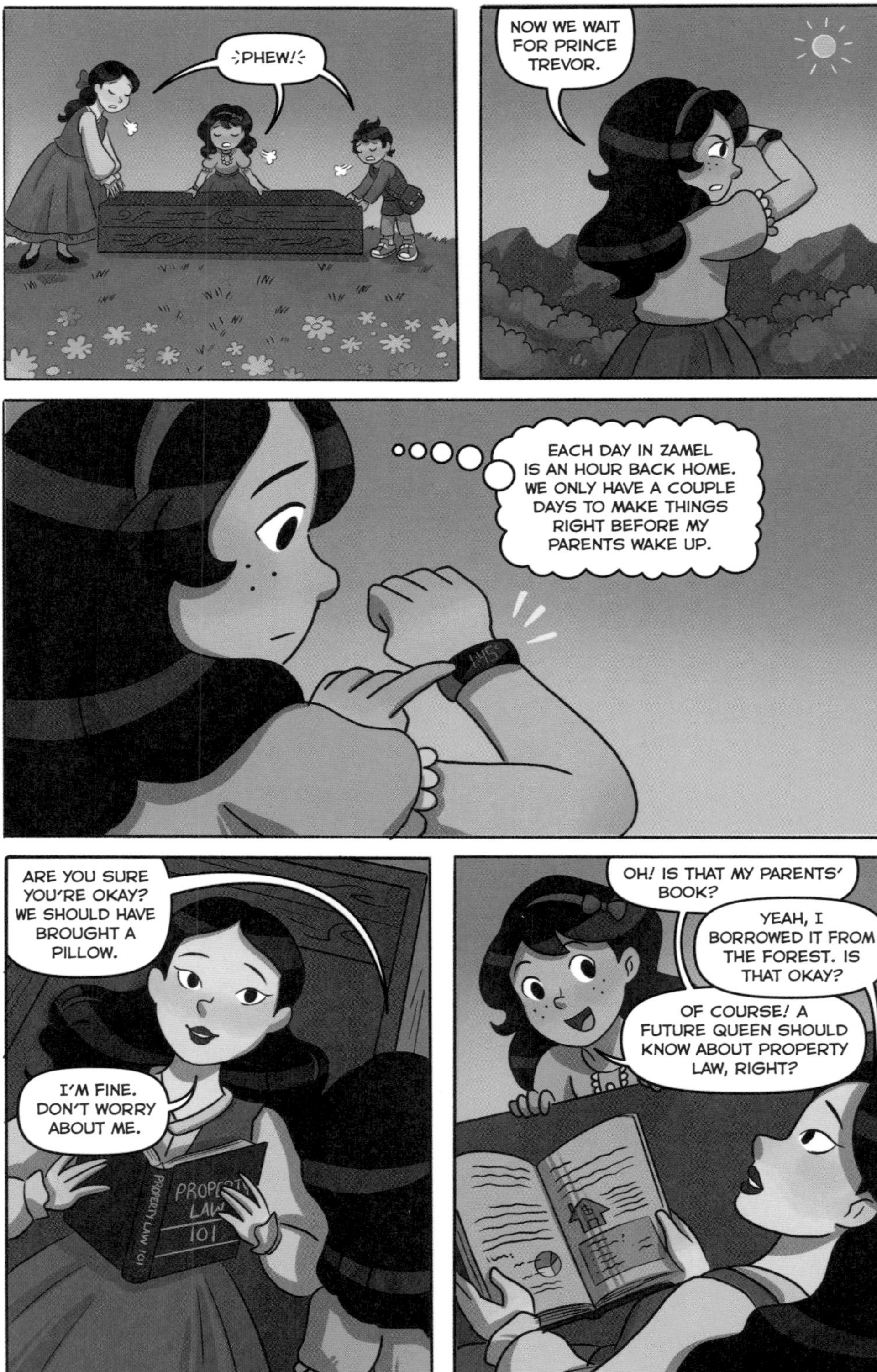
PHEW!
NOW WE WAIT FOR PRINCE TREVOR.
EACH DAY IN ZAMEL IS AN HOUR BACK HOME. WE ONLY HAVE A COUPLE DAYS TO MAKE THINGS RIGHT BEFORE MY PARENTS WAKE UP.
ARE YOU SURE YOU'RE OKAY? WE SHOULD HAVE BROUGHT A PILLOW.
I'M FINE. DON'T WORRY ABOUT ME.
PROPERTY LAW 101
OH! IS THAT MY PARENTS' BOOK?
YEAH, I BORROWED IT FROM THE FOREST. IS THAT OKAY?
OF COURSE! A FUTURE QUEEN SHOULD KNOW ABOUT PROPERTY LAW, RIGHT?

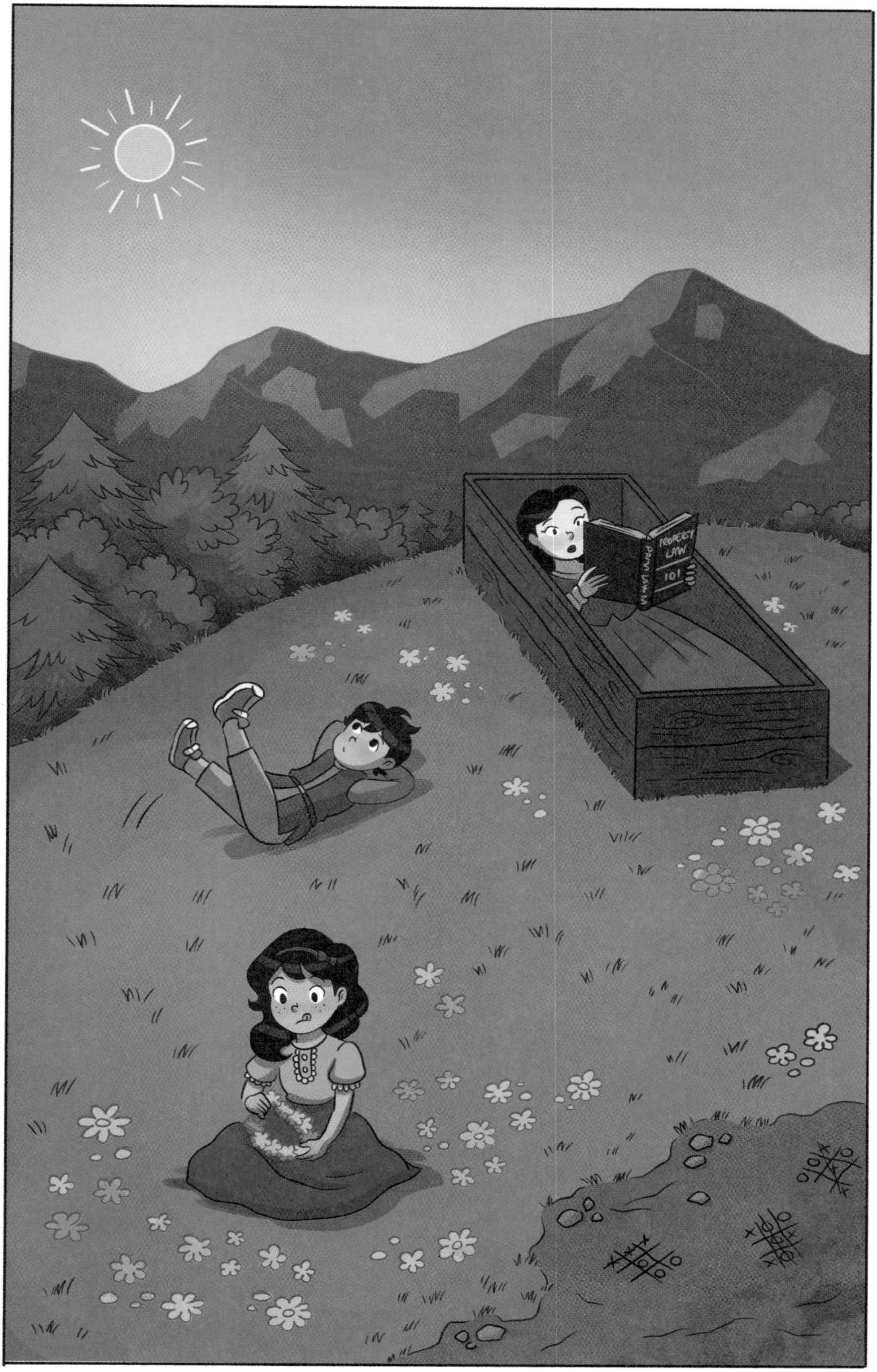
PROPERTY LAW 101

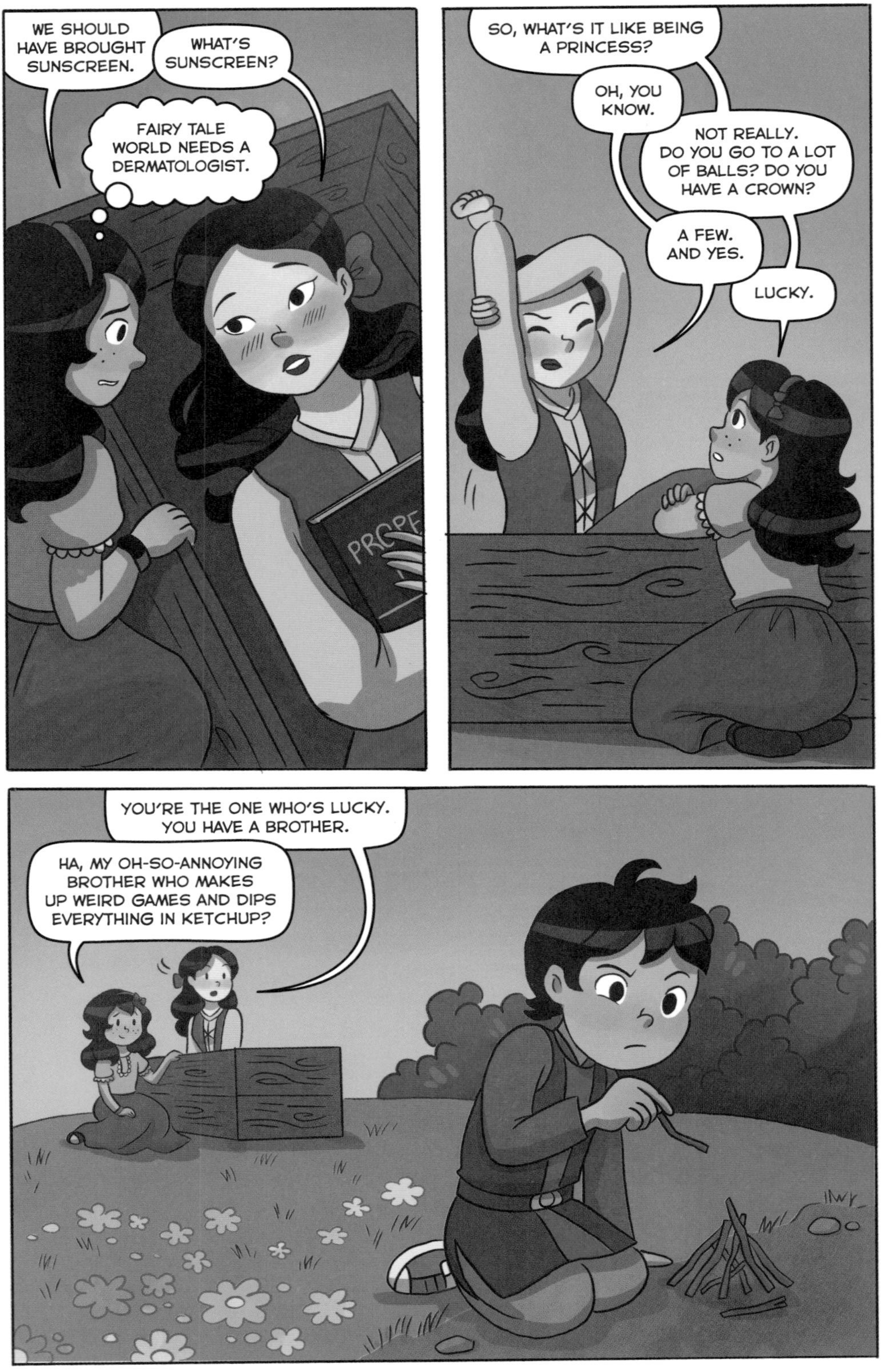
WE SHOULD HAVE BROUGHT SUNSCREEN.
WHAT'S SUNSCREEN?
FAIRY TALE WORLD NEEDS A DERMATOLOGIST.
PROPE
SO, WHAT'S IT LIKE BEING A PRINCESS?
OH, YOU KNOW.
NOT REALLY. DO YOU GO TO A LOT OF BALLS? DO YOU HAVE A CROWN?
A FEW. AND YES.
LUCKY.
YOU'RE THE ONE WHO'S LUCKY. YOU HAVE A BROTHER.
HA, MY OH-SO-ANNOYING BROTHER WHO MAKES UP WEIRD GAMES AND DIPS EVERYTHING IN KETCHUP?

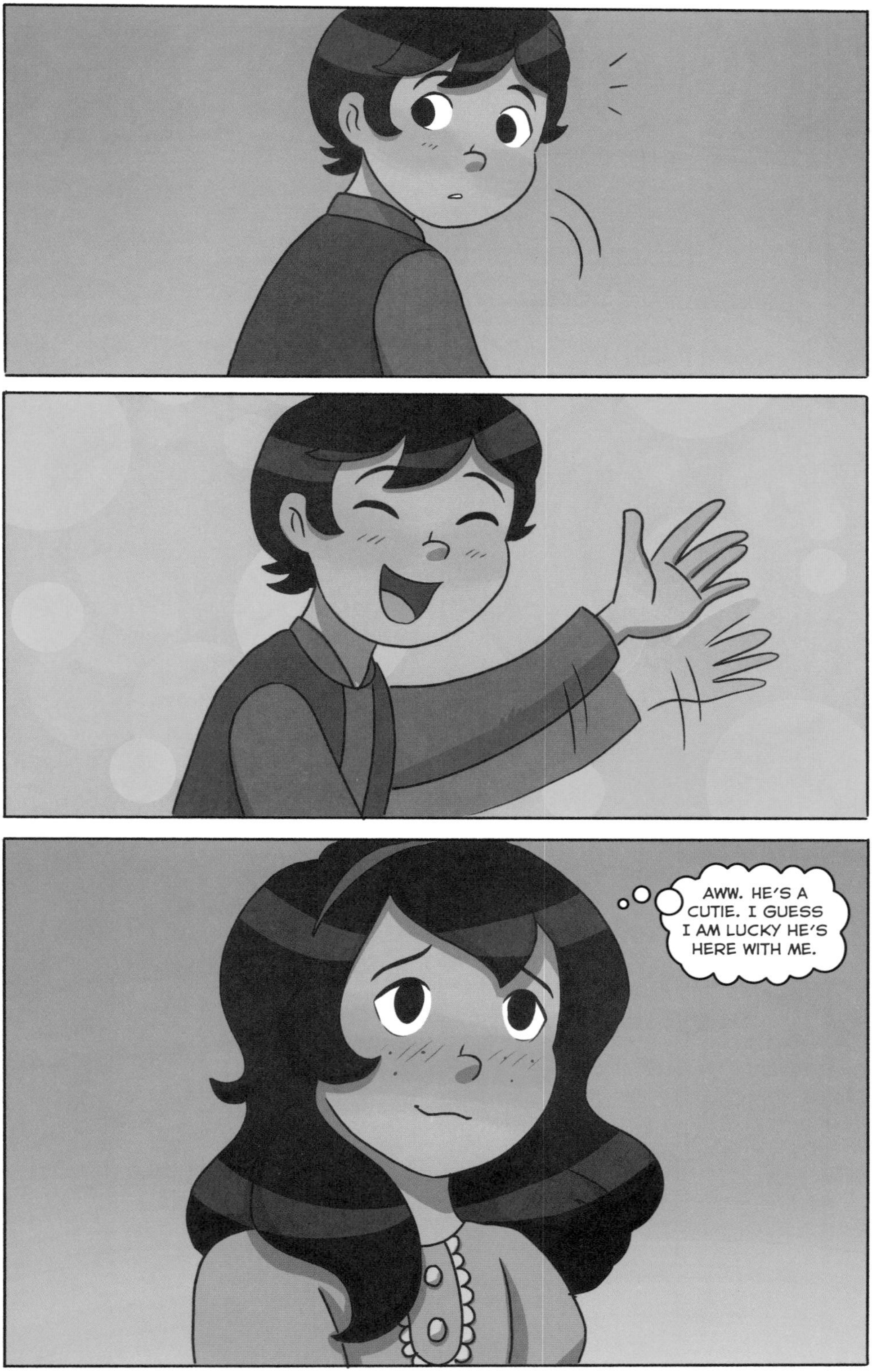
AWW. HE'S A CUTIE. I GUESS I AM LUCKY HE'S HERE WITH ME.

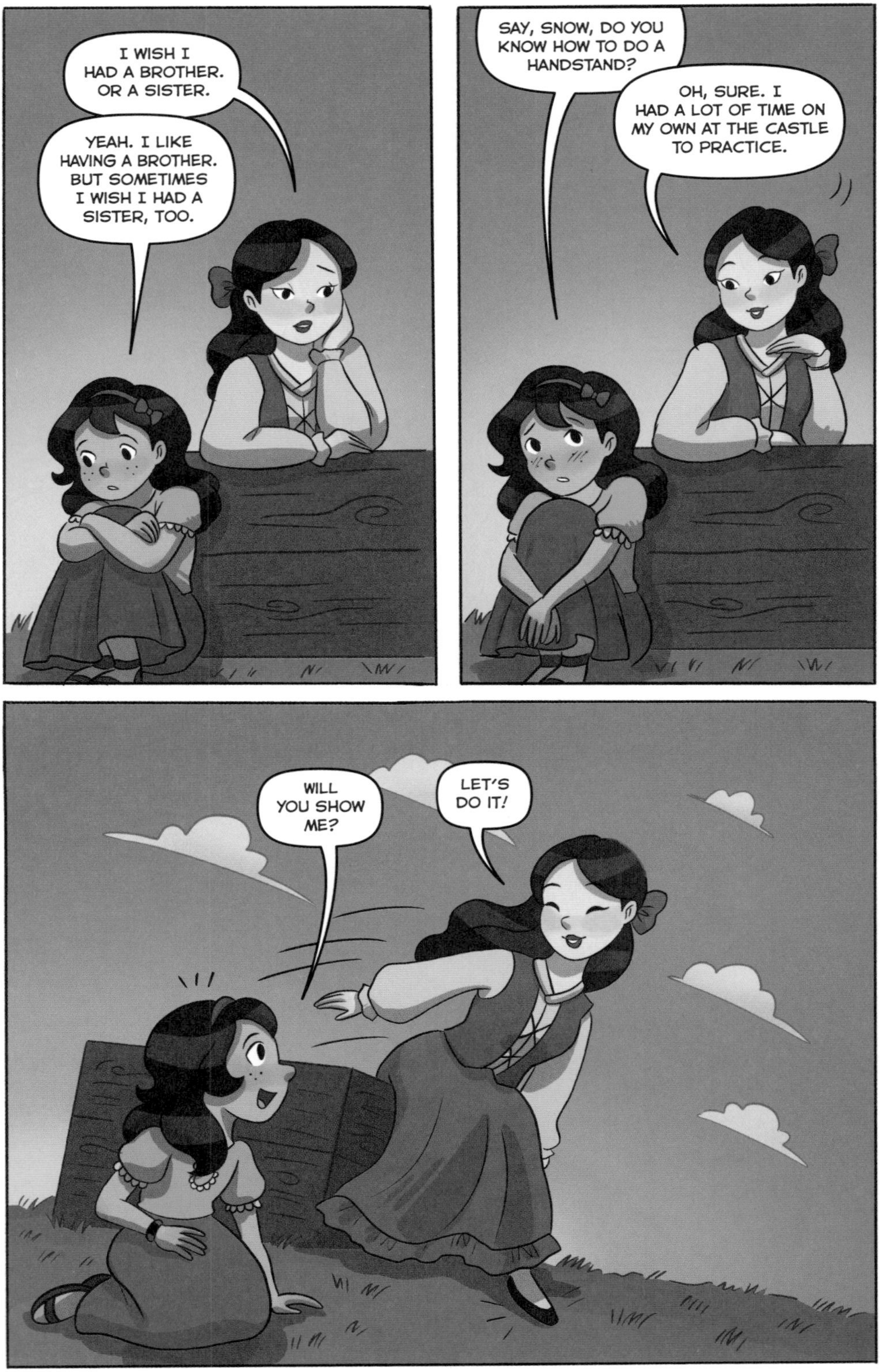
I WISH I HAD A BROTHER. OR A SISTER.
YEAH. I LIKE HAVING A BROTHER. BUT SOMETIMES I WISH I HAD A SISTER, TOO.
SAY, SNOW, DO YOU KNOW HOW TO DO A HANDSTAND?
OH, SURE. I HAD A LOT OF TIME ON MY OWN AT THE CASTLE TO PRACTICE.
WILL YOU SHOW ME?
LET'S DO IT!

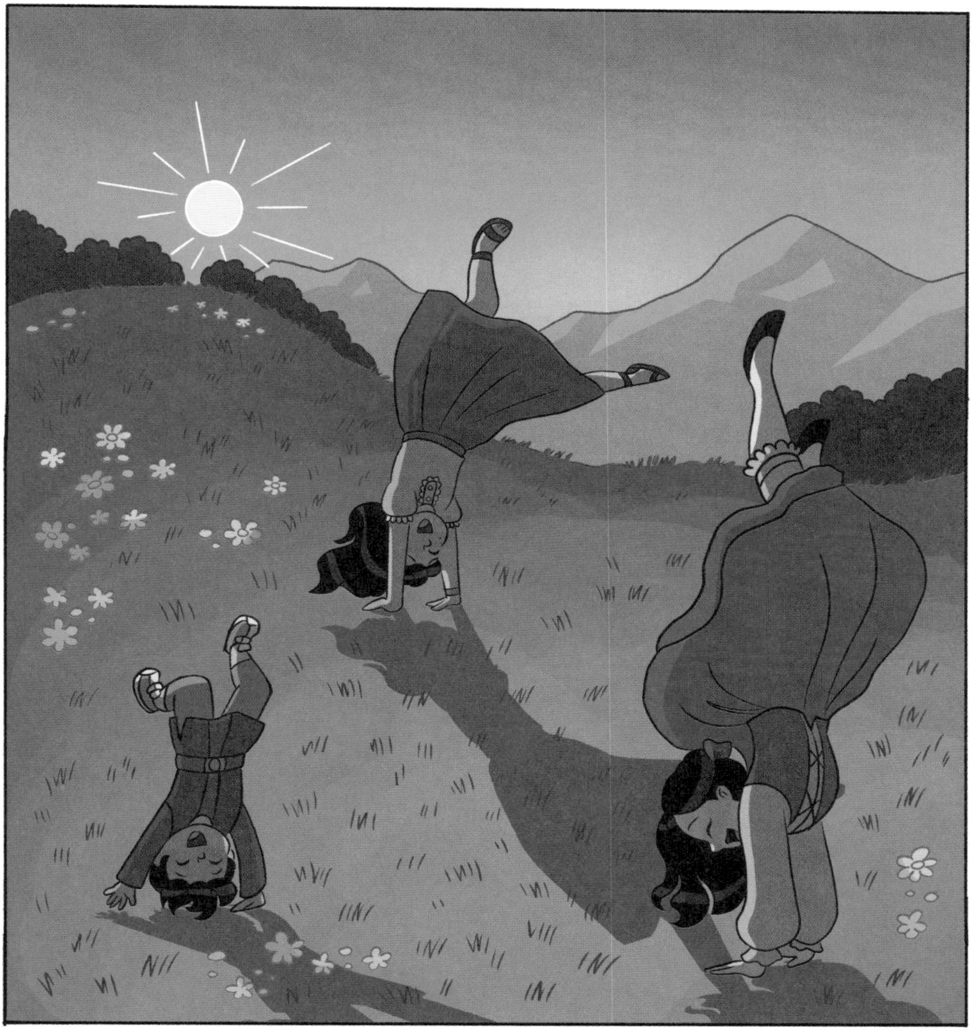

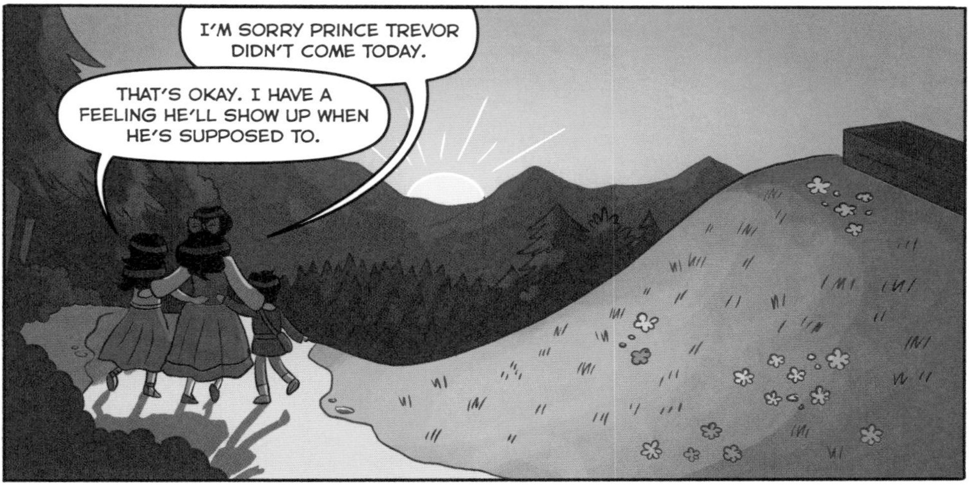
I'M SORRY PRINCE TREVOR DIDN'T COME TODAY.
THAT'S OKAY. I HAVE A FEELING HE'LL SHOW UP WHEN HE'S SUPPOSED TO.

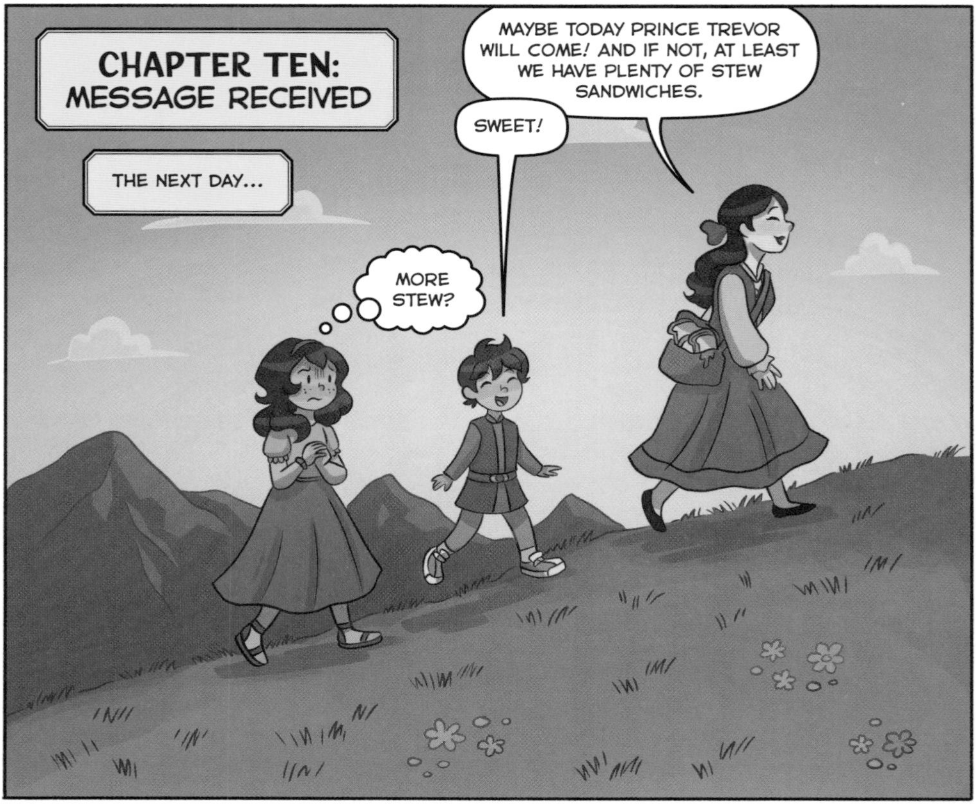
CHAPTER TEN:
MESSAGE RECEIVED
THE NEXT DAY...
MAYBE TODAY PRINCE TREVOR WILL COME! AND IF NOT, AT LEAST WE HAVE PLENTY OF STEW SANDWICHES.
SWEET!
MORE STEW?

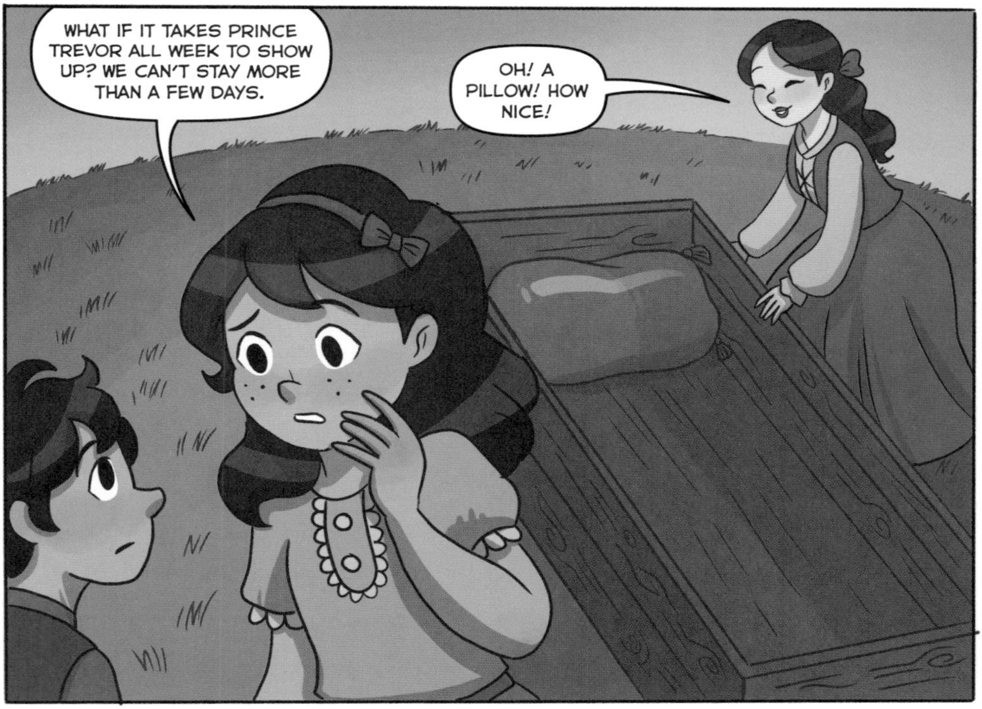
WHAT IF IT TAKES PRINCE TREVOR ALL WEEK TO SHOW UP? WE CAN'T STAY MORE THAN A FEW DAYS.
OH! A PILLOW! HOW NICE!

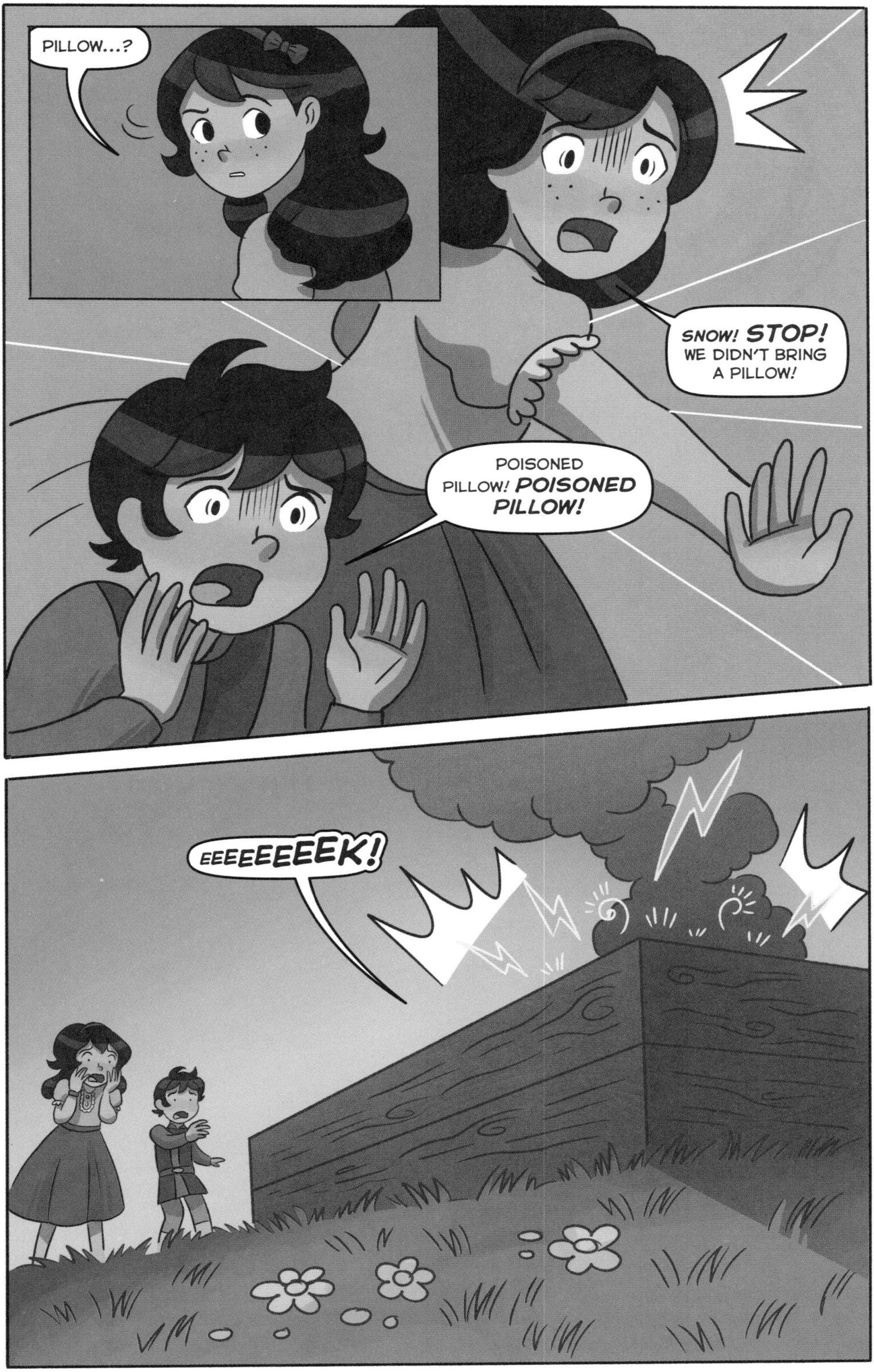
PILLOW...?
SNOW! STOP! WE DIDN'T BRING A PILLOW!
POISONED PILLOW! POISONED PILLOW!
EEEEEEEEK!

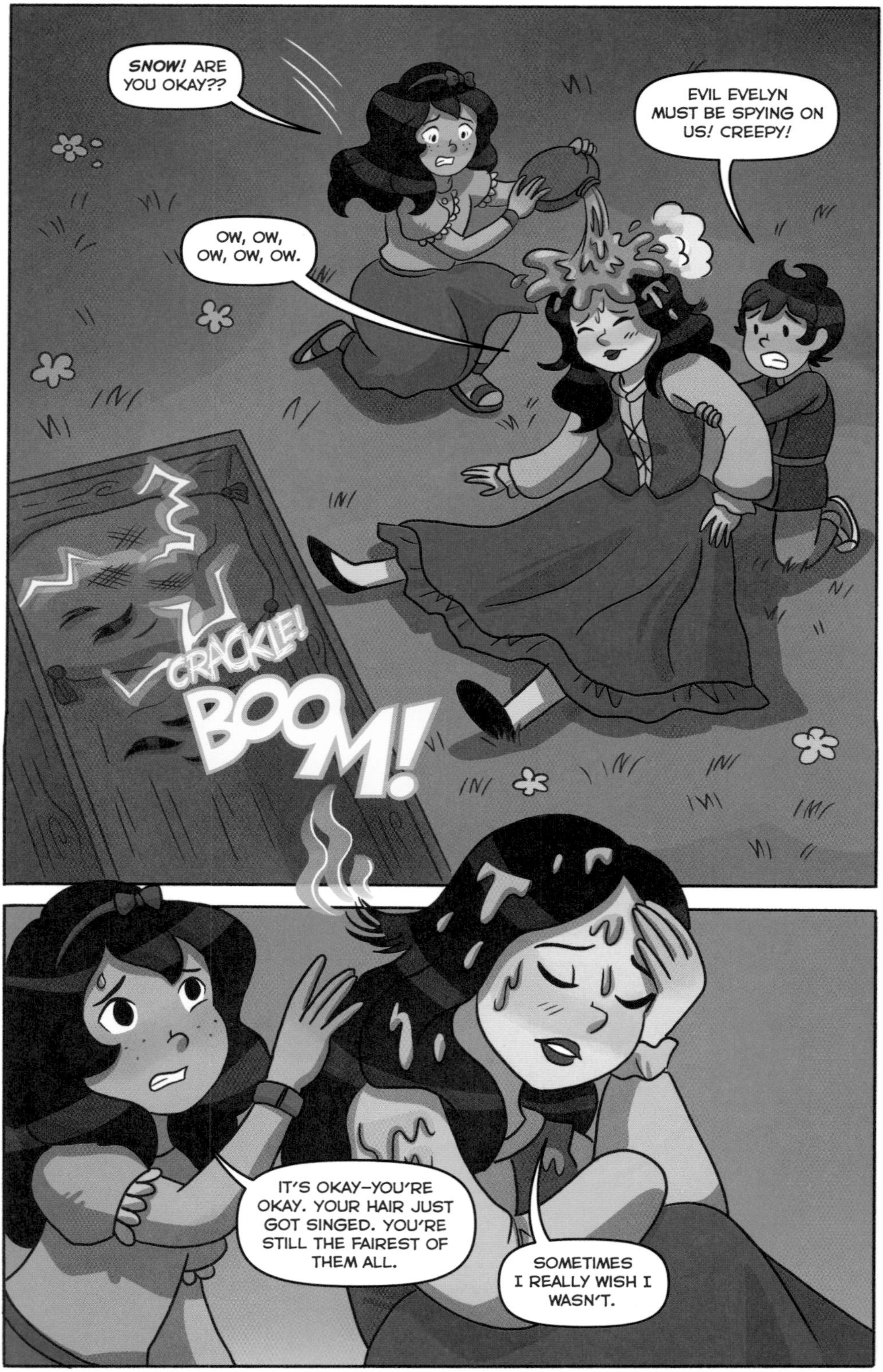
SNOW! ARE YOU OKAY??
EVIL EVELYN MUST BE SPYING ON US! CREEPY!
OW, OW, OW, OW, OW.
CRACKLE!
BOOM!
IT'S OKAY—YOU'RE OKAY. YOUR HAIR JUST GOT SINGED. YOU'RE STILL THE FAIREST OF THEM ALL.
SOMETIMES I REALLY WISH I WASN'T.

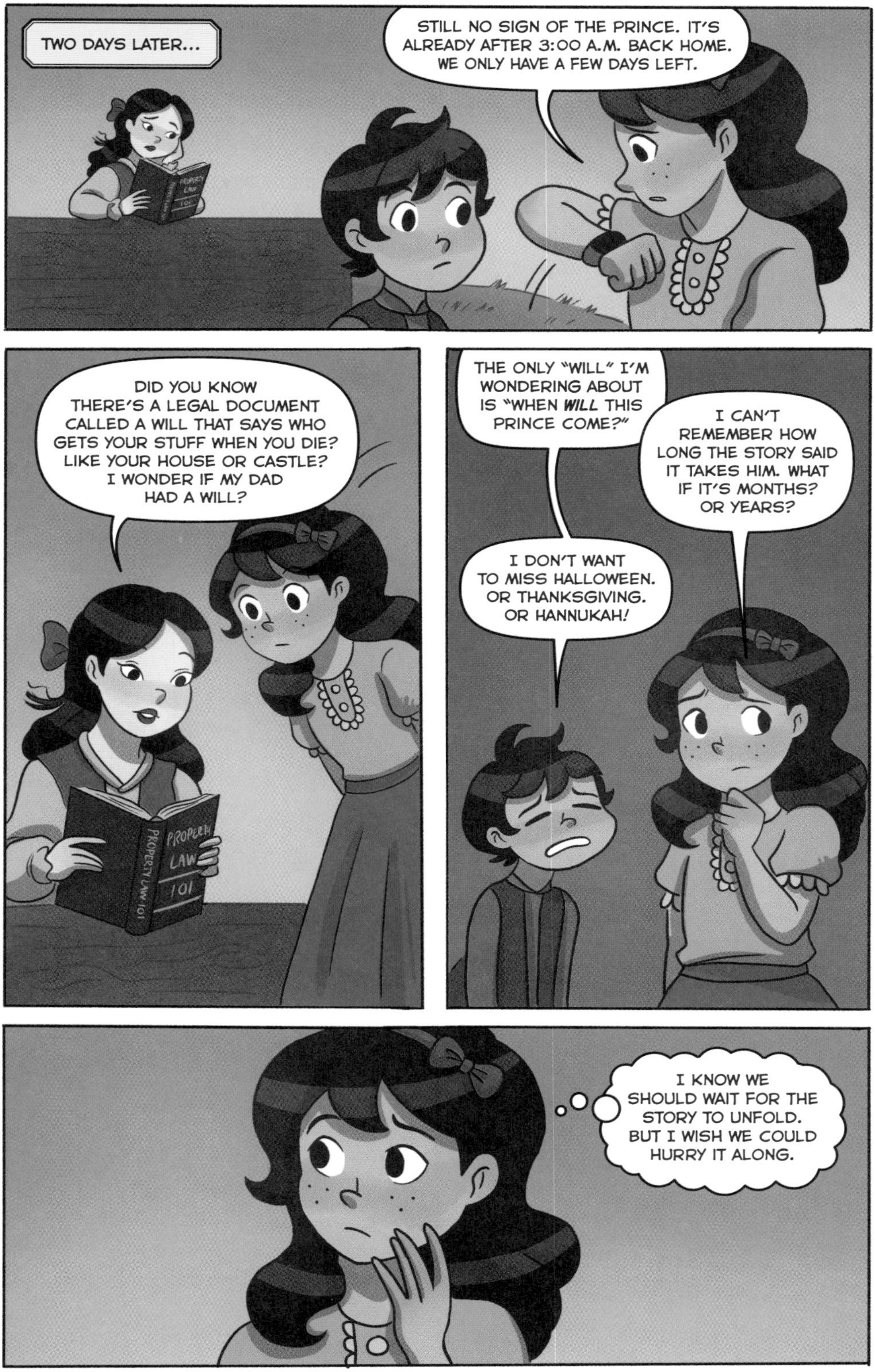
TWO DAYS LATER...
STILL NO SIGN OF THE PRINCE. IT'S ALREADY AFTER 3:00 A.M. BACK HOME. WE ONLY HAVE A FEW DAYS LEFT.
PROPERTY LAW 101
DID YOU KNOW THERE'S A LEGAL DOCUMENT CALLED A WILL THAT SAYS WHO GETS YOUR STUFF WHEN YOU DIE? LIKE YOUR HOUSE OR CASTLE? I WONDER IF MY DAD HAD A WILL?
PROPERTY LAW 101
PROPERTY LAW 101
THE ONLY "WILL" I'M WONDERING ABOUT IS "WHEN *WILL* THIS PRINCE COME?"
I CAN'T REMEMBER HOW LONG THE STORY SAID IT TAKES HIM. WHAT IF IT'S MONTHS? OR YEARS?
I DON'T WANT TO MISS HALLOWEEN. OR THANKSGIVING. OR HANNUKAH!
I KNOW WE SHOULD WAIT FOR THE STORY TO UNFOLD. BUT I WISH WE COULD HURRY IT ALONG.

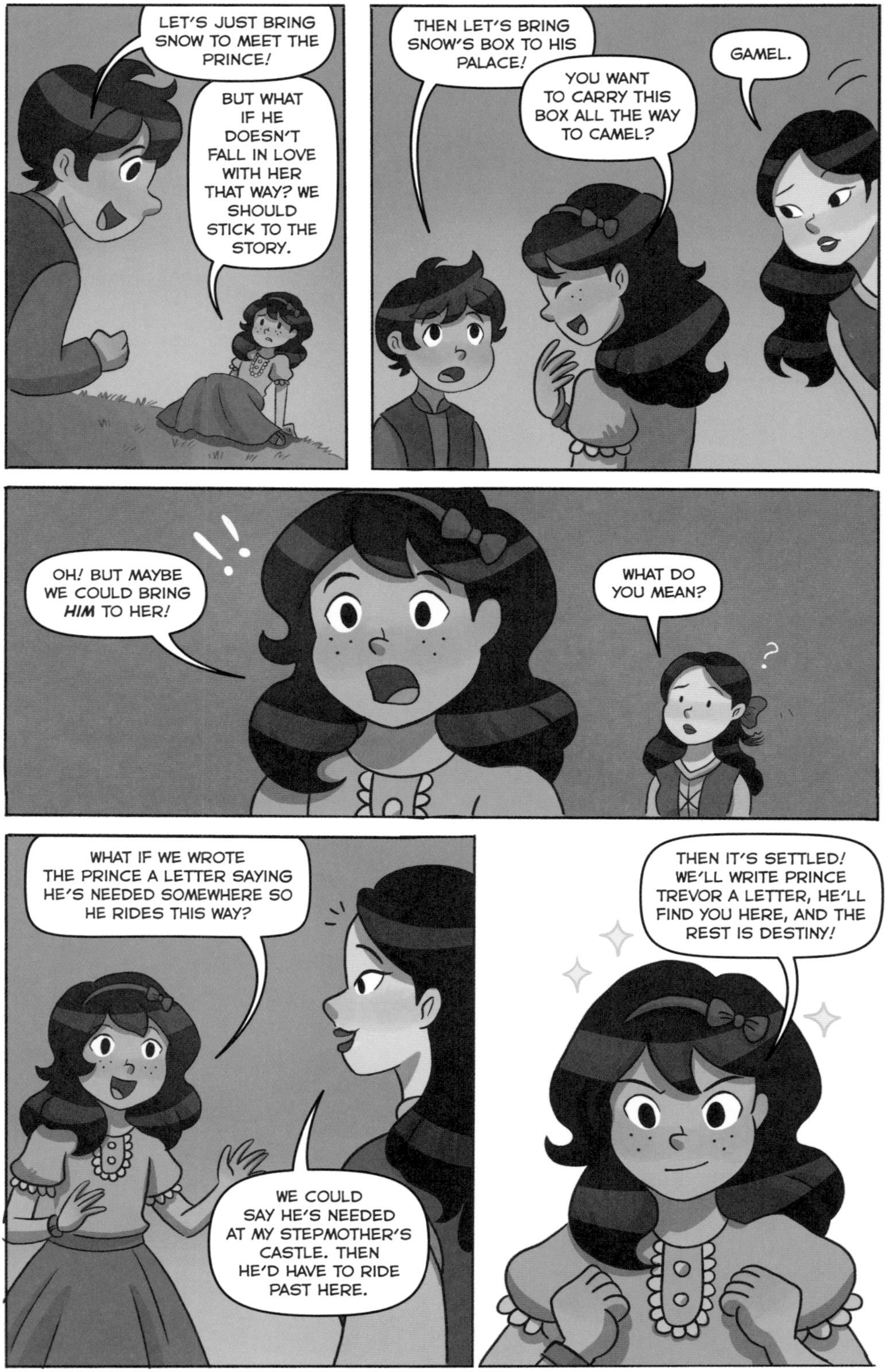
LET'S JUST BRING SNOW TO MEET THE PRINCE!
BUT WHAT IF HE DOESN'T FALL IN LOVE WITH HER THAT WAY? WE SHOULD STICK TO THE STORY.
THEN LET'S BRING SNOW'S BOX TO HIS PALACE!
YOU WANT TO CARRY THIS BOX ALL THE WAY TO CAMEL?
GAMEL.
OH! BUT MAYBE WE COULD BRING *HIM* TO HER!
!!
WHAT DO YOU MEAN?
?
WHAT IF WE WROTE THE PRINCE A LETTER SAYING HE'S NEEDED SOMEWHERE SO HE RIDES THIS WAY?
WE COULD SAY HE'S NEEDED AT MY STEPMOTHER'S CASTLE. THEN HE'D HAVE TO RIDE PAST HERE.
THEN IT'S SETTLED! WE'LL WRITE PRINCE TREVOR A LETTER, HE'LL FIND YOU HERE, AND THE REST IS DESTINY!

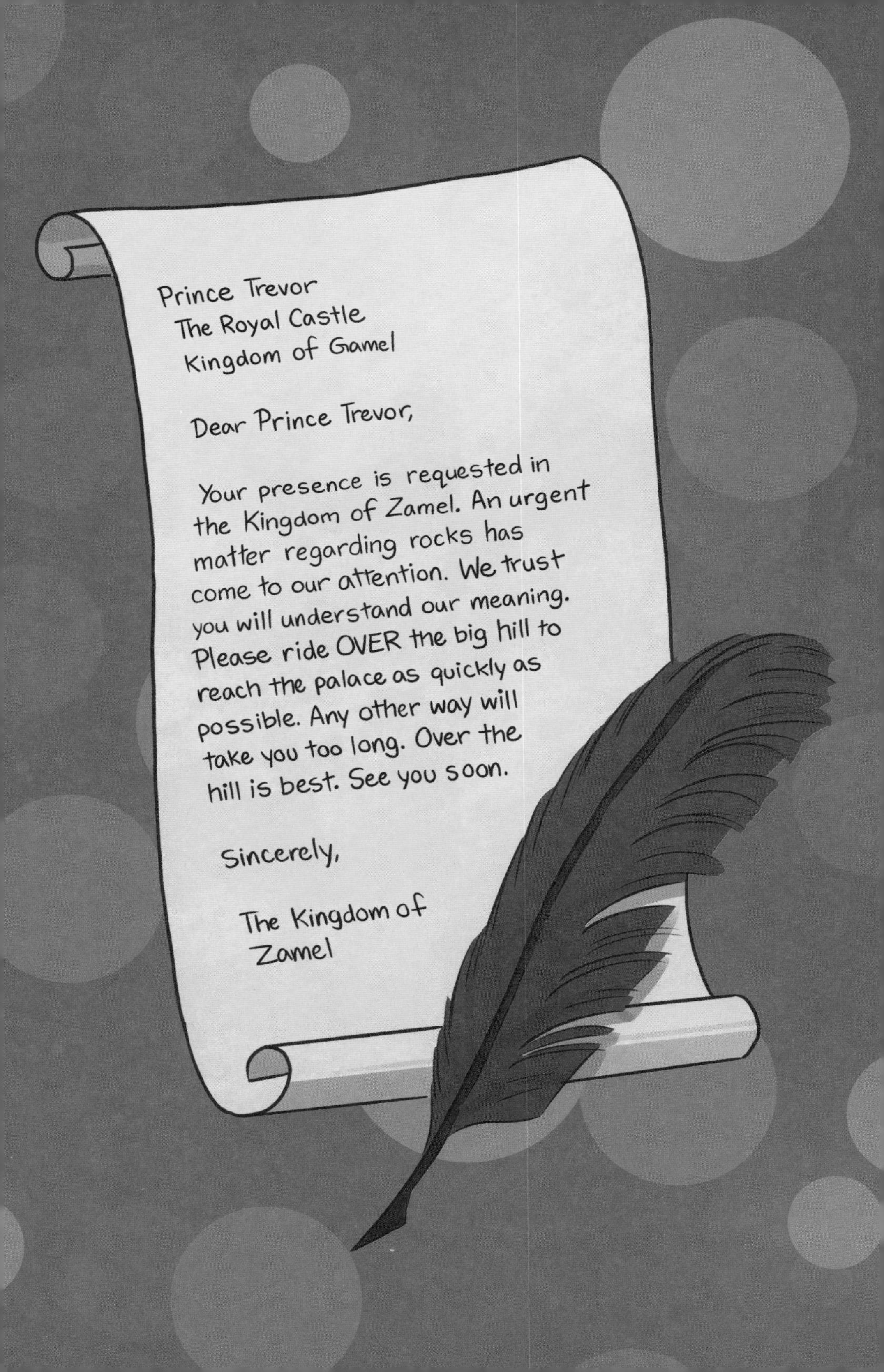
Prince Trevor
The Royal Castle
Kingdom of Gamel

Dear Prince Trevor,

Your presence is requested in the Kingdom of Zamel. An urgent matter regarding rocks has come to our attention. We trust you will understand our meaning. Please ride OVER the big hill to reach the palace as quickly as possible. Any other way will take you too long. Over the hill is best. See you soon.

Sincerely,

The Kingdom of
Zamel

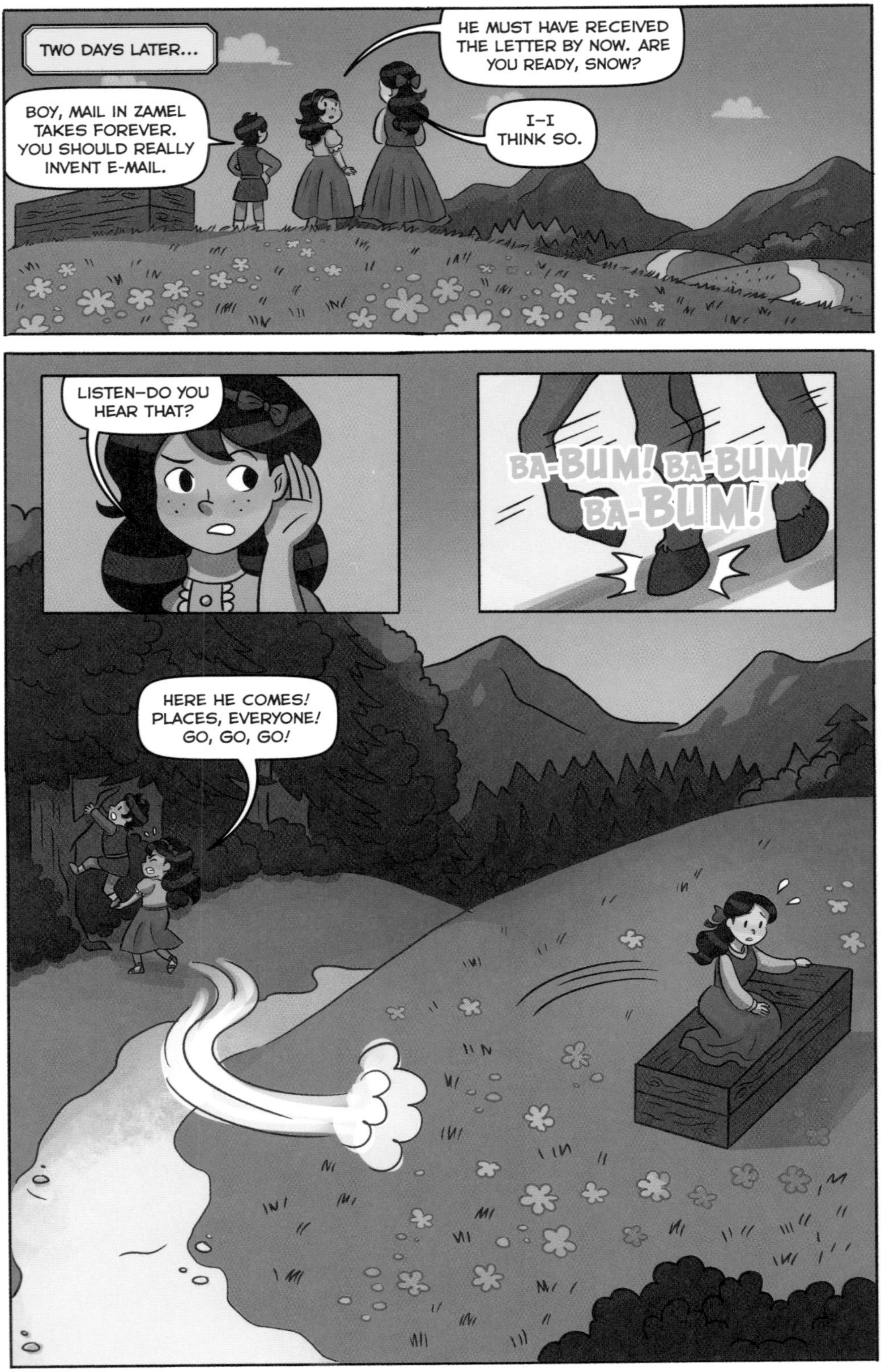
TWO DAYS LATER...
BOY, MAIL IN ZAMEL TAKES FOREVER. YOU SHOULD REALLY INVENT E-MAIL.
HE MUST HAVE RECEIVED THE LETTER BY NOW. ARE YOU READY, SNOW?
I-I THINK SO.
LISTEN-DO YOU HEAR THAT?
BA-BUM! BA-BUM! BA-BUM!
HERE HE COMES! PLACES, EVERYONE! GO, GO, GO!

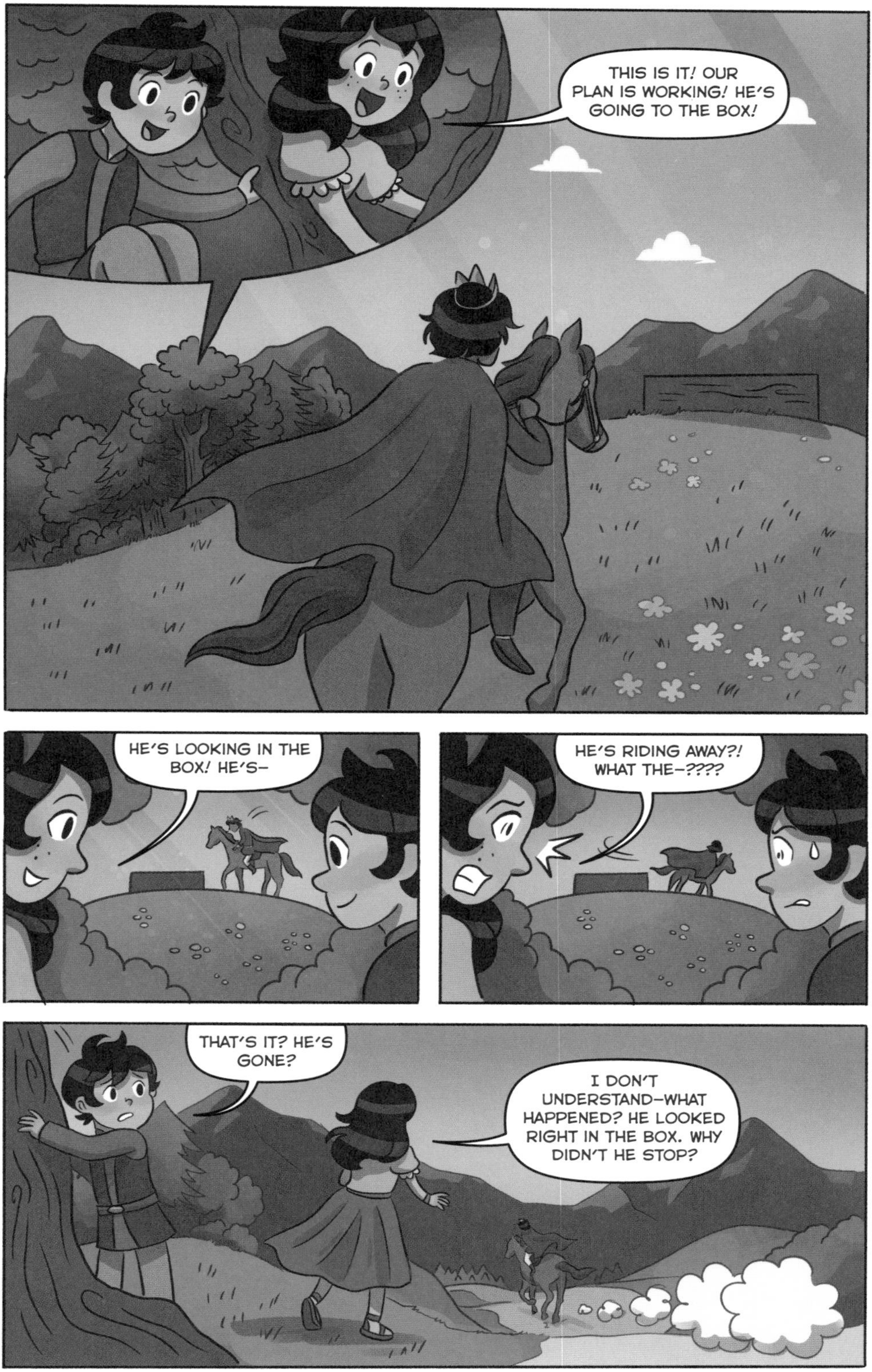
THIS IS IT! OUR PLAN IS WORKING! HE'S GOING TO THE BOX!
HE'S LOOKING IN THE BOX! HE'S–
HE'S RIDING AWAY?! WHAT THE–????
THAT'S IT? HE'S GONE?
I DON'T UNDERSTAND–WHAT HAPPENED? HE LOOKED RIGHT IN THE BOX. WHY DIDN'T HE STOP?

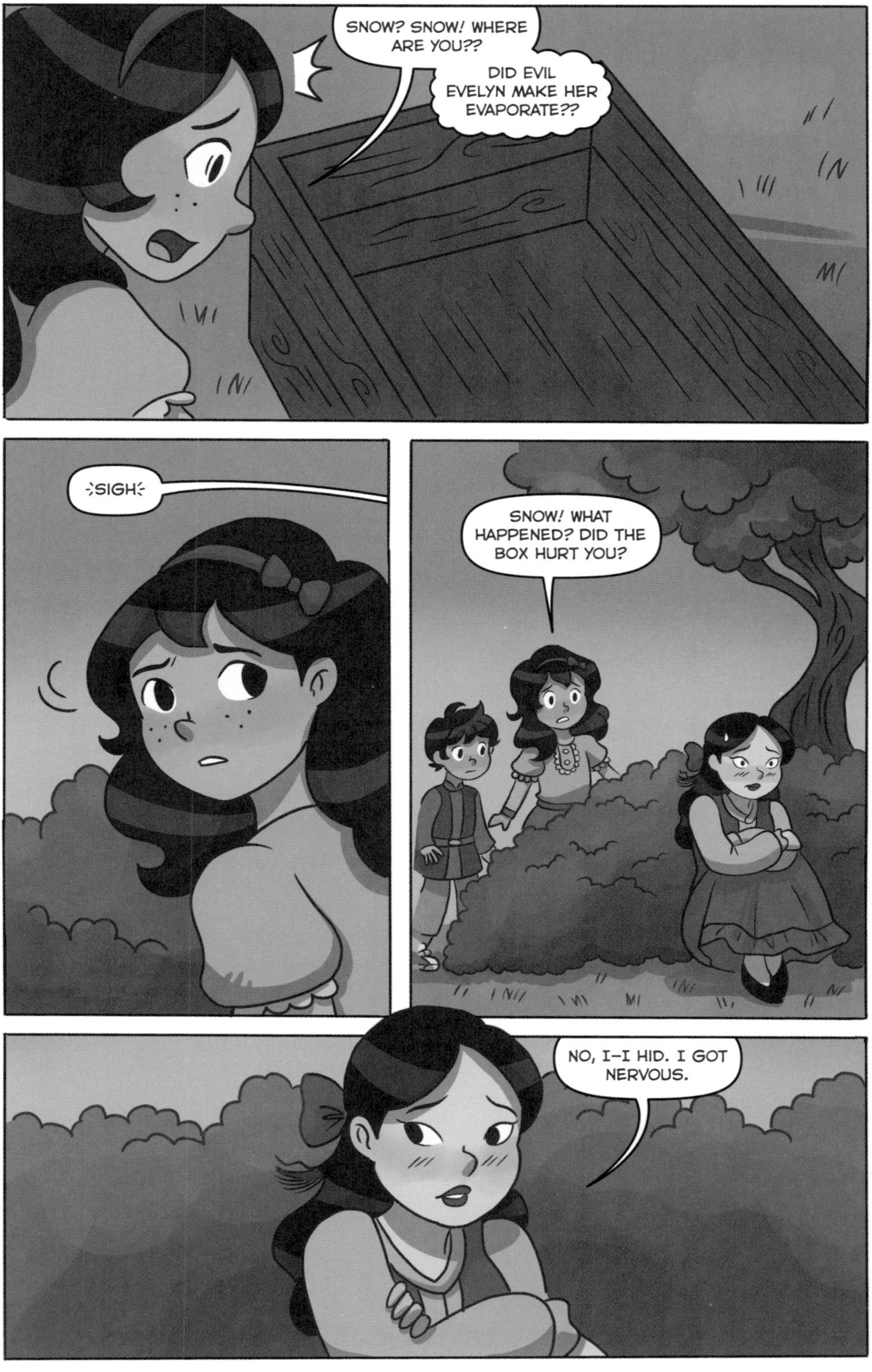
SNOW? SNOW! WHERE ARE YOU??
DID EVIL EVELYN MAKE HER EVAPORATE??
SIGH
SNOW! WHAT HAPPENED? DID THE BOX HURT YOU?
NO, I–I HID. I GOT NERVOUS.

YOU—YOU GOT NERVOUS?

YOU GOT *NERVOUS?!?*

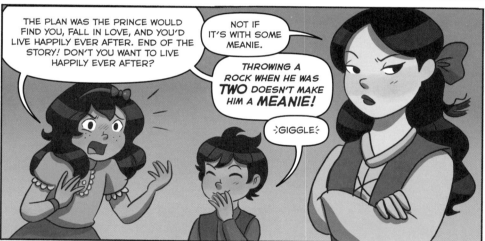

THE PLAN WAS THE PRINCE WOULD FIND YOU, FALL IN LOVE, AND YOU'D LIVE HAPPILY EVER AFTER. END OF THE STORY! DON'T YOU WANT TO LIVE HAPPILY EVER AFTER?

NOT IF IT'S WITH SOME MEANIE.

THROWING A ROCK WHEN HE WAS *TWO* DOESN'T MAKE HIM A *MEANIE!*

÷GIGGLE÷

WHY ARE YOU LAUGHING? THIS IS ALL YOUR FAULT, YOU KNOW!

HEY! WHAT DID I DO?

IF YOU HADN'T STOPPED SNOW FROM EATING THE APPLE—IF YOU HADN'T BEEN PLAYING IN THE BASEMENT IN THE FIRST PLACE— NONE OF THIS WOULD HAVE HAPPENED!

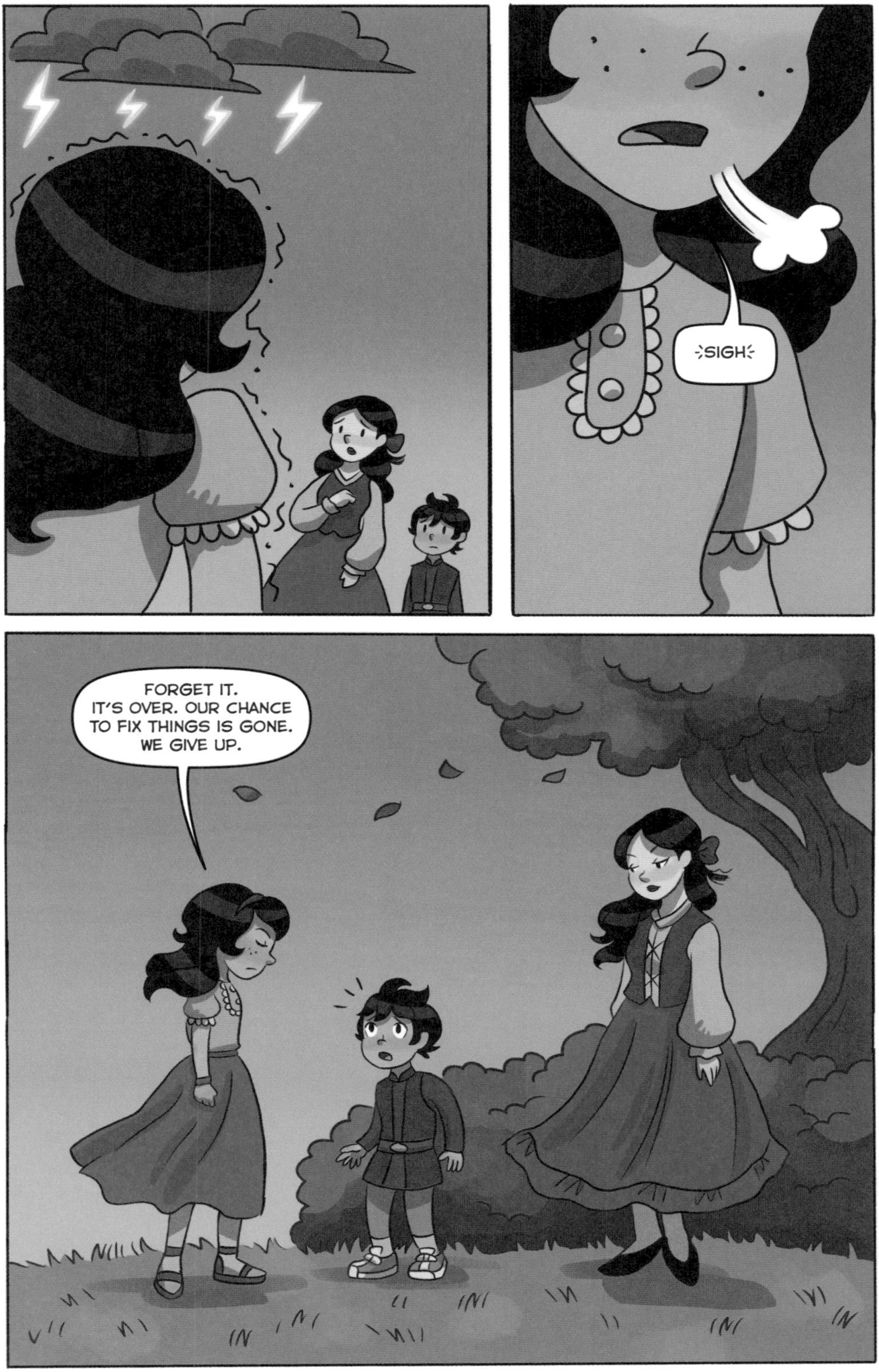

SIGH
FORGET IT. IT'S OVER. OUR CHANCE TO FIX THINGS IS GONE. WE GIVE UP.

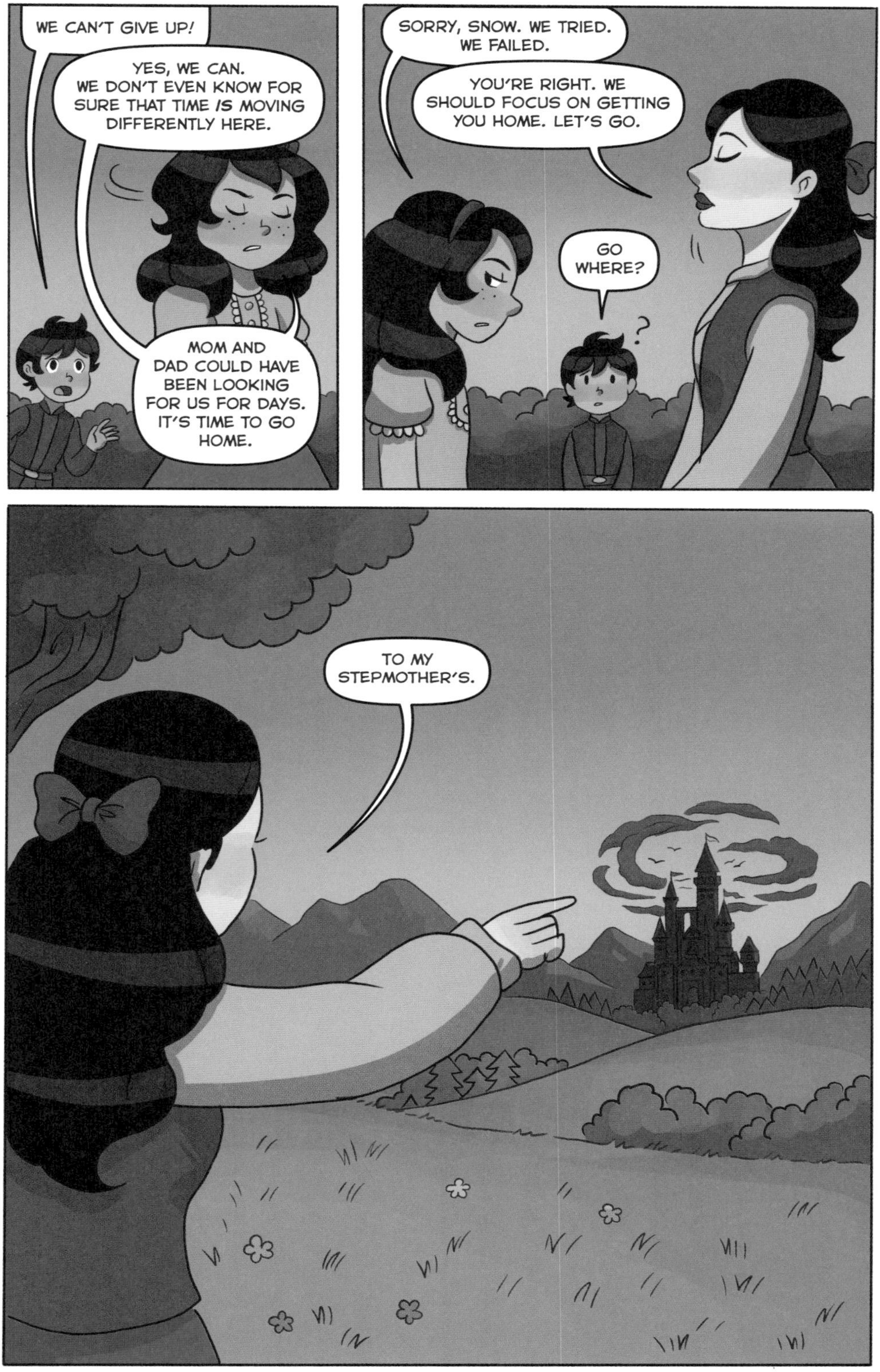
WE CAN'T GIVE UP!
YES, WE CAN. WE DON'T EVEN KNOW FOR SURE THAT TIME *IS* MOVING DIFFERENTLY HERE.
MOM AND DAD COULD HAVE BEEN LOOKING FOR US FOR DAYS. IT'S TIME TO GO HOME.
SORRY, SNOW. WE TRIED. WE FAILED.
YOU'RE RIGHT. WE SHOULD FOCUS ON GETTING YOU HOME. LET'S GO.
GO WHERE?
?
TO MY STEPMOTHER'S.

CHAPTER ELEVEN: PRINCESS IN DISGUISE

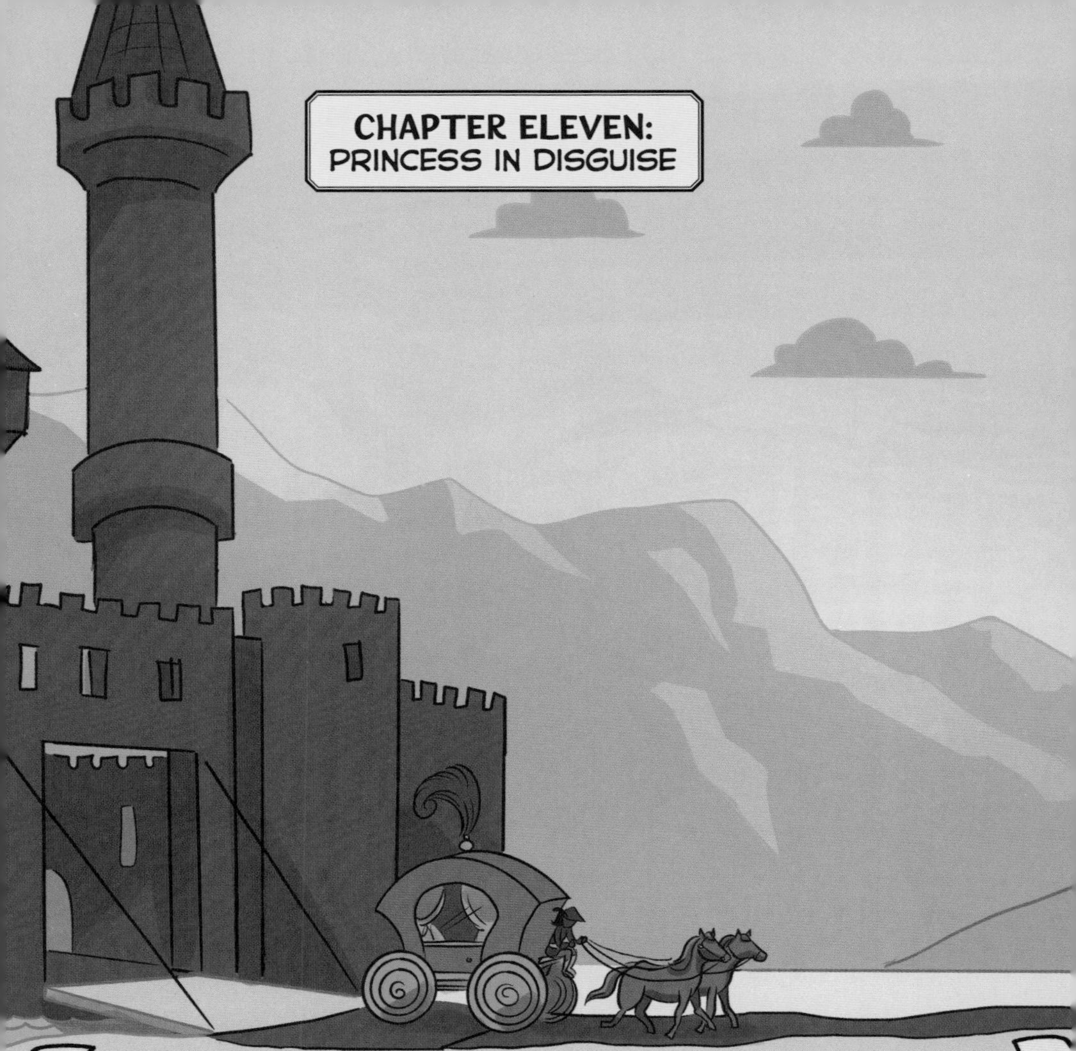

The Plan

STEP 1: Sneak into Evil Evelyn's castle while she's at her weekly massage appointment. (Apparently, being evil is stressful.)

STEP 2: Pretend to be interior decorators. Evil Evelyn LOVES to redecorate.

STEP 3: Snow shows us where to find the mirror.

STEP 4: Jonah and I go home through the mirror. Snow sneaks back out.

STEP 5: The End!

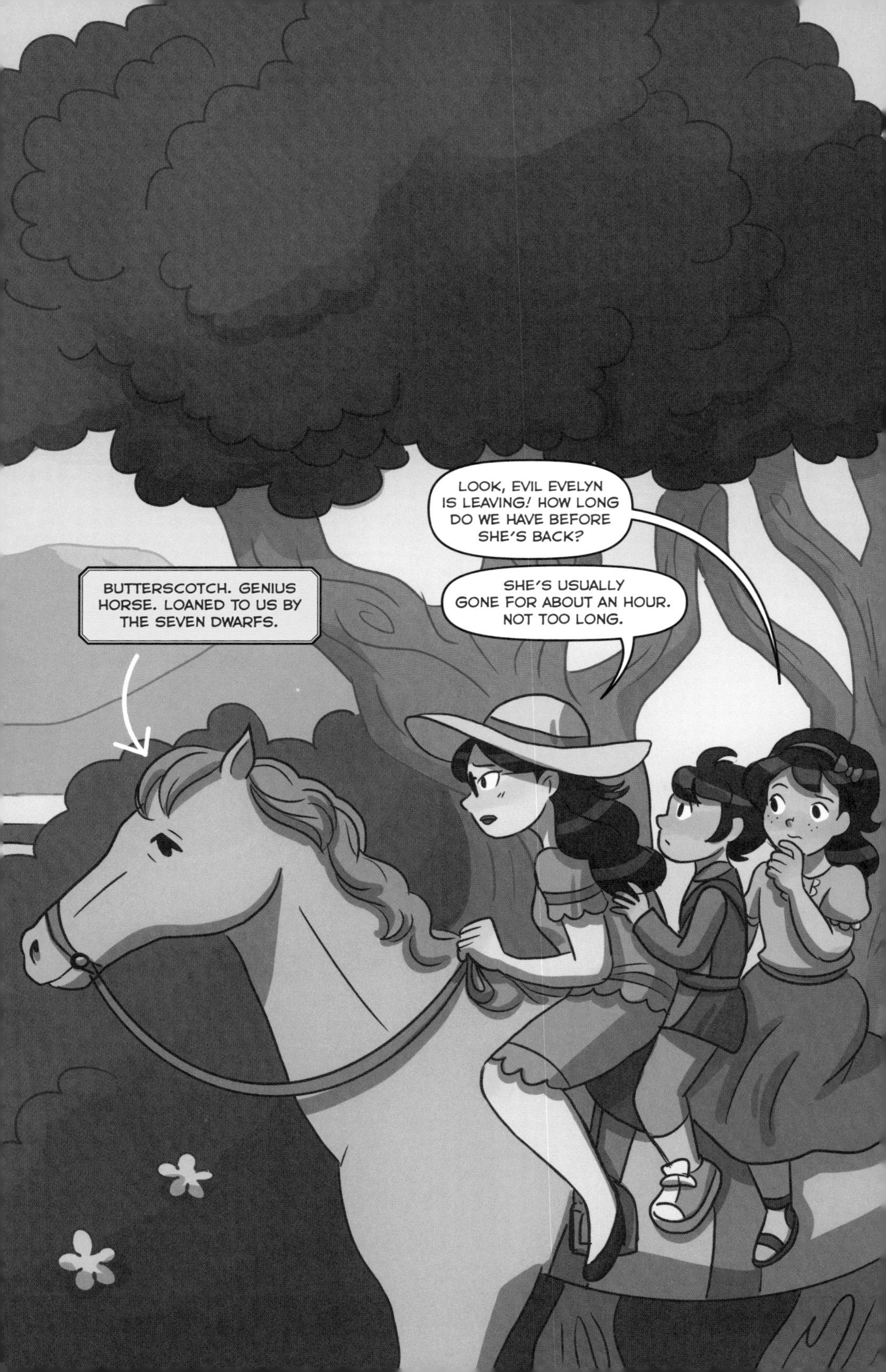
BUTTERSCOTCH. GENIUS HORSE. LOANED TO US BY THE SEVEN DWARFS.
LOOK, EVIL EVELYN IS LEAVING! HOW LONG DO WE HAVE BEFORE SHE'S BACK?
SHE'S USUALLY GONE FOR ABOUT AN HOUR. NOT TOO LONG.

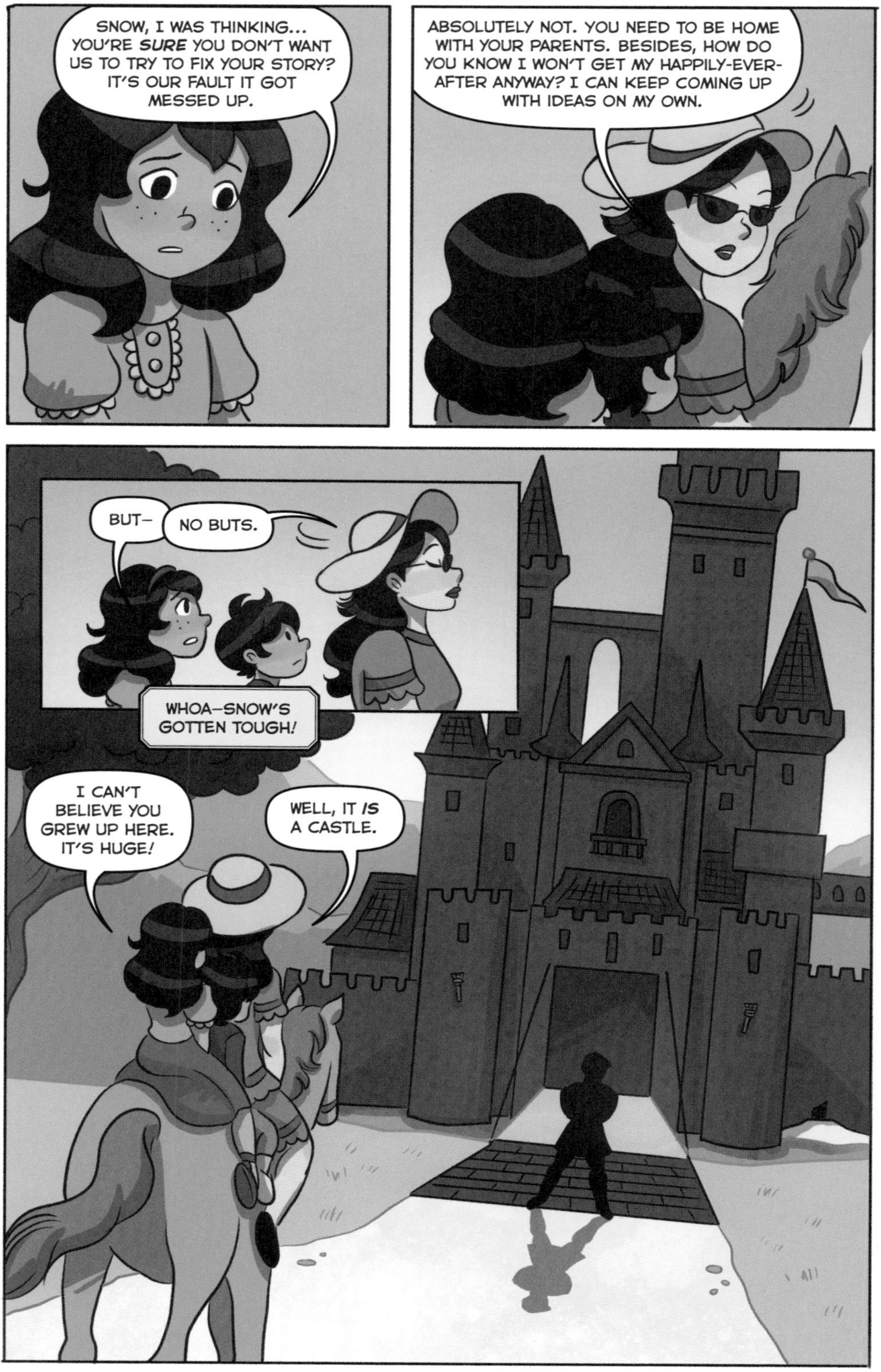
SNOW, I WAS THINKING... YOU'RE **SURE** YOU DON'T WANT US TO TRY TO FIX YOUR STORY? IT'S OUR FAULT IT GOT MESSED UP.
ABSOLUTELY NOT. YOU NEED TO BE HOME WITH YOUR PARENTS. BESIDES, HOW DO YOU KNOW I WON'T GET MY HAPPILY-EVER-AFTER ANYWAY? I CAN KEEP COMING UP WITH IDEAS ON MY OWN.
BUT–
NO BUTS.
WHOA–SNOW'S GOTTEN TOUGH!
I CAN'T BELIEVE YOU GREW UP HERE. IT'S HUGE!
WELL, IT *IS* A CASTLE.

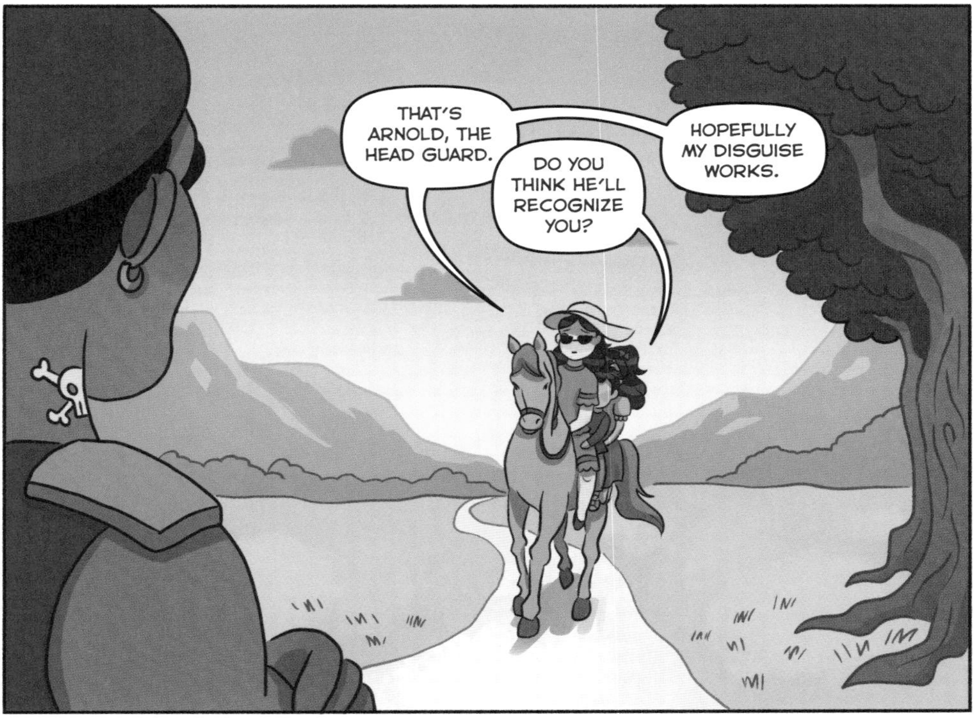
THAT'S ARNOLD, THE HEAD GUARD.
DO YOU THINK HE'LL RECOGNIZE YOU?
HOPEFULLY MY DISGUISE WORKS.

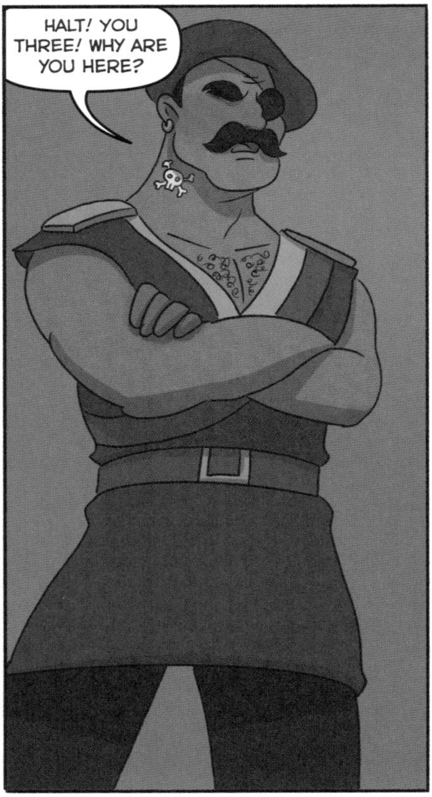
HALT! YOU THREE! WHY ARE YOU HERE?

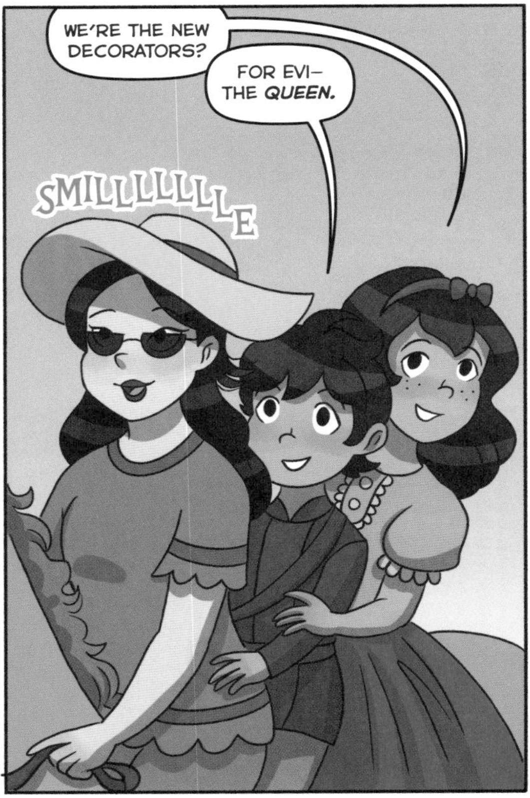
WE'RE THE NEW DECORATORS?
FOR EVI— THE *QUEEN.*
SMILLLLLLLE

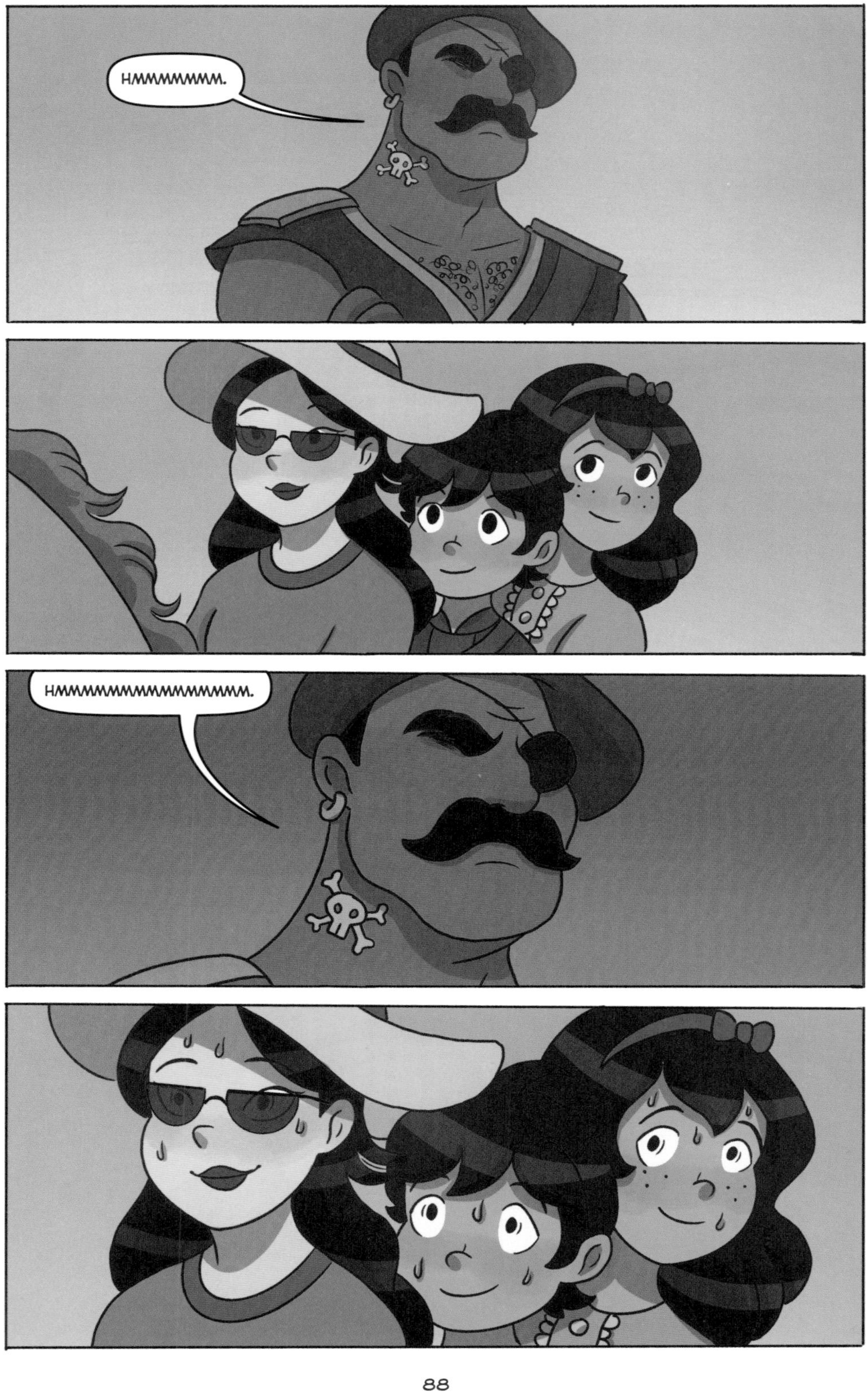
HMMMMMMM.
HMMMMMMMMMMMMMMMMM.

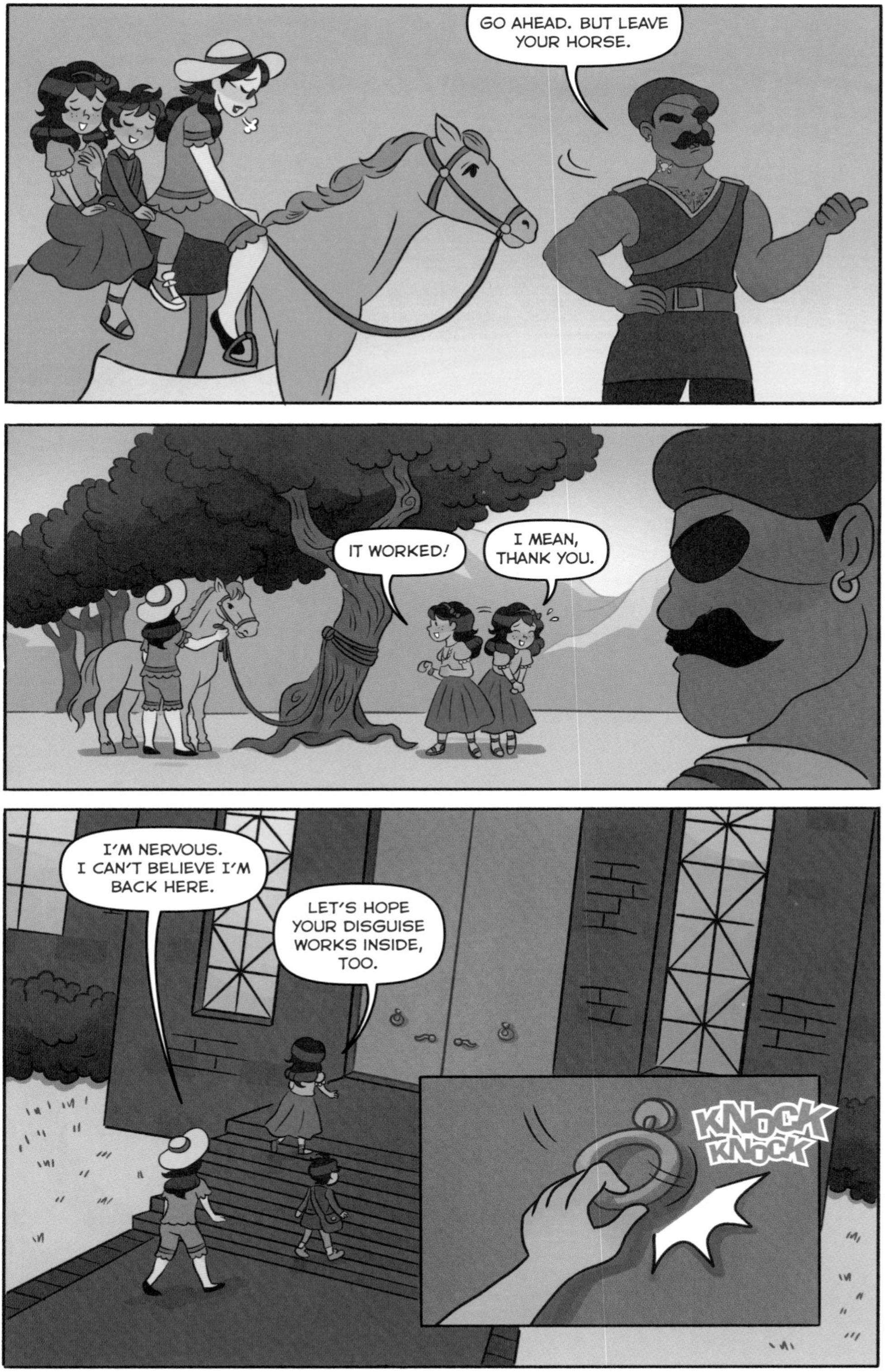
GO AHEAD. BUT LEAVE YOUR HORSE.
IT WORKED!
I MEAN, THANK YOU.
I'M NERVOUS. I CAN'T BELIEVE I'M BACK HERE.
LET'S HOPE YOUR DISGUISE WORKS INSIDE, TOO.
KNOCK KNOCK

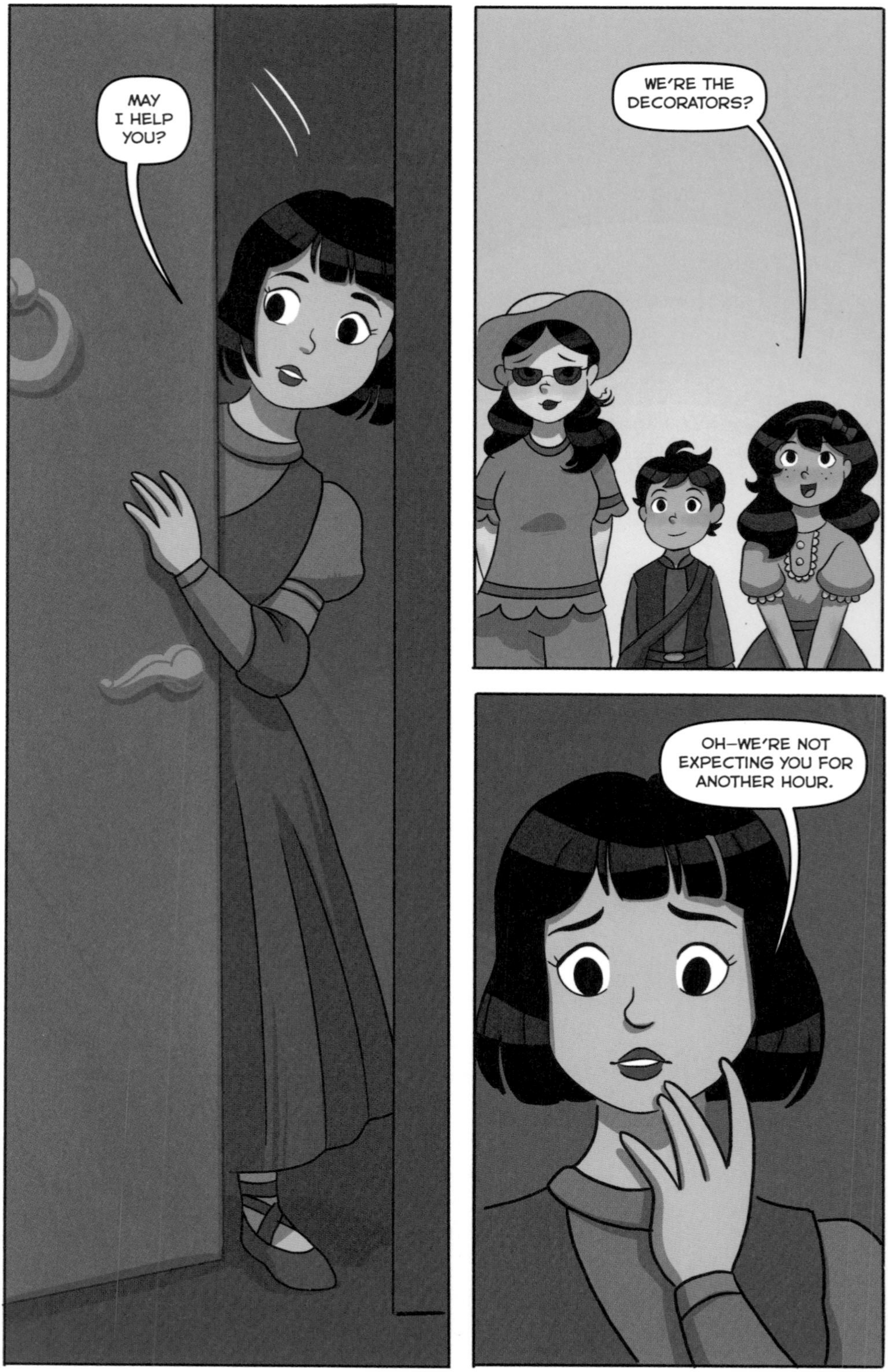
MAY I HELP YOU?
WE'RE THE DECORATORS?
OH—WE'RE NOT EXPECTING YOU FOR ANOTHER HOUR.

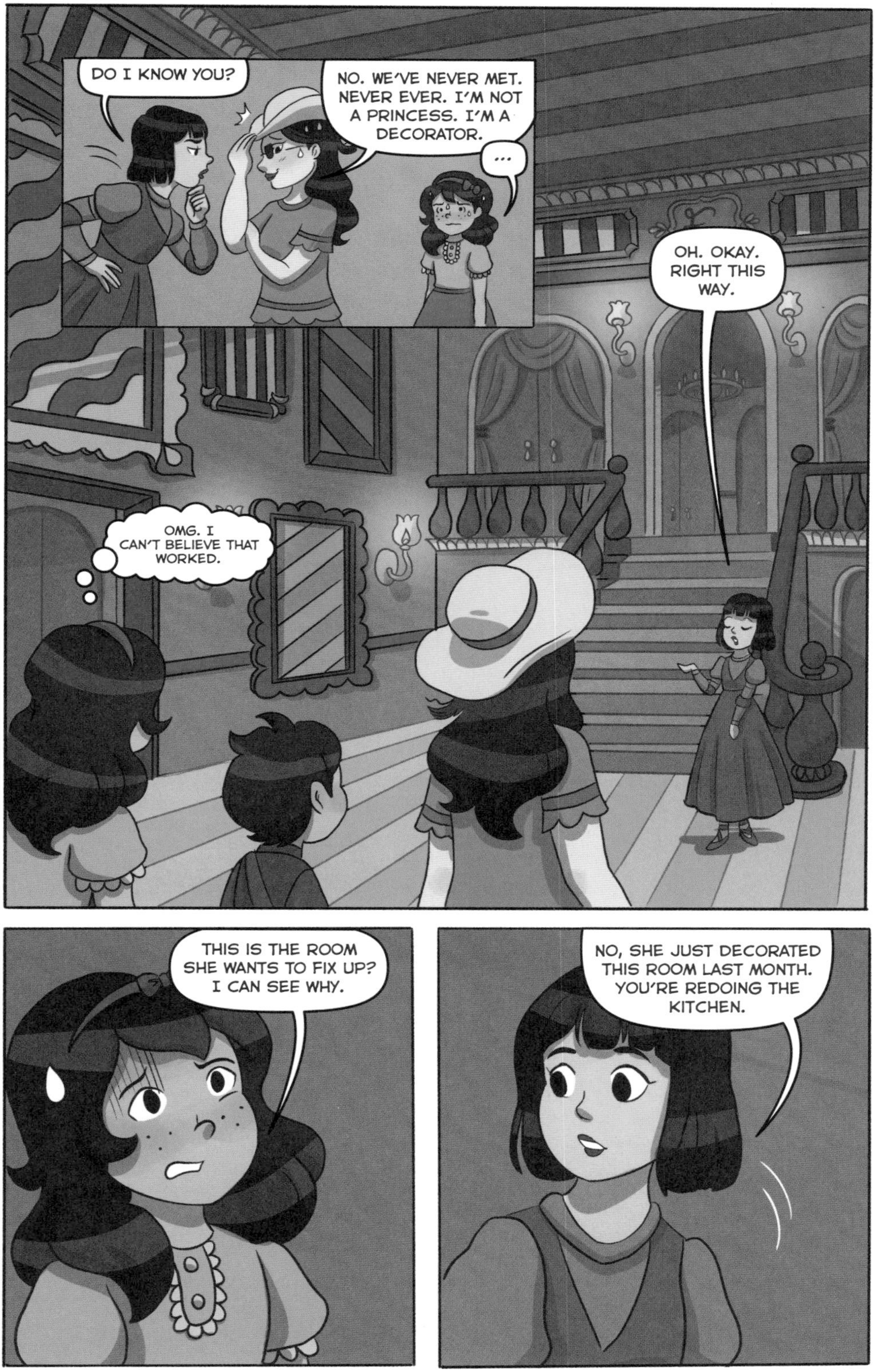
DO I KNOW YOU?
NO. WE'VE NEVER MET. NEVER EVER. I'M NOT A PRINCESS. I'M A DECORATOR.
...
OH. OKAY. RIGHT THIS WAY.
OMG. I CAN'T BELIEVE THAT WORKED.
THIS IS THE ROOM SHE WANTS TO FIX UP? I CAN SEE WHY.
NO, SHE JUST DECORATED THIS ROOM LAST MONTH. YOU'RE REDOING THE KITCHEN.

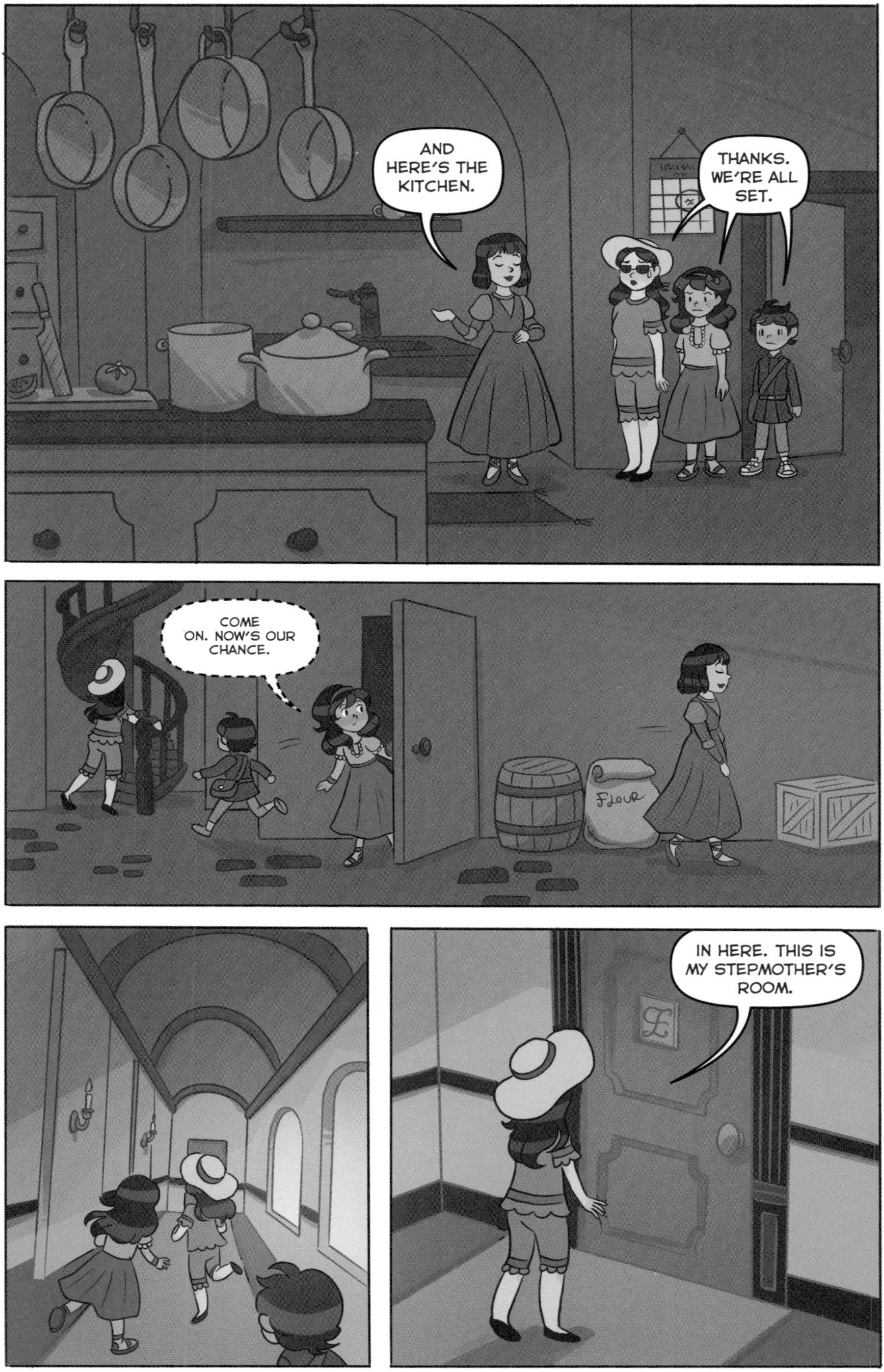
AND HERE'S THE KITCHEN.
THANKS. WE'RE ALL SET.
COME ON. NOW'S OUR CHANCE.
FLOUR
IN HERE. THIS IS MY STEPMOTHER'S ROOM.

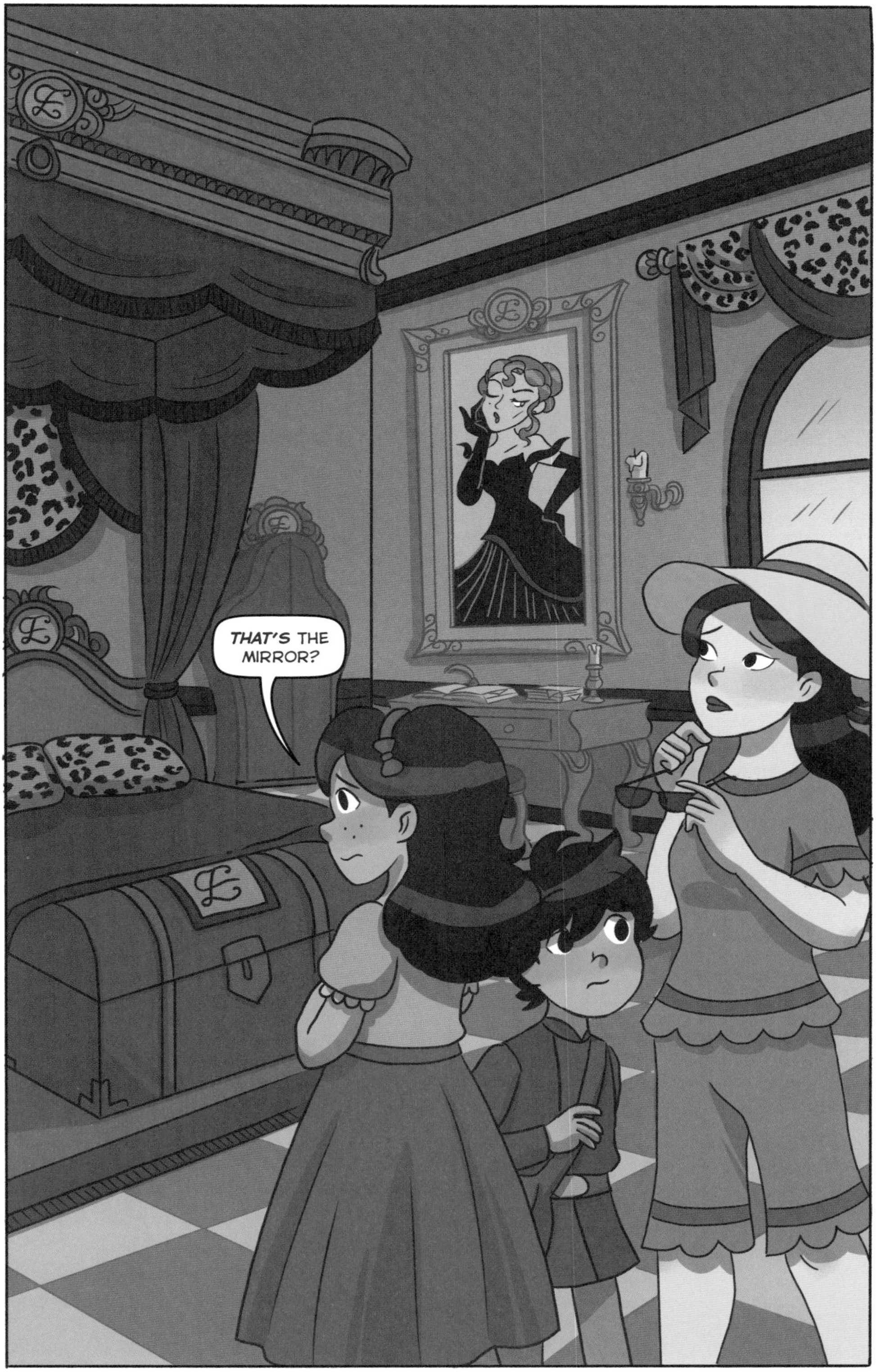
THAT'S THE MIRROR?

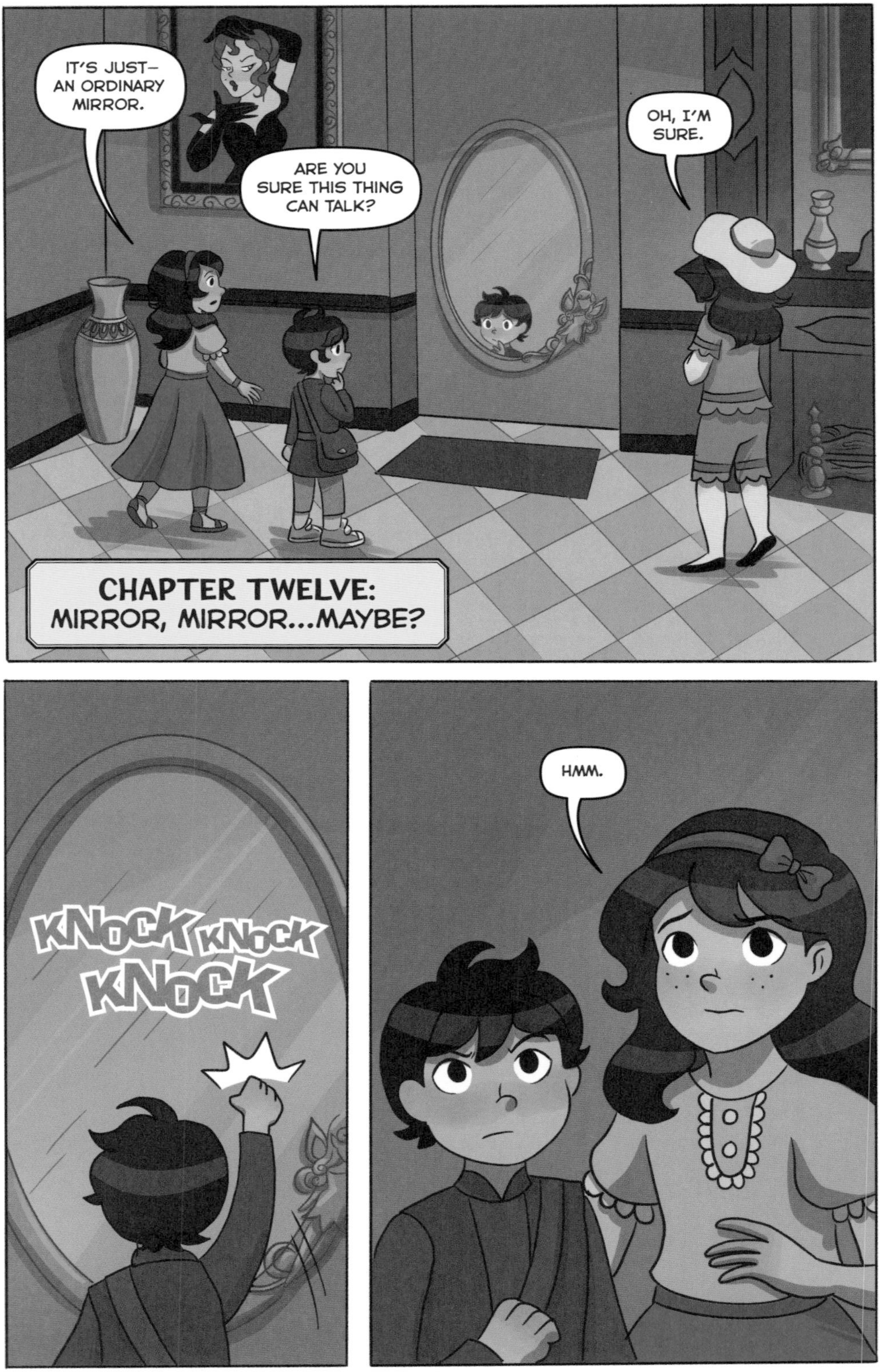
IT'S JUST—
AN ORDINARY
MIRROR.
ARE YOU
SURE THIS THING
CAN TALK?
OH, I'M
SURE.
CHAPTER TWELVE:
MIRROR, MIRROR...MAYBE?
KNOCK KNOCK
KNOCK
HMM.

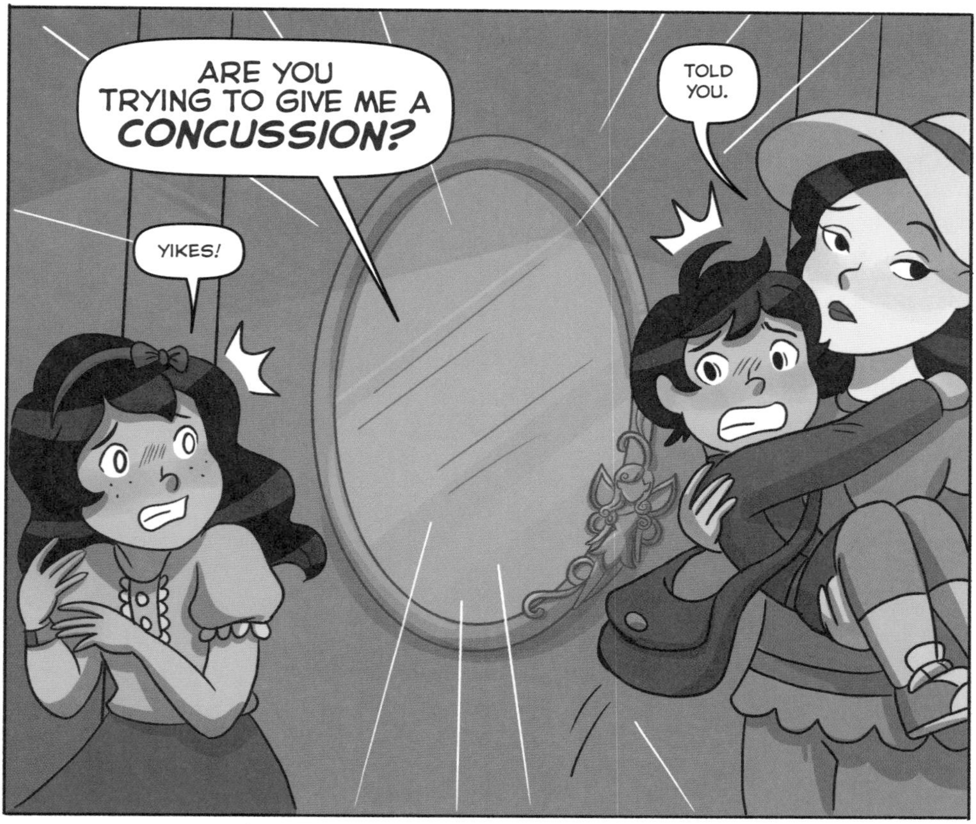
ARE YOU TRYING TO GIVE ME A *CONCUSSION?*
YIKES!
TOLD YOU.

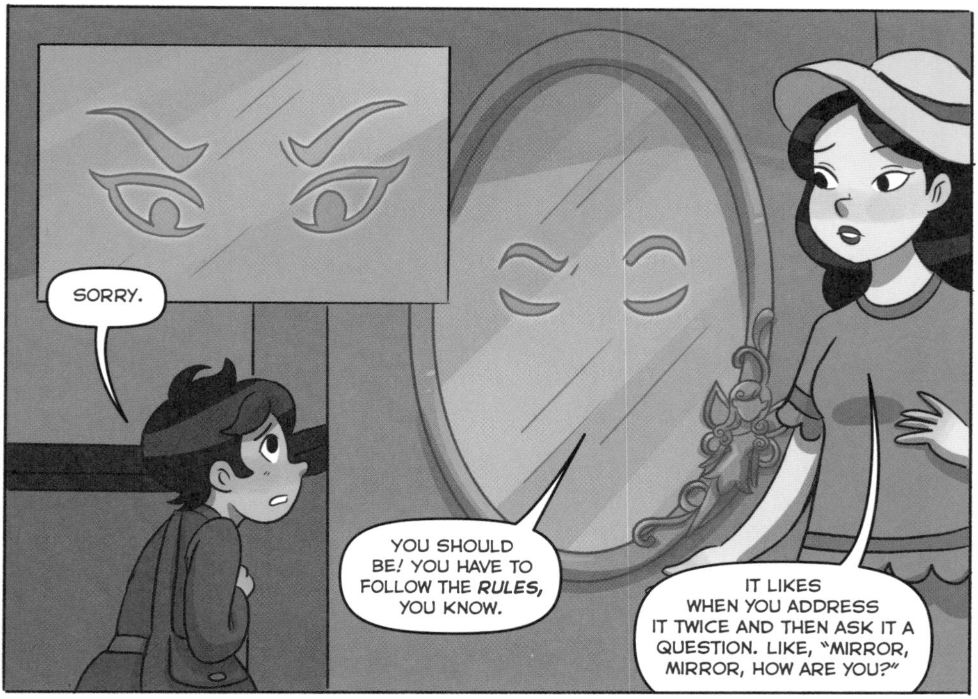
SORRY.
YOU SHOULD BE! YOU HAVE TO FOLLOW THE *RULES,* YOU KNOW.
IT LIKES WHEN YOU ADDRESS IT TWICE AND THEN ASK IT A QUESTION. LIKE, "MIRROR, MIRROR, HOW ARE YOU?"

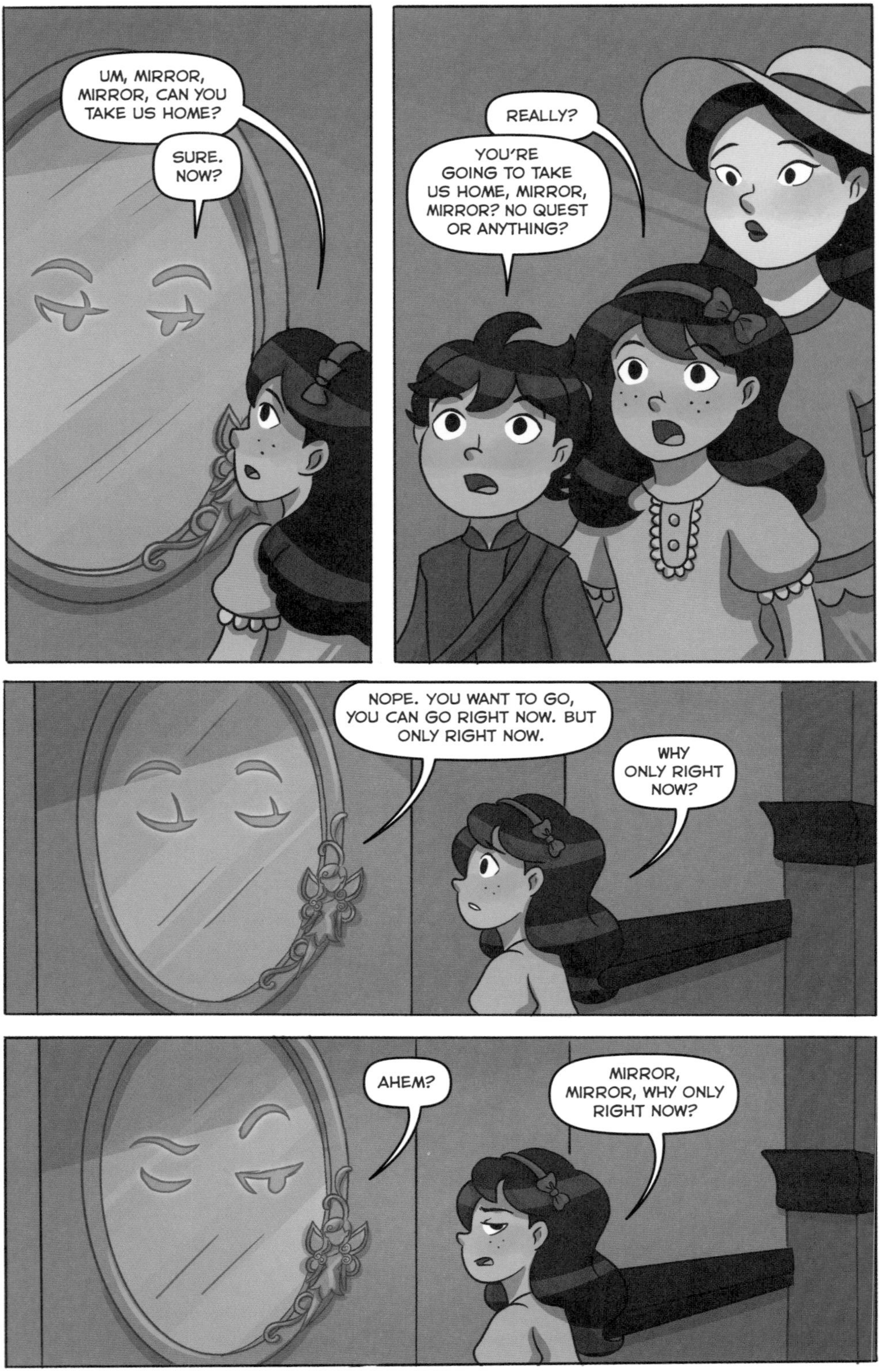
UM, MIRROR, MIRROR, CAN YOU TAKE US HOME?
SURE. NOW?
REALLY?
YOU'RE GOING TO TAKE US HOME, MIRROR, MIRROR? NO QUEST OR ANYTHING?
NOPE. YOU WANT TO GO, YOU CAN GO RIGHT NOW. BUT ONLY RIGHT NOW.
WHY ONLY RIGHT NOW?
AHEM?
MIRROR, MIRROR, WHY ONLY RIGHT NOW?

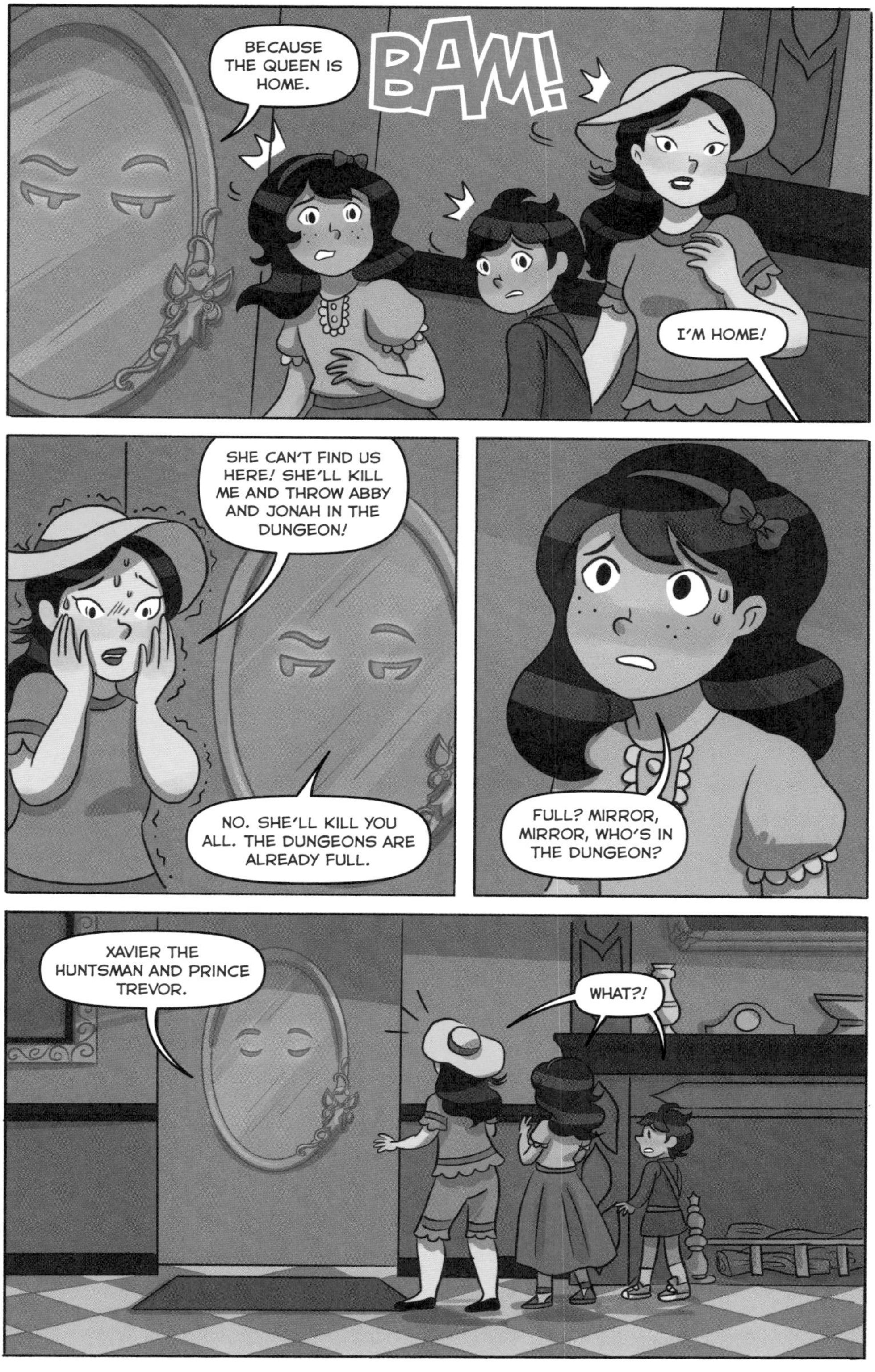
BECAUSE THE QUEEN IS HOME.
BAM!
I'M HOME!
SHE CAN'T FIND US HERE! SHE'LL KILL ME AND THROW ABBY AND JONAH IN THE DUNGEON!
NO. SHE'LL KILL YOU ALL. THE DUNGEONS ARE ALREADY FULL.
FULL? MIRROR, MIRROR, WHO'S IN THE DUNGEON?
XAVIER THE HUNTSMAN AND PRINCE TREVOR.
WHAT?!

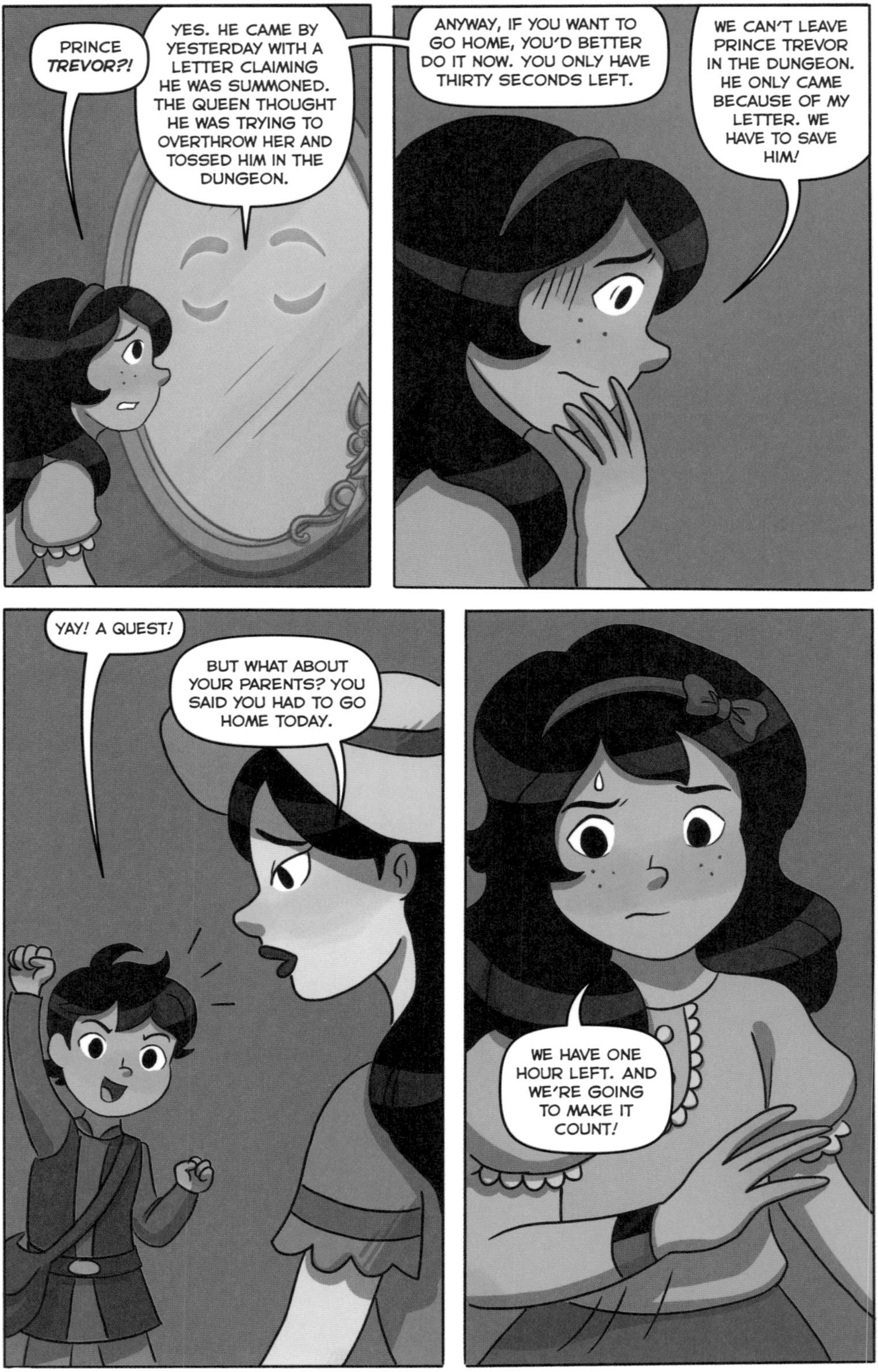
PRINCE *TREVOR?!*
YES. HE CAME BY YESTERDAY WITH A LETTER CLAIMING HE WAS SUMMONED. THE QUEEN THOUGHT HE WAS TRYING TO OVERTHROW HER AND TOSSED HIM IN THE DUNGEON.
ANYWAY, IF YOU WANT TO GO HOME, YOU'D BETTER DO IT NOW. YOU ONLY HAVE THIRTY SECONDS LEFT.
WE CAN'T LEAVE PRINCE TREVOR IN THE DUNGEON. HE ONLY CAME BECAUSE OF *MY* LETTER. WE HAVE TO SAVE HIM!
YAY! A QUEST!
BUT WHAT ABOUT YOUR PARENTS? YOU SAID YOU HAD TO GO HOME TODAY.
WE HAVE ONE HOUR LEFT. AND WE'RE GOING TO MAKE IT COUNT!

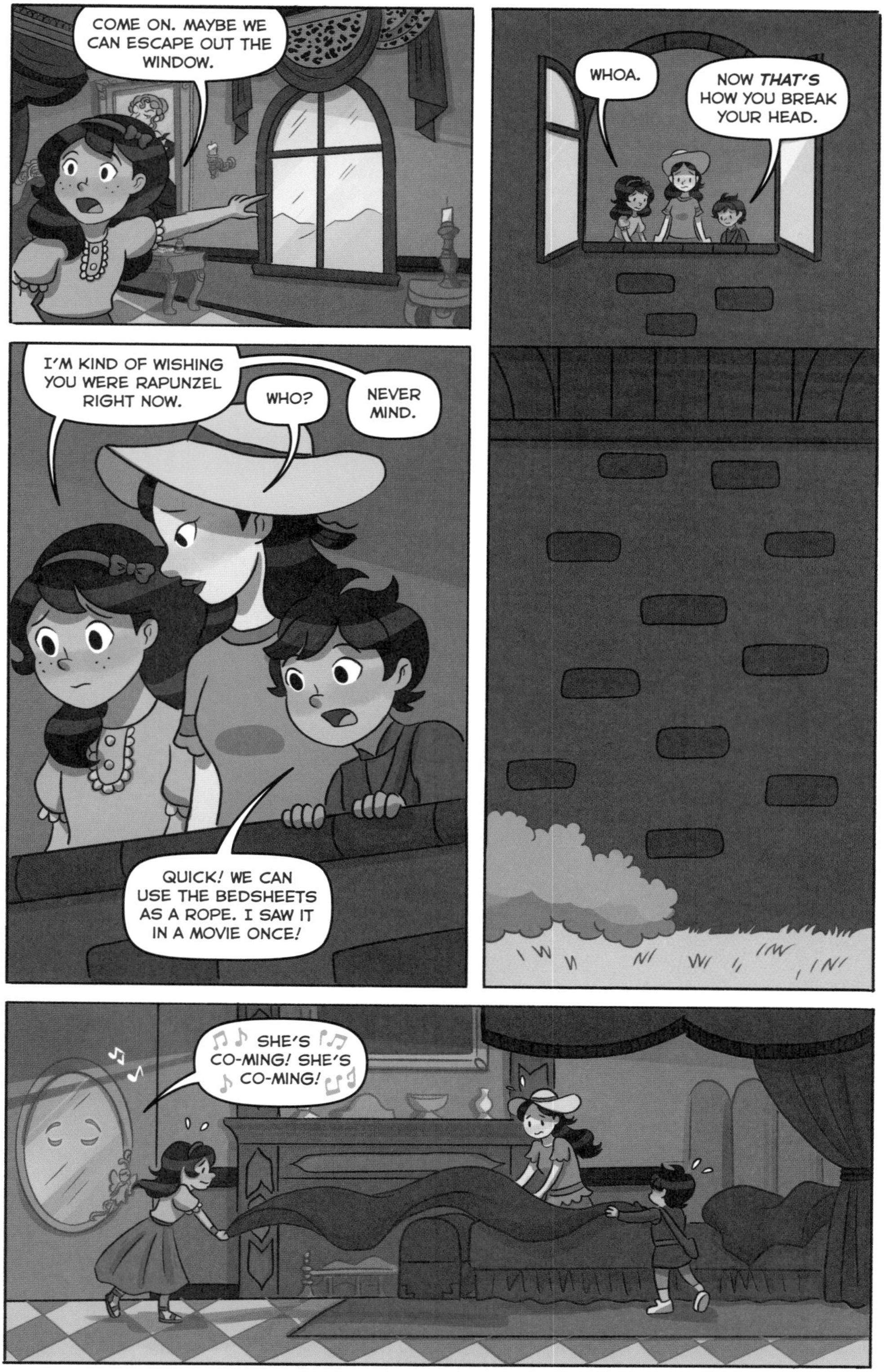
COME ON. MAYBE WE CAN ESCAPE OUT THE WINDOW.
WHOA.
NOW *THAT'S* HOW YOU BREAK YOUR HEAD.
I'M KIND OF WISHING YOU WERE RAPUNZEL RIGHT NOW.
WHO?
NEVER MIND.
QUICK! WE CAN USE THE BEDSHEETS AS A ROPE. I SAW IT IN A MOVIE ONCE!
SHE'S CO-MING! SHE'S CO-MING!

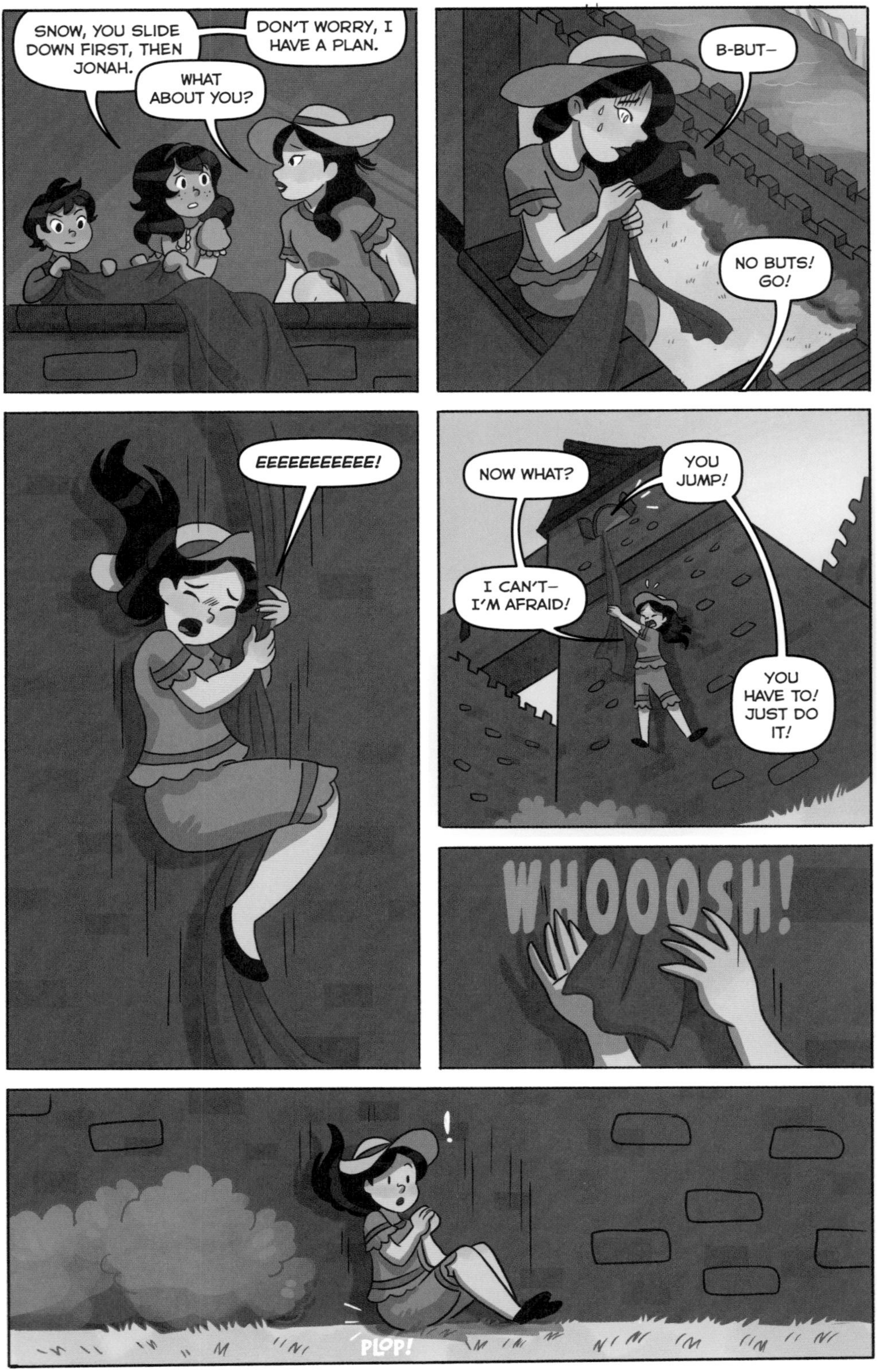
SNOW, YOU SLIDE DOWN FIRST, THEN JONAH.
WHAT ABOUT YOU?
DON'T WORRY, I HAVE A PLAN.
B-BUT—
NO BUTS! GO!
EEEEEEEEEEE!
NOW WHAT?
YOU JUMP!
I CAN'T— I'M AFRAID!
YOU HAVE TO! JUST DO IT!
WHOOOSH!
!
PLOP!

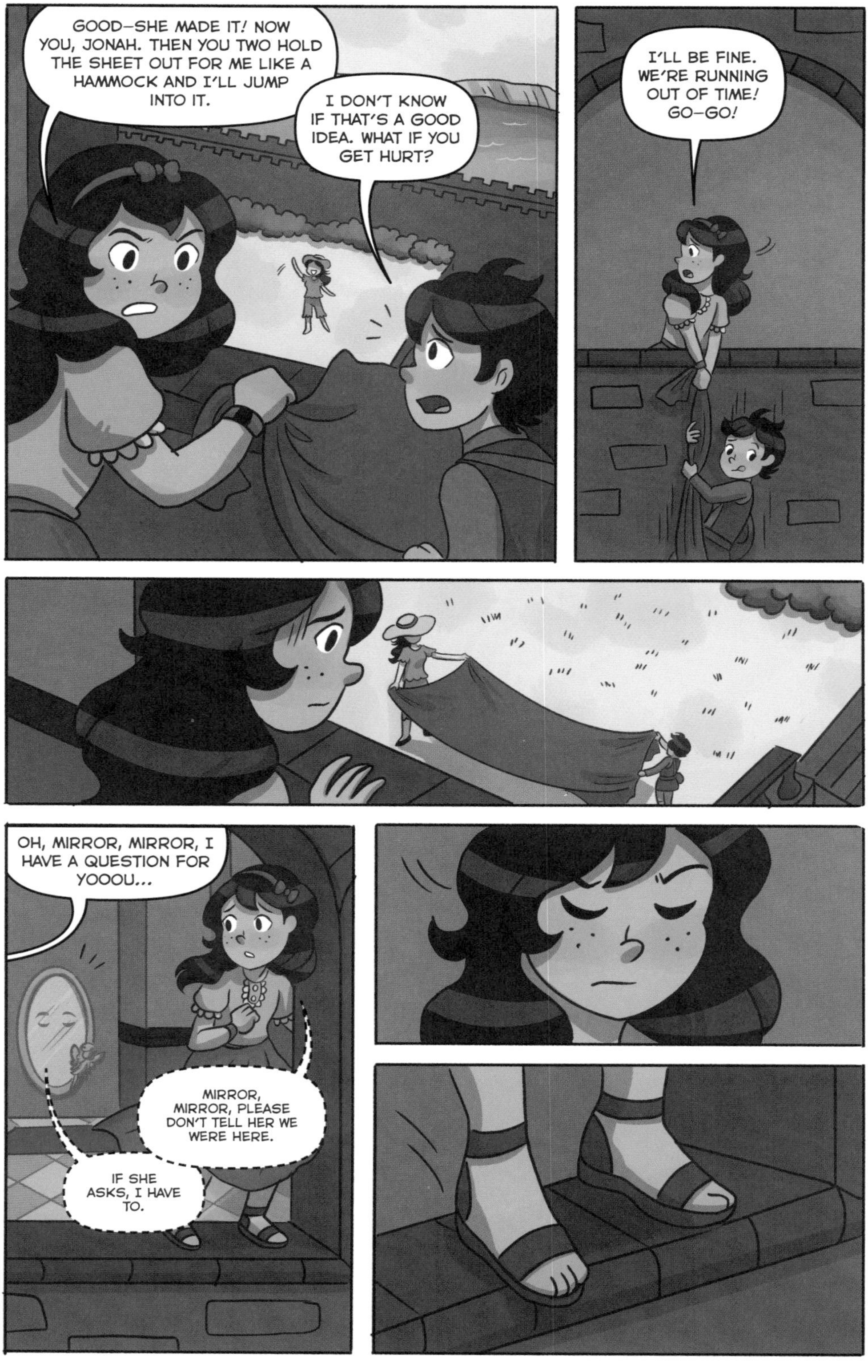
GOOD—SHE MADE IT! NOW YOU, JONAH. THEN YOU TWO HOLD THE SHEET OUT FOR ME LIKE A HAMMOCK AND I'LL JUMP INTO IT.
I DON'T KNOW IF THAT'S A GOOD IDEA. WHAT IF YOU GET HURT?
I'LL BE FINE. WE'RE RUNNING OUT OF TIME! GO—GO!
OH, MIRROR, MIRROR, I HAVE A QUESTION FOR YOOOU...
MIRROR, MIRROR, PLEASE DON'T TELL HER WE WERE HERE.
IF SHE ASKS, I HAVE TO.

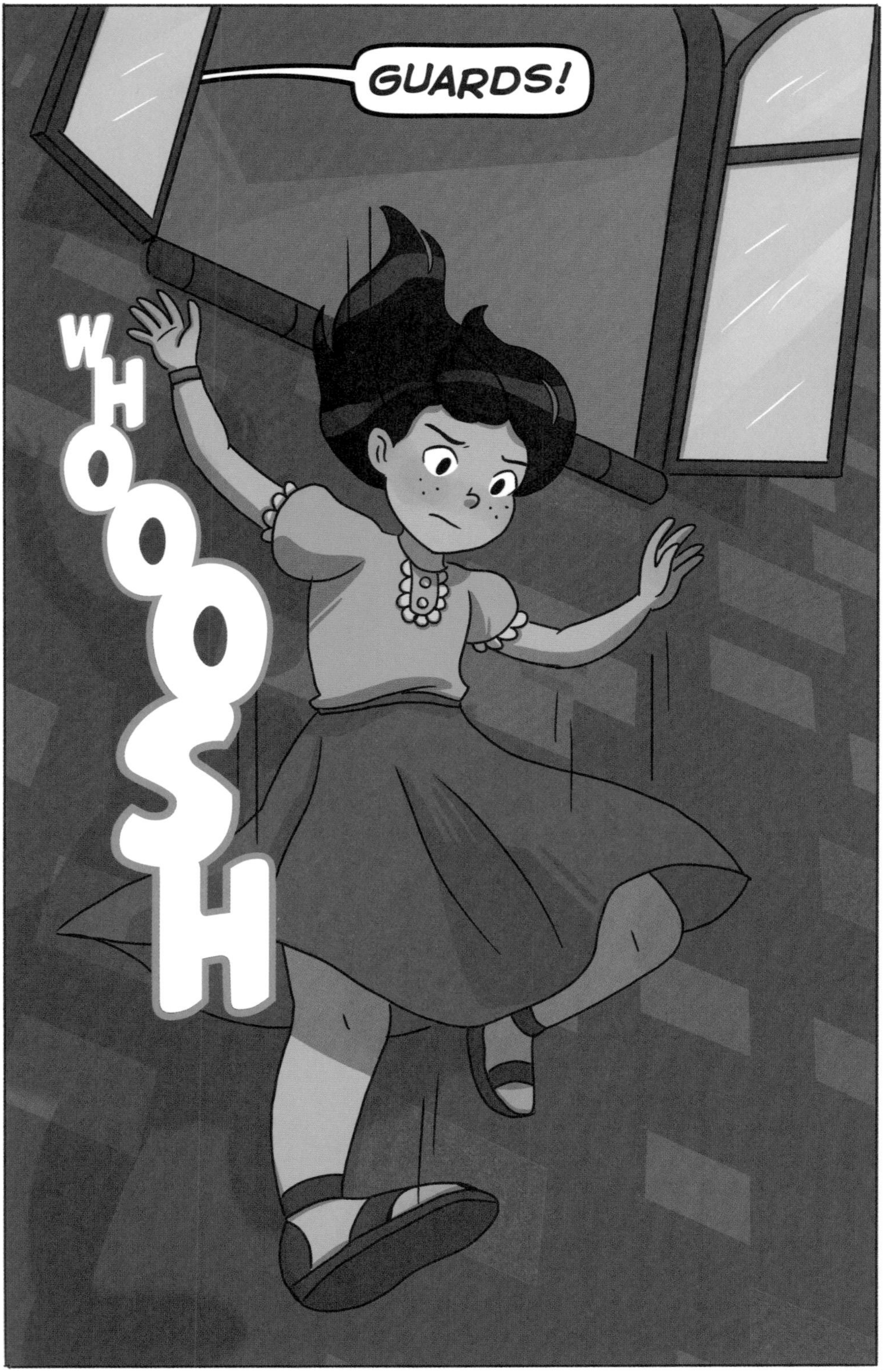
GUARDS!
WHOOOOSH

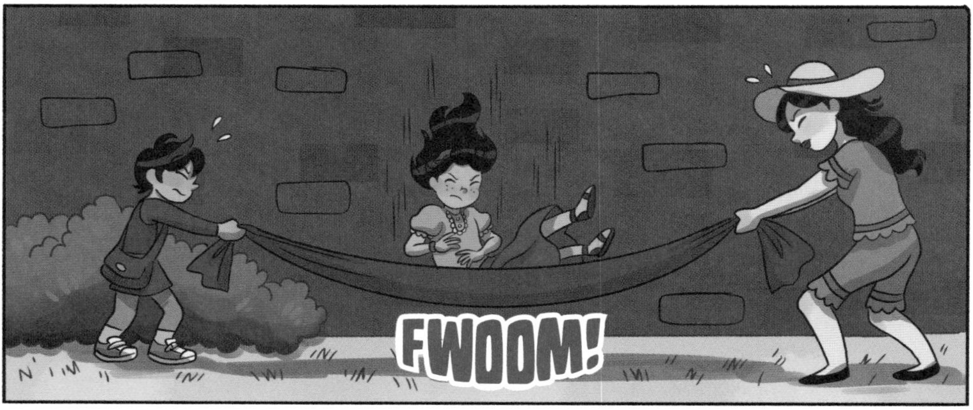
FWOOM!

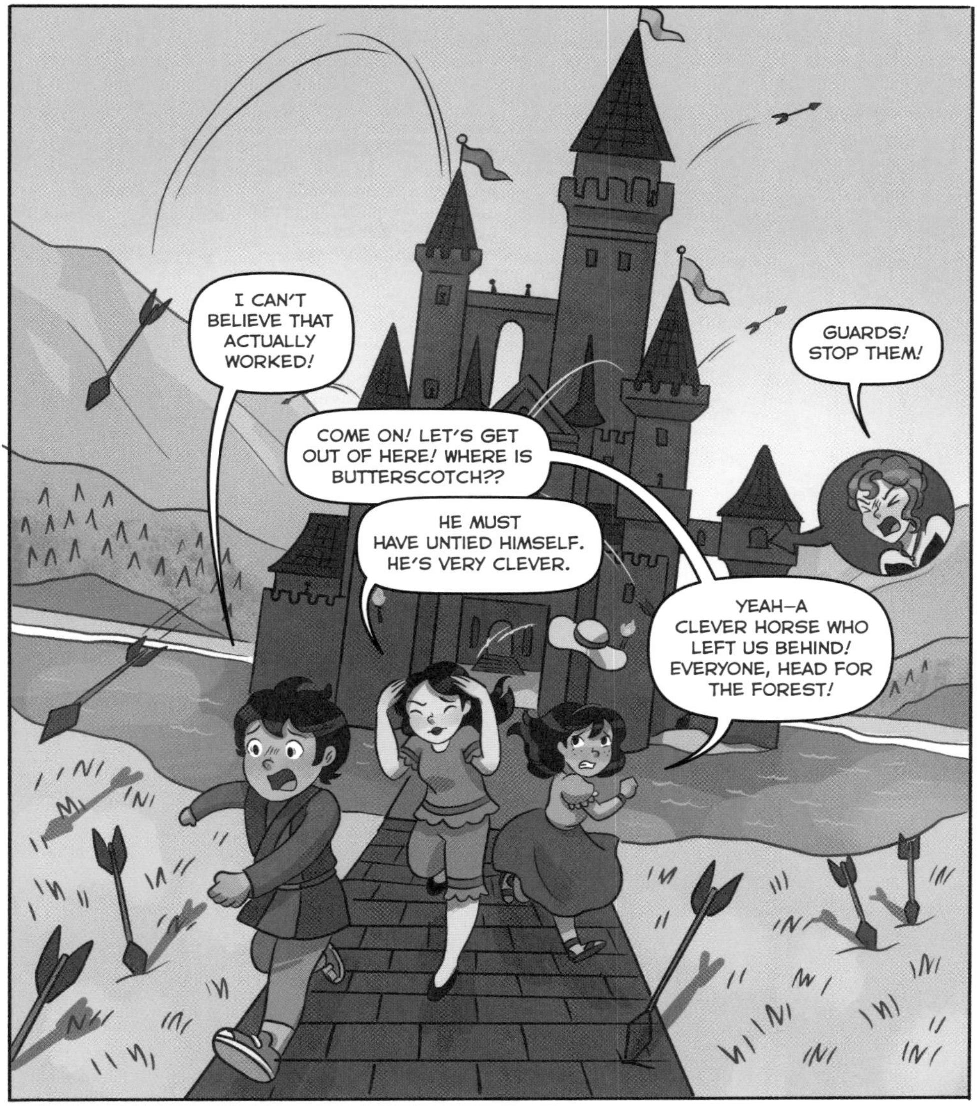
I CAN'T BELIEVE THAT ACTUALLY WORKED!
GUARDS! STOP THEM!
COME ON! LET'S GET OUT OF HERE! WHERE IS BUTTERSCOTCH??
HE MUST HAVE UNTIED HIMSELF. HE'S VERY CLEVER.
YEAH—A CLEVER HORSE WHO LEFT US BEHIND! EVERYONE, HEAD FOR THE FOREST!

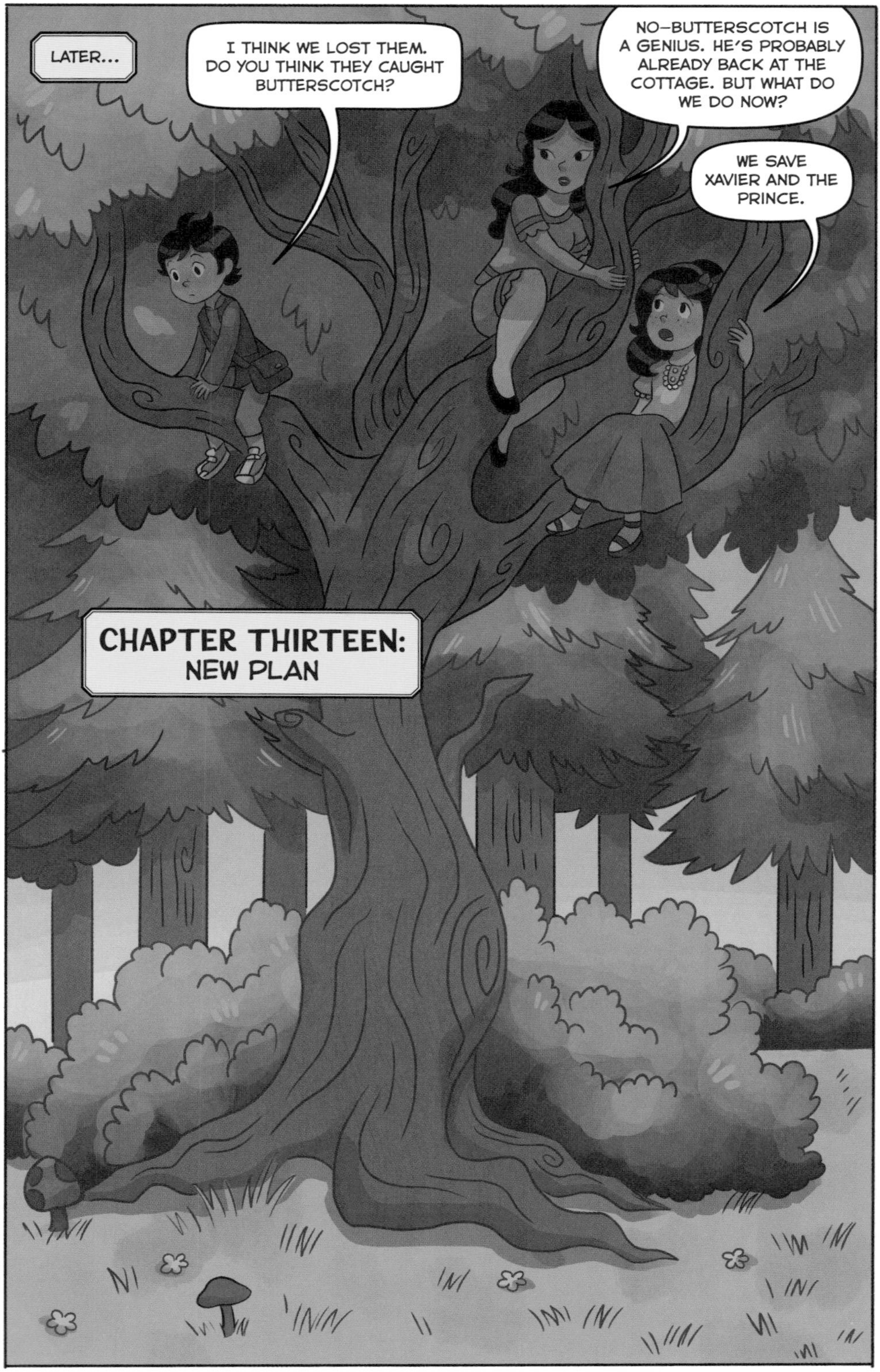
LATER...
I THINK WE LOST THEM. DO YOU THINK THEY CAUGHT BUTTERSCOTCH?
NO—BUTTERSCOTCH IS A GENIUS. HE'S PROBABLY ALREADY BACK AT THE COTTAGE. BUT WHAT DO WE DO NOW?
WE SAVE XAVIER AND THE PRINCE.
CHAPTER THIRTEEN:
NEW PLAN

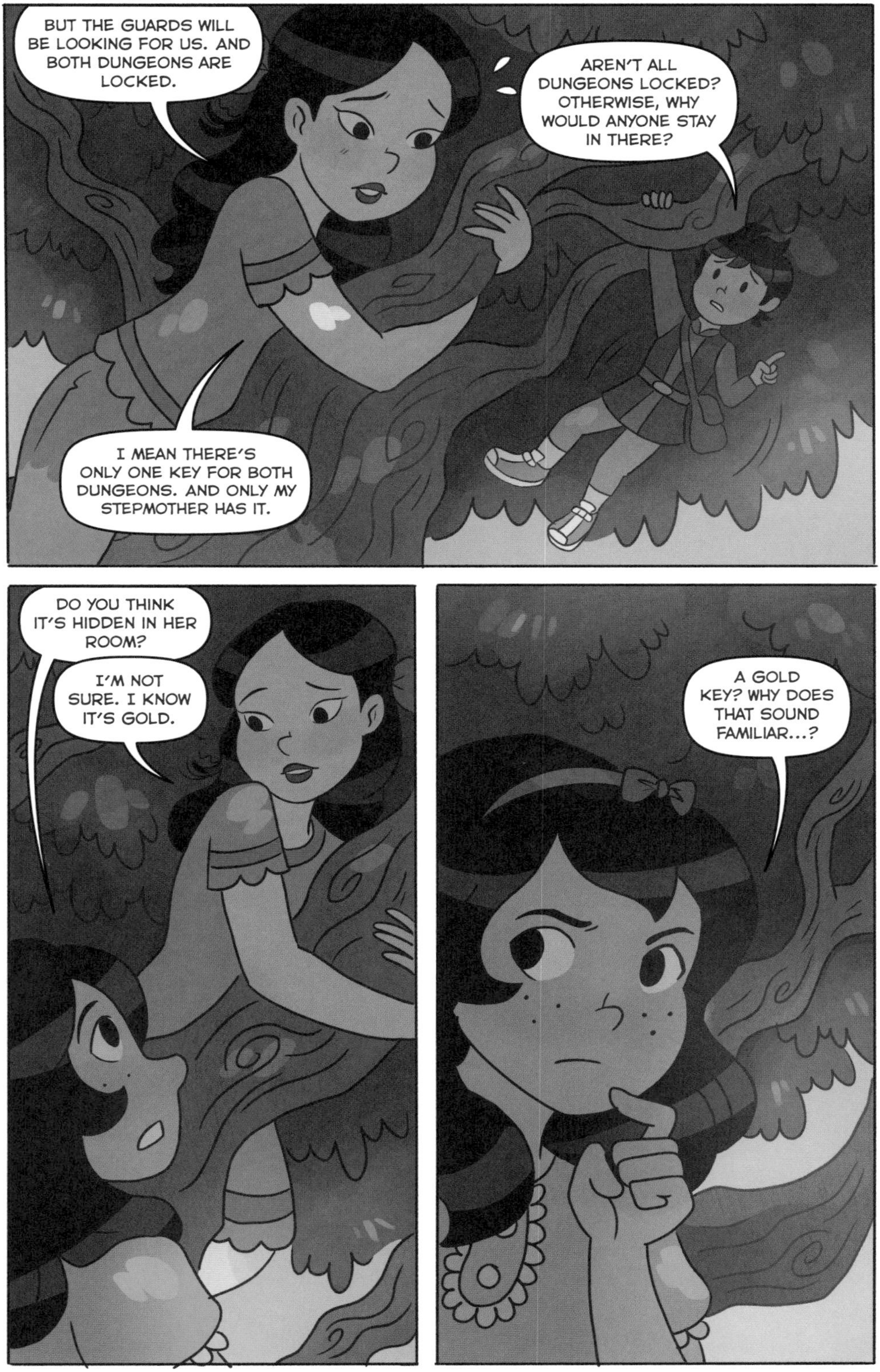
BUT THE GUARDS WILL BE LOOKING FOR US. AND BOTH DUNGEONS ARE LOCKED.
AREN'T ALL DUNGEONS LOCKED? OTHERWISE, WHY WOULD ANYONE STAY IN THERE?
I MEAN THERE'S ONLY ONE KEY FOR BOTH DUNGEONS. AND ONLY MY STEPMOTHER HAS IT.
DO YOU THINK IT'S HIDDEN IN HER ROOM?
I'M NOT SURE. I KNOW IT'S GOLD.
A GOLD KEY? WHY DOES THAT SOUND FAMILIAR...?

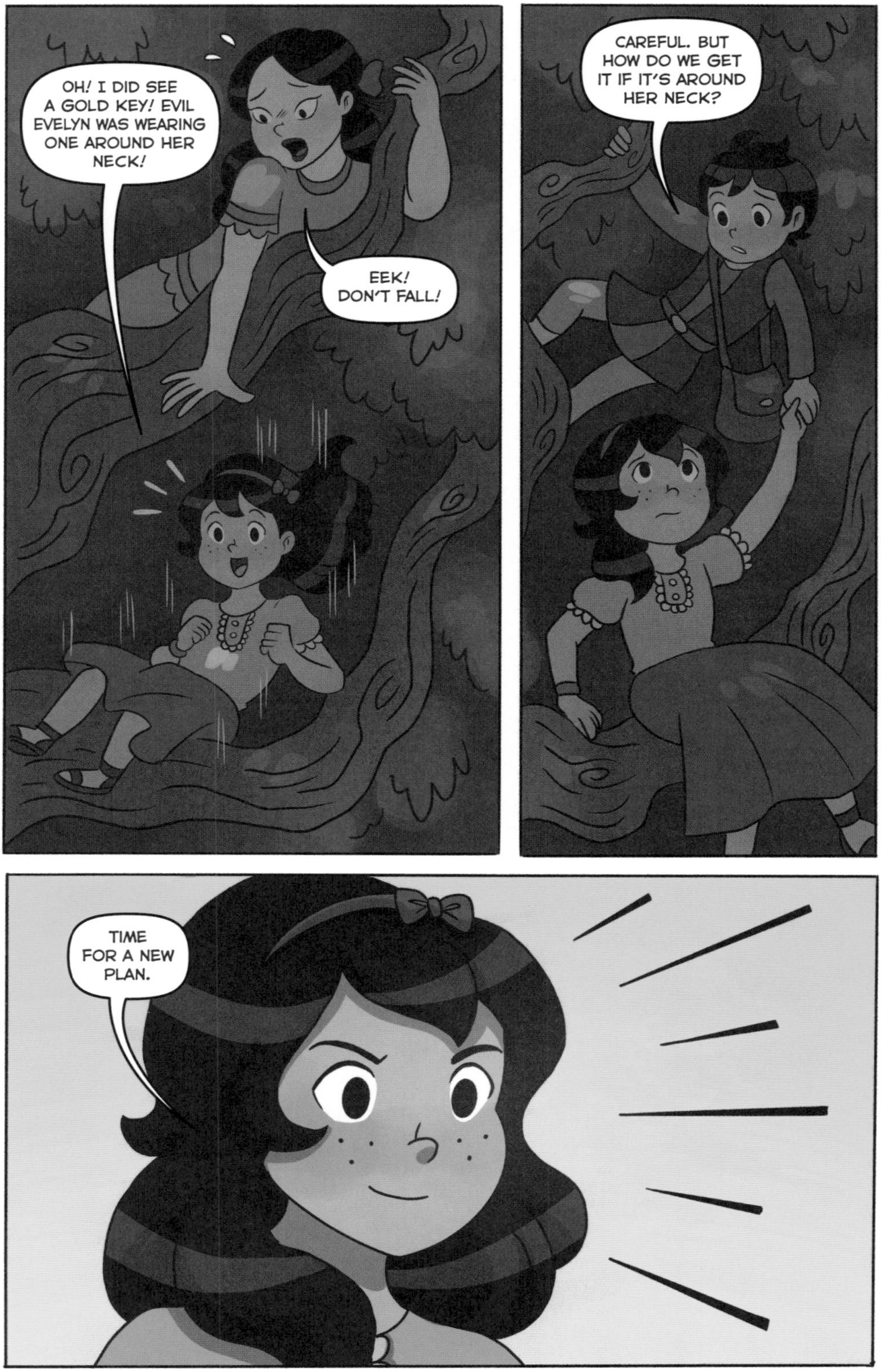
OH! I DID SEE A GOLD KEY! EVIL EVELYN WAS WEARING ONE AROUND HER NECK!
EEK! DON'T FALL!
CAREFUL. BUT HOW DO WE GET IT IF IT'S AROUND HER NECK?
TIME FOR A NEW PLAN.

The ~~New~~ Plan

STEP 1: Sneak into Evil Evelyn's castle while she's at her weekly massage appointment. ~~asleep.~~
(Apparently, being evil is stressful.)

↙ Get the key.
STEP 2: ~~Pretend to be interior decorators.~~
~~Evil Evelyn LOVES to redecorate.~~

↙ Save Xavier the Huntsman and Prince Trevor.
STEP 3: ~~Snow shows us where to find the mirror.~~

STEP 4: Jonah and I go home through the mirror.
Snow sneaks back out. with Xavier and Trevor.

STEP 5: The End!
(For real this time!)

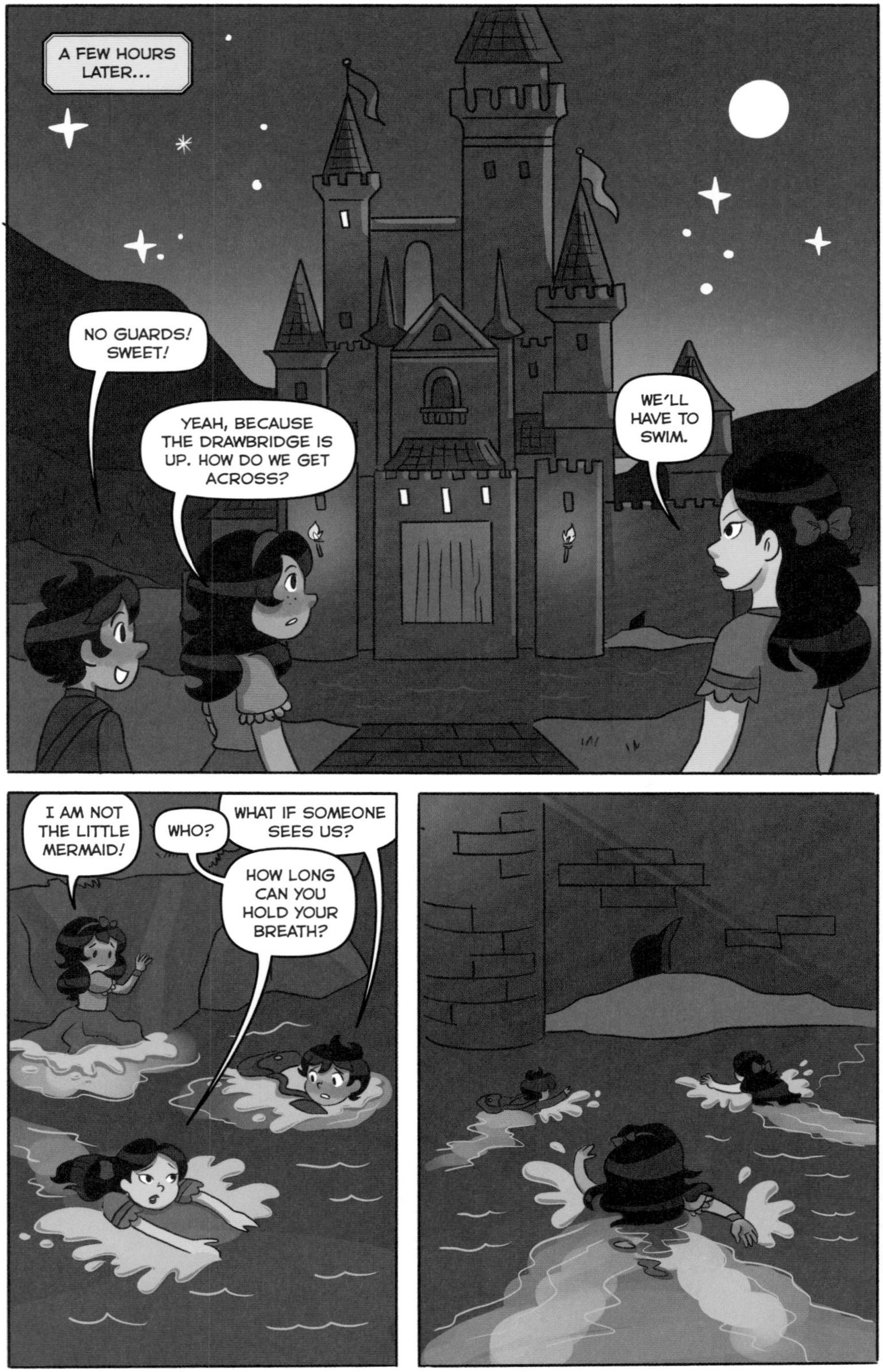
A FEW HOURS LATER...
NO GUARDS! SWEET!
YEAH, BECAUSE THE DRAWBRIDGE IS UP. HOW DO WE GET ACROSS?
WE'LL HAVE TO SWIM.
WHAT IF SOMEONE SEES US?
HOW LONG CAN YOU HOLD YOUR BREATH?
WHO?
I AM NOT THE LITTLE MERMAID!

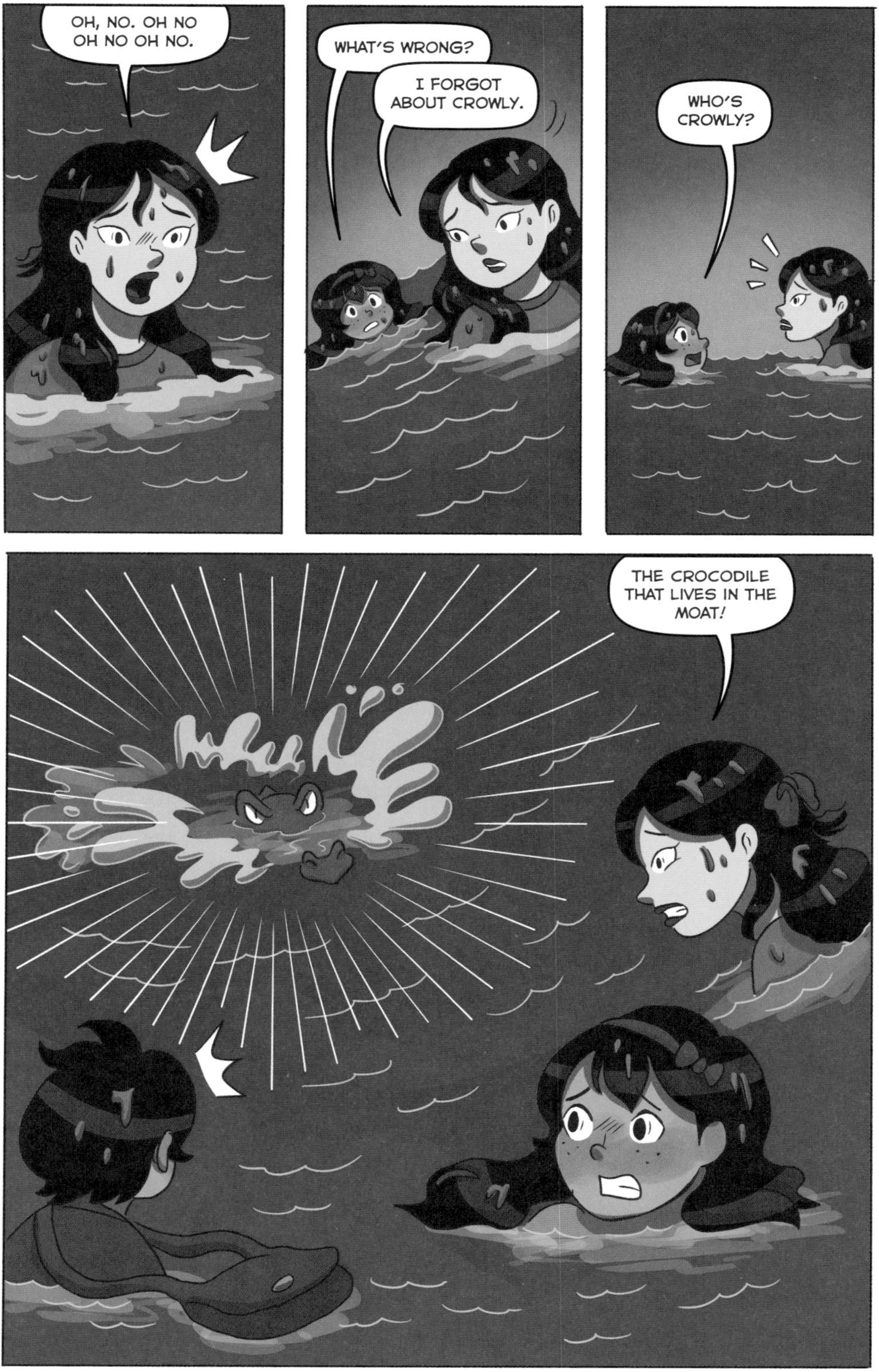
OH, NO. OH NO
OH NO OH NO.
WHAT'S WRONG?
I FORGOT ABOUT CROWLY.
WHO'S CROWLY?
THE CROCODILE THAT LIVES IN THE MOAT!

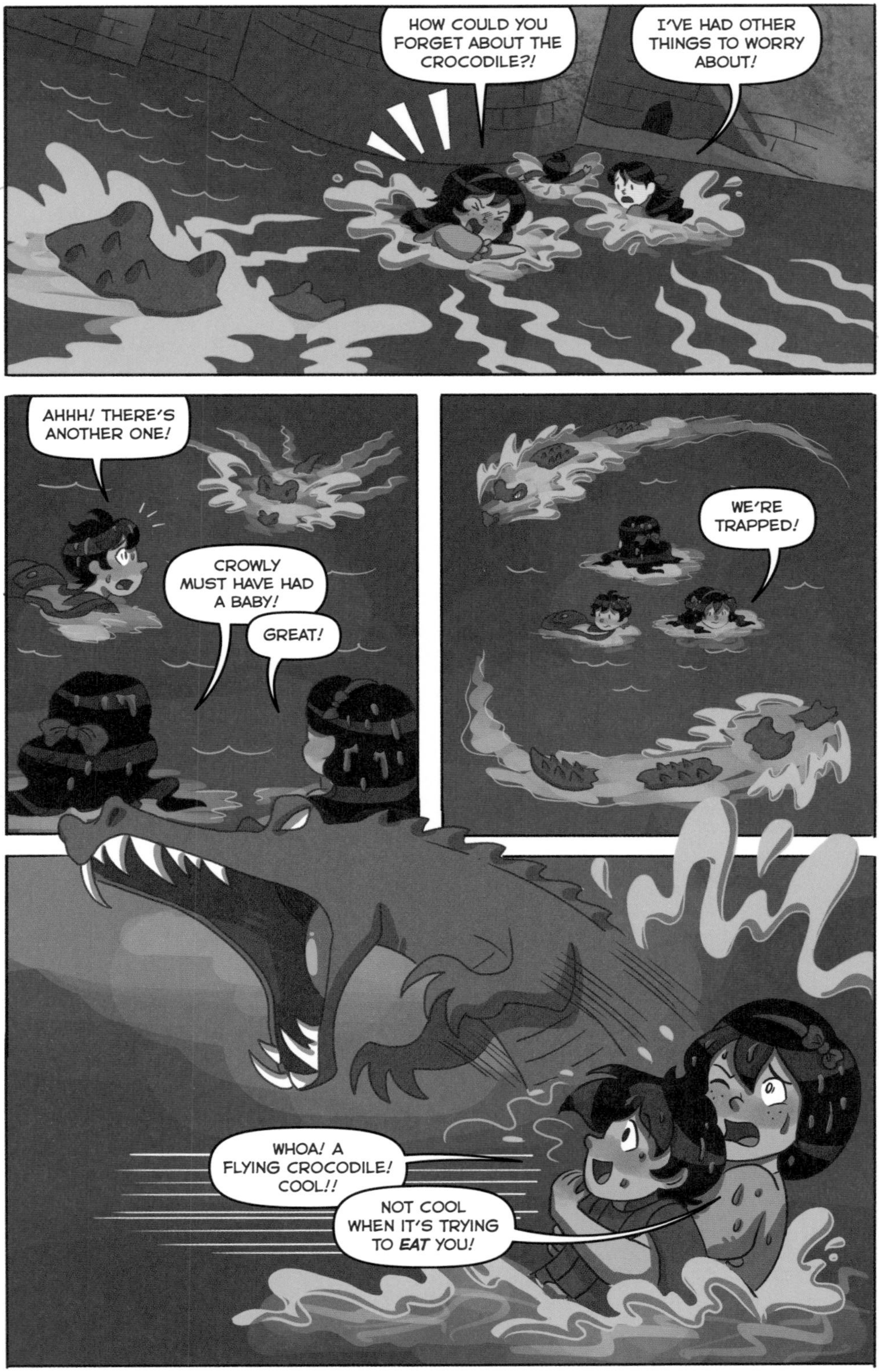
HOW COULD YOU FORGET ABOUT THE CROCODILE?!
I'VE HAD OTHER THINGS TO WORRY ABOUT!
AHHH! THERE'S ANOTHER ONE!
CROWLY MUST HAVE HAD A BABY!
GREAT!
WE'RE TRAPPED!
WHOA! A FLYING CROCODILE! COOL!!
NOT COOL WHEN IT'S TRYING TO *EAT* YOU!

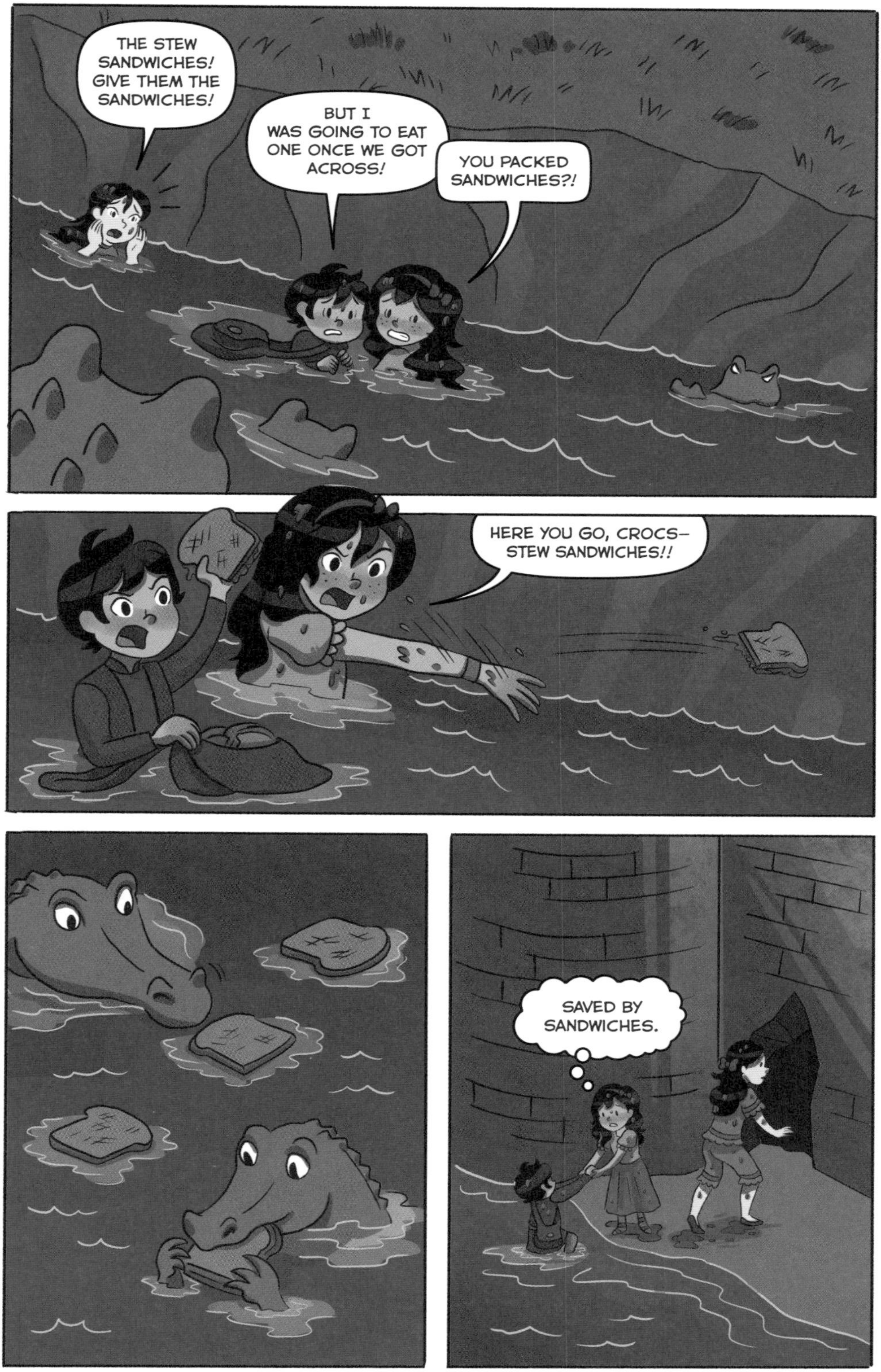
THE STEW SANDWICHES! GIVE THEM THE SANDWICHES!
BUT I WAS GOING TO EAT ONE ONCE WE GOT ACROSS!
YOU PACKED SANDWICHES?!
HERE YOU GO, CROCS— STEW SANDWICHES!!
SAVED BY SANDWICHES.

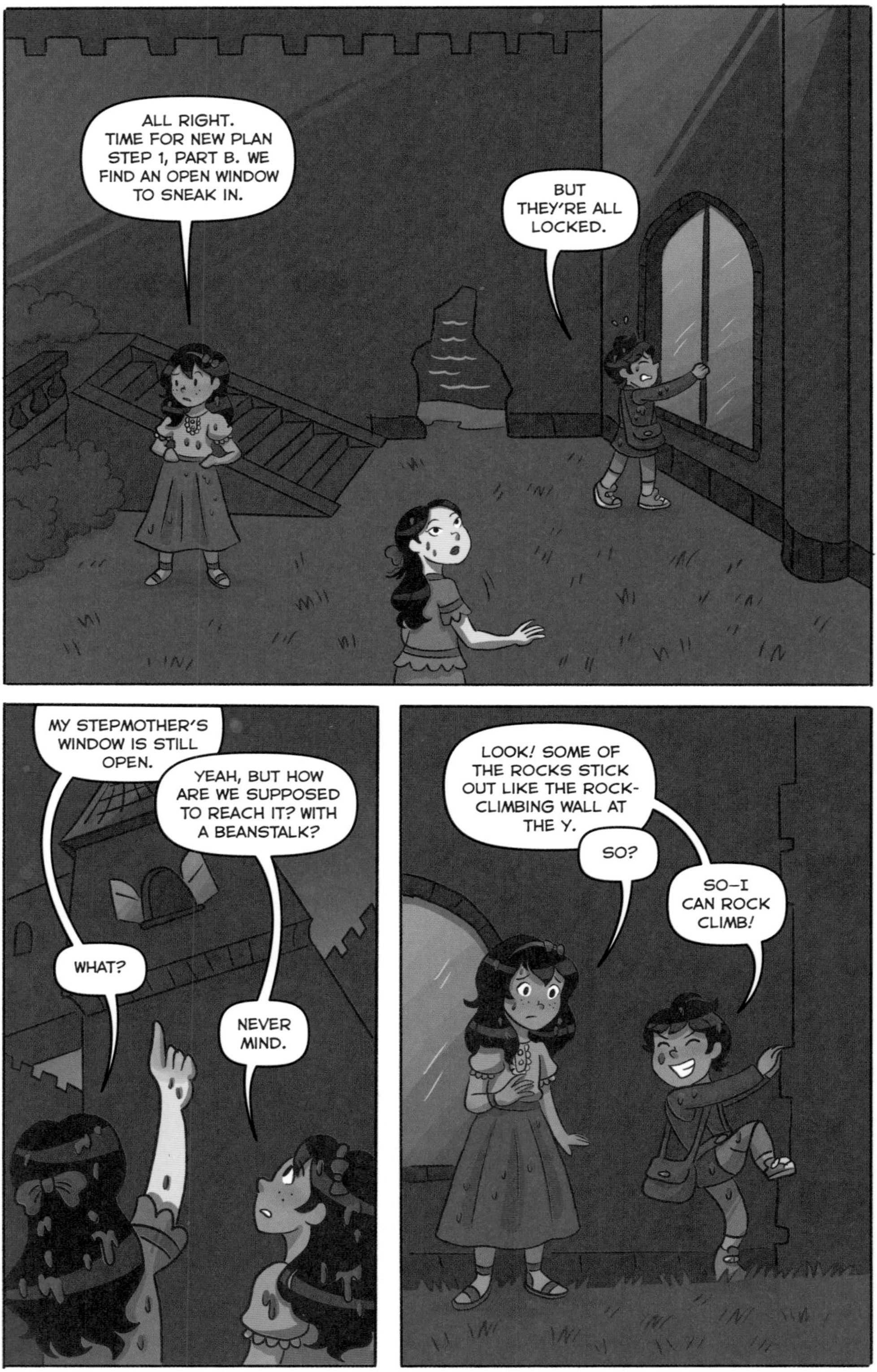
ALL RIGHT. TIME FOR NEW PLAN STEP 1, PART B. WE FIND AN OPEN WINDOW TO SNEAK IN.
BUT THEY'RE ALL LOCKED.
MY STEPMOTHER'S WINDOW IS STILL OPEN.
YEAH, BUT HOW ARE WE SUPPOSED TO REACH IT? WITH A BEANSTALK?
WHAT?
NEVER MIND.
LOOK! SOME OF THE ROCKS STICK OUT LIKE THE ROCK-CLIMBING WALL AT THE Y.
SO?
SO—I CAN ROCK CLIMB!

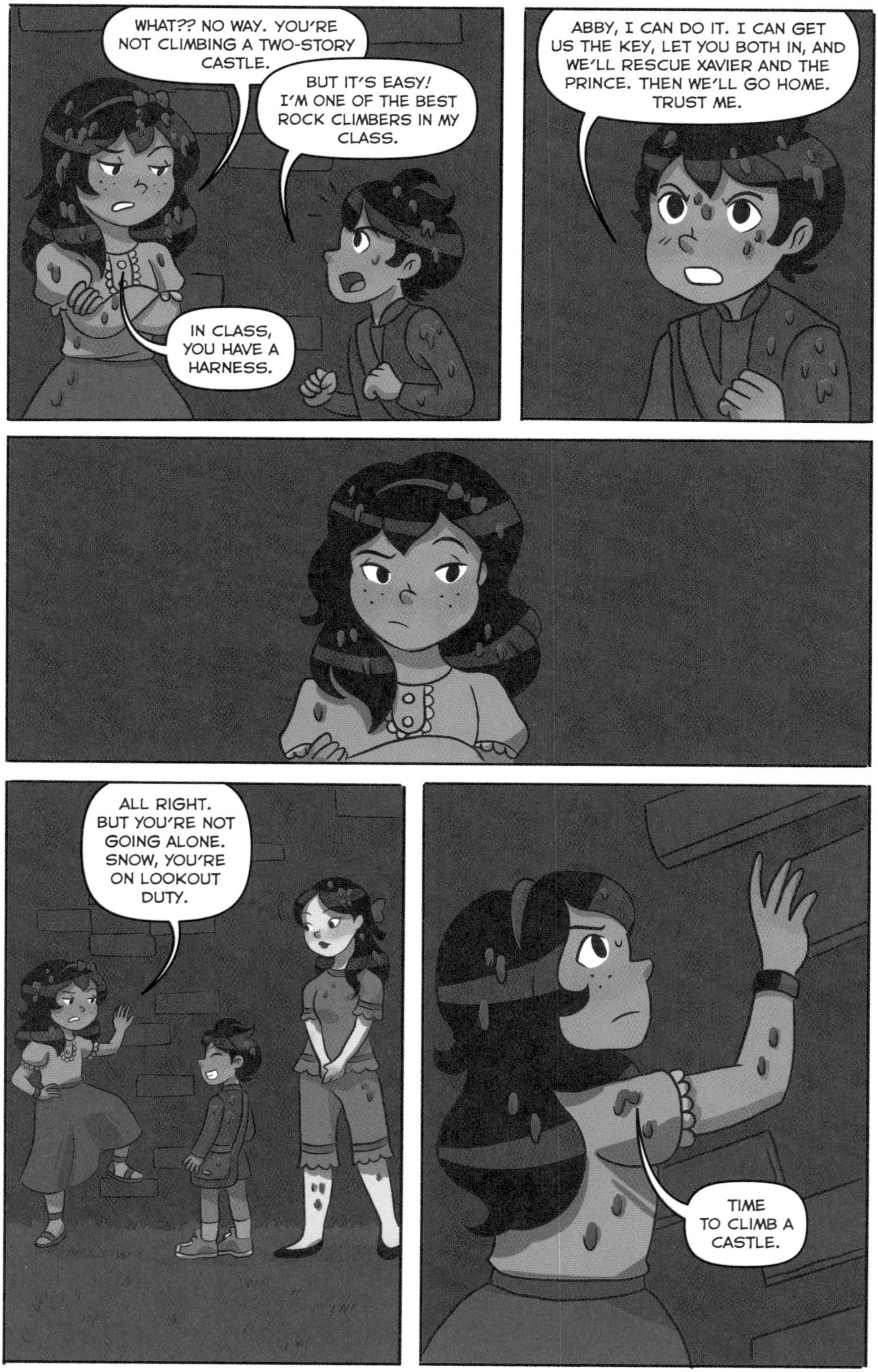
WHAT?? NO WAY. YOU'RE NOT CLIMBING A TWO-STORY CASTLE.
BUT IT'S EASY! I'M ONE OF THE BEST ROCK CLIMBERS IN MY CLASS.
IN CLASS, YOU HAVE A HARNESS.
ABBY, I CAN DO IT. I CAN GET US THE KEY, LET YOU BOTH IN, AND WE'LL RESCUE XAVIER AND THE PRINCE. THEN WE'LL GO HOME. TRUST ME.
ALL RIGHT. BUT YOU'RE NOT GOING ALONE. SNOW, YOU'RE ON LOOKOUT DUTY.
TIME TO CLIMB A CASTLE.

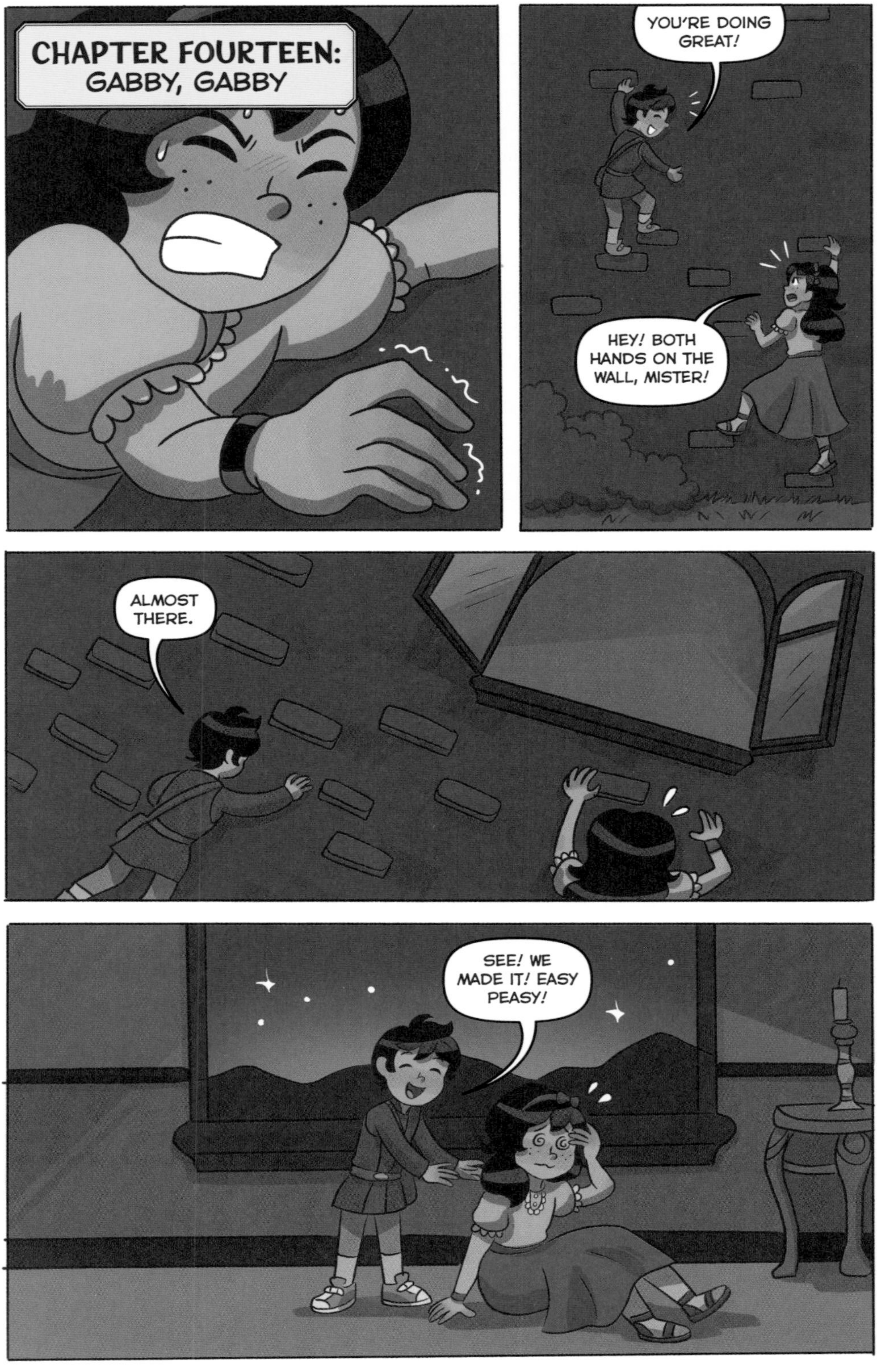
CHAPTER FOURTEEN:
GABBY, GABBY
YOU'RE DOING GREAT!
HEY! BOTH HANDS ON THE WALL, MISTER!
ALMOST THERE.
SEE! WE MADE IT! EASY PEASY!

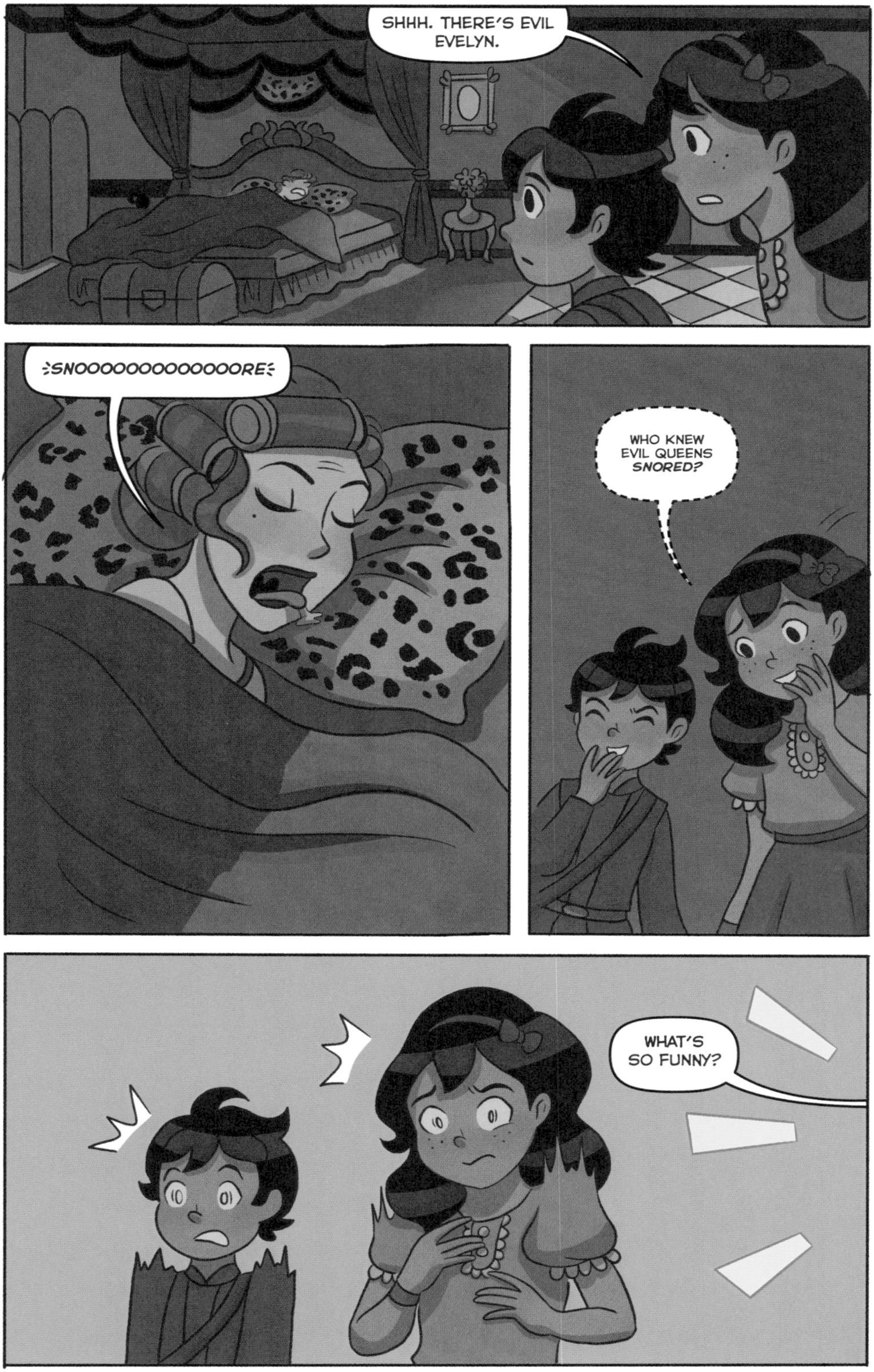
SHHH. THERE'S EVIL EVELYN.
SNOOOOOOOOOOOOOORE
WHO KNEW EVIL QUEENS SNORED?
WHAT'S SO FUNNY?

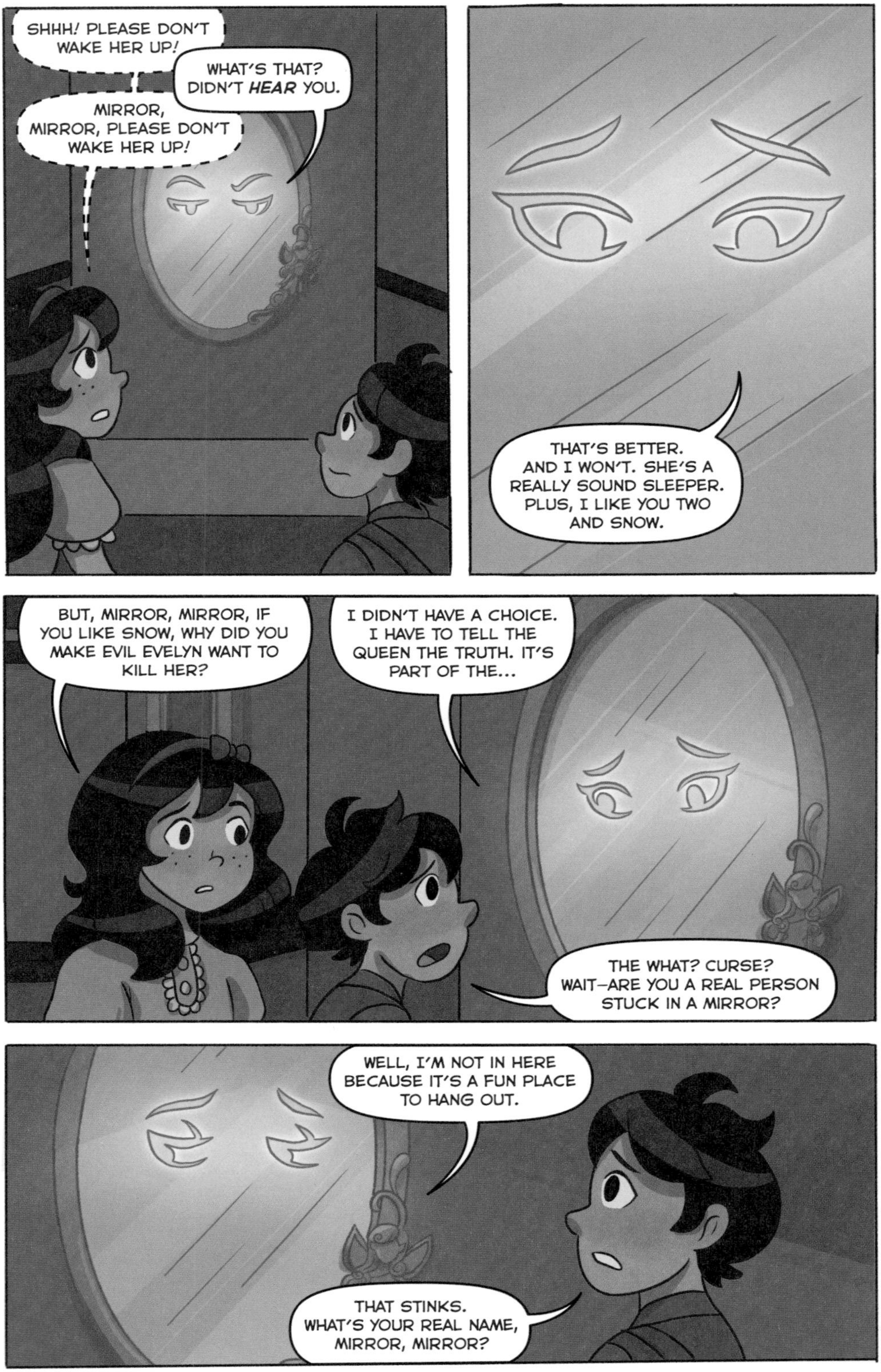
SHHH! PLEASE DON'T WAKE HER UP!
WHAT'S THAT? DIDN'T **HEAR** YOU.
MIRROR, MIRROR, PLEASE DON'T WAKE HER UP!
THAT'S BETTER. AND I WON'T. SHE'S A REALLY SOUND SLEEPER. PLUS, I LIKE YOU TWO AND SNOW.
BUT, MIRROR, MIRROR, IF YOU LIKE SNOW, WHY DID YOU MAKE EVIL EVELYN WANT TO KILL HER?
I DIDN'T HAVE A CHOICE. I HAVE TO TELL THE QUEEN THE TRUTH. IT'S PART OF THE...
THE WHAT? CURSE? WAIT—ARE YOU A REAL PERSON STUCK IN A MIRROR?
WELL, I'M NOT IN HERE BECAUSE IT'S A FUN PLACE TO HANG OUT.
THAT STINKS. WHAT'S YOUR REAL NAME, MIRROR, MIRROR?

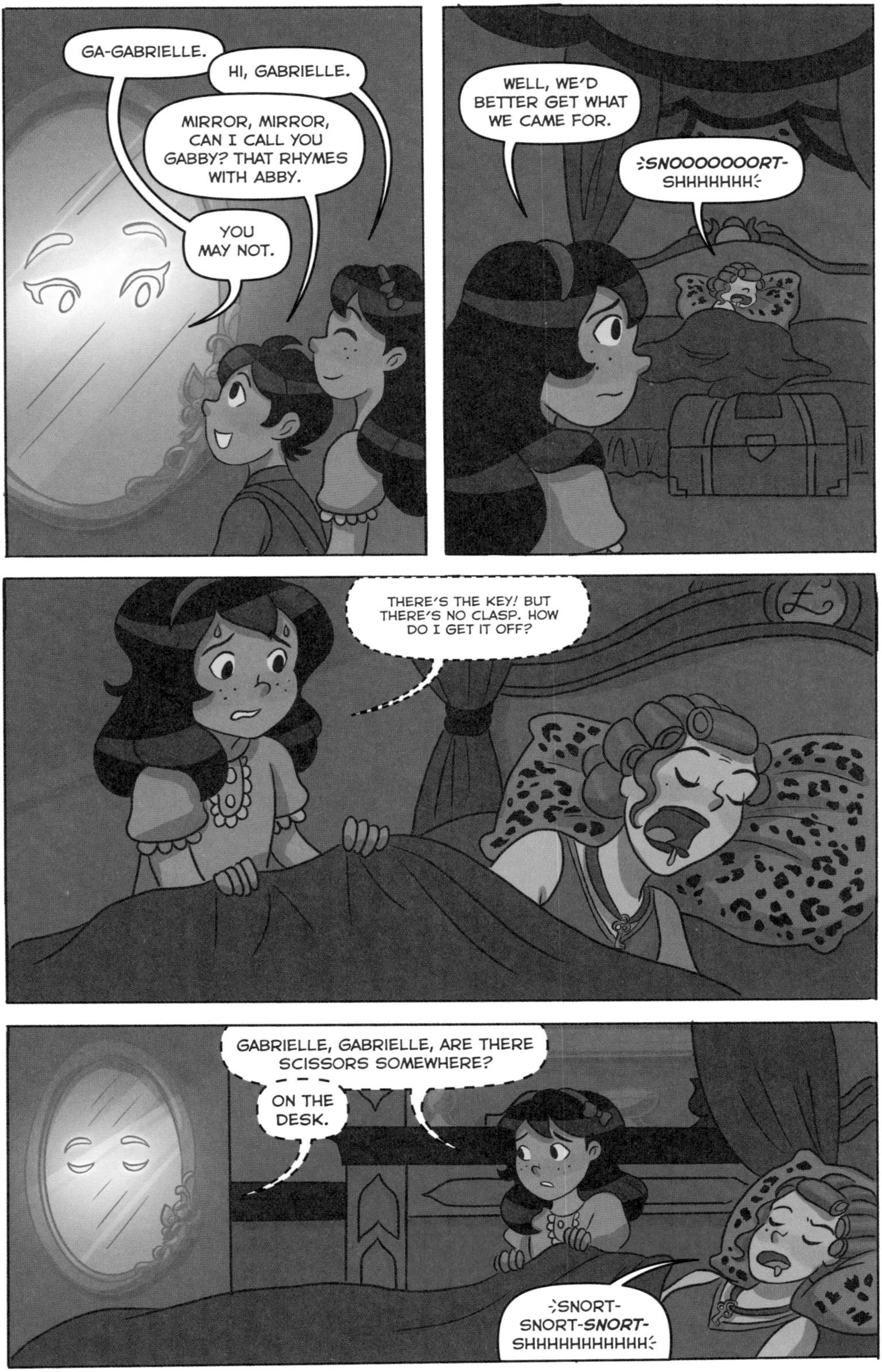
GA-GABRIELLE.
HI, GABRIELLE.
MIRROR, MIRROR, CAN I CALL YOU GABBY? THAT RHYMES WITH ABBY.
YOU MAY NOT.
WELL, WE'D BETTER GET WHAT WE CAME FOR.
SNOOOOOOORT-SHHHHHHH
THERE'S THE KEY! BUT THERE'S NO CLASP. HOW DO I GET IT OFF?
GABRIELLE, GABRIELLE, ARE THERE SCISSORS SOMEWHERE?
ON THE DESK.
SNORT-SNORT-SNORT-SHHHHHHHHHH

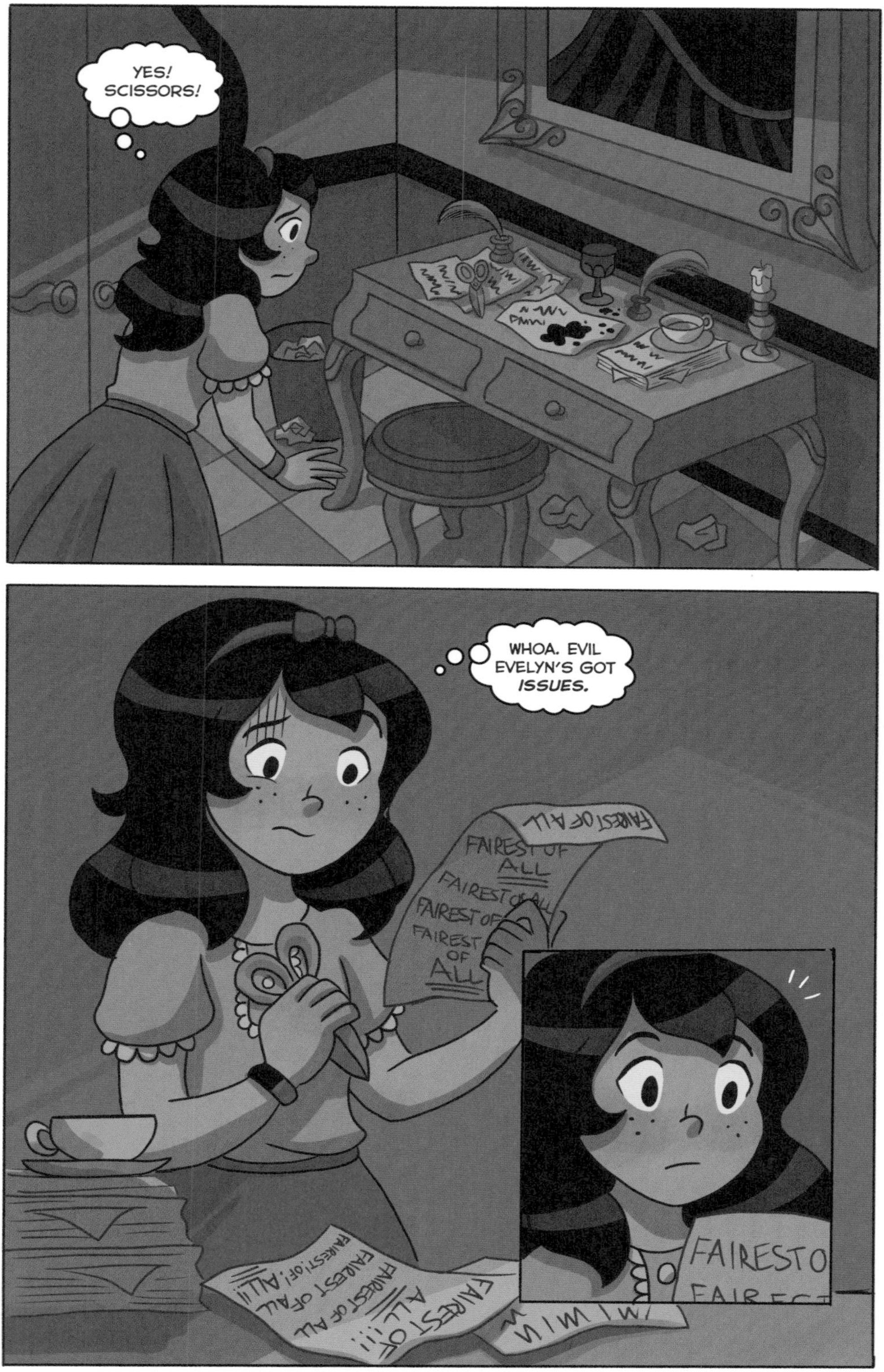
YES! SCISSORS!
WHOA. EVIL EVELYN'S GOT *ISSUES.*
FAIREST OF ALL
FAIREST OF ALL
FAIREST OF ALL
FAIREST OF
FAIREST OF ALL
FAIRESTO

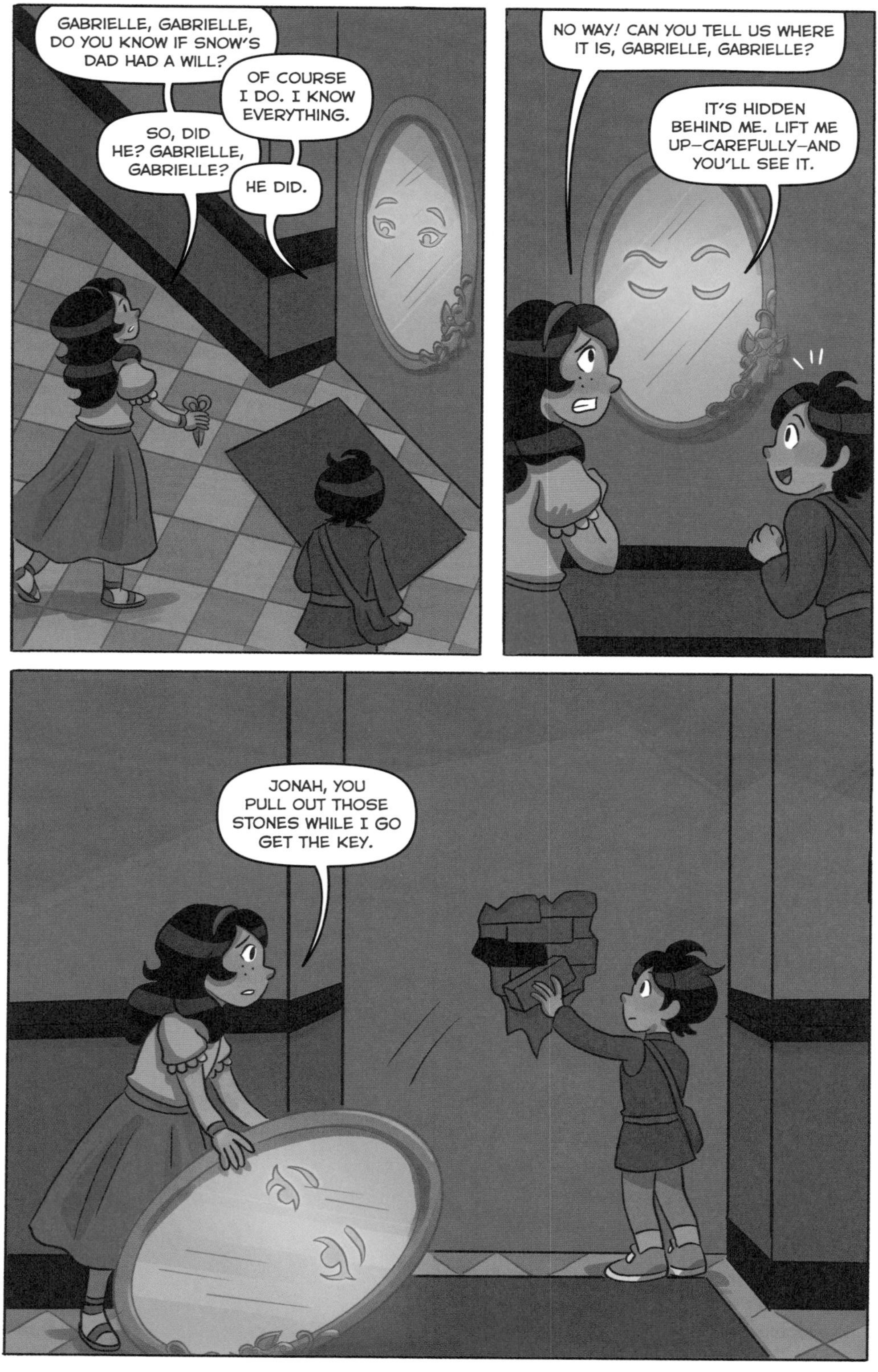
GABRIELLE, GABRIELLE, DO YOU KNOW IF SNOW'S DAD HAD A WILL?
OF COURSE I DO. I KNOW EVERYTHING.
SO, DID HE? GABRIELLE, GABRIELLE?
HE DID.
NO WAY! CAN YOU TELL US WHERE IT IS, GABRIELLE, GABRIELLE?
IT'S HIDDEN BEHIND ME. LIFT ME UP—CAREFULLY—AND YOU'LL SEE IT.
JONAH, YOU PULL OUT THOSE STONES WHILE I GO GET THE KEY.

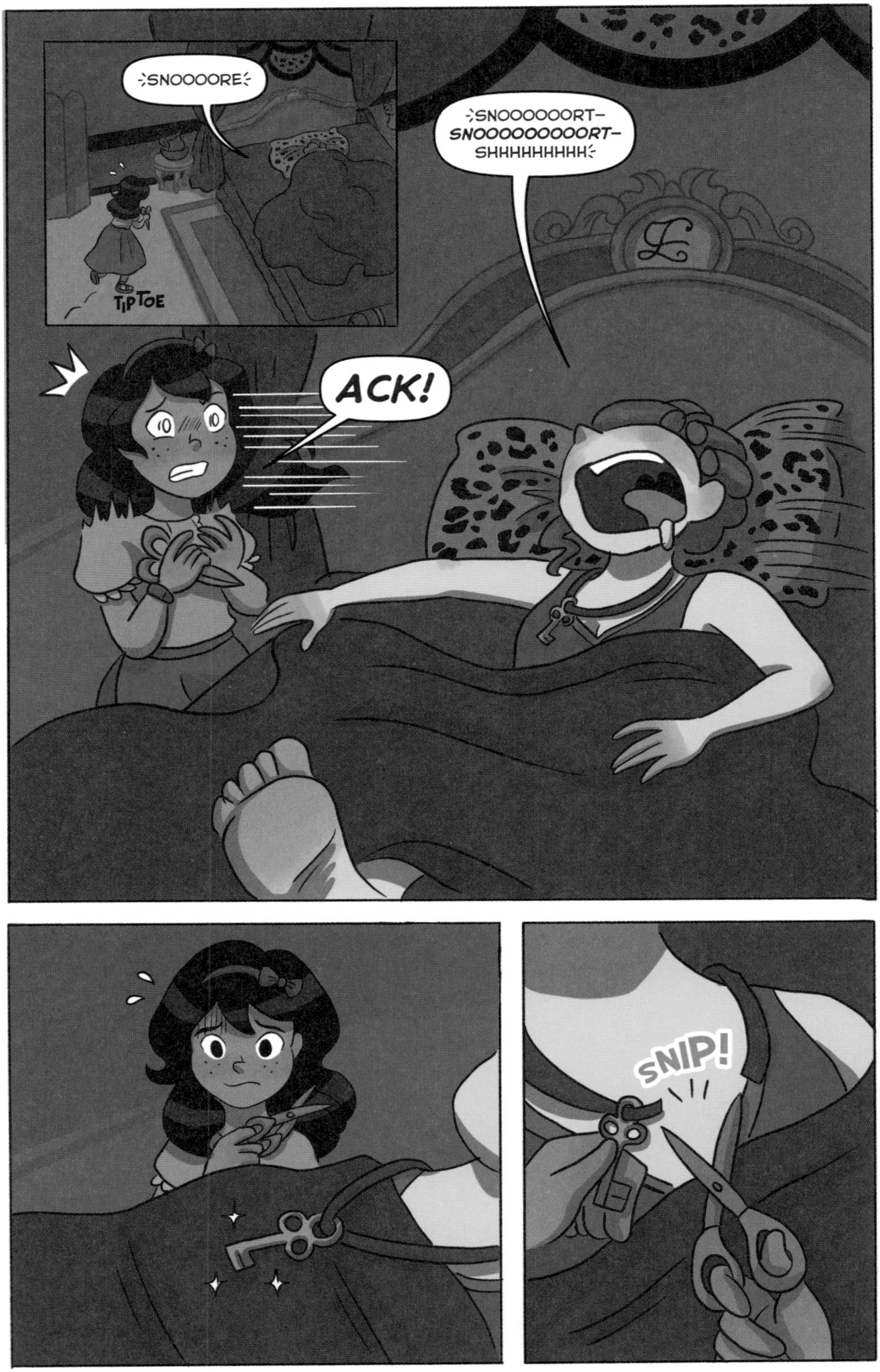
SNOOOORE
TIPTOE
SNOOOOOORT–
SNOOOOOOOOORT–
SHHHHHHHHH
ACK!
SNIP!

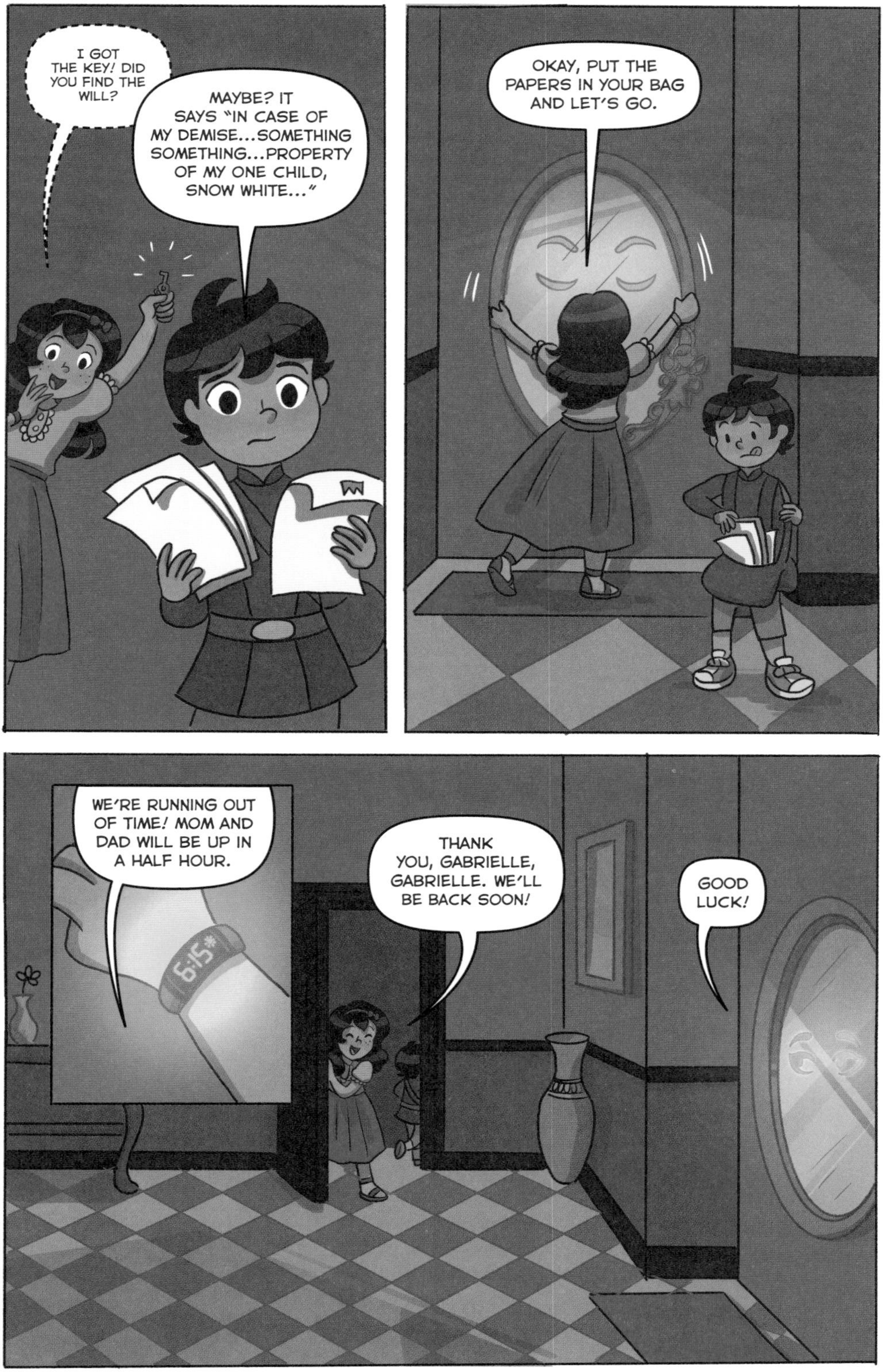
I GOT THE KEY! DID YOU FIND THE WILL?
MAYBE? IT SAYS "IN CASE OF MY DEMISE...SOMETHING SOMETHING...PROPERTY OF MY ONE CHILD, SNOW WHITE..."
OKAY, PUT THE PAPERS IN YOUR BAG AND LET'S GO.
WE'RE RUNNING OUT OF TIME! MOM AND DAD WILL BE UP IN A HALF HOUR.
6:15
THANK YOU, GABRIELLE, GABRIELLE. WE'LL BE BACK SOON!
GOOD LUCK!

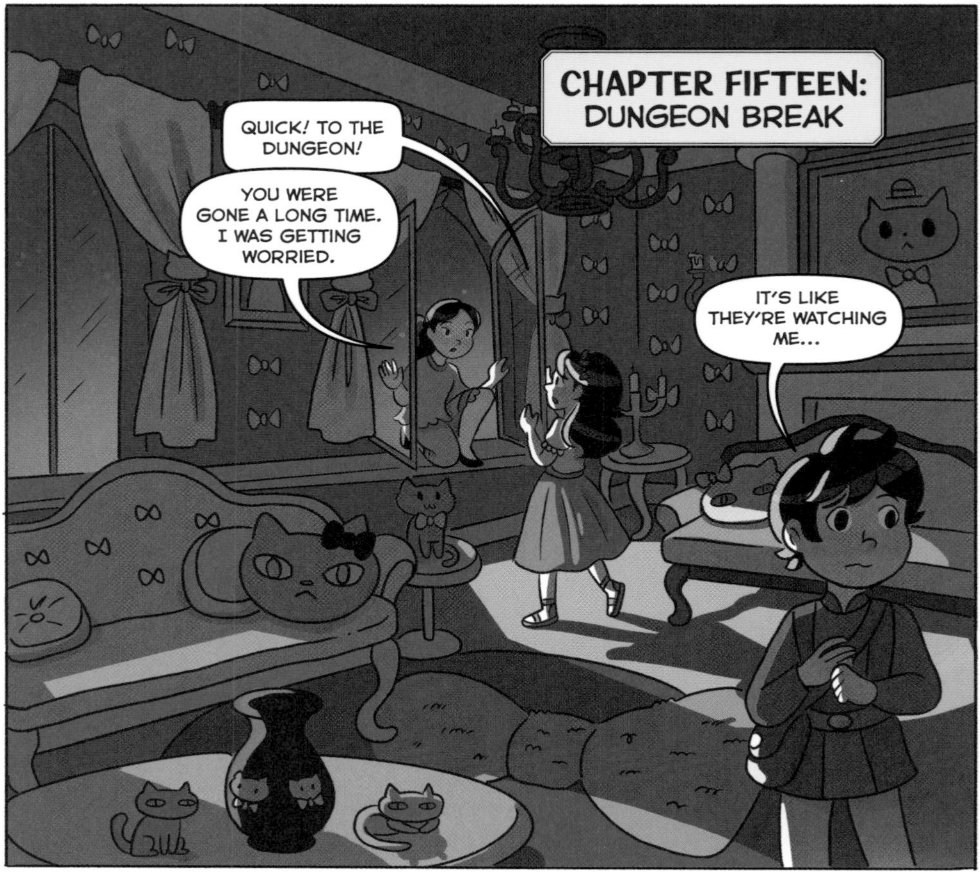
CHAPTER FIFTEEN:
DUNGEON BREAK
QUICK! TO THE DUNGEON!
YOU WERE GONE A LONG TIME. I WAS GETTING WORRIED.
IT'S LIKE THEY'RE WATCHING ME...

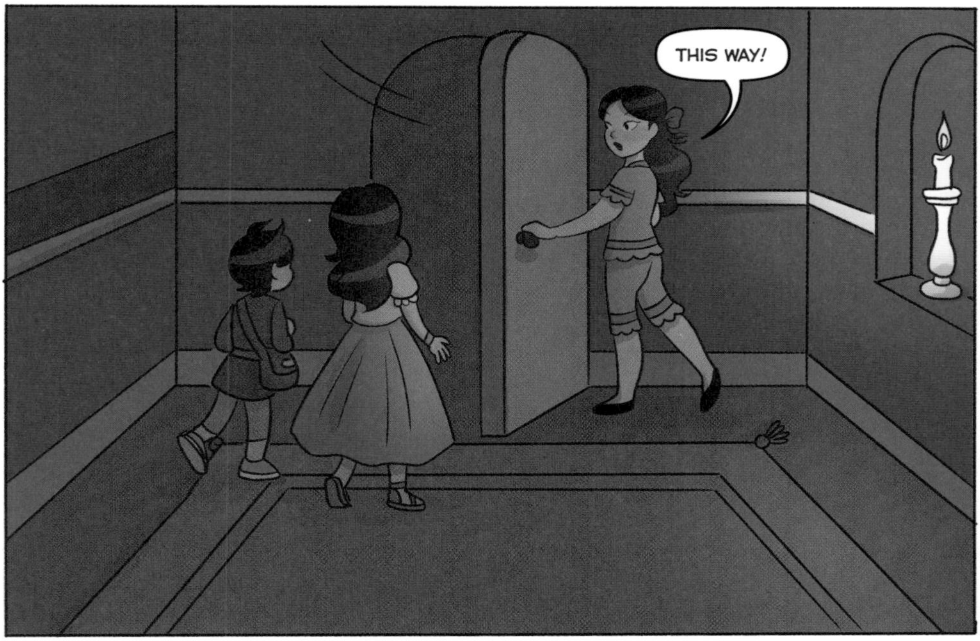
THIS WAY!

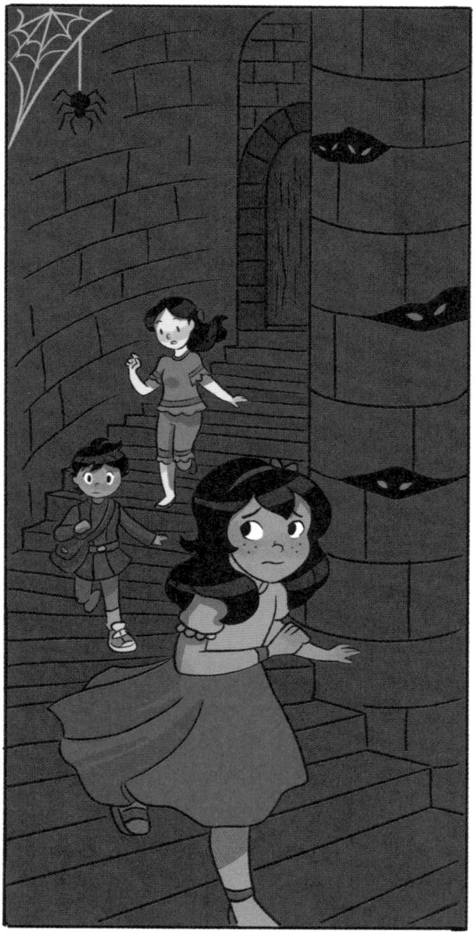

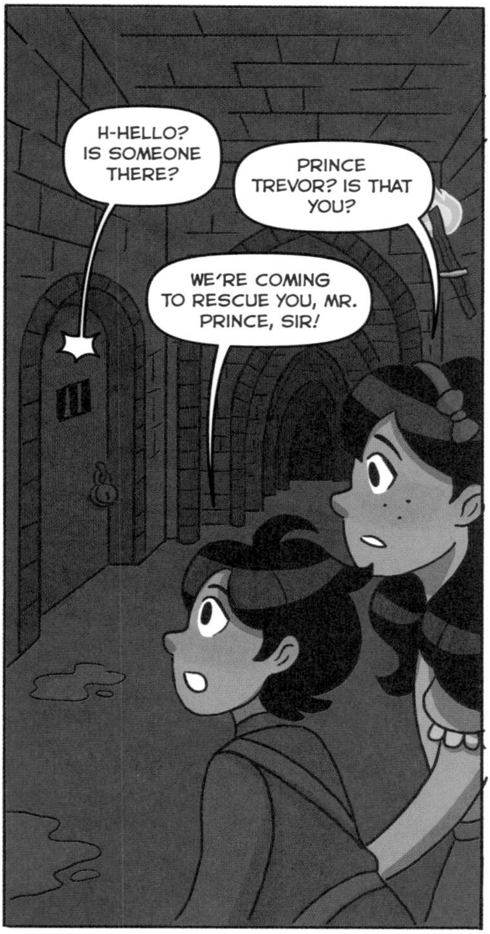
H-HELLO? IS SOMEONE THERE?
PRINCE TREVOR? IS THAT YOU?
WE'RE COMING TO RESCUE YOU, MR. PRINCE, SIR!

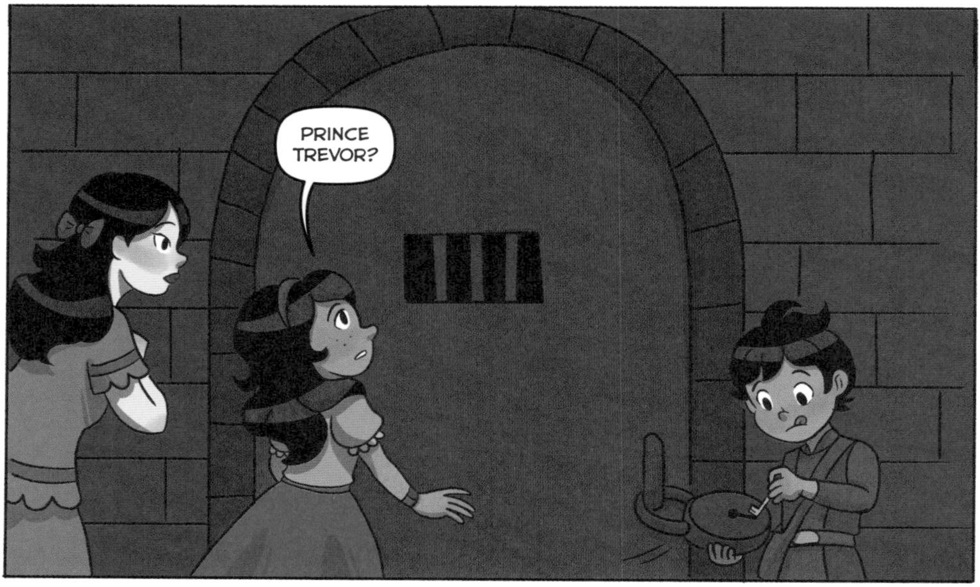
PRINCE TREVOR?

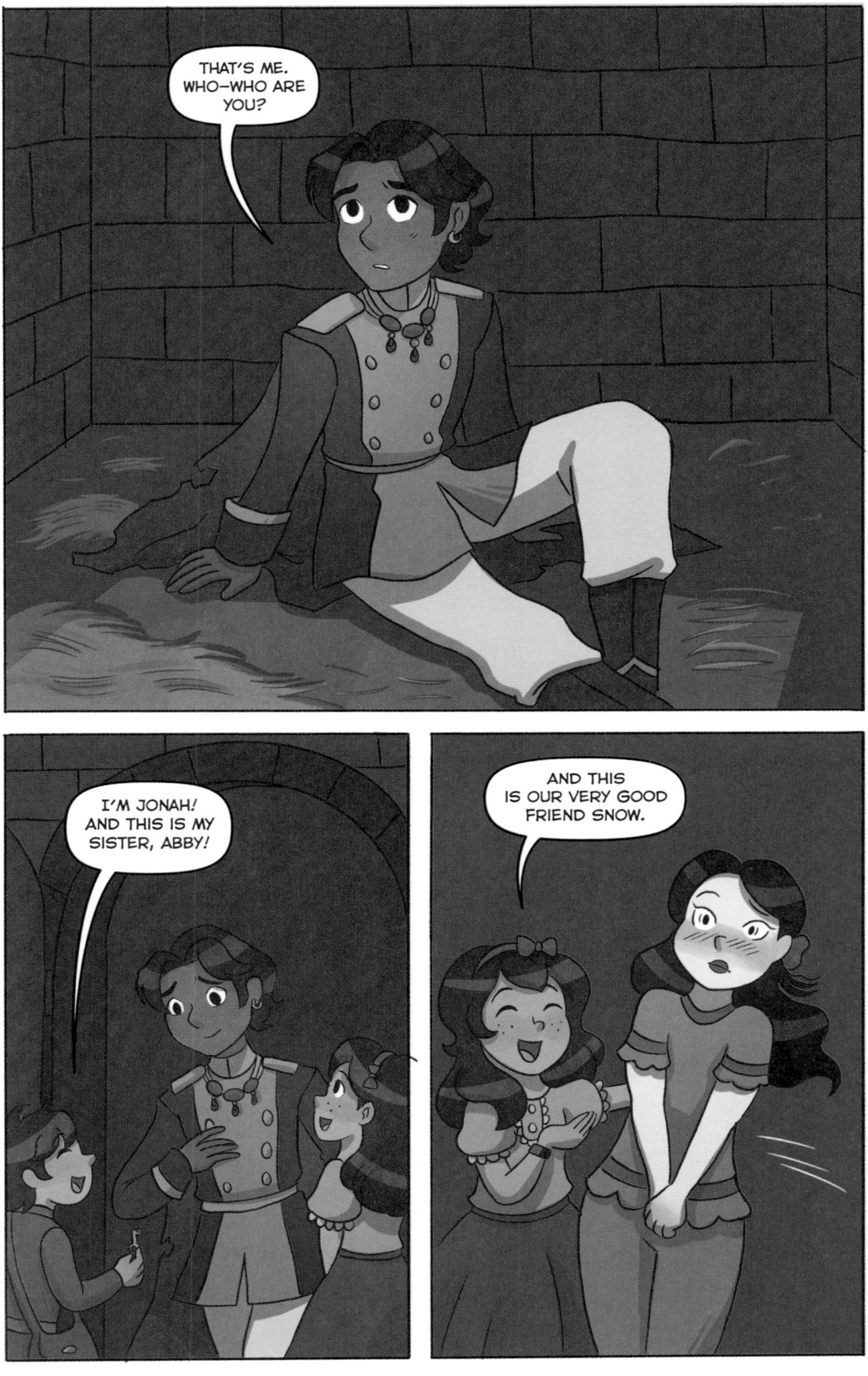
THAT'S ME. WHO—WHO ARE YOU?
I'M JONAH! AND THIS IS MY SISTER, ABBY!
AND THIS IS OUR VERY GOOD FRIEND SNOW.

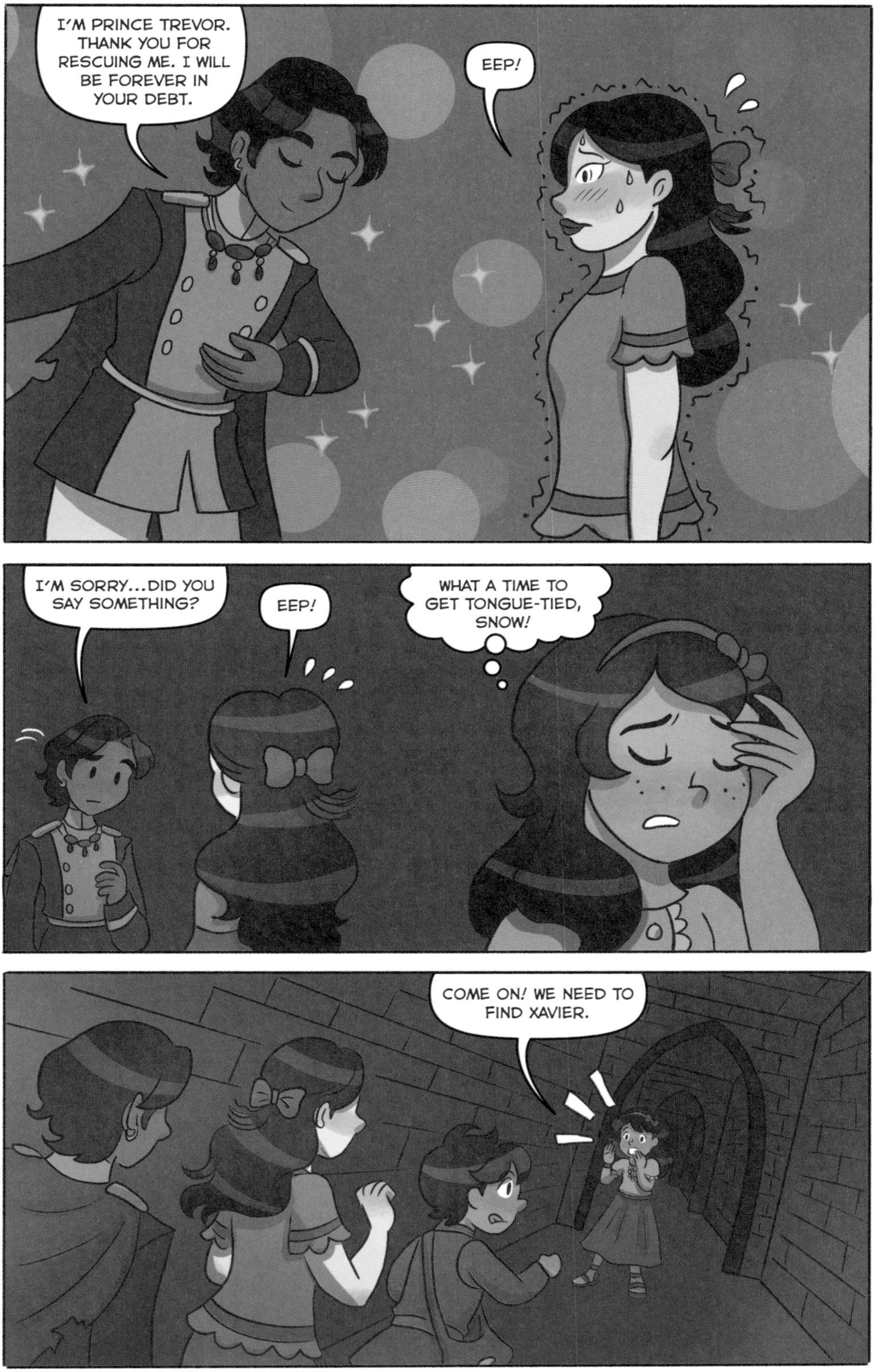

I'M PRINCE TREVOR. THANK YOU FOR RESCUING ME. I WILL BE FOREVER IN YOUR DEBT.
EEP!
I'M SORRY...DID YOU SAY SOMETHING?
EEP!
WHAT A TIME TO GET TONGUE-TIED, SNOW!
COME ON! WE NEED TO FIND XAVIER.

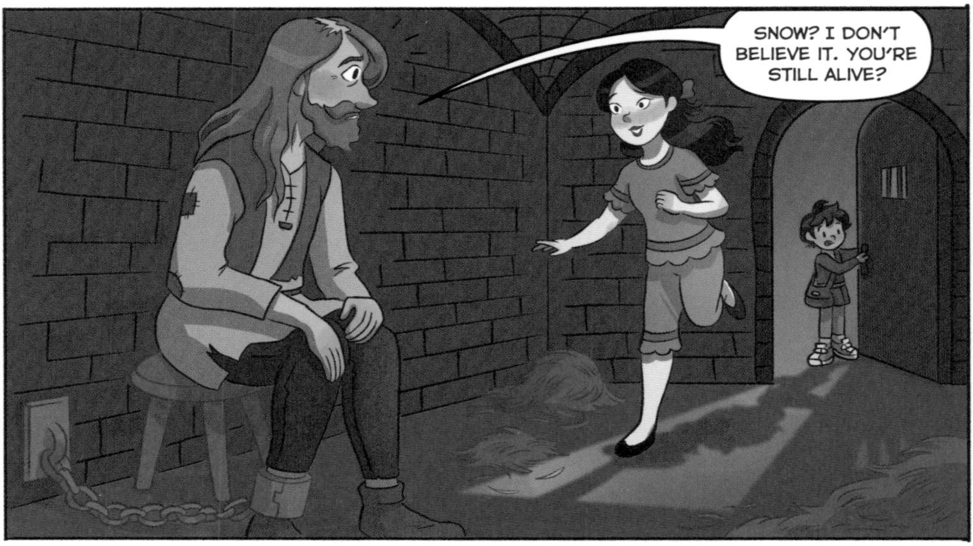
SNOW? I DON'T BELIEVE IT. YOU'RE STILL ALIVE?

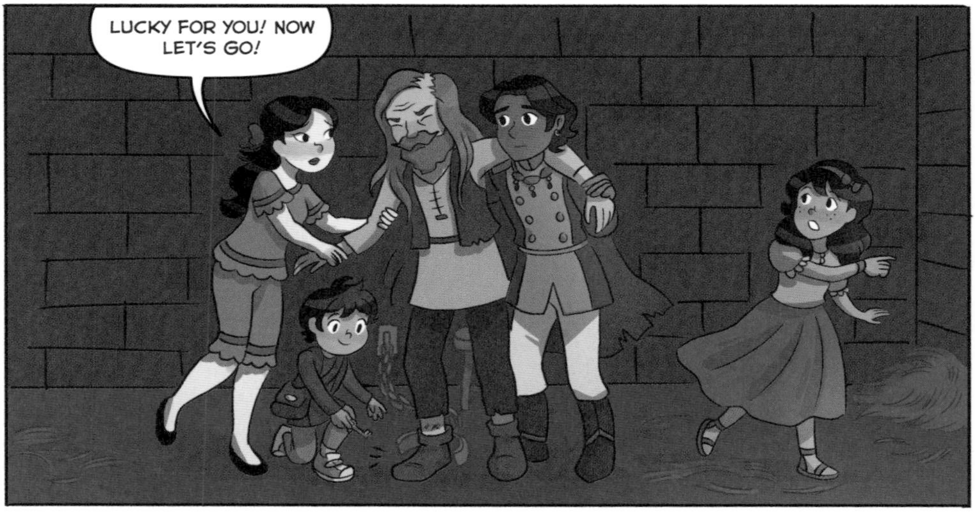
LUCKY FOR YOU! NOW LET'S GO!

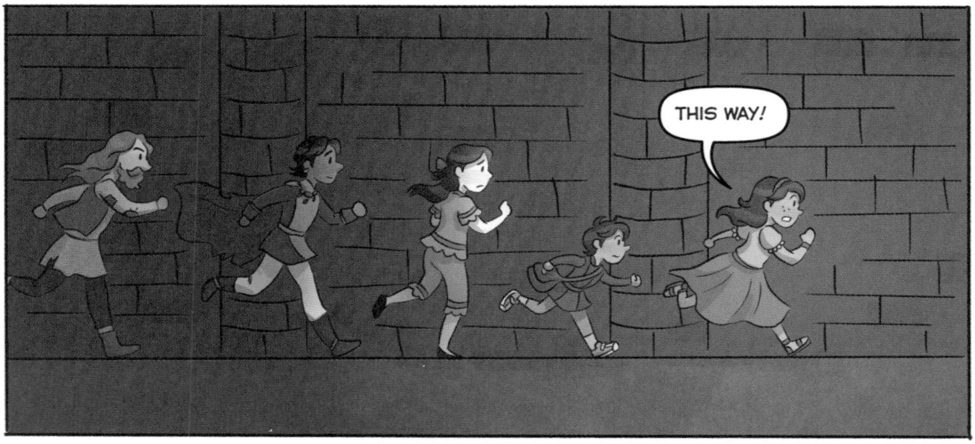
THIS WAY!

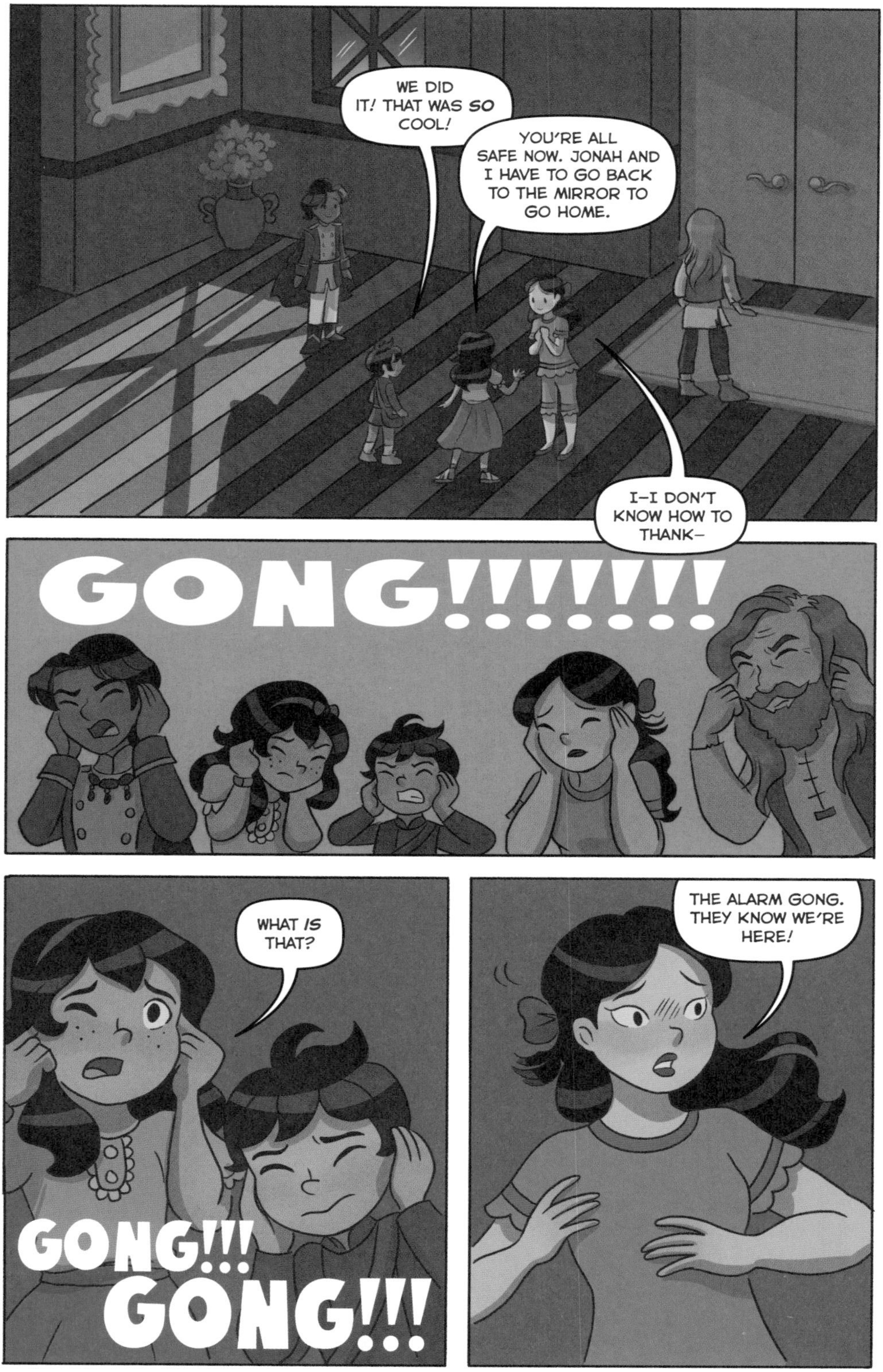
WE DID IT! THAT WAS SO COOL!
YOU'RE ALL SAFE NOW. JONAH AND I HAVE TO GO BACK TO THE MIRROR TO GO HOME.
I–I DON'T KNOW HOW TO THANK–
GONG!!!!!!!
WHAT IS THAT?
GONG!!!
GONG!!!
THE ALARM GONG. THEY KNOW WE'RE HERE!

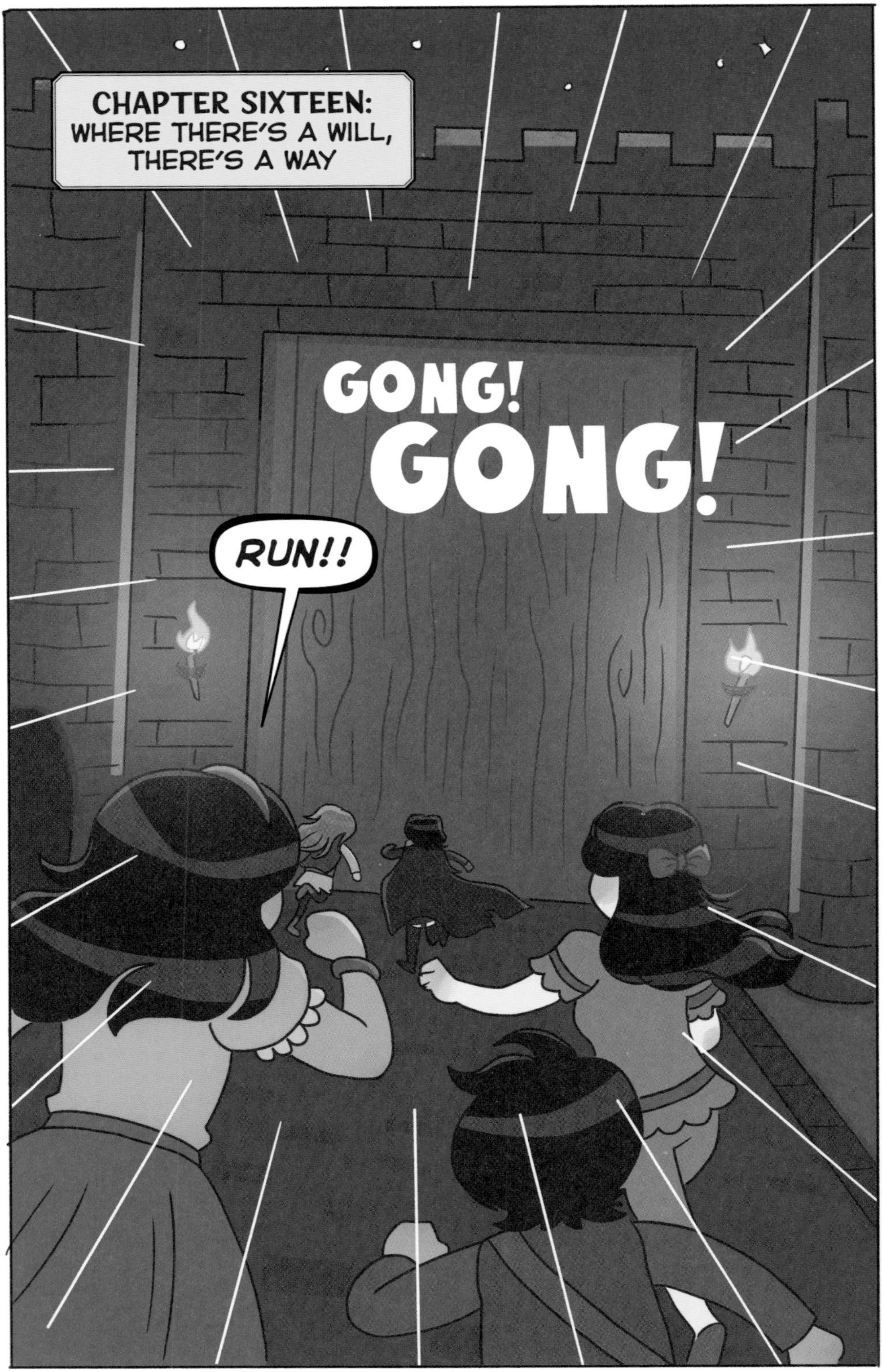
CHAPTER SIXTEEN:
WHERE THERE'S A WILL, THERE'S A WAY
GONG! GONG!
RUN!!

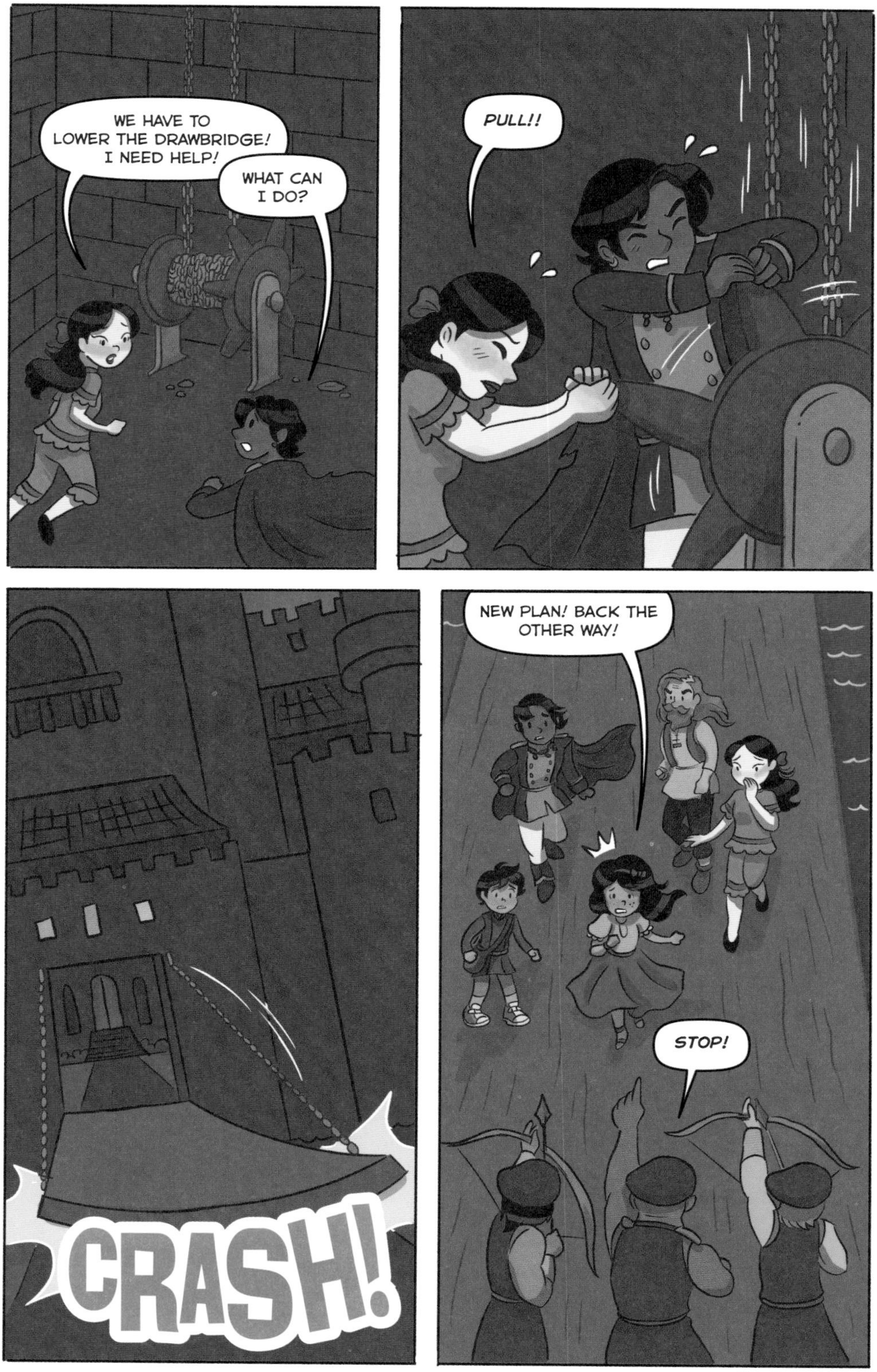
WE HAVE TO LOWER THE DRAWBRIDGE! I NEED HELP!
WHAT CAN I DO?
PULL!!
CRASH!
NEW PLAN! BACK THE OTHER WAY!
STOP!

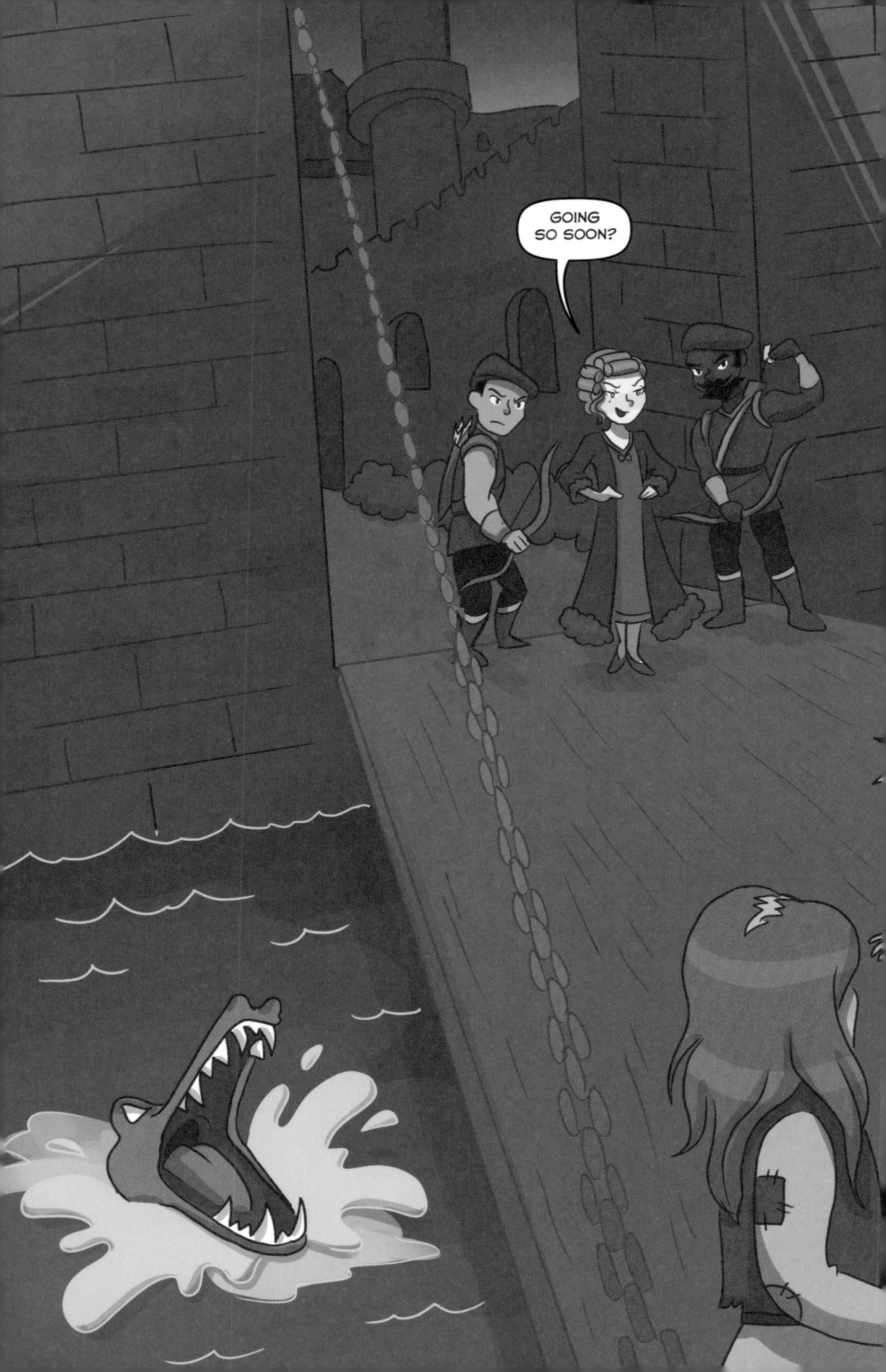
GOING
SO SOON?

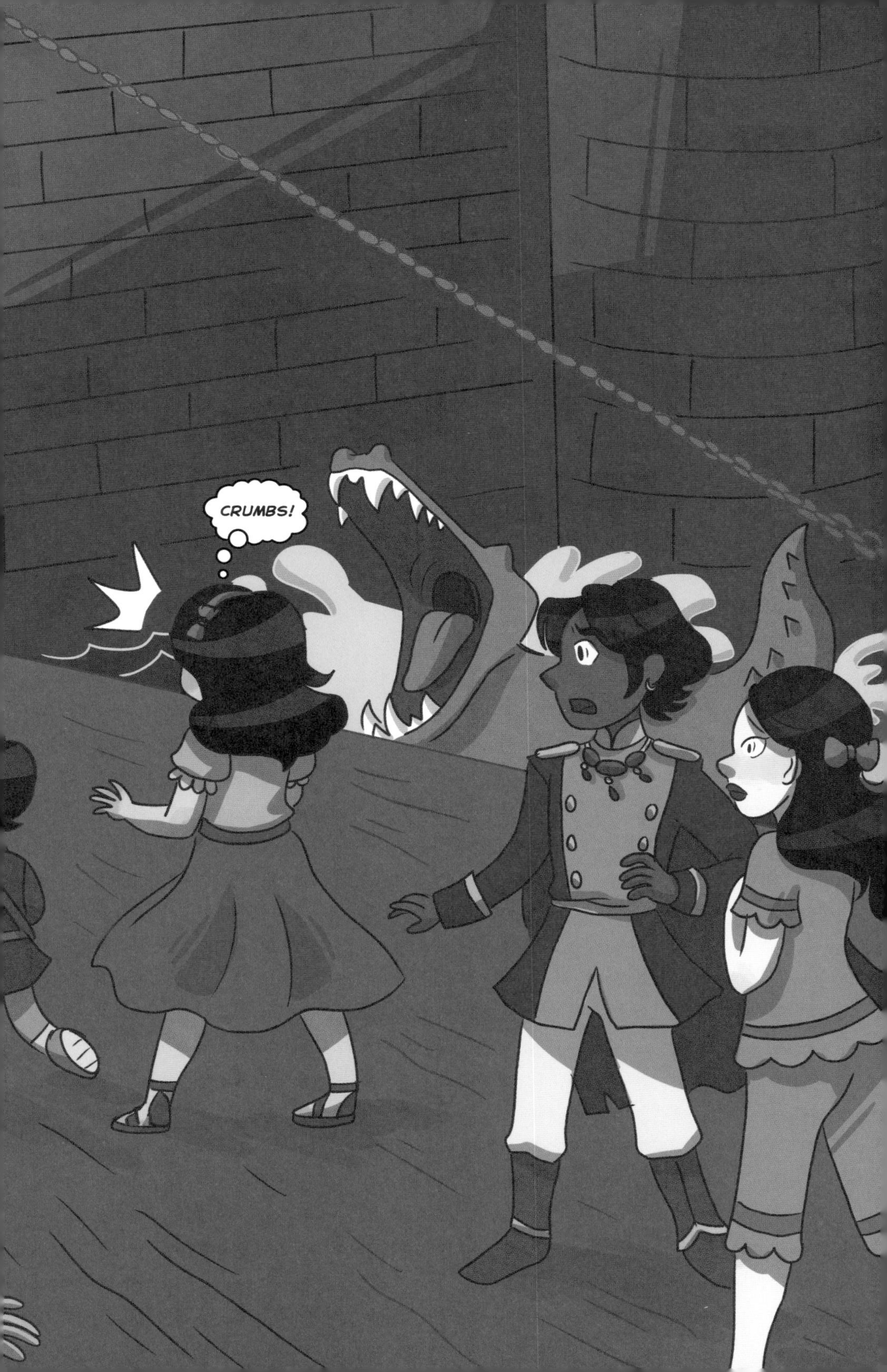
CRUMBS!

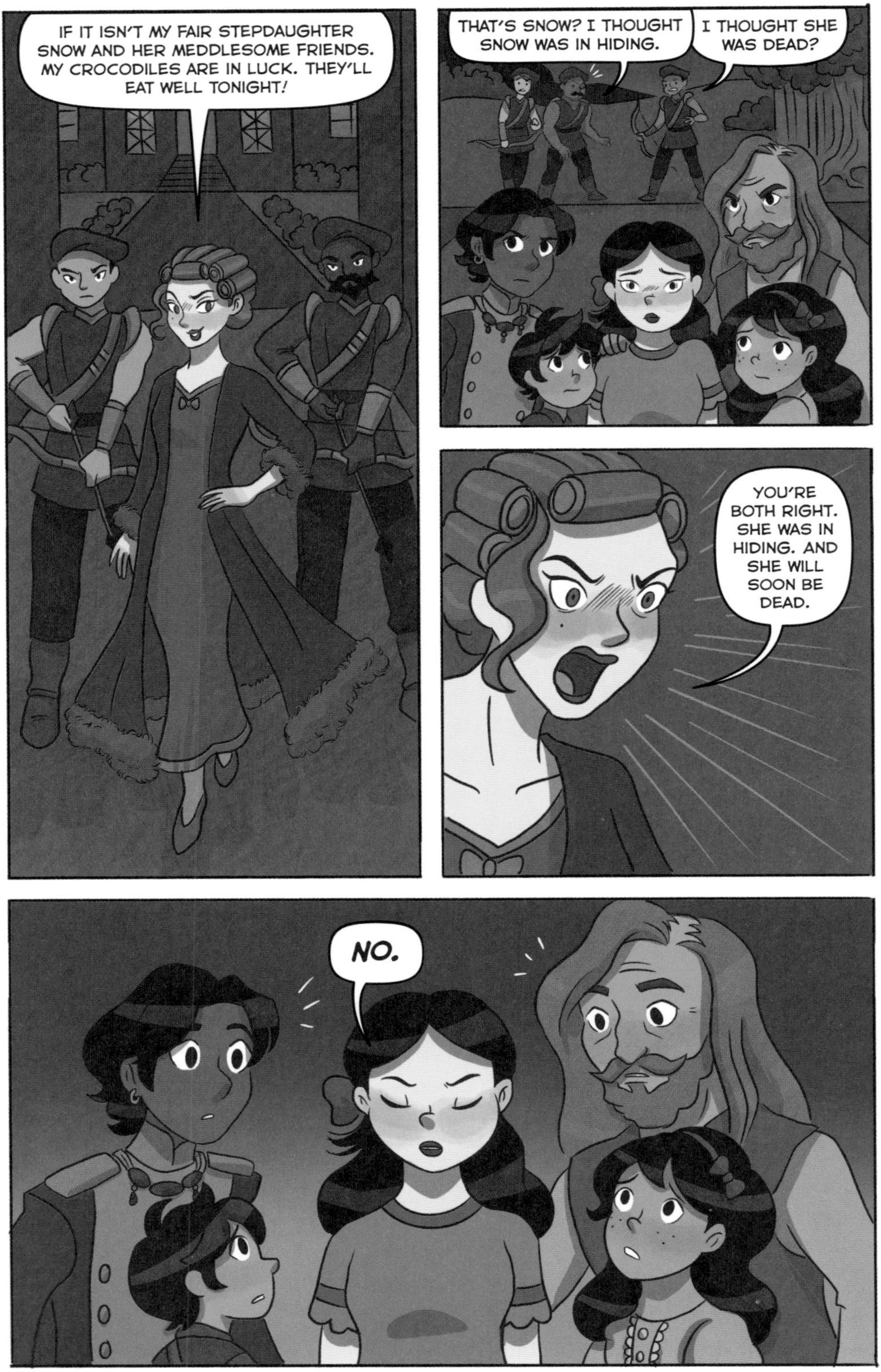
IF IT ISN'T MY FAIR STEPDAUGHTER SNOW AND HER MEDDLESOME FRIENDS. MY CROCODILES ARE IN LUCK. THEY'LL EAT WELL TONIGHT!
THAT'S SNOW? I THOUGHT SNOW WAS IN HIDING.
I THOUGHT SHE WAS DEAD?
YOU'RE BOTH RIGHT. SHE WAS IN HIDING. AND SHE WILL SOON BE DEAD.
NO.

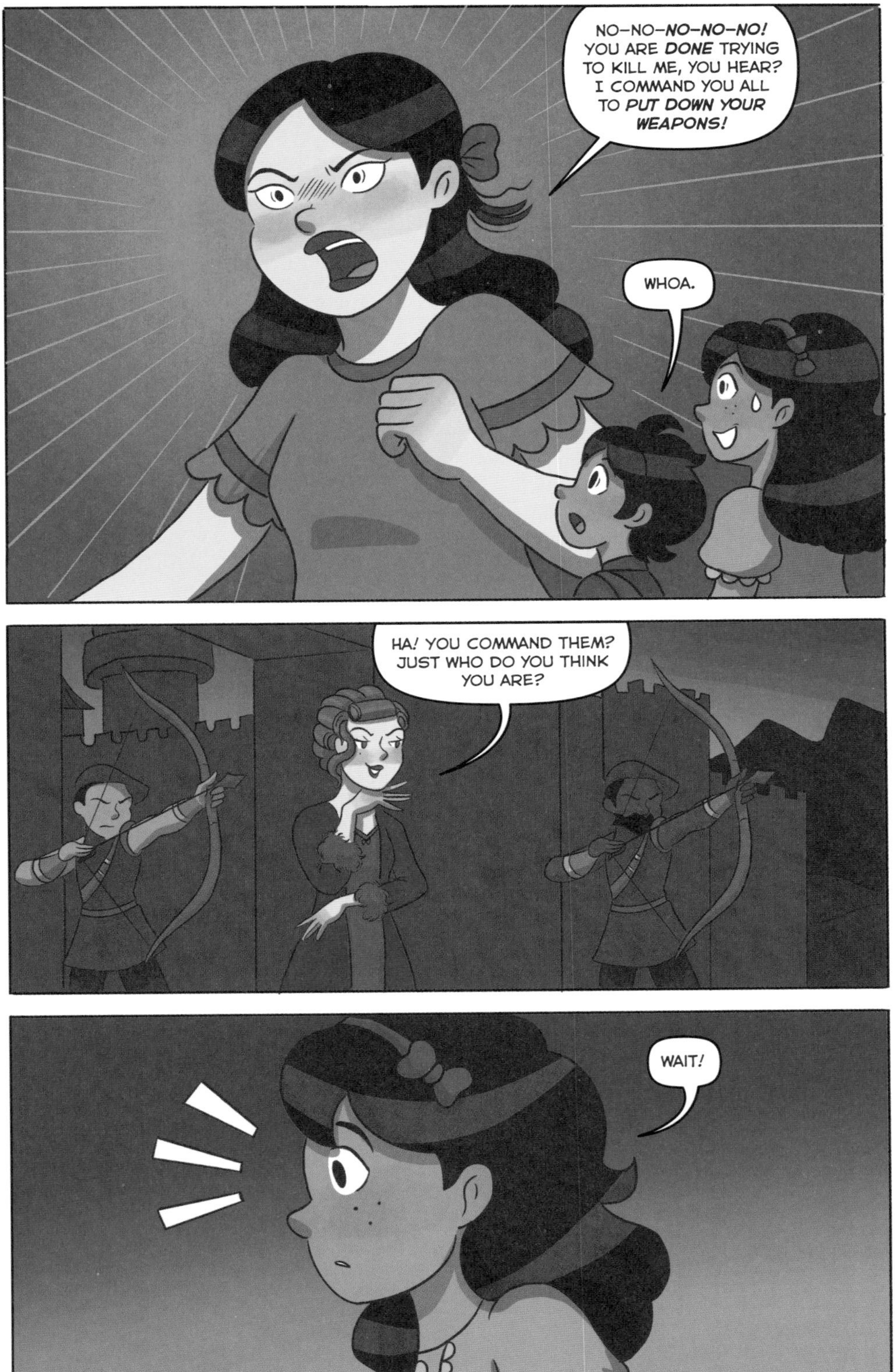
NO—NO—NO—NO—NO! YOU ARE DONE TRYING TO KILL ME, YOU HEAR? I COMMAND YOU ALL TO PUT DOWN YOUR WEAPONS!
WHOA.
HA! YOU COMMAND THEM? JUST WHO DO YOU THINK YOU ARE?
WAIT!

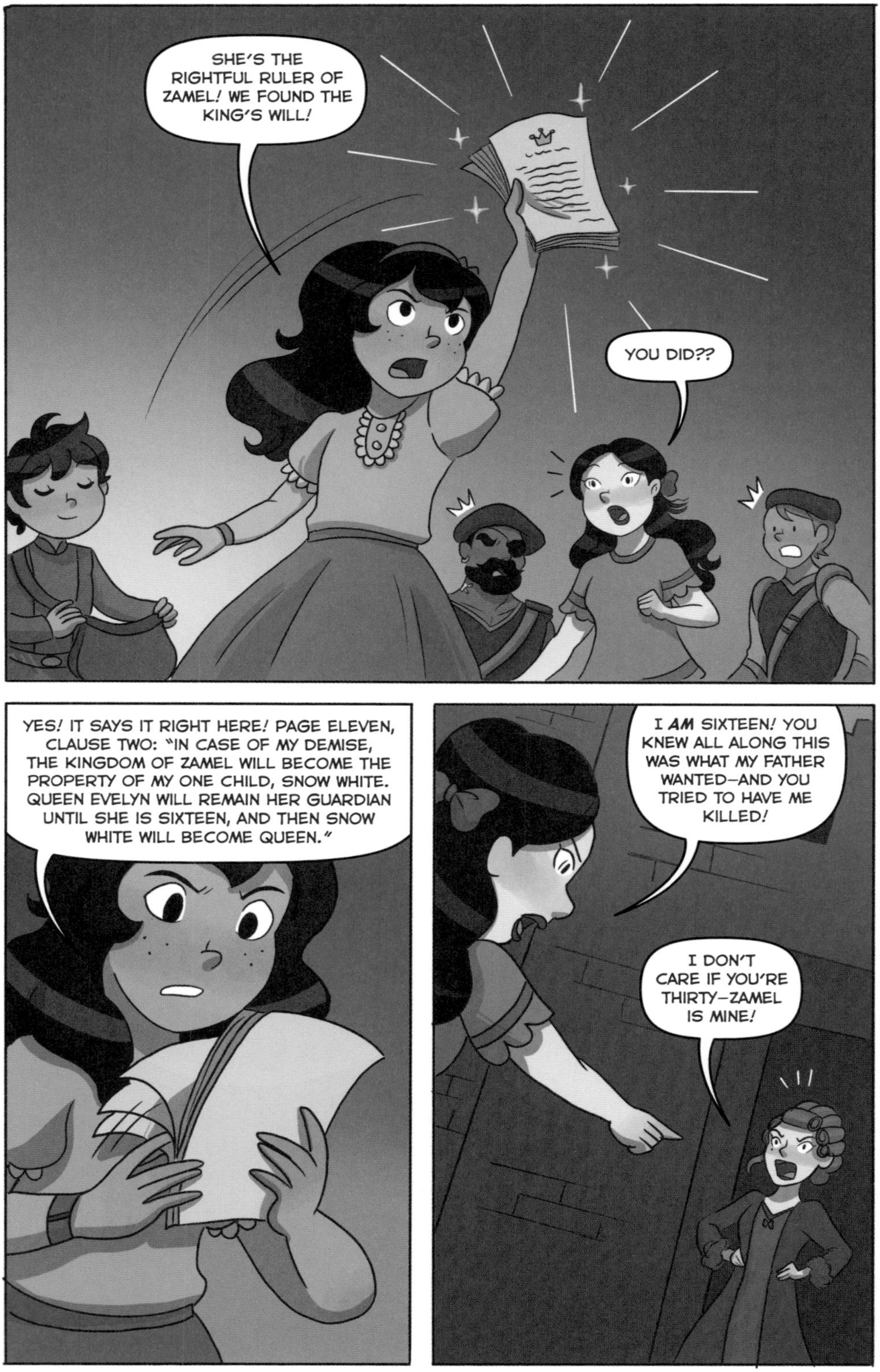
SHE'S THE RIGHTFUL RULER OF ZAMEL! WE FOUND THE KING'S WILL!
YOU DID??
YES! IT SAYS IT RIGHT HERE! PAGE ELEVEN, CLAUSE TWO: "IN CASE OF MY DEMISE, THE KINGDOM OF ZAMEL WILL BECOME THE PROPERTY OF MY ONE CHILD, SNOW WHITE. QUEEN EVELYN WILL REMAIN HER GUARDIAN UNTIL SHE IS SIXTEEN, AND THEN SNOW WHITE WILL BECOME QUEEN."
I ***AM*** SIXTEEN! YOU KNEW ALL ALONG THIS WAS WHAT MY FATHER WANTED—AND YOU TRIED TO HAVE ME KILLED!
I DON'T CARE IF YOU'RE THIRTY—ZAMEL IS MINE!

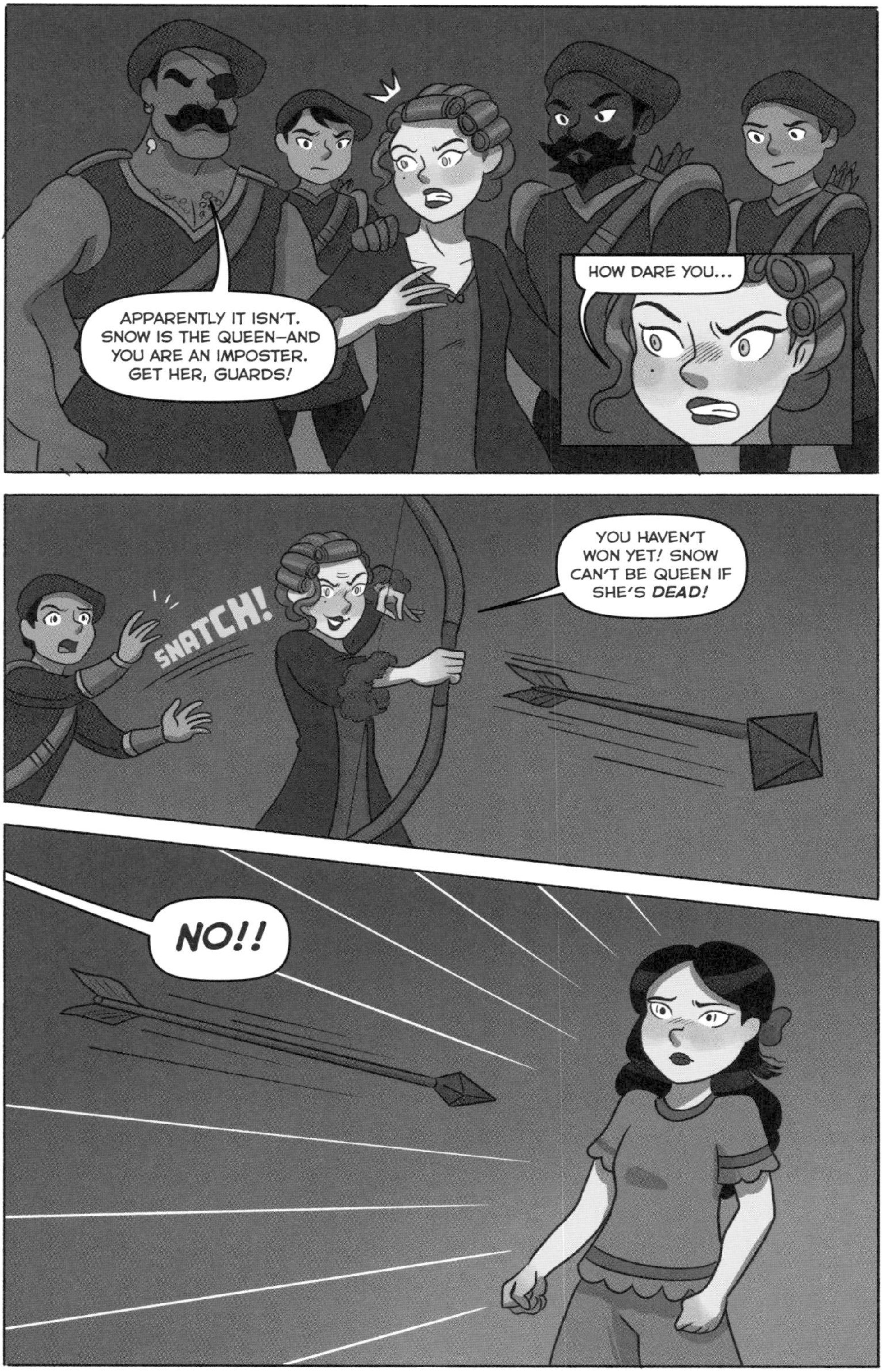
APPARENTLY IT ISN'T. SNOW IS THE QUEEN—AND YOU ARE AN IMPOSTER. GET HER, GUARDS!
HOW DARE YOU...
SNATCH!
YOU HAVEN'T WON YET! SNOW CAN'T BE QUEEN IF SHE'S *DEAD!*
NO!!

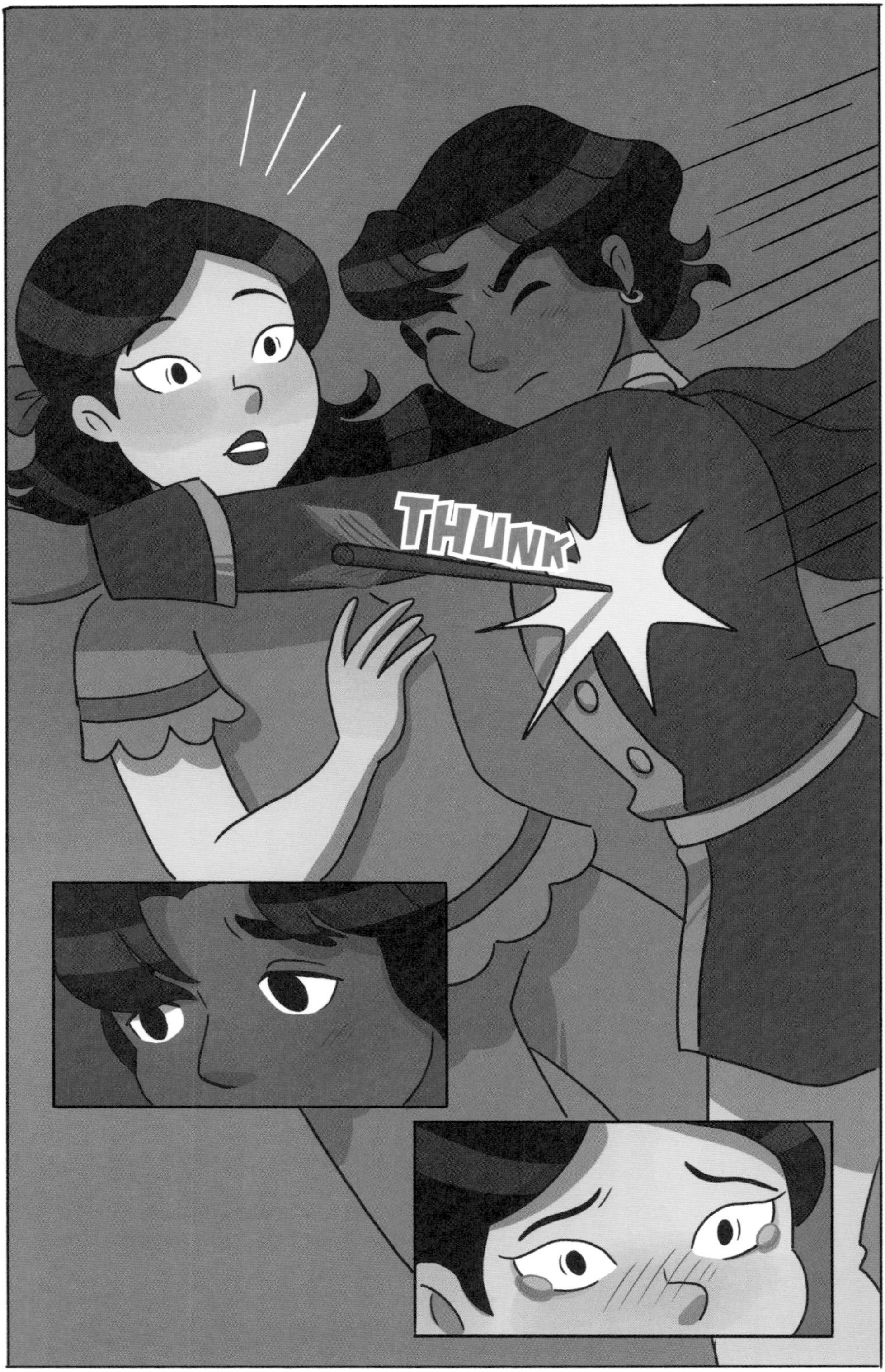
THUNK

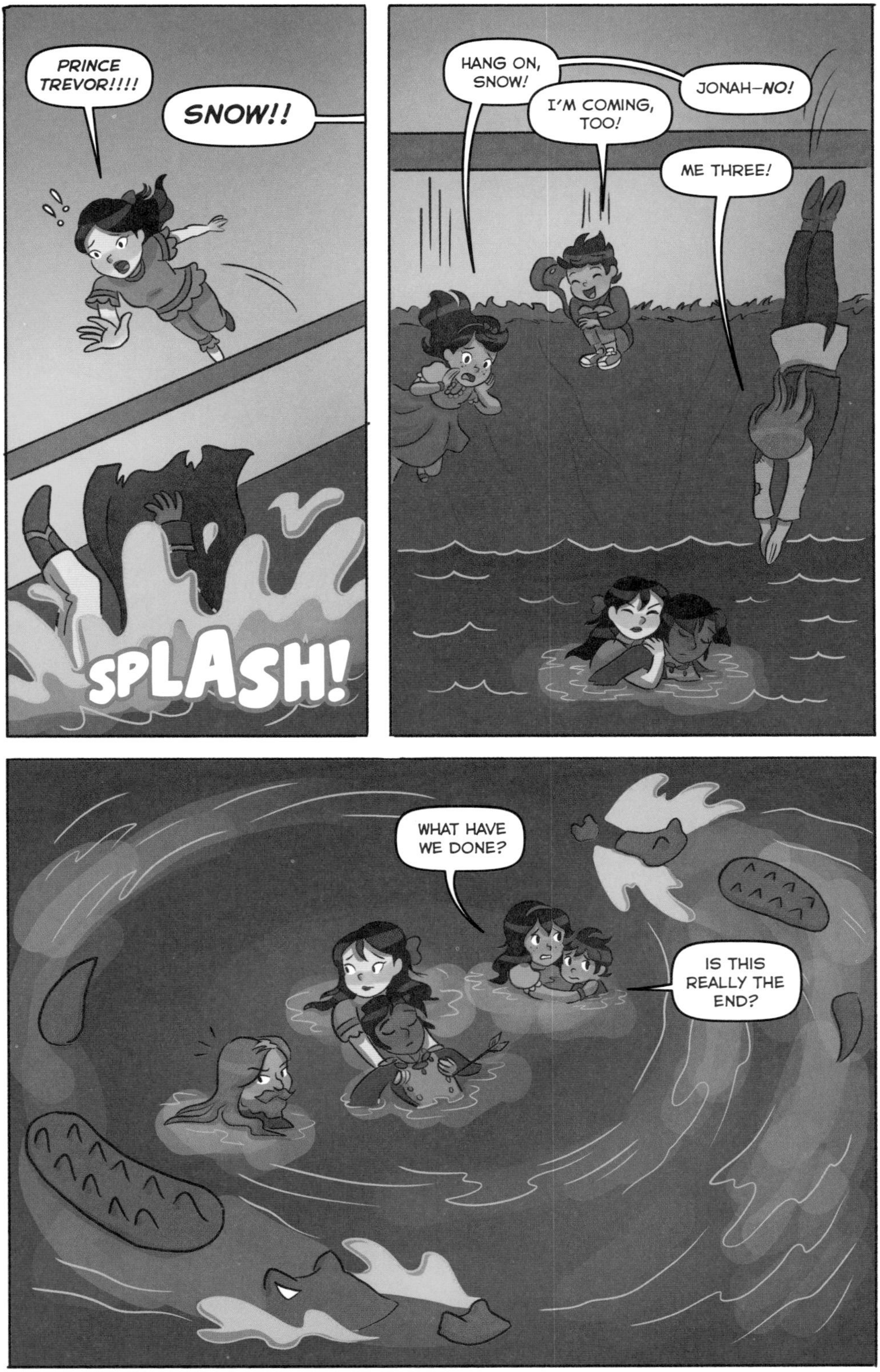
PRINCE TREVOR!!!!
SNOW!!
SPLASH!
HANG ON, SNOW!
I'M COMING, TOO!
JONAH—NO!
ME THREE!
WHAT HAVE WE DONE?
IS THIS REALLY THE END?

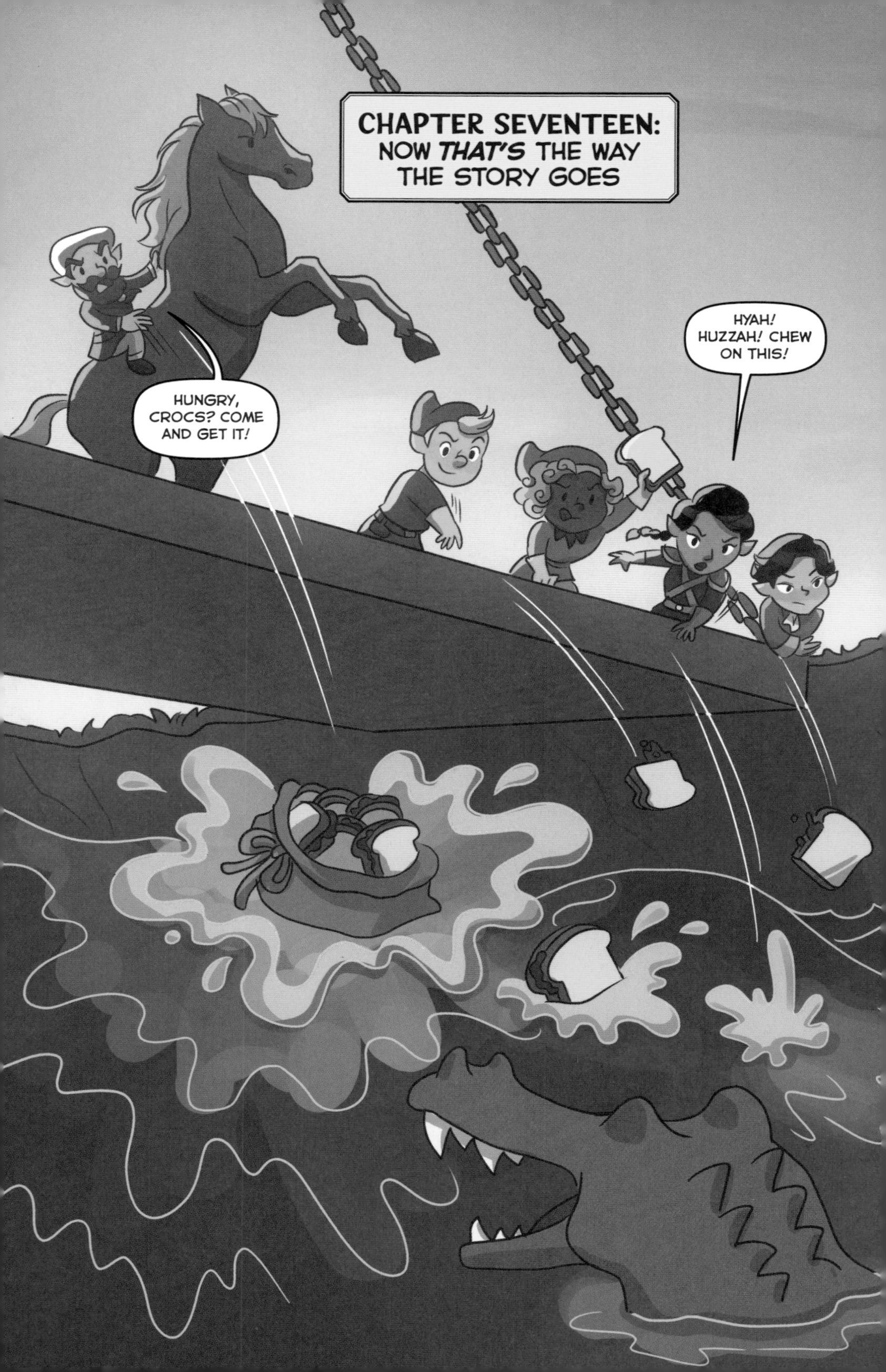

CHAPTER SEVENTEEN:
NOW *THAT'S* THE WAY THE STORY GOES
HUNGRY, CROCS? COME AND GET IT!
HYAH! HUZZAH! CHEW ON THIS!

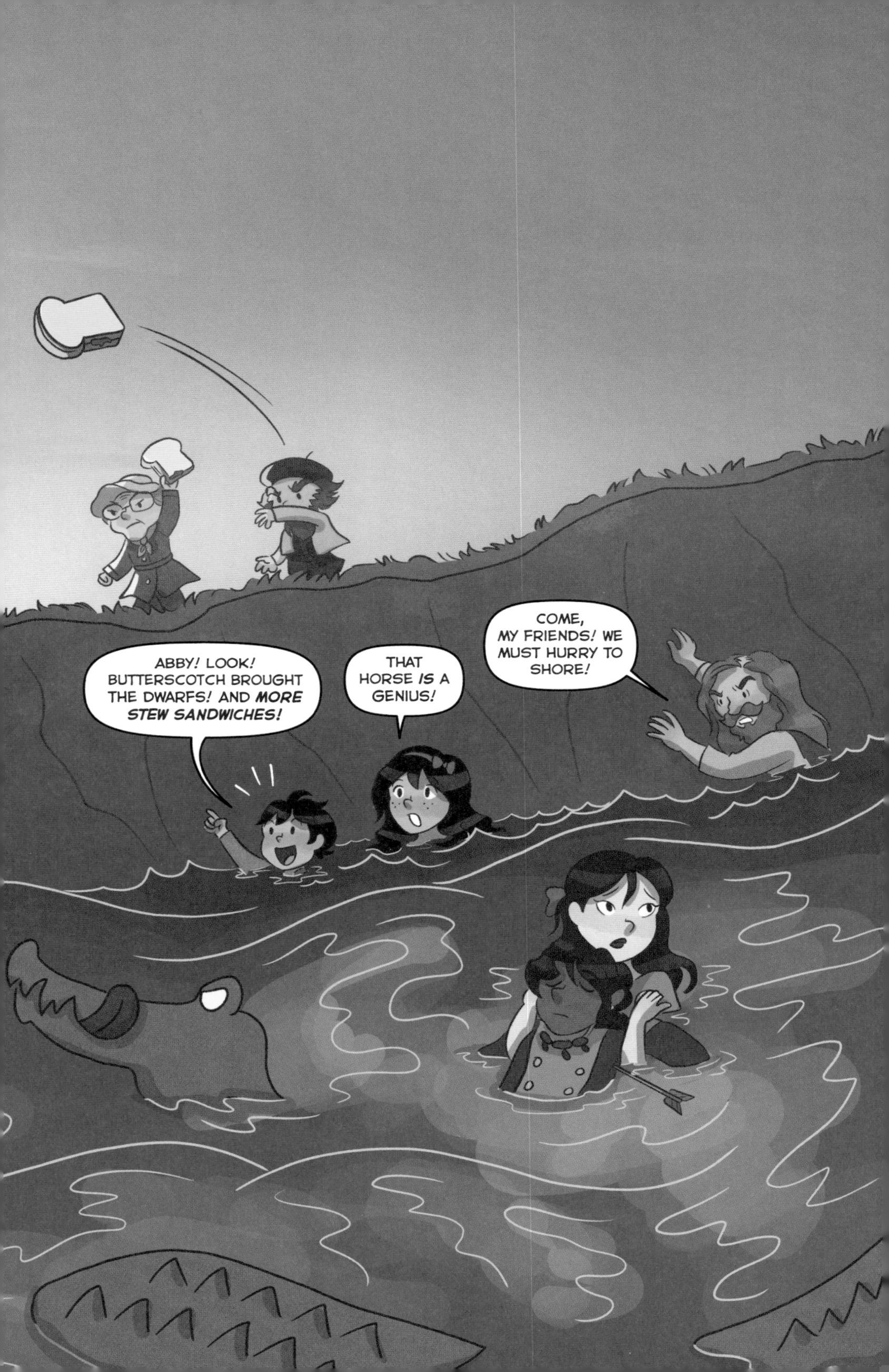
ABBY! LOOK! BUTTERSCOTCH BROUGHT THE DWARFS! AND MORE STEW SANDWICHES!
THAT HORSE IS A GENIUS!
COME, MY FRIENDS! WE MUST HURRY TO SHORE!

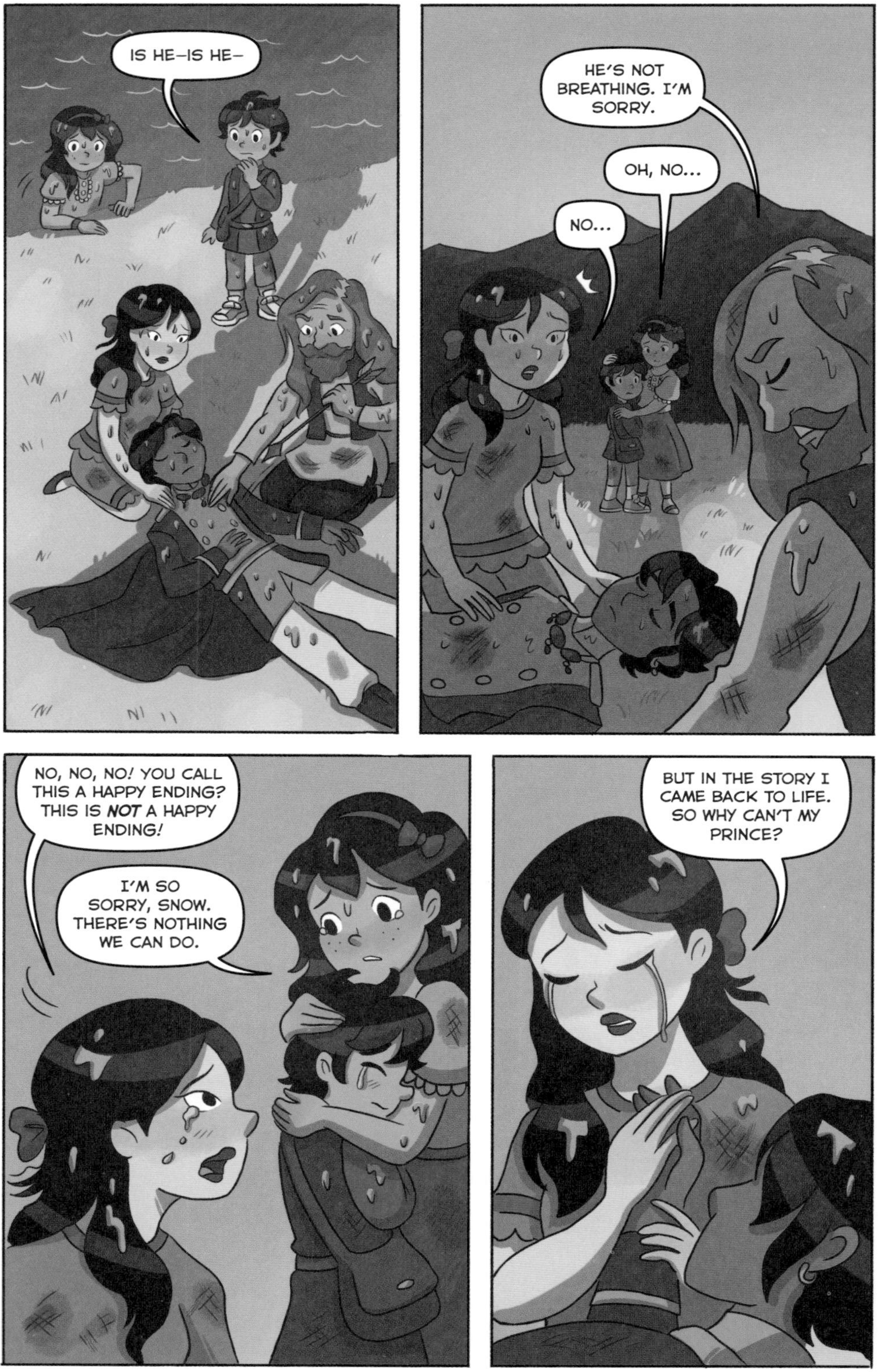
IS HE—IS HE—
HE'S NOT BREATHING. I'M SORRY.
OH, NO...
NO...
NO, NO, NO! YOU CALL THIS A HAPPY ENDING? THIS IS *NOT* A HAPPY ENDING!
I'M SO SORRY, SNOW. THERE'S NOTHING WE CAN DO.
BUT IN THE STORY I CAME BACK TO LIFE. SO WHY CAN'T MY PRINCE?

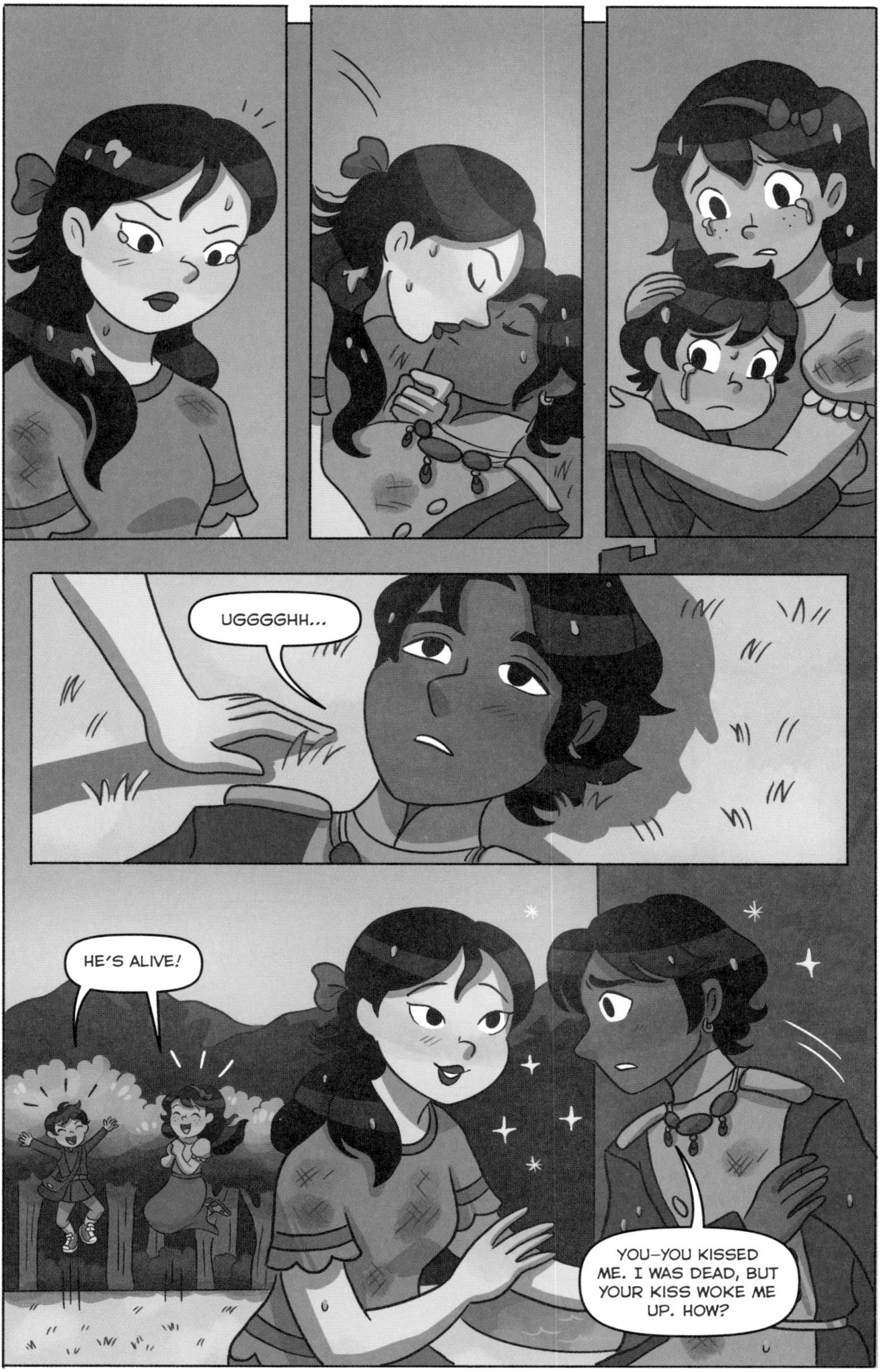
UGGGGHH...
HE'S ALIVE!
YOU—YOU KISSED ME. I WAS DEAD, BUT YOUR KISS WOKE ME UP. HOW?

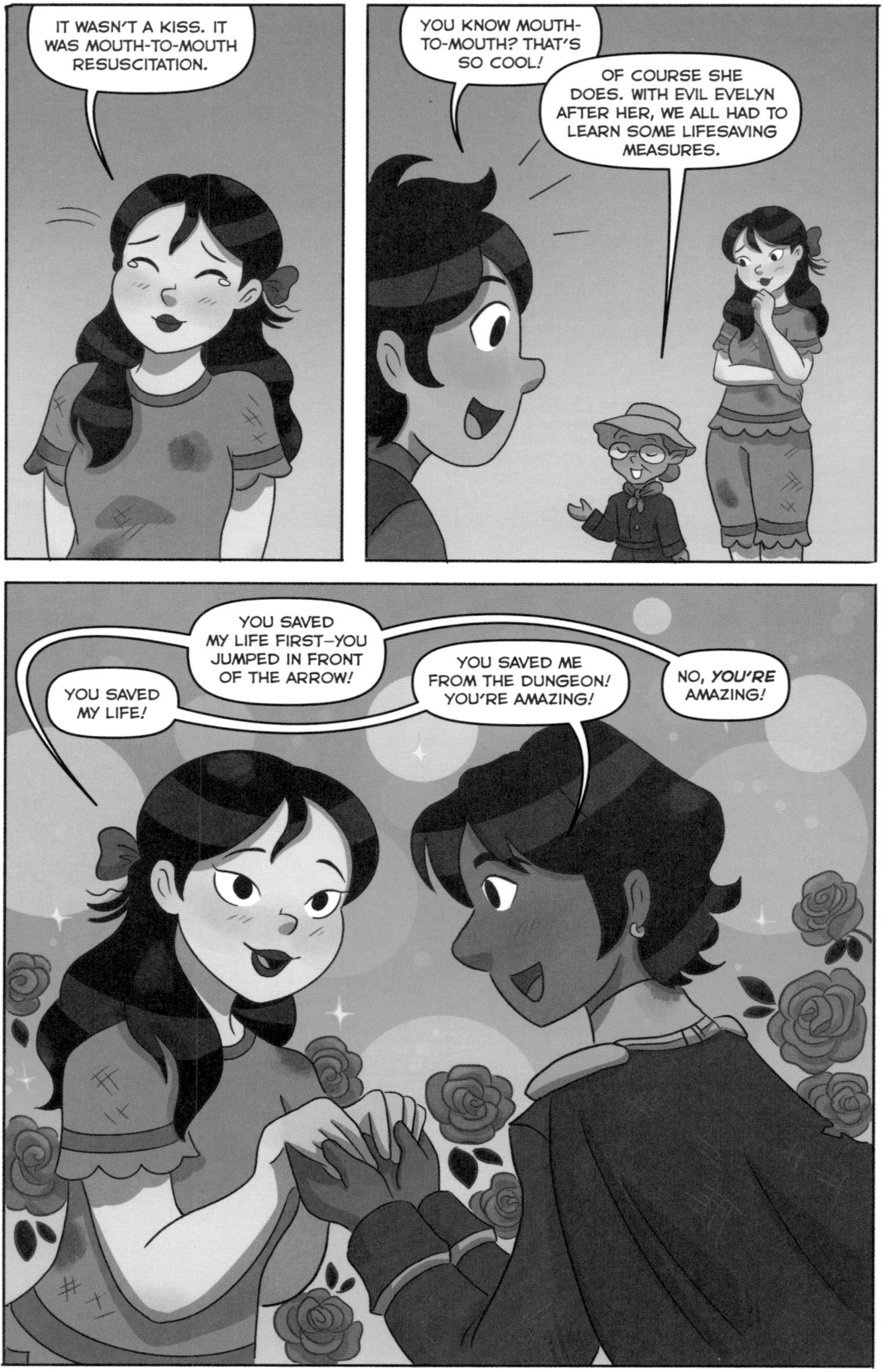
IT WASN'T A KISS. IT WAS MOUTH-TO-MOUTH RESUSCITATION.
YOU KNOW MOUTH-TO-MOUTH? THAT'S SO COOL!
OF COURSE SHE DOES. WITH EVIL EVELYN AFTER HER, WE ALL HAD TO LEARN SOME LIFESAVING MEASURES.
YOU SAVED MY LIFE!
YOU SAVED MY LIFE FIRST—YOU JUMPED IN FRONT OF THE ARROW!
YOU SAVED ME FROM THE DUNGEON! YOU'RE AMAZING!
NO, ***YOU'RE*** AMAZING!

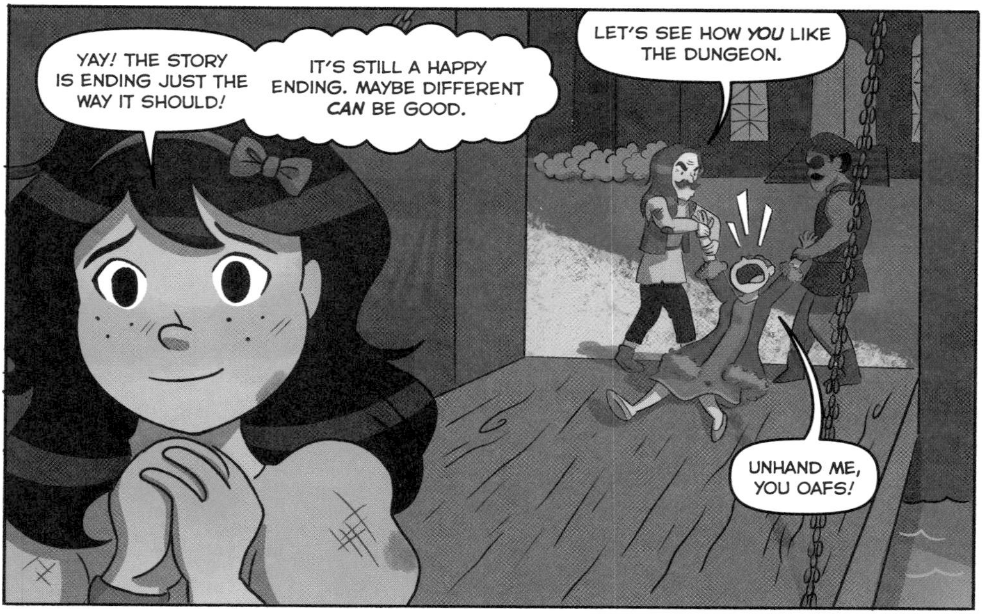
YAY! THE STORY IS ENDING JUST THE WAY IT SHOULD!
IT'S STILL A HAPPY ENDING. MAYBE DIFFERENT CAN BE GOOD.
LET'S SEE HOW YOU LIKE THE DUNGEON.
UNHAND ME, YOU OAFS!

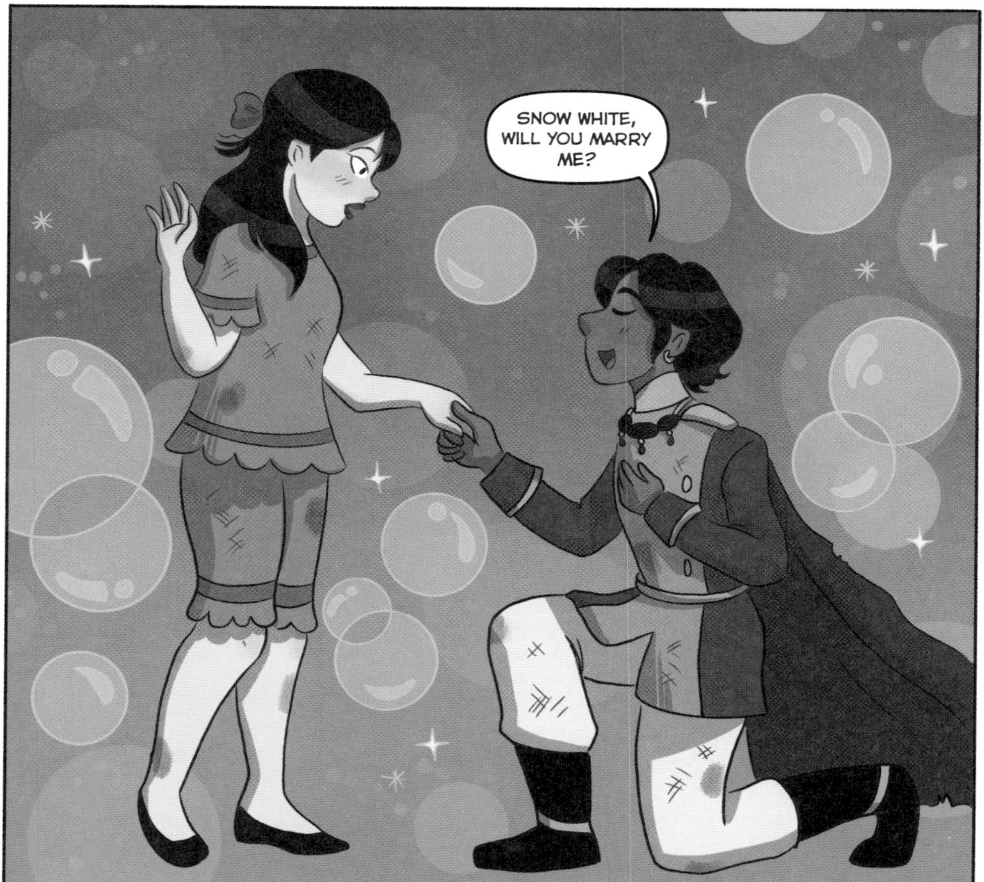
SNOW WHITE, WILL YOU MARRY ME?

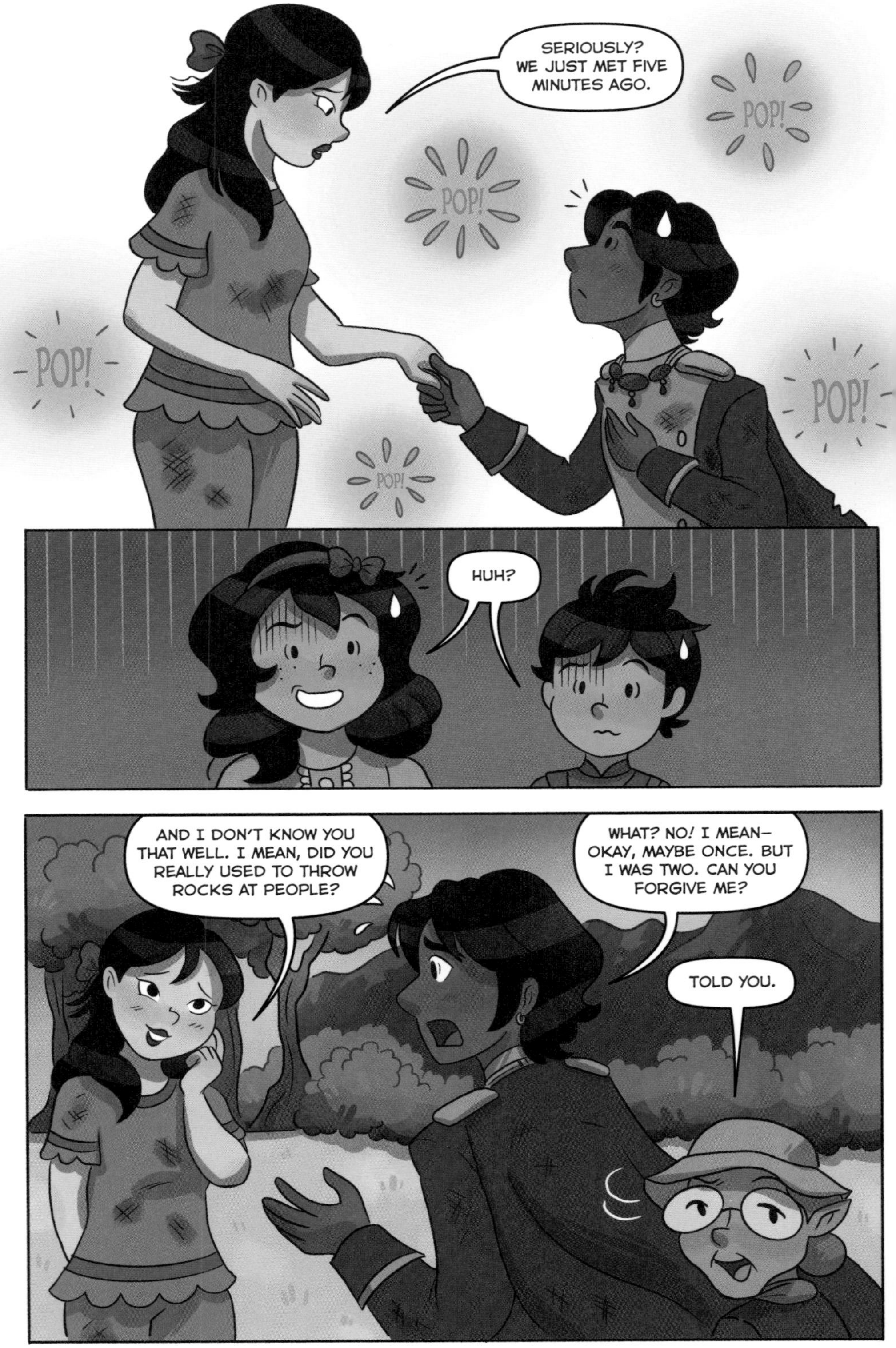
SERIOUSLY? WE JUST MET FIVE MINUTES AGO.
POP!
POP!
POP!
POP!
POP!
HUH?
AND I DON'T KNOW YOU THAT WELL. I MEAN, DID YOU REALLY USED TO THROW ROCKS AT PEOPLE?
WHAT? NO! I MEAN— OKAY, MAYBE ONCE. BUT I WAS TWO. CAN YOU FORGIVE ME?
TOLD YOU.

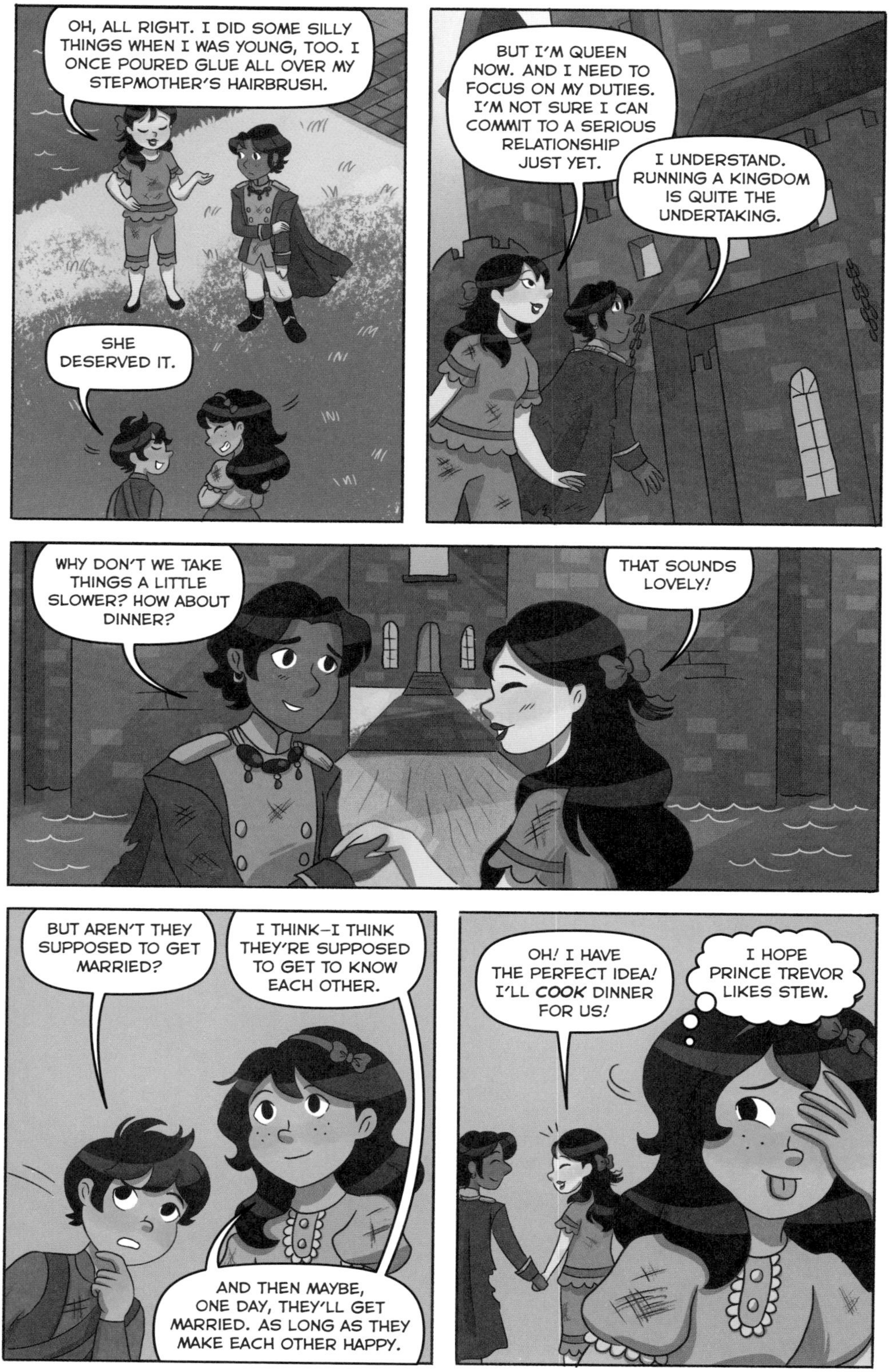
OH, ALL RIGHT. I DID SOME SILLY THINGS WHEN I WAS YOUNG, TOO. I ONCE POURED GLUE ALL OVER MY STEPMOTHER'S HAIRBRUSH.
SHE DESERVED IT.
BUT I'M QUEEN NOW. AND I NEED TO FOCUS ON MY DUTIES. I'M NOT SURE I CAN COMMIT TO A SERIOUS RELATIONSHIP JUST YET.
I UNDERSTAND. RUNNING A KINGDOM IS QUITE THE UNDERTAKING.
WHY DON'T WE TAKE THINGS A LITTLE SLOWER? HOW ABOUT DINNER?
THAT SOUNDS LOVELY!
BUT AREN'T THEY SUPPOSED TO GET MARRIED?
I THINK—I THINK THEY'RE SUPPOSED TO GET TO KNOW EACH OTHER.
AND THEN MAYBE, ONE DAY, THEY'LL GET MARRIED. AS LONG AS THEY MAKE EACH OTHER HAPPY.
OH! I HAVE THE PERFECT IDEA! I'LL ***COOK*** DINNER FOR US!
I HOPE PRINCE TREVOR LIKES STEW.

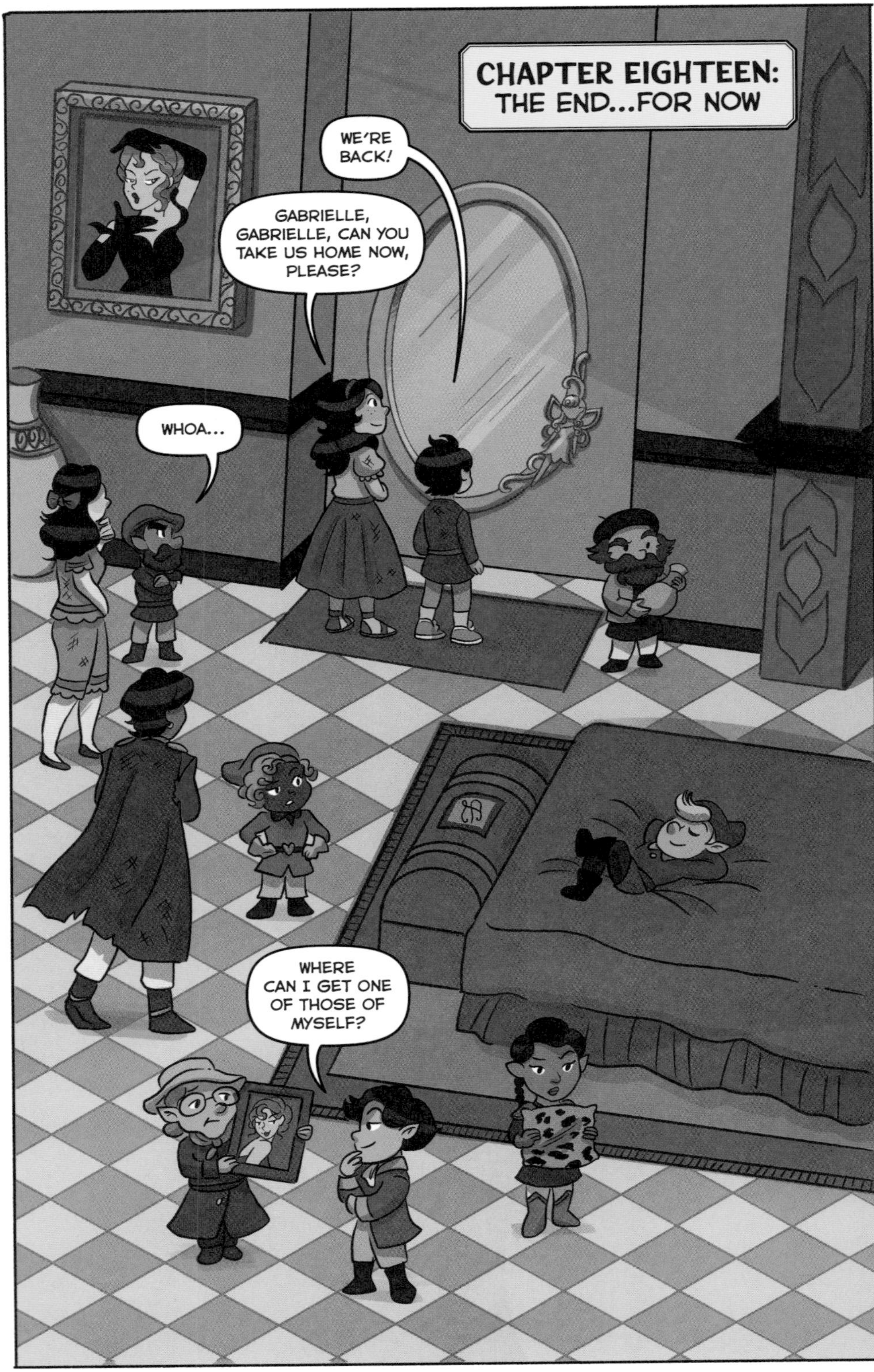
CHAPTER EIGHTEEN:
THE END...FOR NOW
WE'RE BACK!
GABRIELLE, GABRIELLE, CAN YOU TAKE US HOME NOW, PLEASE?
WHOA...
WHERE CAN I GET ONE OF THOSE OF MYSELF?

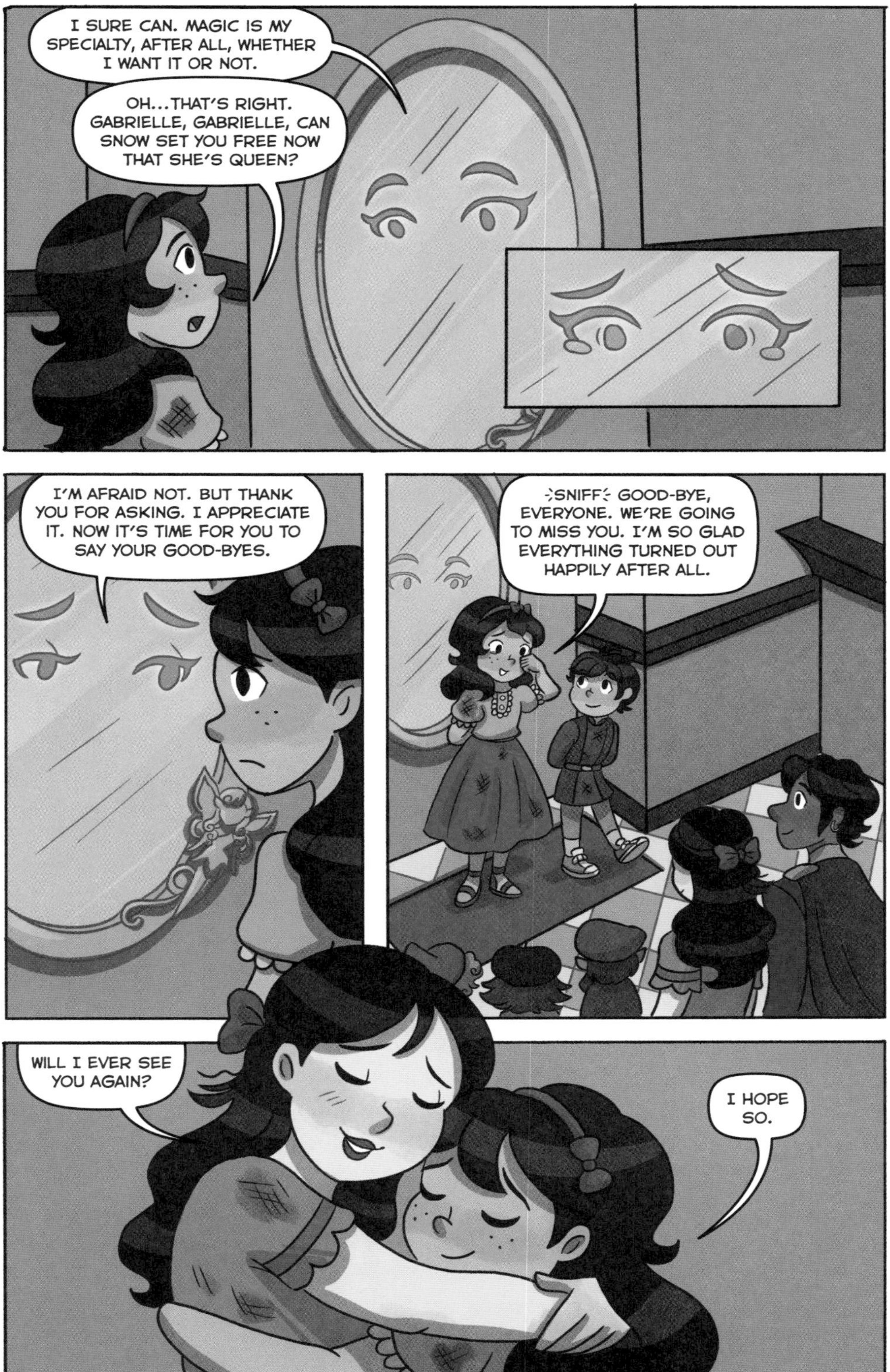
I SURE CAN. MAGIC IS MY SPECIALTY, AFTER ALL, WHETHER I WANT IT OR NOT.
OH...THAT'S RIGHT. GABRIELLE, GABRIELLE, CAN SNOW SET YOU FREE NOW THAT SHE'S QUEEN?
I'M AFRAID NOT. BUT THANK YOU FOR ASKING. I APPRECIATE IT. NOW IT'S TIME FOR YOU TO SAY YOUR GOOD-BYES.
SNIFF GOOD-BYE, EVERYONE. WE'RE GOING TO MISS YOU. I'M SO GLAD EVERYTHING TURNED OUT HAPPILY AFTER ALL.
WILL I EVER SEE YOU AGAIN?
I HOPE SO.

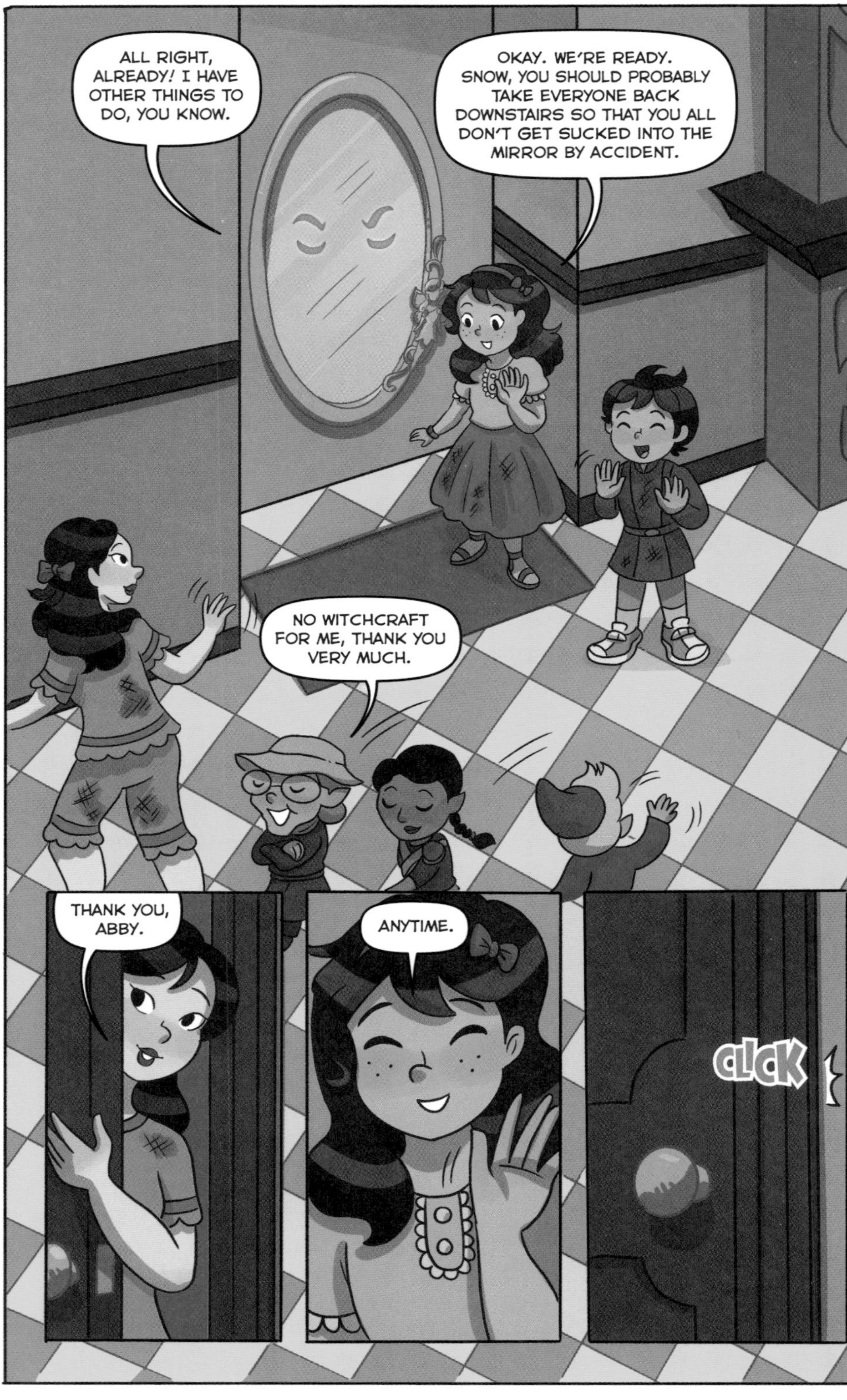
ALL RIGHT, ALREADY! I HAVE OTHER THINGS TO DO, YOU KNOW.
OKAY. WE'RE READY. SNOW, YOU SHOULD PROBABLY TAKE EVERYONE BACK DOWNSTAIRS SO THAT YOU ALL DON'T GET SUCKED INTO THE MIRROR BY ACCIDENT.
NO WITCHCRAFT FOR ME, THANK YOU VERY MUCH.
THANK YOU, ABBY.
ANYTIME.
CLICK

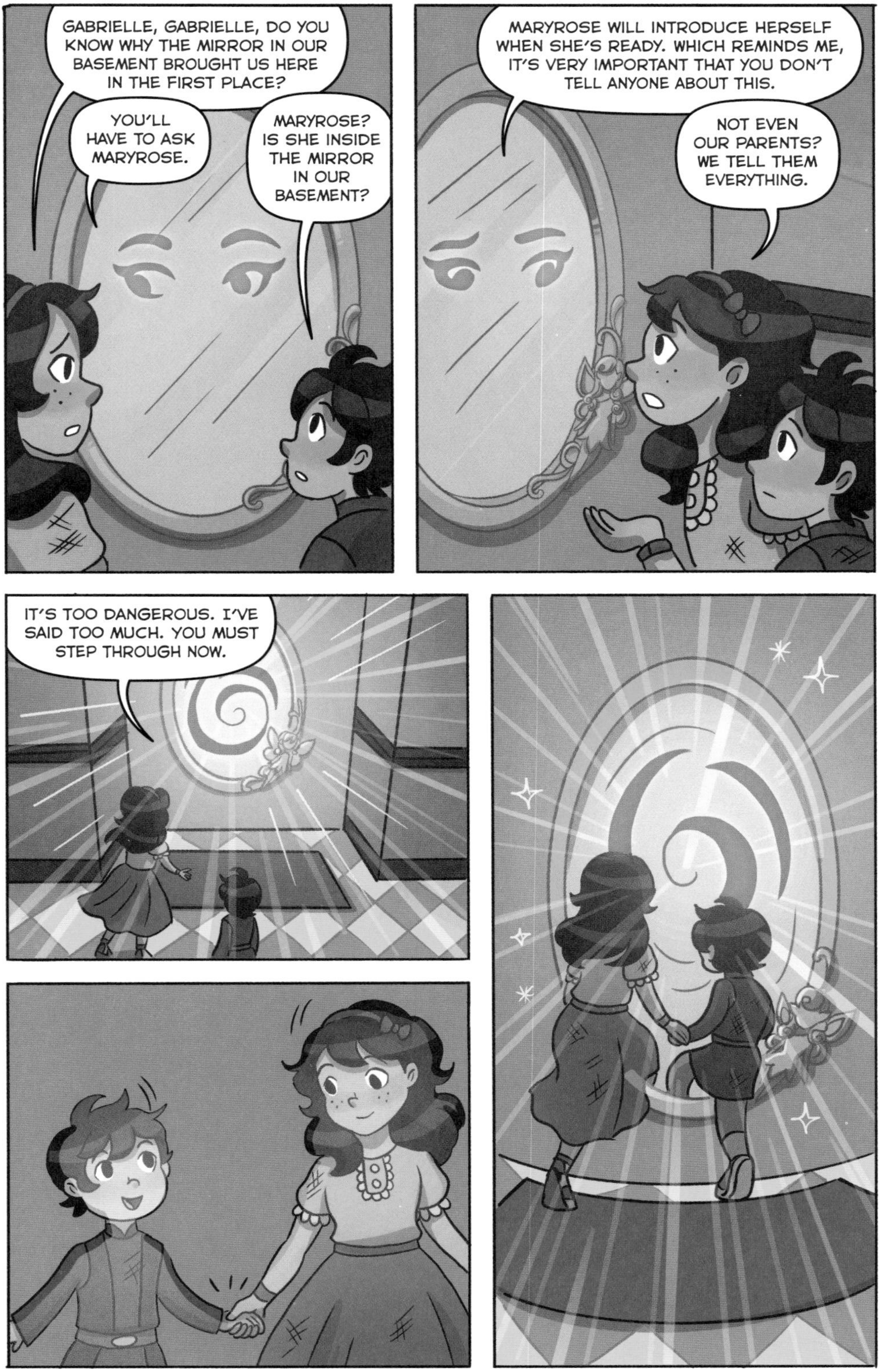
GABRIELLE, GABRIELLE, DO YOU KNOW WHY THE MIRROR IN OUR BASEMENT BROUGHT US HERE IN THE FIRST PLACE?
YOU'LL HAVE TO ASK MARYROSE.
MARYROSE? IS SHE INSIDE THE MIRROR IN OUR BASEMENT?
MARYROSE WILL INTRODUCE HERSELF WHEN SHE'S READY. WHICH REMINDS ME, IT'S VERY IMPORTANT THAT YOU DON'T TELL ANYONE ABOUT THIS.
NOT EVEN OUR PARENTS? WE TELL THEM EVERYTHING.
IT'S TOO DANGEROUS. I'VE SAID TOO MUCH. YOU MUST STEP THROUGH NOW.

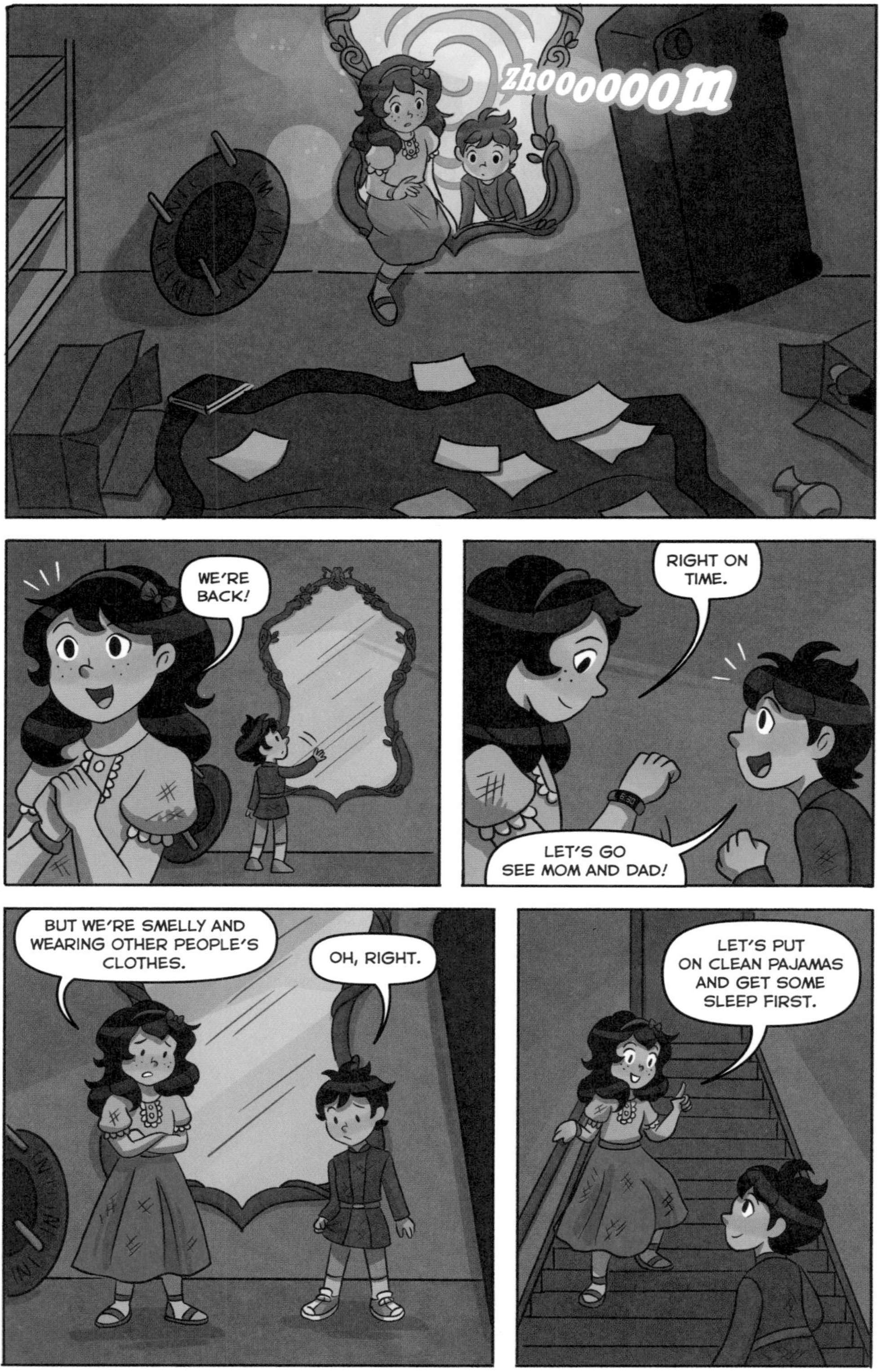
Zhoooooom
WE'RE BACK!
RIGHT ON TIME.
LET'S GO SEE MOM AND DAD!
BUT WE'RE SMELLY AND WEARING OTHER PEOPLE'S CLOTHES.
OH, RIGHT.
LET'S PUT ON CLEAN PAJAMAS AND GET SOME SLEEP FIRST.

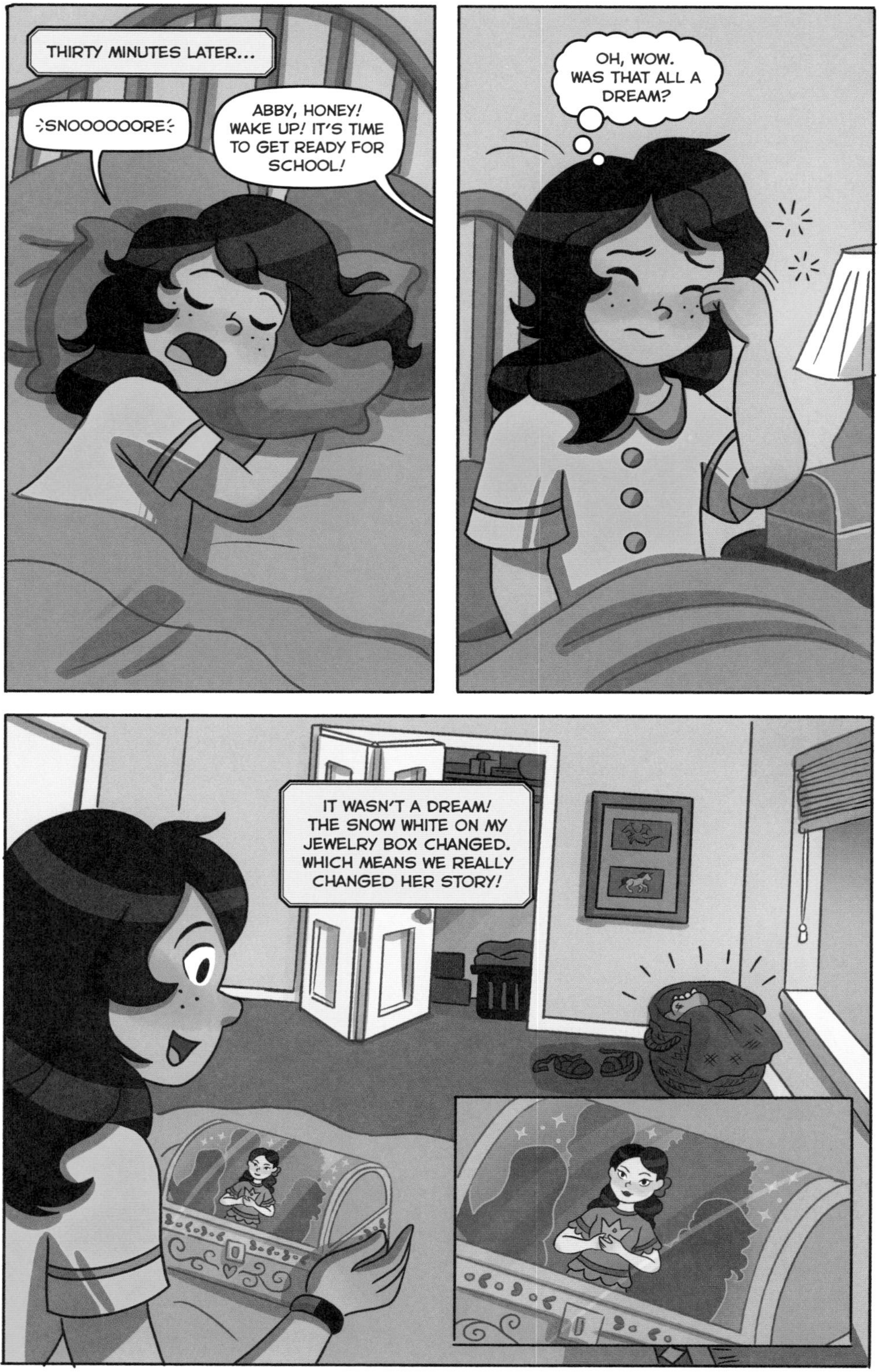
THIRTY MINUTES LATER...
SNOOOOOORE
ABBY, HONEY! WAKE UP! IT'S TIME TO GET READY FOR SCHOOL!
OH, WOW. WAS THAT ALL A DREAM?
IT WASN'T A DREAM! THE SNOW WHITE ON MY JEWELRY BOX CHANGED. WHICH MEANS WE REALLY CHANGED HER STORY!

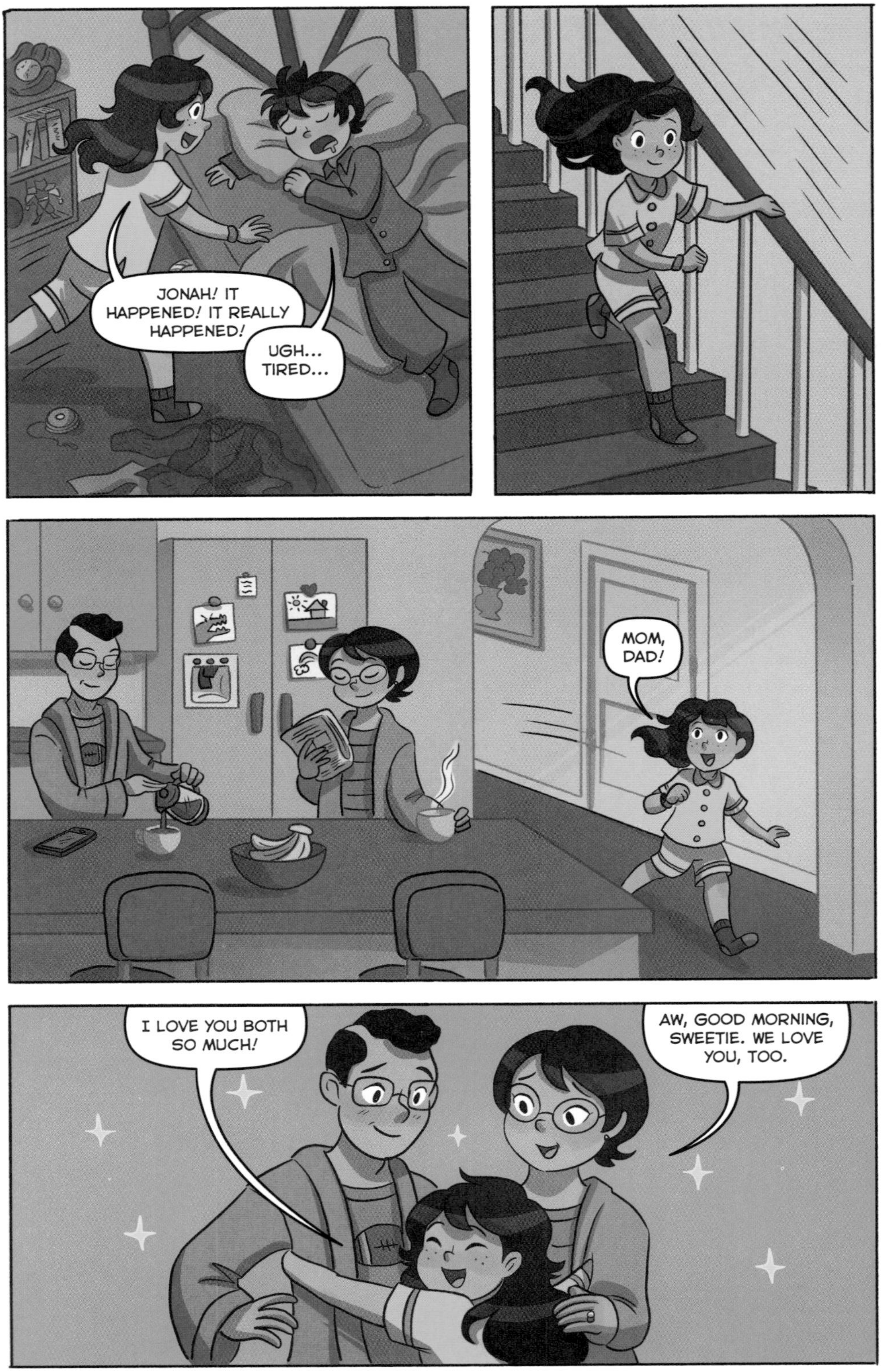
JONAH! IT HAPPENED! IT REALLY HAPPENED!
UGH... TIRED...
MOM, DAD!
I LOVE YOU BOTH SO MUCH!
AW, GOOD MORNING, SWEETIE. WE LOVE YOU, TOO.

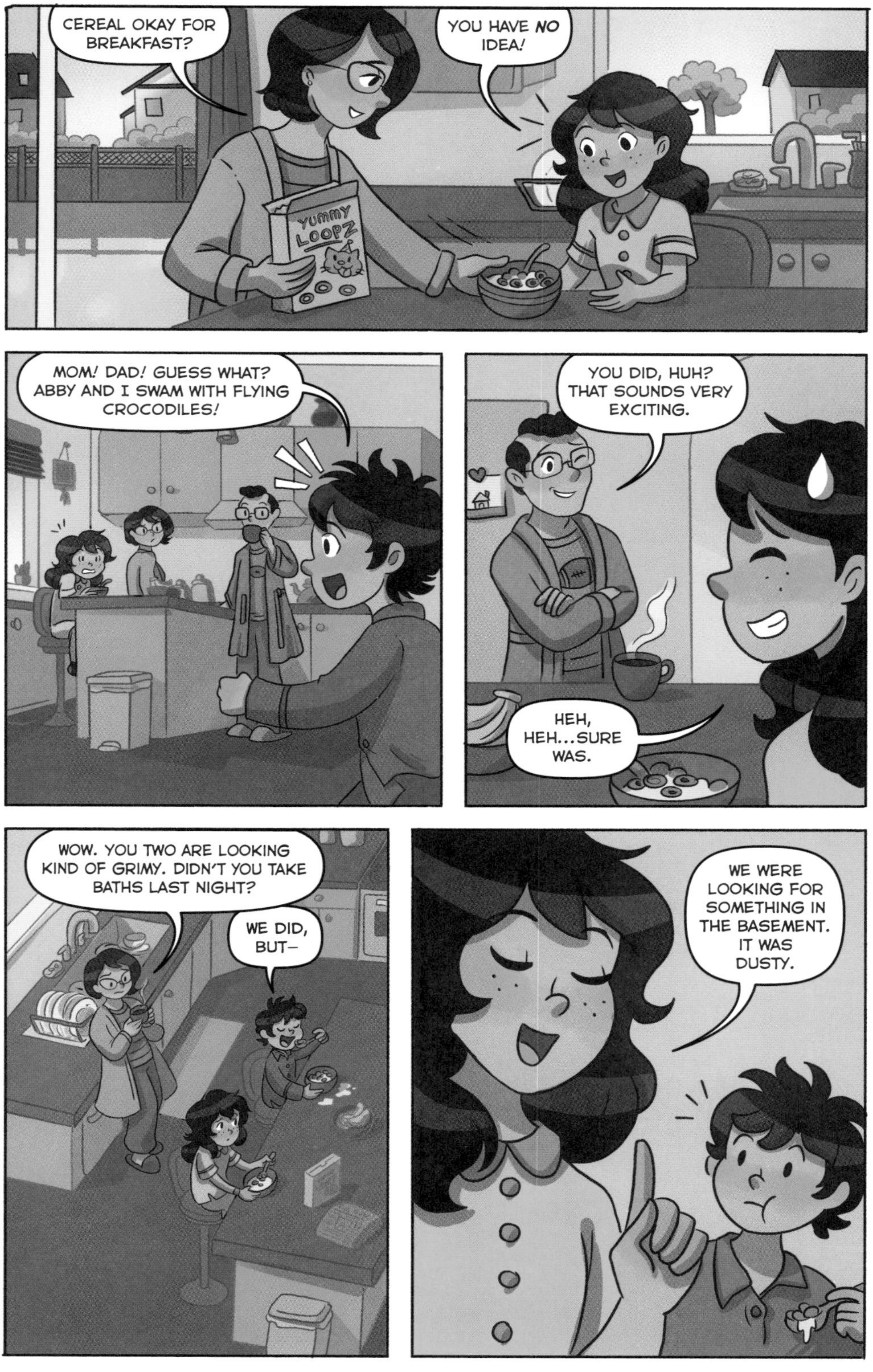
CEREAL OKAY FOR BREAKFAST?
YOU HAVE **NO** IDEA!
MOM! DAD! GUESS WHAT? ABBY AND I SWAM WITH FLYING CROCODILES!
YOU DID, HUH? THAT SOUNDS VERY EXCITING.
HEH, HEH...SURE WAS.
YUMMY LOOPZ
WOW. YOU TWO ARE LOOKING KIND OF GRIMY. DIDN'T YOU TAKE BATHS LAST NIGHT?
WE DID, BUT–
WE WERE LOOKING FOR SOMETHING IN THE BASEMENT. IT WAS DUSTY.

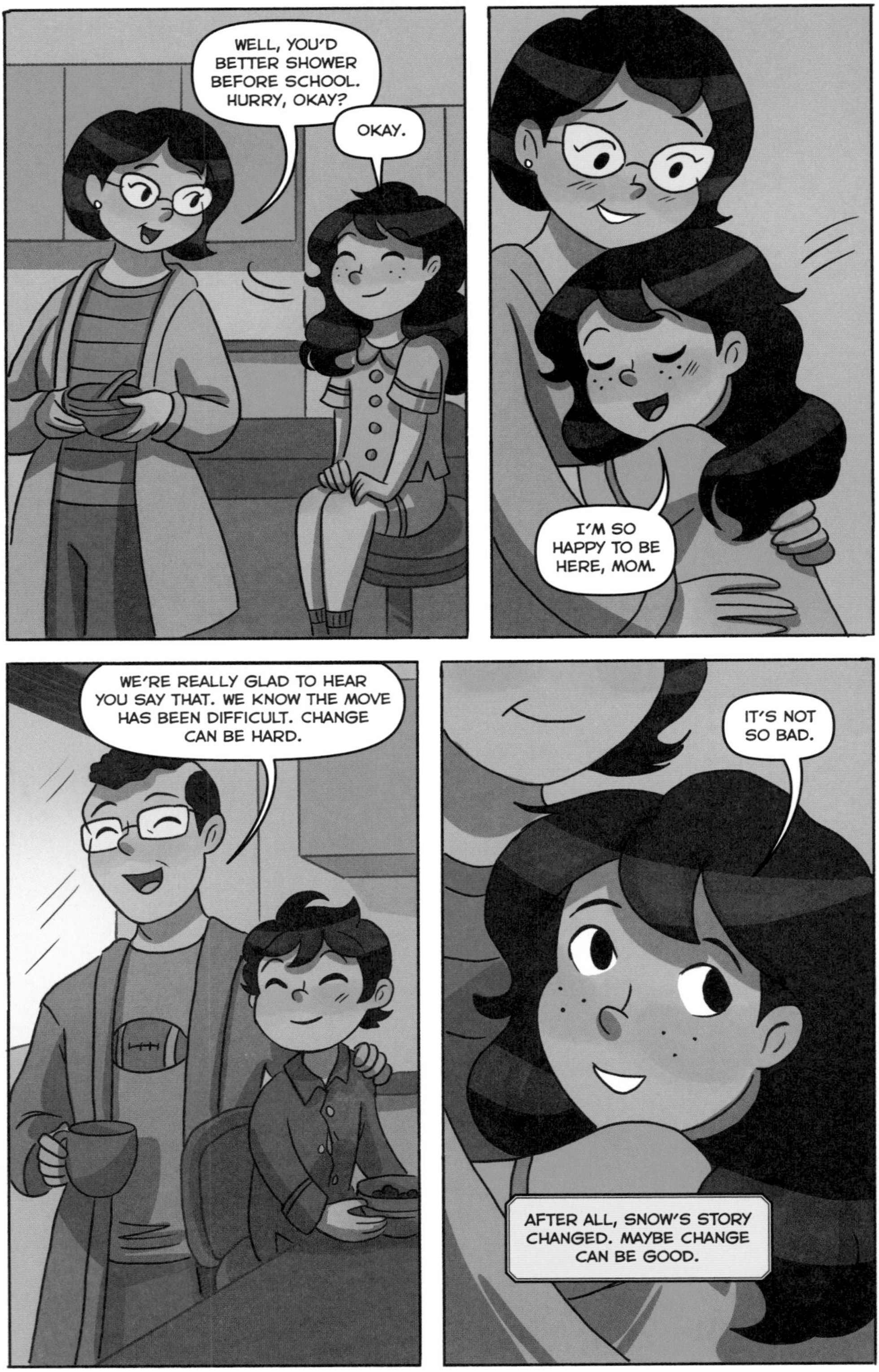
WELL, YOU'D BETTER SHOWER BEFORE SCHOOL. HURRY, OKAY?
OKAY.
I'M SO HAPPY TO BE HERE, MOM.
WE'RE REALLY GLAD TO HEAR YOU SAY THAT. WE KNOW THE MOVE HAS BEEN DIFFICULT. CHANGE CAN BE HARD.
IT'S NOT SO BAD.
AFTER ALL, SNOW'S STORY CHANGED. MAYBE CHANGE CAN BE GOOD.

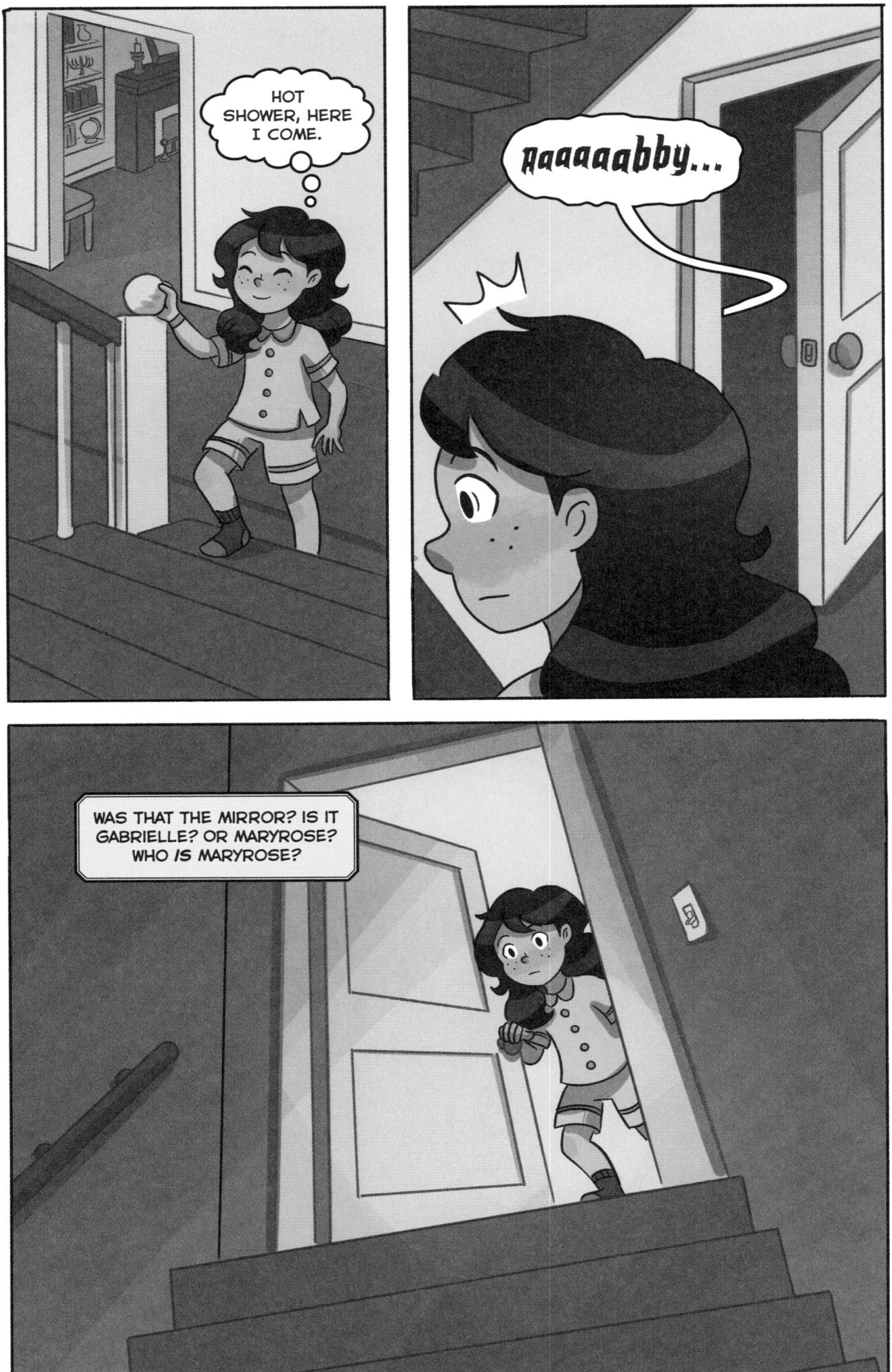
HOT SHOWER, HERE I COME.
Aaaaaabby...
WAS THAT THE MIRROR? IS IT GABRIELLE? OR MARYROSE? WHO *IS* MARYROSE?

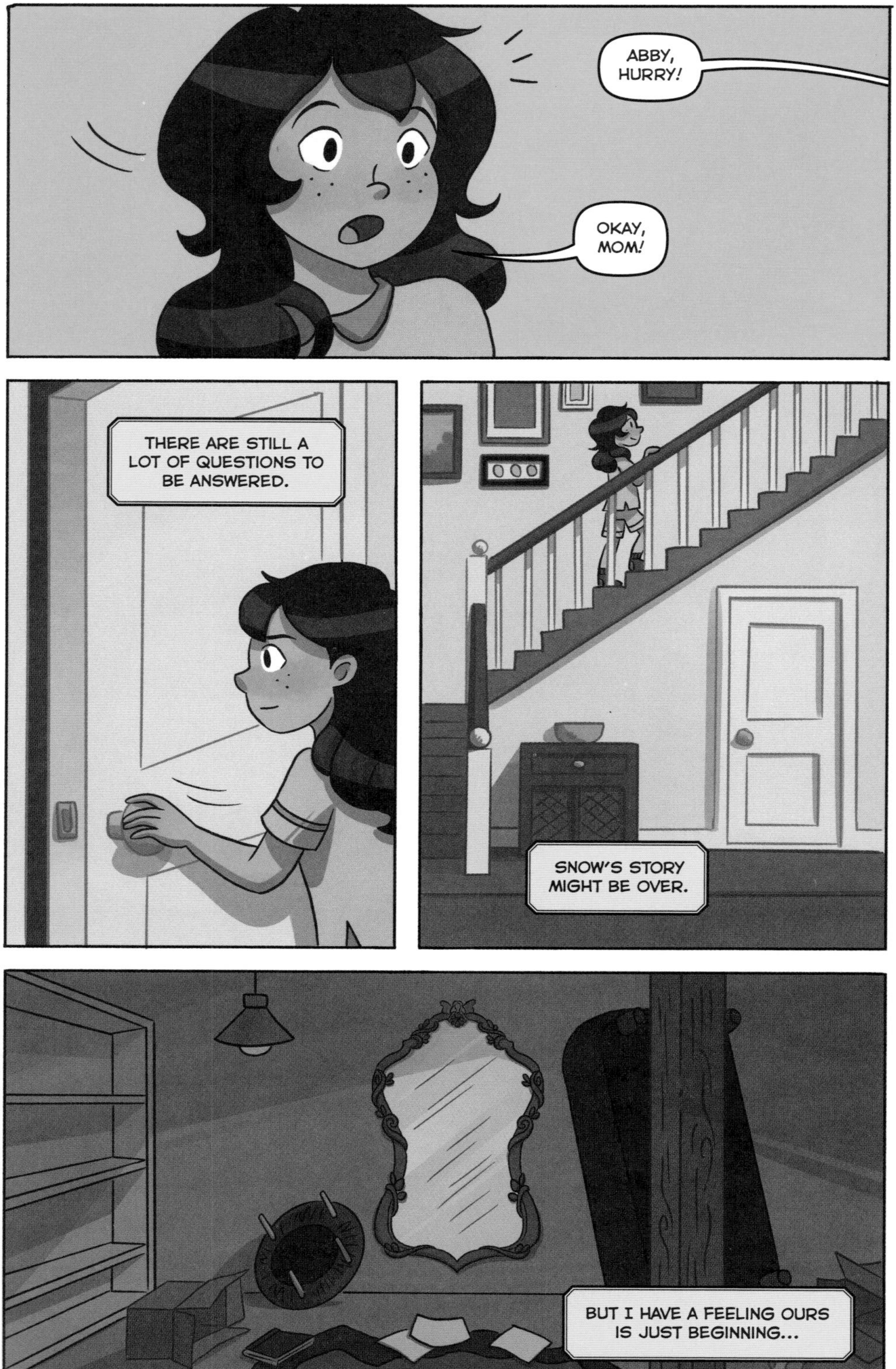
ABBY, HURRY!
OKAY, MOM!
THERE ARE STILL A LOT OF QUESTIONS TO BE ANSWERED.
SNOW'S STORY MIGHT BE OVER.
BUT I HAVE A FEELING OURS IS JUST BEGINNING...

Don't miss Abby and Jonah's next adventure, where they fall into the story of *Cinderella!*

Whatever After
The Graphic Novel
∽ If the Shoe Fits ∽

Coming Soon

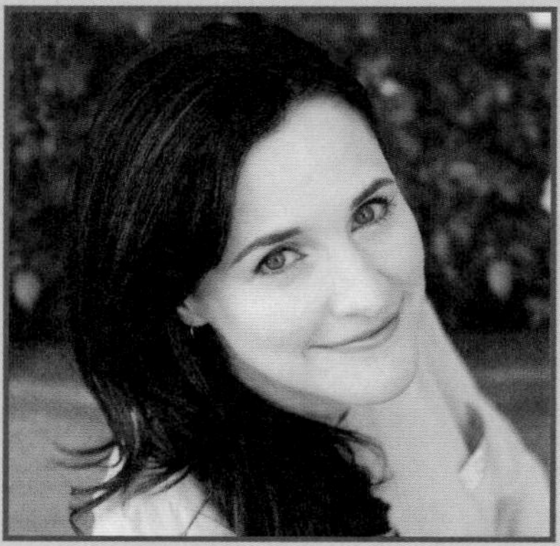

Photo by Heather Waraksa

SARAH MLYNOWSKI is the *New York Times* bestselling author and coauthor of lots of books for teens and tweens, including the Whatever After series, the Best Wishes series, and the Upside-Down Magic series, which was adapted into a Disney Channel movie. Born in Montreal, Sarah now lives in Los Angeles with her family. Visit her online at sarahm.com.

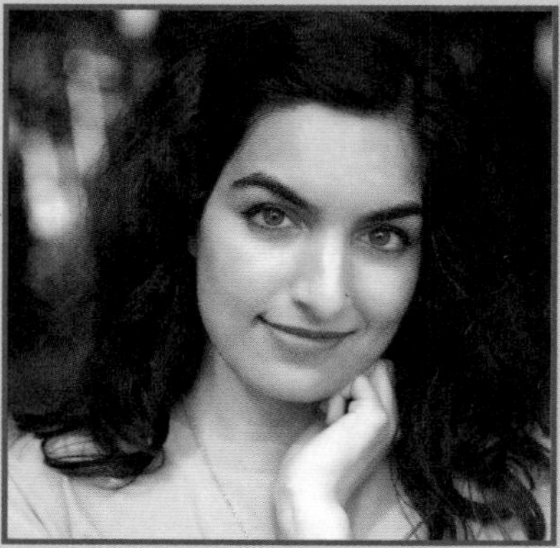

Photo by Ishu Kler

ANU CHOUHAN is a Canadian illustrator and art director. A trained animator with a background in video game development, Anu often puts her love of her Punjabi cultural heritage into her art and draws inspiration from anime, nature, and fashion. She illustrated the graphic novel adaptation of the *New York Times* bestselling book *Aru Shah and the End of Time*. Learn more at anumation.ca.